A KING'S PASSION

He spoke into the supercharged silence. "Do you know why I didn't ask for you?" he said at last.

At first she didn't respond. Then she turned to stare at him, her black eyes leaden and filmy, her face streaked with sweat and blood and tears. "No . . ."

He held her eyes. He wanted her to understand. "It was when I met your sister. Spirits Walking Woman."

Her eyelids flickered. "I should have strangled that bitch when she was born." She paused. "I thought about it later."

He shuddered. He knew she meant every word. "I need a wife, a Queen. . . ." he said.

Her voice was harsh. "I would have been a great Queen," she said.

He shook his head. "You don't see it, do you?"

A fire was rekindling in her eyes now. "See what?"

He laughed softly. "You're not a Queen. Spirits is a Queen. You—I can have *you* any time I want. . . ."

Her teeth and claws raked out again, but this time he was ready for her. In more ways than one . . .

SPIRITS WALKING WOMAN

Margaret Allan

AN ONYX BOOK

ONYX
Published by the Penguin Group
Penguin Putnam Inc., 375 Hudson Street,
New York, New York 10014, U.S.A.
Penguin Books Ltd, 27 Wrights Lane,
London W8 5TZ, England
Penguin Books Australia Ltd, Ringwood,
Victoria, Australia
Penguin Books Canada Ltd, 10 Alcorn Avenue,
Toronto, Ontario, Canada M4V 3B2
Penguin Books (N.Z.) Ltd, 182–190 Wairau Road,
Auckland 10, New Zealand

Penguin Books Ltd, Registered Offices:
Harmondsworth, Middlesex, England

First published by Onyx, an imprint of Dutton Signet,
a member of Penguin Putnam Inc.

First Printing, January, 1998
10 9 8 7 6 5 4 3 2 1

For
Desmond Tan
Health, Wealth, Happiness
Love

A civilization is destroyed only when its gods are destroyed.

—E. M. Cioran

And again: No more gods! no more gods! Man is King, Man is God! But the great Faith is Love!

—Arthur Rimbaud

AUTHOR'S NOTE

This is a work of fiction, and on a particularly problematic subject: the lives of those who comprised that ancient Mesoamerican culture we now call the Olmec. Current understanding of these people is changing with great rapidity; what was considered settled knowledge only a few years ago has been overturned in the light of ever more recent discoveries. Moreover, to confuse matters further, this work of fiction contains elements of fantasy and is not intended as historically realistic.

Harvest Mountain Lord, for instance, is a historical figure depicted on a pre-Mayan stela; but his time is a thousand years after the setting of this book. Similarly, a version of the tale of Quetzalcoatl is retold here; whether the Olmec knew of the Feathered Serpent is an equally problematic issue. Even Great Head City is a composite of two actual Olmec centers: San Lorenzo and La Venta.

I have been greatly aided by Dr. Paul Pettennude, an archeologist who has been doing work in the Mayan area for over thirty years. His help and advice have been invaluable. I am particularly indebted to him for his explication of the relationship between lightning and the Feathered Serpent. If, then, anything in this novel conforms to current archeological knowledge of the Olmec, it is Paul's doing. Errors and simple fancies are plainly my own.

—Margaret Allan

CHAPTER ONE

I

Spirits Walking Woman had a frightening dream the night before the Great King came to Holy Stone City looking for a wife.

She didn't remember the dream after she woke, only knew it had happened from the vague sense of fear it left as its residue. She rose in the morning with the sun in her eyes, and though the morning was clean and bright, she felt brushed by wisps of dread.

Something had come to her in the cold hours before dawn and touched her, but she couldn't remember it. Yet she felt a sense of foreboding, and for a moment she thought of the place she had sealed off forever inside herself. Only for an instant, though, and then the morning sun burned it all away.

Out of the corner of her eye, she saw her sister, Green Water Woman, sneaking up behind her. For one short breath—sharply inhaled—she wished for the power of the Hidden Ones, to make herself invisible. She could think of no other way to escape. Instead, she sighed, gritted her teeth, and pretended she didn't see what was coming. Sometimes the mouse escapes the hawk by playing dead . . .

She was standing at the outermost wall, overlooking the hidden trail that snaked up the side of the cliff to

Holy Stone City. She wasn't tall, five feet and an inch or so, but her shoulders were broad for a woman, her waist narrow, and she stood so straight it looked as if somebody were pushing her backward. Her inky hair fell shining below her shoulders, a single thick braid woven with blue feathers.

She peered out at the world through eyes like round black agates, over the top of a straight, narrow nose, an unconscious frown on full, wide lips. Her cheekbones were like high shelves, supporting her almond-shaped eye sockets, and her deeply tanned skin showed hints of red beneath dark gold. She wore a simple white skirt cinched about her waist with a turquoise brooch, and several necklaces of amber, turquoise, and feathers, beneath a gorgeous cape of feathers. As she moved, her upper body became visible through the front of the cape, revealing budding breasts and dark pink nipples.

She held herself as regally as a princess, for so she was, although she mostly thought of herself as merely a girl. Older men already eyed her sideways and wondered what she would look like when she was fully grown. Women instinctively deferred to her, and would have even if her family was not royal.

She kept on looking down, ignoring the sounds of her sister's skulking approach, trying to concentrate on the beauty of the day—for the day was beautiful . . .

In the blazing heat of the morning, colors lay draped in filmy agate bands across the high plateau: sapphire sky above, gray, sun-parched stone between, dusky emerald jungle below. The river trailed its brown scarf heedlessly, turgidly powerful in the hazy distance.

Spirits Walking shielded her eyes against the morning sun and listened to the cries of the Great King's courtiers as they made their way toward the cliff wall beneath her perch. She could hear the throb of drums, the harsh, snakelike rattle of shaken gourds. Already she could see the bright plumage of feathered headpieces on the advance guard, bobbing like jeweled birds up the steep path which led to her father's citadel. A soft footstep intruded.

"You won't have him, you know. He will be mine." Venom.

Even though she'd expected it, the familiar hiss of that voice, silken as a caress and brutal as a knife in the back, startled her. She forced herself not to turn. Her knuckles turned white against the stones of the parapet wall. Then, suddenly, agony lanced through her skull as strong fingers gripped her ear lobe and twisted; sharp fingernails dug into her tender skin.

"Oh, I'm sorry," the voice continued in its sinister purr. "Did I frighten you? But you shouldn't be frightened of me, little sister. Unless you actually believe the Great King Harvest Mountain Lord would be interested in someone like . . . *you*?"

Spirits Walking slowly lifted her chin, but didn't turn, didn't acknowledge the pain. She knew that to do so would only inflame her sister to greater feats of punishment.

"Green Water Woman, I'm not interested in the Great King," she said through teeth clenched against the pain. It was a lie, but she would never admit it to her older sister.

Green Water Woman released her sister's ear and stepped back, abruptly bored with her sadistic play. "Oh? Then why have you put on your best robe? Not that it will help. When the Great King sees me, he'll have no eyes for little girls dressed up in childish feathers."

Spirits Walking sighed and turned to face her.

Green Water wore a spectacular feathered and beaded cape that covered her from neck to toes. It hung open in the front, showing provocative glimpses of hard, tight muscle, undulating belly, a high, tight waist. She was a few inches taller than Spirits; her hair, so black it was almost blue, flowed to her hips, framing her wide shoulders and upper body like a shimmering fan.

Her head was oval, tapering to a pointed chin, with features pushed just a bit to the center, foxy and concentrated; bones prominent beneath slick, smooth skin, each feature as if carved with a sharp knife from hard wood. Her nose was thin and high, with wide nostrils. Her mouth also wide, lips roughened from where she continually chewed them to make them swell sensually.

She moved like a snake, tough, sinuous, controlled, and with her slanted eyes, gimlet stare, and open nostrils, she seemed constantly to be seeing—and smelling—something she didn't like. The expression was pronounced now, but even so, her exotic beauty was still stunning. Men watched her every step, and she knew it.

"You *are* very pretty, Green Water." Spirits tilted her head, rubbed her ear, and examined the older girl carefully. "That robe is Mother's, isn't it?"

Green Water Woman spread her arms to reveal the full glory of the robe she wore, intricately worked with feathers and tiny colored beads that caught the light and refracted it in a rainbow of glittering hues. "Yes. Isn't it beautiful?"

"Oh, yes," Spirits said, speaking the truth. It was a glorious creation that her mother and her handmaids had worked on for many turnings of the moon. The sight of it draped across Green Water's slender shoulders made her stomach flutter, though. Mother had not offered her anything half so beautiful to wear for the Great King's visit. Did it mean, then, that mother favored Green Water as a suitor for the Great King's honor?

Green Water accepted the compliment as her due, as she did all compliments, and sneered down the fine length of her nose at the younger girl, satisfied and mocking at the same time. Her eyes raked Spirits up and down.

"I'm prettier than you, little sister. The king will want a woman, not an ugly child who knows nothing of men and their ways, or how to make them happy . . . in case you had other thoughts."

With that, Green Water thrust her chin up, gathered her robe about her, and turned to stalk away. Spirits Walking watched her go, unaware that her lips moved as she whispered to herself, "The Great King will want what the Great King wants . . ."

But she feared Green Water was right. Her older sister was beautiful, with her high cheekbones and uncharacteristically thin, straight nose setting off wide, slanted eyes that sparkled like obsidian in noonday light. And her sister certainly was more knowledgeable about the ways of men. Spirits had discovered that long before, when by accident she'd intruded on a tangle of naked, thrashing limbs in one of the hidden rooms of the Jaguar Temple and, fascinated, had concealed herself to watch. Her shock had been both real and delicious when she discovered that one of the pair making those strange, grunting noises, those half-swallowed moans of passion was Green Water Woman, her own sister.

But she'd never mentioned the encounter. She knew too well what would be the result; swift blows, hissed threats, the terrible rage of which only she knew the full extent. Her sister was clever enough to reveal only her sweetest side to others; it was for Spirits Walking, whom she deemed helpless, that she reserved the true horror of her unbridled rage.

But what can I do? Spirits thought suddenly. *If I could just get out of this place, this home that's nothing more than a trap now. If only the Great King . . .*

If only. It was hopeless. But she had to succeed. Not for herself, but for all of them. *Oh, Father, what have you done?*

"Spirits! There you are. I've been looking all over . . ."

At the familiar, distracted tones, Spirits turned and forced a smile onto her forlorn features. "Yes, Mother, I've been right here. Watching for the Great King to arrive."

The first wife of the King of Holy Stone City was a short, dumpy woman who bustled up and hugged the girl close to breasts like warm, comfortable pillows. She looked incongruous in her feathered finery, like some awkward, flightless bird. Two of Queen Blue Parrot's serving women followed her, one of them carrying a sunshade, the other trying without a great deal of success to control the long train of crimson-and-white feathers that flowed in her mistress's agitated wake.

"Well, look at you! Don't you look like a young princess?" her mother said, taking her by the shoulders and pulling her close for better examination. "Do you like your robe, my daughter?"

"Oh, yes, Mother," Spirits said, even as she yearned to ask why Green Water Woman wore one of the Queen's own royal capes. But she did not ask, for the mere question would have revealed too much of her own intentions.

Her mother peered myopically into her face—the older woman's vision had been cloudy for years—and now she put her nose almost onto the tip of her daughter's and said, "Is that paint I see around your eyes, Spirits?"

This close, Spirits could see the small white god marks floating in her mother's dark eyes, the spirit-veils that obscured her vision. "Yes, Mother," she whispered.

"Ah. Well, good," the older woman replied, releasing Spirits and stepping back. "I was afraid you'd forget the proper appearance. After all, you've never been to the court of the Great King. Did you do it yourself?"

Spirits nodded, then remembered her mother had difficulty in detecting small movements. "Yes," she said again. "I asked Bright Moon to help me."

"Oh. That old woman? Though she has been to the High Court many times, of course. She was your father's nurse." The queen paused a moment, and her rounded features went still, as if she were recalling days she'd almost forgotten.

"Good, then," she said finally, "that's well enough. You must hurry, Spirits, for the Great King will be at the walls soon, and you must be there with us to greet him." She raised a feathery fan and absently swished it at her face, ignoring the small rain of feathers that ensued. "Now. Have you seen your elder sister?"

"Yes. She was just here, but she left. She didn't tell me where she was going."

"Oh, I could slap that girl. Well, I just have to find her, and quickly. Come, women," she said smartly to her escorts. The one with the fan, a middle-aged courtier named Snake Knees, took the Queen's pudgy arm and prepared to lead her away, adjusting the sunshade so it shielded the Queen's face from the broiling light overhead.

The older woman paused and glanced over her shoulder at the girl who watched her with wide, silent eyes. Her motherly heart went out to her daughter then, for she, too, had been a quiet girl in her youth. Sometimes the flamboyance and beauty of her elder daughter disturbed her, although in her own way, this younger daughter might well be as beautiful as her elder sister. It was perhaps too soon to tell, for Spirits Walking had only seen twelve summers. But she was also, unlike her mother, slender and large-eyed, and already her breasts were showing obvious hints of future bounty. Sometimes Queen Blue Parrot wondered how such lissome creatures as her two daughters could have sprung from her own thick and stolid thighs.

And there were other times when she wondered if Green Water Woman was truly what she seemed; on occasion it seemed to her that this hard and willful girl might have come from another womb than her own. Maybe it was only an old woman's fancy, but she found more comfort in Spirits Walking, and in a sudden flash of unasked-for insight she wondered if the Great King—But no. Of course not. Green Water was truly the beautiful one, the one who could snare this great prize, this necessary prize.

Queen Blue Parrot knew that some others thought her a stupid and dithering old woman, and that contented her. Let them think her harmless who would, the better for her own plots. That her elder daughter was numbered among those who underestimated her was not a secret to her. Daughters often knew least about their own mothers. But she was certain Spirits Walking was not deceived by the bumbling, good-hearted front she put up.

Still, let Green Water catch the Great King, and leave the fastness of Holy Stone City for the lowland sprawl of Great Head City, the Great King's seat near the ocean. From what she'd heard, the match might not be a bad one, at that. Harvest Mountain Lord was searching for a wife, but little was spoken about his first marriage, or the woman who had birthed his offspring. Strange things were murmured about that poor woman's untimely death, and not for the first time Blue Parrot whispered a silent prayer of thanks for her own good luck in husbands, for even if her husband was a fool, he was a kindly one.

It was a hard thing, to consign even an undutiful daughter like Green Water to a man—though he was a Great King—about whom so many odd and disquieting rumors swirled. But if it could be done, the ascendance of Holy Stone City and its sacred quarries

and workshops would be assured, something the
Queen understood with far more clarity than many of
her detractors. It seemed to her that her husband,
King Sky Wind Warrior, was dabbling in dangerous
things, both for himself and for those who depended
on him. A marriage between her eldest girl and the
Great King would surely put an end to that.

She stared at the blurry form of her second daughter another long moment, then said, "Be sure you
don't forget. Be at the gate in time. I'll see you there."

"I'll be there, Mother," Spirits replied, her voice
calm and soothing. "In fact, I'll leave now."

"That's good, dear," her mother said and, reas-
sured, turned away a final time. It was such a bother,
having to be led around by Snake Knees or one of
her other handmaids, but there was no help for it. At
least she wasn't totally blind yet, and her mind—it
wasn't cloudy at all.

II

The Great King Harvest Mountain Lord turned to
his general, the Lord Skull Breaker, who strode at his
side and said, "This befouled headdress itches like
crazy. I hate this ceremonial pigeon dung."

Harvest Mountain wore only a white woven skirt
and rough sandals, leaving his high, round chest open
to the sun. A sheen of sweat glistened on his tight,
smooth muscles. Tall for a man of his people, he
moved with the assured balance of a born athlete.

He wore his straight black hair to his neck, cut in
a smooth bowl, like a helmet. His eyes, like raisins in
slightly yellow bowls, stared aimlessly about, filmy
with boredom. His face was smoothed by a thin layer
of fat, his high forehead unlined. When he smiled, he
showed a mouthful of white teeth and one dark spot,
lower left, where a single tooth had been lost to a
nearly forgotten accident.

The little finger on his left hand was also missing;
there were calluses on his palms from weapons practice, but otherwise he was unmarred. He moved with
strength, but there was an air of repulsion about him,
as if he unconsciously resisted being touched.

People tended to look away from him. They might
have done so even if he weren't the Great King . . .

Lord Skull Breaker, commander of the Great King's
army, nodded sourly. He was an older man, once
heavily built, now sagging and sweating at the exer-
tions of the climb. His granite-colored hair, roughly
chopped, did nothing to conceal the stretch of naked
skin on the top of his pear-shaped head.

He wiped his broad forehead with a rough cloth he
carried for that purpose, and glanced up at the inhab-
itants of Holy Stone City, who lined the rim of the
cliff wall overhead. "Not far now, Lord. I hope they
have some beer up there."

Harvest Mountain Lord, who had visited Holy
Stone City in his youth, grinned. "Oh, yes. I'm sure
they do. They make very good beer here, or so I remember. Fit for a Great King."

A cloud of gnats buzzed up from the thick green
brush along the narrow path and began to orbit the
Great King's head. He brushed irritably at the inva-
sion, glanced about, and said, "You! Fan waver!"

The startled courtier who, preoccupied with crashing through the bushes in order to keep his place near
the Great King, had missed the sudden insectile on-
slaught, turned and saw it now. The man's face
drained of color. Instantly he leaped forward, fan
beating frantically.

Harvest Mountain Lord stared at the hapless under-
ling for a long moment. Then he shrugged and turned
to Skull Breaker. "Kill that one," he said.

Lord Skull Breaker nodded. "Of course, Lord." He
raised his hand and brought the procession to a halt.
"Kneel, you," he told the errant courtier.

Shrieking, the man turned and lurched back down the trail, straight into the arms of the warriors hurrying to their lord. They dragged the screaming man back.

"Hold him," Skull Breaker said grimly as he undid the thong that fixed his war club to a belt at his waist. The guards forced the man to his knees and, with a single mighty swing, Skull Breaker lived up to his name.

Calmly, he cleaned his weapon on the clout of the unfortunate fan waver, then replaced it at his belt. The Great King stepped gingerly around the mess, and the march continued.

As if nothing had occurred—which wasn't strange, for nothing really had occurred—the Great King said, "I wonder how many ugly royal daughters they'll have waiting for me in this city?"

The General, who knew his Lord would cheerfully insert the royal member into the hind end of a snake, was unimpressed by this show of cynicism. He was already mightily tired of this seemingly endless progression from city to city. It had been going on for moons now, and all the Lord Skull Breaker really desired at this point was a swift return to Great Head City and the cool comforts of his own open-walled, thatch-roofed home and the three wives who maintained it for him. Nevertheless, the military part of his attention was focused on his surroundings, and he found himself impressed. This was not a place he would enjoy trying to capture.

They had camped the night before at the base of the cliff, surrounded by vast basalt quarries and a labyrinth of shops where skilled artisans worked the stone into great sculptures, or prepared it for shipment on huge sledges cross-country to the rivers where it could be floated to other cities, Great Head City itself not the least among them.

The quarries and shops were a relatively easy target—the taking of them, at least (holding them would be an entirely different matter)—but this city clinging to the top of the cliff was different. The only access to it was by this cursed narrow path, and Lord Skull Breaker could easily envision that arrows and boulders from above would make the narrow trail impassable. Further, from their high vantage point, the people of Holy Stone City could deny the use of the quarries to anybody else without actually risking direct conflict on the plains surrounding the stone works.

The commander of Holy Stone City's army, Lord Skull Breaker decided, had an enviably easy task. He wished his own were so agreeable.

Lord Skull Breaker's spies had kept him informed, even upon the trail, and the news he'd received of late was not reassuring. The King's brother-in-law, Lord Night Thunder Shaker, had set himself up in Rising Moon City, called the Old City, far up the rivers in the heartland away from the coasts, and malcontents were flocking to him. The most recent reports said the army he was raising was now almost equal in size to the Great King's own, and that worried Skull Breaker much more than whether Harvest Mountain Lord found a new Queen. Sadly, the Great King had a disturbing propensity for thinking with his cock at times, and this insane meander seemed to be one of those times. However much he protested, his master still ignored his concerns.

Ah, well. Praise be to Nameless Duality, and their mighty son, the Lord Jaguar, who would either watch over their chosen people or not. Which fact made Holy Stone City so important, for it was from these very quarries that came the gifts which ensured the continued favor of the Gods.

Nor did it help that Lord Skull Breaker's spies brought disquieting news on precisely this subject. It seemed that Lord Night Thunder Shaker had sent emissaries here, offering protection and wealth in exchange for sole access to the sacred stone hidden in the earth. If this mountain king in his high aerie decided to accept, things might begin to go very badly for Harvest Mountain Lord—and for his loyal general as well.

Viewed from this end of his very cynical forty-two years, it seemed to Lord Skull Breaker the Gods didn't much care who gave them sacrifices, as long as someone did. And that the loyalties of the Gods were even more changeable than those of their creatures, men. If Lord Night Thunder Shaker found himself able to offer bigger stone heads and more ornately carved altars to the glory of Lord Jaguar than the Great King did, then the mantle of the Great King might find itself moved from Great Head City to Rising Moon City. Along with the head of the Great King himself—but only his head, for without doubt, as custom demanded, the former brother-in-law would dine on what remained.

"Hey, old friend! Why the sour face? What are you thinking?"

The Great King's words jerked Lord Skull Breaker from his reverie. "Ah, Lord. Maybe you will find a beautiful maiden here." He glanced hopefully at his master.

"Mmph. I'd settle for a hot night. Those women they offered at the last place, they all had faces like muddy river rocks. Did you notice?"

Inwardly, Skull Breaker sighed. The King was young, true, but it seemed a particularly bad joke that the fate of the kingdom might hinge on whether Harvest Mountain Lord found a bedmate to suit his overly particular lust. Still, his Lord was the son of a mighty father, and must have in some way received a portion of that great man's skills and talents.

Lord Skull Breaker would not mind at all returning home, raising the full royal army, and proceeding to Rising Moon City with the object of stringing Lord

Night Thunder Shaker's guts from the city walls, before that worthy's army became too large and well-trained.

"Oh, look!" the king said. "There they are, the women!" He shaded his eyes against the glare. "All covered with feathers, of course. Can you see anything, Skull Breaker? Any good-looking ones?"

The General, whose eyes, though old, were still sharp as those of a hawk, followed the King's pointing finger. "No, my Lord, as you say, the feathers. I wonder if they itch as much as ours do?"

But the King was preoccupied with the vision of new female flesh, and so only replied, "Who cares what women feel? They are merely women, fit only for the use of a man. Besides, their feathers will come off soon enough."

A few moments later, in a fog of drums and rattles, and a sudden burst of welcoming song from the people of Holy Stone City, the Great King arrived at the latest stop on his wifely quest. Was it only chance, Lord Skull Breaker was later to wonder, that at that very moment a black crow flew low over the city gates, cawed harshly three times, and then vanished?

CHAPTER TWO

I

Spirits stood motionless, caught between elation and misery. On the one hand, she loved dressing up and displaying herself in glowing colors, but on the other hand, the feathery robe made her skin itch in the steamy air.

She managed to keep a smile pasted on her face, but all she really wanted to do was throw off the robe and indulge herself in an orgy of scratching. She could not, of course; her mother would have been appalled, and her entire family shamed.

The Great King stood several strides from her, flanked by his club-faced, bald general on one side, deep in conversation with her father on the other. As far as she could tell, the King had barely glanced at her, though she'd seen him stare long and hard at Green Water when he'd entered the ceremonial ball field for the first time.

As usual, Spirits felt left out. The men—the Great King, her father Sky Wind Warrior, Skull Breaker, any others sufficiently important to draw close—stood in front of her father's table throne. Her father, of course, in deference to the exalted status of his guest, did not seat himself on the throne, for this would place him high above the Great King, and was unthinkable.

Nor did the Great King attempt to usurp the seat of his lesser royal brother. She pondered on that a moment, wondering, trying to puzzle out the intricate dance she knew she was seeing without really understanding the movements of it.

She—and the rest of the royal women—waited at a distance, running with sweat, fanned ineffectually by bored courtiers. Overhead the sun beat down on their huddled group like a whip.

Finally the Queen sighed. "They'll get drunk," she said softly. "It will take a while. Let us seat ourselves." She turned, squinted myopically, made a gesture, and slaves hurried over with woven seating mats. Taking care not to disturb their finery, the three women seated themselves cross-legged on the soft grass.

Behind them, the rest of the women—consorts, second and third and fourth wives and their daughters, did likewise. It was like watching a sudden flowering of blossoms on the royal greensward.

Sunlight glinted painfully through leafy branches, making Spirit's eyes water. Most turned their faces down, but Spirits narrowed her eyes and continued to watch the festivities in front of the throne. Male slaves hurried to and fro, bearing clay pots full of warm pulque. The men, kings and their courtiers, laughed. Their mouths were red, their teeth white. The colors of bone and blood.

She felt a curious shifting then, and not a comfortable one. It reminded her of childhood things, things she no longer wished to remember. Its effect was strange: the voices of the men faded, and a heavy buzzing seemed to fill the saturated air. The sun blazed, flooding the mesa with light. The people who passed there became almost translucent, ghostlike. Their passage left filmy trails. She felt her heartbeat, heard it as a dull, world-filling thud. For a moment everything stopped, and she waited in breathless anticipation of she knew not what, her limbs baked into the hard clay of fear.

This stasis of vision held for only a moment and then it vanished, leaving her wide-eyed and running with cold sweat. Where had it come from? From the past, surely, but hadn't she already slain it? Why now, when she most needed her mind sharp, clear and untroubled by old terrors, did it return?

Was it a portent of things to come?

She licked her lips and tasted salt. The steaming air covered her like a blanket. A final flicker, dark and cold in the smothering heat, like the flash of a fish's tail as it dives into deep water, welled up; but this time she forced it back into its cave of hidden memories. She knew how to do this. She had learned long before, and learned so well she'd almost forgotten that this secret void still existed within her. Was it an omen? She stared at the group of men and hoped that it wasn't, that it was merely a trick of her sun-blasted eyes and heart.

II

The Great King, Harvest Mountain Lord, stepped closer to his general, Skull Breaker, and spoke in soft, musing tones while he pinched the tip of his sharp chin between thumb and forefinger. "So this one would betray me to my brother-in-law who calls himself Thunder Shaker?"

Skull Breaker nodded slowly. "I heard it once as a whisper, and then twice more as screams from one I tortured for the truth. I believe what I heard. Sky Wind Warrior plots against you, Lord."

They both stared thoughtfully at Sky Wind Warrior, the object of their concerns. He was lounging near the edge of his throne table, laughing, surrounded by a dense circle of his courtiers.

He was by far the tallest man in the Long Courtyard, nearing six feet, his broad shoulders and thick neck setting off a tightly muscled frame cured by sun and time to the consistency of old leather.

He was blind in his left eye, an old war injury, but his right eye, a curious blue-green color, sparkled with intensity when he laughed, which was often. And while his laughter was warm, his smile alone was cold, almost frightening. He wore his salt-and-pepper hair long, tied in a pair of braids he wore across his broad chest. He carried himself haughtily, as a true king, and moved like a big cat despite the way he limped slightly off his left leg, another old battle injury.

"Ambitious, my Lord," Skull Breaker murmured.

"Hm. Yet he seems friendly enough, and his words— you heard him speak, Skull Breaker—are of nothing but loyalty to me, and his love for me." He released his chin and sighed. "My father always trusted him."

Yes, thought the General, but your father Tall Mountain was a strong man, strong enough to make men like this country king fear him. And out of that fear came loyalty, for men such as this only trust what they cannot overcome. But he does not fear you, Lord.

So Skull Breaker thought, but he said nothing of it, and instead shrugged. "He plots against you, Lord," he repeated.

But Harvest Mountain seemed not to hear him. His sharp, darting gaze slid from King Sky Wind's broad back and now rested on the flock of downed forest birds that was the cluster of royal women.

"The first daughter, did you see the tits on her? And for once, a face that doesn't look like yours, my General."

"Yes, Lord. She is very beautiful."

"What do you think, Skull Breaker? Is she fit for the royal thunder stick?"

Skull Breaker stared at his Great King. "That is for you to say, my Lord."

"I say yes," Harvest Mountain Lord told him.

III

Spirits felt hot breath on the back of her neck. She moved her head slightly and whispered, "What?"

Her sister's voice was barely loud enough to hear, but the force of it was more than sufficient to bring Spirit's attention to full alertness.

"What are you staring at?"

Spirits moved her shoulder slightly, and tilted her head toward her mother, Queen Blue Parrot. "Mother . . ."

"I don't care about her," Green Water replied. "And don't think she'll protect you from me."

Now Spirits turned to face her older sister. "Green Water, what is wrong with you?"

"You're staring at the Great King, aren't you?"

"No, I'm not. Green Water, I don't think he's even aware that we exist. Look at him—he's half drunk already."

"Yes, I noticed." A knowing smile played on Green Water's full lips.

Spirits stared at this odd expression. Suddenly she remembered the sweating tangle of limbs she'd discovered in the temple a while back. No doubt her sister had similar designs on, and plans for, the Great King. And how could she compete with that? Her eyes flickered toward the honeyed swell of Green Water's full breasts. She had nothing similar with which to wage her own battle. Inwardly, she sighed. Well, there was always more than one way to skin a dog.

"Leave me alone, Green Water. I don't care about your schemes." With that, she turned her face firmly toward the front, and after a moment she felt her sister's fiery breath recede from the back of her neck.

Spirits could feel sweat coursing in rivulets down her body. She stared at the men, who had thrown off their finery, and now stood gulping pulque in front of the throne. The Great King's body was fine and slender. She felt a strange stirring at the bottom of her belly.

The Great King had lost his stiff dignity, and now capered about like the youth he was. Spirits found her gaze drawn to the mysterious bulge beneath his white clout. Whatever he had there, it was sizable. She was no innocent. She knew what men did to women. Now, for the first time, she imagined the Great King doing the same thing to her.

The hilarity in front of the throne was growing more pronounced. She watched her father slap the young Great King on the back, hard enough to make the King spill his gourd of pulque. But the boy didn't seem to mind, only laughed and gestured at one of the slaves for a refill.

Now she looked at his eyes. They were bright and sharp as chipped flint. The tiniest of sunburned lines crinkled from their edges, and when he laughed, he seemed barely old enough to be standing with the full-grown men who surrounded him. Yet he was obviously the center of their universe; even if he had been invisible, she would have known he was there from the way the others moved in unconscious orbit around him.

Still, this boy-King possessed dark secrets and a hidden past, or so it was said. And there was something frightening about him. She couldn't quite figure out what it was, but it was there. A shadow, a sense of darkness.

And this was the man she had decided to marry. She had not quite yet worked out how she intended to accomplish this, but it had to be done. The survival of her family depended upon her success. She knew her sister too well: that selfish girl cared about nothing but herself. Spirits had no doubt Green Water would cheerfully watch her entire family fed to dogs, as long as her own position was assured.

And Spirits could not allow that to come to pass.

But how had things reached this terrible point? She knew more than she wished, more than any girl her age should know. Always shy, people tended not to notice her even when she stood right next to them. And even if they did see her, what they noticed was only a small, pretty child—certainly nobody who would understand the things they whispered softly to each other. And so, piece by piece, she had gradually picked up, if not the whole truth, certainly enough to understand the peril in which her father had placed all of them.

Sometimes she wondered what her father could possibly be thinking of. They lived well. Their city was safe, those in it well fed, their future assured. It was more than most people could expect. And yet her father, with his treachery, risked it all.

"Spirits, what's wrong with you? If I didn't know better, I'd say you've gone to sleep. Are you dreaming awake?" Queen Blue Parrot's tone was worried. This was no time for her younger daughter to suffer one of her spells.

Spirits turned and smiled at her mother. "This is very boring, isn't it? I thought it would be more exciting."

"Spirits, don't say things like that." But Blue Parrot couldn't help a quick smile. "Actually, these High Court things are always that way. The men get drunk, and we get pushed off to the side and forgotten."

"Mother," Green Water broke in, "perhaps Spirits is . . . tired." She nodded knowingly. "After all, she is quite young. No doubt the excitement has exhausted her. Perhaps it would be better to have one of the handmaids take her away for a while now. That way she will be well rested for the feast."

Blue Parrot nodded. "Yes, that's a very good idea, Green Water."

She patted Spirits on the shoulder. "You go along

now, dear, and try to get some rest. I'll make sure
you're awake well in time for the feast."

"Mother, I'm not tired at all. Don't make me leave.
Green Water's only trying to get rid of me."

She winced as sharp-nailed fingers pinched her back
viciously. But the Queen didn't notice, only shook her
head and said, "A nap will do you good, daughter.
Run along while nobody is looking. Now, don't make
a scene, Spirits. I will see you at the feast."

Grumbling inwardly, but knowing there was no use
in protesting, Spirits climbed gradually to her feet.
One of the older woman kneeling behind them rose
at the same time and came forward to escort her away.
"Sleep well, daughter," the Queen said absently. Only
Spirits saw the evil gleam of triumph glitter from
Green Water's eyes. She stared at her older sister
blankly, then turned and allowed herself to be led off.

Like a dog to the slaughter, she thought, and then
reproached herself for being overly dramatic. It was
only a nap, after all, and, truth be told, sleep was the
last of her intentions.

IV

Green Water watched her younger sister depart, the
triumphant expression slowly fading from her beautiful features. Her eyes narrowed. She had gotten rid
of the meddling bitch, but she was no closer to realizing her aims than before.

She glared at her mother's back, but Blue Parrot
remained sweetly oblivious. No help there. Not that
she had expected anything. Her mother was a fat old
fool, stupid and nearly blind. She knew better than to
hope for anything from that quarter.

Out on the grass in front of the throne, the men
sank deeper into the clutches of their drink. Her eyes
found the lithe frame of the Great King. She had not
missed the loosely jiggling bulge in his clout, and

licked her lips at the sight of it. If she could only get her talented fingers on that, she knew she could stop worrying about any competition from Spirits.

Unfortunately, it was a long reach from her place here on the mat to where her prize lounged, wobbling and glazed-eyed, against the edge of the table throne. One good thing—after as much pulque as he'd drunk, the Great King would be an easy mark.

"Mother!"

Blue Parrot's eyes were shut, her face turned up toward the sun. She was humming under her breath, and did not seem to hear her daughter's whispered demand.

"Mother! Listen to me!"

"What? What is it, dear?"

Green Water pointed at the cluster of drunken men. "Look at the Great King. See how the sweat runs off him. He must be terribly hot. Where are his fan wavers?"

Queen Blue Parrot shrugged. "I'm sure he's fine, dear. He's a young man, after all."

"But shouldn't we do something?" Green Water paused as if thinking. "I know . . . I'll bring him something to eat . . . That should cool him off."

The Queen's faded eyes slid gently toward her daughter's eager face. She could not make out those features very clearly, but her ears served her as well as most people's perfect vision. She understood that Green Water had no intention of cooling off the King; if anything, she planned on doing exactly the opposite. However, since this fit in nicely with her own plans, the older woman smiled and said, "I think that's a wonderful idea. Yes, take some of the women and bring the men a bit of food to go with their pulque." She fluttered her pudgy fingers. "No doubt our visitors are hungry after the long climb up the cliff."

V

Harvest Mountain Lord paused, chest heaving, head spinning. He crouched forward, hands on knees, and shook his head. Sweat flew from his brow. He looked up, then turned, and dug a sharp elbow into Skull Breaker's ribs. "Well, look what we have here. The feast has come to me."

Skull Breaker understood his meaning perfectly and grinned. At the head of the small procession making its way along the length of the Long Court toward him, Green Water strode proudly, shoulders back, head high, breasts out-thrust. Her dark hair rippled in the gentle breeze of her passage. Her full lips curved up in a faint smile. When she felt the gaze of the Great King fall on her, she slowly ran the pink tip of her tongue across the moist surface of her lips.

"Great Jaguar, would you look at that?" Harvest Mountain breathed softly.

Skull Breaker nodded slowly. "Yes," he said.

The two men glanced at each other. The moment stretched, caught in the widening length of the early afternoon. Overhead, a boiling rank of ragged cumulus clouds advanced across the vacant blue arc of the sky. Fierce shards of sunlight pierced the clouds, burning hard-edged blocks of shadow into the central courtyard.

And into that creaking moment crept a sudden breath of bright green terror. Skull Breaker felt it and shivered, despite the sheen of sweat on his flabby shoulders. Harvest Mountain sensed it as well, but his reaction was a soft, dreamy smile, as if he'd just remembered something now fondly recalled but long forgotten.

"The breath of the God," Harvest Mountain murmured.

A crow—perhaps the same one as before, Skull Breaker thought uneasily—flapped noisily over their heads and screamed once into the sudden silence.

"It looks good, doesn't it?" Harvest Mountain said, his smile twitching.

Skull Breaker stared at him, breathless, and nodded, not knowing what looked good at all—whether the approaching girl, or the feast borne on wide platters by the train of slaves behind her. Or perhaps something else, something only his King could see.

Somewhere in the distance the pipers and drummers had started up again, their rhythm like a speeding heartbeat, the pipes whining their thin cries of pleasure.

"My Lord, I thought you might be hungry after your long journey. I hope this will be . . . sufficient." Green Water Woman stood very close, her words a sultry whisper of invitation.

Skull Breaker felt the jolt that passed between the two of them, woman and king, as a sudden electric contraction beneath his breastbone. He inhaled softly and stepped back.

She had an animal smell to her, hot and musky. Inhaling it brought an answering twitch beneath the white folds of his clout. But she wasn't for the likes of him, no, not this creature whose black eyes burned, whose very flesh seemed to emit waves of heat.

Harvest Mountain Lord seemed entirely unaffected by her, however. He bobbed his head slightly, and said, "Yes, very nice. Don't you think you should bow to me?"

At which point Green Water did one of the strangest things Skull Breaker had ever seen. A slow smile, the equal of the one drifting back and forth on Harvest Mountain's lips, transformed her features. Wordlessly she stepped back, dropped to all fours, and touched the earth at the Great King's feet with her head. In theory it was a proper obeisance, but in fact, she never lowered her eyes. She turned her head instead, so that during the entire process her own gaze never broke its link with Harvest Mountain's eyes.

Somehow her bow became both mocking and complicit, as if the two of them were sharing some sort of private joke. Nevertheless, Skull Breaker was shocked, and even more so when the shameless woman leaned forward and ran her tongue lightly across the top of Harvest Mountain's foot. Like a cat . . .

"My Lord," he hissed, as the woman rose slowly to her feet, but the Great King raised his right hand and fluttered his fingers for silence.

"Very good," he told Green Water. "You show your loyalty as you should."

She faced him and once again threw her shoulders back so that her magnificent breasts jutted out, their nipples dark and full of hot blood. "I am your slave, Lord," she whispered.

Harvest Mountain Lord nodded. "We shall see," he said.

VI

Dusk brought with it a general quickening: the breezes which had vanished during the long hours of the afternoon returned, touching the leaves with a sound like distant applause. As the sun balanced, a swollen and bloody ball just atop the distant green horizon, flocks of birds began to explode from the darkness of the forest. The musicians, who had succumbed to a surfeit of pulque, woke fuzzy-eyed and bemused from their afternoon siestas, and groped for their instruments. A ragged tune began to sound from where they lay slumped near the edge of the Long Courtyard.

In the kitchens of the royal enclosure, situated on mounds to the inner side of the courtyard, dozens of slaves rushed frantically about, finishing up preparations for the feast shortly to begin.

Spirits Walking awoke with a start. For a moment she felt disoriented; she shook her head and brought herself up on one elbow, her nose full of the smell of roasting pig and turtle, her ears ringing with shouts from the nearby kitchens.

Despite her earlier protests, she was, like almost everybody else, accustomed to sleeping through the hottest hours of the afternoon. But the shadows which filled the interior of the woman's sleeping house, usually so familiar and comforting, now seemed ominous.

Then she remembered—the feast!

With that small epiphany came a sharp sense of dread. How long had she been sleeping? However long it had been, that time was now lost forever. What opportunities had she missed to carry out her plans? And, in her absence, what opportunities had Green Water seized?

She rubbed the sleep from her eyes and called for a woman to help her dress. It seemed as if it took forever to get the formal robe properly fitted to her slender form, and the time it took her maid, Bright Moon, to paint her face was a further agony.

"Hurry up," Spirits begged, but the old woman only made a hissing sound deep in her wattled throat and told her to hold still.

Finally, after what seemed like half a sun's daypassage, Spirits was ready. Bright Moon held up a plate of polished onyx, and Spirits eyed her shadowy reflection in the guttering light of the torches ringed around the open sides of the enclosure. "It's all right, isn't it, Bright Moon?"

The crone nodded, her toothless gums stretched in a yawning pink smile. "You look wonderful, dear," she said.

"Help me out, then," Spirits said, rising to her full height, wishing fervently that she was just a little taller. Once again, though, her native good sense came to her rescue. She wasn't as tall, as developed, as good-looking as Green Water, and wouldn't be for a while yet. Which meant that in the meantime, she had

to make do with what she did have. The only problem
was, she couldn't think what that might be.

She sighed. "I'm ready, Bright Moon," she said
softly.

Nodding, the handmaid, her knees creaking with the
effort, bent down and caught the ends of the feathered
robe in her clawed fingers and lifted it off the ground.
A final pause while Spirits breathed deeply, hoping to
calm herself, and off they went.

VII

"Sit over here, next to me, Spirits," Queen Blue
Parrot said as Spirits came into the Long Court, which
had been transformed for the great feast.

A thousand torches blazed, tied to posts set into the
ground, or held by motionless servants and slaves.
Two huge bonfires, the smell of their burning aromatic
in the night air, added to the illumination.

The music makers, their numbers swelled twice
over, made a great racket in front of the throne area.
Despite their determined noise, however, they could
barely be heard over the buzzing roar of the crowd.

Spirits settled herself on a mat near her mother,
then looked about, amazed. She'd never seen so many
people gathered together in one place. Not only were
all the members of the court here—ten hands' worth,
each of them pushing as close to the two Kings as
they could get—but also the rest of the people of the
city proper, as well as the leaders of every village
under Holy Stone City's sway, their families, and what
looked to be most of their villagers, too. Add to that
the servants, traders visiting from other cities, and a
horde of slaves, and Spirits guessed there were perhaps two hundred hands of people jostling, talking,
eating, singing, drinking, dancing, and screaming in the
shadowy green stretch of the Long Courtyard.

A servant knelt before her, bearing a wooden tray

piled high with bits of spiced, broiled pig. Spirits sniffed, and suddenly realized she was ravenous. Her mouth watered as she snatched out several steaming chunks of meat onto a thick green leaf which she held as a plate.

"Spirits . . ." her mother whispered. "Slow down. The High King will think we don't feed you at all!"

Spirits nodded as she chewed and swallowed. The meat was almost too hot to eat. Her fingers tingled from the smoky grease. "Yes, Mother, I'm sorry." She paused, looking around.

"Mother, where's Green Water?"

The Queen waved one stubby hand vaguely. "Oh . . . over there somewhere . . ."

Over there appeared to be in the general direction of the throne. Spirits craned her head, trying to see. The flickering orange glow of the torches made vision difficult, and though the night was clear enough, there was no moon to add to the light. The figures before the throne were nearly indistinguishable from each other. Only her father, because of his height, was easy to pick out.

"Mother, I'm going over there, to Father."

"Spirits . . ."

"Don't worry. I won't be a bother. But I want to see."

Her mother turned, her dim gaze seeming to become suddenly sharp. "Leave your sister alone."

Well, that's plain enough, Spirits thought. "Yes, Mother," she replied softly. "Don't worry, I won't interfere."

Blue Parrot held her examination for a beat, then nodded, evidently satisfied. "Mind your manners, Spirits. Remember who you are."

Spirits climbed to her feet, trying not to disturb her fancy robe. She pulled it tighter around her shoulders and smiled down on Blue Parrot.

You want her to snare the King, she thought, but she only said, "I'll be good, Mother. I promise."

Queen Blue Parrot watched her as she picked her way through the seated women, heading toward the throne. She trusted Spirits, but couldn't shake a feeling of apprehension. The girl had something on her mind. What was it?

She was so young. Too young for all this.

She shook her head. If only her husband weren't such a *fool* . . .

VIII

The humid night air was drenched with the smell of tightly packed, sweating bodies, but most of the revelers fell back from her as they recognized the youngest of the royal daughters. And when she reached the area near the throne, she found that soldiers had pushed the crowds back, clearing a space for the two Kings and their attendants. She stepped past one glowering brute she vaguely recognized—his spear, held horizontally across his chest, like a fence, dipped to let her through—and walked up to Sky Wind Warrior, who lounged with his elbows propped on the top of his table throne.

"Father . . ." she said softly as she approached, her head demurely bowed.

He seemed startled. "Spirits . . . ?"

His words were soft, slurred. He was very drunk. "Yes, Father?" She stepped close to him, so they couldn't be overheard.

He leaned forward and put his lips close to her ear. She got a strong whiff of sour pulque as he whispered, "You shouldn't be here."

"Oh, Father, please don't send me away. I haven't met the Great King yet."

He straightened, eyeing her carefully. "It's not a proper time."

She looked into his one good eye. "Why, Father? Green Water is here. She's with him now."

He glanced over her shoulder with a guilty start. So he's in on it, too, she thought with sudden dismay. "That's . . . different," he said at last.

She knew better than to argue with him, so she sidestepped the question entirely. "Father, please? Let me meet him, and then I'll go right back to Mother. I promise."

Sky Wind's good eye, which had begun to wander, snapped back to her face. As if he'd just remembered she was there. He shook his head in irritation. "Your sister . . ."

"I won't say a word, Father."

"All right. Come on with me. No, take my hand. Keep your head down, and remember your manners."

She put her hand in his, and let him lead the way. His palm felt dry and rough, and for an instant she felt like a little girl again. Sky Wind took slow, careful steps, but stayed in front of her, shielding her with his body. It made her feel small and protected, and for a moment, despite all his failings, she loved her father very much.

She felt the silence that suddenly surrounded them as if she'd stepped into a pocket of chill, damp air. It was a *watchful* silence . . .

"Lord," Sky Wind Warrior said softly. "This is my youngest daughter. Her name is Spirits Walking Woman." He tugged her forward. She kept her head down, dropped to her knees, carefully bumped her forehead on the trampled earth.

"My Lord King," she whispered. He was only a boy. She'd seen him, drunk, laughing like any boy. But her words trembled in her throat. That silence, surrounding him . . .

His voice was a clear tenor, each word crisp and distinct, as if none of the pulque she'd seen him drink had touched him at all.

Still on her knees, she raised her head, and started slightly as his long fingers made a cup beneath her chin. He lifted up her face and said, "But . . . you're beautiful."

Beside him, Green Water Woman's eyes blazed like coals just before they burst into flame: filmy and ashen on the surface, scorching red-black cracks beneath.

"My Lord," she hissed.

"Be quiet," he said, without looking at her.

And to Spirits, "Stand up, girl, and let me look at you." It was strange to hear a voice so arrogant and so youthful at the same time.

She rose to her feet, feeling the heat of Green Water's hatred like a fire smoldering off to her right, murder in the shadows. Then her eyes snagged on Harvest Mountain's dark gaze, caught, held, and—

Green Water Woman uttered a choked cry of rage, lurched forward, and splashed a full gourd of pulque into Spirits's face. Spirits felt the sticky warmth drench her, cascade down the feathers of her cape, glue them together into a sodden, dripping mass.

"*Sorry,*" Green Water said over and over again, "*sorry, sorry.*"

The High King had instinctively jerked back. Now he stepped forward again, his hand reaching for Spirits, who was trying to wipe the stinging liquid from her eyes. She could feel the clay-based paint smearing beneath her fingers, and knew she must look like a fool.

Green Water was still babbling hysterically. "*Sorry, my Lord, oh, sorry, one of the servants pushed me, sorry . . .*"

"Which one?" Sky Wind Warrior grated.

She stared at him, then flapped her right arm. ". . . that one."

It could have been anybody. Or nobody.

Sky Wind Warrior faced the High King. "I apologize, my Lord. All you all right?"

The young man grinned. "Pulque, Sky Wind? Nobody was ever harmed by pulque—at least not from having it poured on them . . ." He cut his eyes toward Green Water, then turned serious. "But, Spirits, I'm afraid her robe is ruined." Awkwardly, he tried to smooth the feathers over her shoulders, but where his fingers touched, clumps of blue came away and fell to the ground.

"My Lord . . ." Spirits protested softly. "It's only a robe."

Harvest Mountain wiped his fingers absently on his thigh, leaving blue streaks. "Your face is a mess, little one."

She touched her cheeks. "I must go now, Lord. I'm sorry." She was already backing away, her face lowered to hide her confusion and anger. Behind Harvest Mountain, Green Water glared, head thrown back, her wide nostrils quivering in triumph.

"Yes, little sister. Go change your filthy clothes before you disgrace us any further . . . and when you come back, keep yourself with the rest of the *children,* out of harm's way."

Spirits felt her cheeks burning. "Yes, dear sister," she whispered. "I'm sorry for making such a scene . . ."

Harvest Mountain reached out, brushed his fingertips across her chin. "It's all right, Spirits Walking. Perhaps I will see you again . . ."

She nodded, lowered her head in a final bow, and backed away.

Beautiful, she thought. *He said I was beautiful.*

Green Water Woman stopped a passing servant, then turned back, one exposed breast pressing lightly against Harvest Mountain's arm as she offered a fresh gourd of pulque.

"My Lord," she said. "Where were we?"

He laughed, took the gourd, and swallowed heavily. "We were right here, I think," he said. "But maybe not for much longer . . ."

IX

Green Water felt a thrill of fear—and anticipation. Harvest Mountain had set up his royal enclosure at the foot of the Long Court, a quickly built compound made of poles set into the ground and loosely covered with a thatch of dark green palm fronds. The freshly cut fronds, called *coyol*, breathed a thick, spicy scent into the air as Harvest Mountain, finally showing a few signs of intoxication—he stumbled once, and laughed for no apparent reason—led her by the hand deep into the interior of the makeshift royal pavilion.

Out of the corner of her eye, Green Water saw faces turn to follow them, like white mushrooms growing in the shadows—courtiers curious about their master's choice of bedmates for the night.

She paid no attention. In the close-knit world of her people, privacy was nearly impossible—she'd grown up under the careful observation of relatives, servants, and slaves, and for her this watchfulness held no more importance than if those eyes had been painted on otherwise blank stones.

"Here . . ." Harvest Mountain said, tugging her toward his bed. She let herself be pulled off her feet, and flopped as gracefully as she could onto a mound of straw that was covered with woven mats and a layer of white cotton blankets. A cloud of clean-smelling straw dust rose up around her. He stood over her, hands on his narrow hips, staring down. She could see the white glint of his teeth, and a faint sparkle where his eyes hid in the shadow of his cheekbones.

"My Lord . . ." she said, raising her arms in invitation.

"You want me," he said. There was no question in his voice.

She nodded, and slowly spread the front of her robe, until her pale nakedness lay framed in the feathers, like a gift. She ran her fingers down across her breast, stroked her burning nipples, licked her lips . . .

"Come to me, Lord . . ."

He exhaled slowly, then shrugged out of his own cape and let it fall unheeded. It made a feathery rustle in the darkness. He stripped off his skirt and clout, and she saw his penis, tall and dark against the lighter skin of his belly. It was huge—she hadn't been wrong. So large it was almost a deformity, the big round knob twitching well above his navel.

"Yes . . ." he said, lowering himself. She spread her legs to receive him, feeling the hot wetness leaking from her secret places, dripping and cooling on her inner thighs.

"Uhmmm . . ." he moaned as she took his weight, felt the length of his club caught between them, pressing on her soft belly, like a third presence in their bed.

She thrust up against him, grinding her hips. He smelled of pulque and sweat. His tongue, thrust deep inside her mouth, tasted of salt; he ground his lips against hers, crushing her lips against his teeth until she tasted blood.

It enraged her. She began to buck beneath him, her engorged nipples scraping against his smooth chest, sliding back and forth on a film of sweat.

He thrust his great member into the darkness between her legs, and she felt the hard roundness, sliding on its own lubrication, batter against her entrance.

She spread her legs wider, felt him enter her, felt her tender flesh stretching . . . It was pain and it was wonderful and she ran her long fingernails down the cool gooseflesh of his back, her head thrown back, eyes wide and blank, mouth open, gasping. As he clawed and thrust at her, and she at him, biting, tearing, bruising.

Like animals. It was the most pleasure she'd ever found.

And just before the long, rhythmic shudders caught her up and lifted her away, some still sane part of her thought: "What can Spirits do to compete with this?"

Then the hot, sweet darkness took her, and inside herself she screamed, *Mine! He's mine . . .*

His weight crushed down on her, and she remembered nothing more.

CHAPTER THREE

I

Always an early riser, Spirits loved the morning best of all. While the rest of the city slept, she preferred to be up and about, wandering down the Long Court, perhaps stopping near the parapets and looking down across the great stone quarries in the filmy light of dawn, or just standing in the woods near the Royal Pavilions, listening to the birds and smelling the thick scent of dew on the grass.

On this morning she was near the northern edge of the city proper, peering over the cliff top, watching the brown snake of the river curl past the edge of the quarries. Down below, the slaves were already up, being urged on by their overseers, as they worked to load a huge stone shape onto roller logs near the riverbank.

From this distance it was hard to make out the workings on that immense stone, just that it was a rectangular block as long as two men, as tall as a tall man standing upright. The thin cries of the overseers, and the snap of their whips, wavered on the morning breeze.

"That's mine, you know . . ."

"*What*! Oh . . . my Lord. I'm sorry, you startled me." She felt her cheeks burning, and thought: this is ridiculous, all I ever do with him is embarrass myself. Then, suddenly, she realized how naked she was; as was her wont on these morning strolls, she wore only a skirt. Her hair was unbound, falling down to her shoulder blades, and her upper body was exposed to the morning air. She was suddenly conscious of her tiny breasts, and instinctively placed her hands across them.

He seemed not to notice. In fact, he wasn't looking at her at all, but instead stared dreamily off across the cliff top, a faint smile quirking his lips. Like her, he wore only sandals and a skirt. She noticed deep red ridges, like claw marks, running down the tight muscles of his back.

"I ordered that one made two rainy seasons ago, when my father died and I ascended to the throne. His throne, that is. That one will be mine." He nodded toward the huge stone moving an inch at a time toward the river. "Have you seen it yet?"

"No . . . You're up early, my Lord."

He laughed softly. "You mean after last night? I'm lucky, I guess. Pulque doesn't seem to affect me. And I wanted to see your city without an army of courtiers and guards trailing along behind."

She nodded. He looked different this morning, dressed simply, his face unmarked by the previous night's revels. Younger—there wasn't that creepy feeling of watchfulness about him today. He seemed almost like any other boy.

Careful, she warned herself. He may seem that way, but he's still the High King. She wanted desperately to ask him about Green Water, but instinctively knew that would be a mistake. She didn't want him thinking about her sister, not now. Not when she had her own . . .

She shook her head slightly. "My father doesn't let me go down to the quarries," she said.

"Ah. Well, would you like to?"

She turned and looked at him. He was smiling; the missing tooth in his lower jaw made him seem even more boyish.

"My Lord . . ."

"Oh, don't worry. I'll escort you myself. Surely your father wouldn't mind."

She thought that Sky Wind Warrior, with his intricate schemes, most definitely would mind. Which was why she had no intention of asking him.

"I'm sure, Lord." She smiled. "What better escort could I ask for?"

His grin widened. "Good. It's settled, then. Do you know the way?"

"Of course, Lord. The top of the trail is right over here . . ." As she led him to a break in the rough stone wall, she noticed that he limped slightly, like her father did, but off a different leg. There was a long, twisty, pink scar on his right thigh, beginning somewhere beneath his skirt and running down almost to the back of his knee. Her father had gotten his scar in battle. She wondered what had happened to Harvest Mountain, but didn't think she knew him well enough to ask.

"Careful going down," she said. "It's narrow."

"You lead the way," he told her.

II

The path down the cliff to the quarries was even narrower and steeper than the main path Harvest Mountain had climbed to enter Holy Stone City the day before. It took only a cursory examination to see that from a military standpoint, a handful of strategically placed men could stop an army here forever. He shook his head and turned his thoughts to other things.

This modest girl beside him, for instance, with her hands still cupped demurely across her childish breasts.

For a moment he wondered what she would do if he grabbed those thin wrists, ripped them away, and threw her down . . .

No.

There was something more to her than that. Just a feeling, but he'd sensed it the night before, and now, in the clear, fresh morning air, he felt it even more strongly. Something different . . .

Her elder sister, of course, was another story. His thoughts drifted to her as he'd left her earlier, sprawled on her back on his bed, legs spread wide, no doubt proclaiming her wantonness even in her sleep. For a moment or two he forgot about the pristine young woman at his side as he remembered the almost frighteningly pleasurable experience of the night before.

He could still smell the sharp odor of her musk, taste the salt of her sweat, the blood on her lips. It had been like having sex with a she-jaguar, all claws and hot breath and writhing muscle. Her frenzy had been contagious; when he'd rammed himself inside her and felt her arch beneath him, it was as if he'd lost himself. His world had expanded suddenly, and he'd floated in a great, bloodshot darkness, feeling himself melting into her as they battered and slashed each other, nerve endings screaming, until she'd *sucked* his essence into her . . .

He shivered involuntarily, thinking of it. The woman was possessed . . .

"My Lord?" Spirits said.

"Um. Sorry, wasn't paying attention." He glanced down at her and thought it was amazing how different two sisters could be. Of course, Spirits was younger, and perhaps in time she would become like her elder sister. But he doubted it. There was an air of sturdy innocence about her, and he couldn't picture her shrieking, bucking, raking her fingernails down his back . . .

He realized he was growing erect. And it wasn't at the memories of the night before, but from trying to imagine Spirits in a similar position.

She would scream, but . . .

He shook his head. Hot already, and the day hardly begun. They reached a switchback in the trail, a small open space that looked out over the quarries and to the river beyond. Mist swirled along the surface of the brown water, slowly melting. The sun was well above the horizon now, shrinking into a hot, blazing ball. Across the river, the forest was dissolving into a wavering green line as heat mirages drifted up, obscuring the individual trees. He squinted against the buttery yellow light, and shaded his eyes to get a better view of the activity below.

The shouts of the men straining against the huge chunk of hard gray basalt were sharper, more distinct. The overseers were the loudest, shouting gutteral threats and urging the slaves to "Push harder! Harder!"

"They've almost got it to the edge of the river," Harvest Mountain said.

Spirits watched the scene below with interest. "Yes." As she watched, a phalanx of naked men put their shoulders to the stone and shoved. The stone moved perhaps an inch, hard to tell from this far away. "They say the hardest part is getting it onto the raft."

Harvest Mountain nodded. They must be getting close, then, because a huge raft made of logs tied together with tough woven vines was anchored right at the edge of the bank, only an arm's length from the leading edge of the stone.

"Two of the slaves were crushed the other day," Spirits noted softly.

"Ah," Harvest Mountain agreed. He didn't care about slaves.

"Do you want to go closer?" Spirits asked.

He took her hand. He did it so naturally that Spirits

hardly noticed that her fingers were touching the
Great King for the first time in her life. Or that she'd
dropped her palms from her breasts, and that Harvest
Mountain was eyeing her with renewed interest.

"Yes, let's go on down. I want to see it up close."
He tugged at her, and she looked up at him.

"Should you call your guards, Lord? I mean, they
are slaves . . ."

He grinned. Wouldn't her father love it if he managed to get himself killed down there? But it was a
challenge, somehow, and for some reason it mattered
what this girl with her wide, clear gaze thought of him.
He would not show her anything that might be called
cowardice. And her concern touched him in a way
that made him wonder . . .

"No, no. We'll be fine. Come on."

III

Of course, their arrival in the quarries completely
disrupted the work. She squeezed his hand in dismay.
"Oh, Lord, I didn't think . . ."

All around them, overseers were bumping their
heads on the ground, or whipping the slaves into suitable obeisance. Harvest Mountain brought them to a
halt at the edge of the main area of activity, said,
"Sorry. I should have known," and squeezed her hand
in reply.

The quarry master hurried toward them, summoned
from his pavilion some distance away. He was short
and stocky, with the familiar upside-down-pear-shaped
skull of the Old People, just like Skull Breaker. He
wore only a clout; his fat round belly jiggled as he ran
toward them, sweat streaming down his blocky face.
Two servants hurried along with him, one carrying a
colorful woven robe that flapped in the breeze.

The quarry master reached them, flung himself

down, and banged his forehead in submission with
such vigor Spirits worried he would split his skull.

"Arise . . . servant," Harvest Mountain said
absently.

"Yes, Broken Carver, get up," Spirits added.
"You'll hurt your knees, down there like that."

Harvest Mountain turned to grin at her. "You
know, I never thought about that . . ."

She realized what she'd done. "Oh, Lord, I'm sorry.
I didn't think—"

"No, it's all right." He paused, still grinning, then
bent down to whisper in her ear: "You can call me
Harvest Mountain if you'd like." His nostrils widened
slightly; her black hair smelled clean and fresh. She
must have washed it when she got up.

"Oh . . . yes, my Lord—Harvest Mountain."

"That's better," he told her.

Broken Carver, helped to his feet by his servants,
donned his robe. His eyes flicked uncertainly back and
forth between them.

"The High King would like to see his stone," Spirits said.

"Ah . . . yes. Of course. What would you like to
see, your Highness?"

Harvest Mountain stared at him. "Oh . . . whatever."

"Lead the way," Spirits added cheerfully.

They stood at the edge of a broad, cleared area at
the foot of the quarry wall proper. The ground was
beaten into dust by the tramp of hundreds of feet, the
scrape of great stones, the pressure of countless rolling
logs and wedges. At the far edge of this space began
the jumbled village where the slaves lived; the stench
was overwhelming, even at this distance. The sun
blazed down on all this like a furnace; Spirits felt
sweat prickling on her skin.

Broken Carver, his dignity restored with his robe,
cleared his throat, bowed halfway, and pointed toward

the huge stone, partly concealed by the crowd of slaves now standing slack-jawed around it.

"Come with me, please," he said. His voice was thick with phlegm, the consequence of breathing years of stone dust. They followed him until he stopped a few feet from the stone itself, the mob of slaves parting silently to let them through.

"We began the excavation of this particular stone two turnings of the seasons ago, my Lord," he said, bowing once again in Harvest Mountain's direction. "As you can see, it is a fine stone, hard-grained, strong. I personally selected it, and supervised the initial cuts."

Harvest Mountain stepped closer, squinting his eyes against the sunlight that sparked off a million tiny facets in the rock. Of course, he'd seen much of this kind of work before; his capital, Great Head City, held more of the great sculptures—the heads, the altars, the table thrones—than any other location in the empire. But what he'd seen was finished work. He'd never examined, up close, the naked hulking rock, barely worked, as it was wrenched from the ground like a protesting tooth, and dragged by brute force to the river for its long journey to the capital.

Broken Carver's rough, liquid voice faded to a minor buzzing as Harvest Mountain examined what would one day be his own throne, set in its high place at the top of the Grand Court in Great Head City.

It was a single chunk of dark gray volcanic basalt, roughly hacked into a rectangular shape with a flat top whose edges overhung the massive base by perhaps the length of his forearm. In the middle of the base some skilled carver had already roughed out a niche, and within the niche a squat figure was seated cross-legged. Only vague details were yet visible; the figure, and all the fine decorations of the throne, would be finished by the master artisans in the capital. Even so, this gigantic rock was impressive; it seemed

to contain within its gray-black skin a sense of brooding, of hidden power.

He slowly ran his fingertips across the surface. Hot,
slightly rough. He sighed.

"Very good . . . carver," he said absently. "You've
done well."

He paid no attention to the sucking sounds of
breath suddenly inhaled, and he didn't even bother to
look at the man who had dropped to the ground and
banged his forehead in gratitude for praise from the
High King himself.

"Hear me now," he continued, still staring at the
table throne before him. "I require another of the
god-rocks, this one larger than any you have ever
made before. It will be my own image, and you must
send it to me before two more full turns of the seasons. Do you understand?"

Broken Carver, overcome with joy, continued to
pound his forehead into the dirt. A dark, sweaty depression was forming before him in the dust. Even
Spirits gasped; it was a huge demand, one that would
require many servants and slaves, and would command a huge price from this boy before her. Enough,
perhaps, to assure the riches of Holy Stone City for
years to come.

Harvest Mountain turned away from his throne-to-
be with a soft sigh. "Well, Spirits Walking, what do
you think? Have I done well?"

"My Lord . . . Harvest Mountain. It is a great thing.
My father . . ."

"Oh, blast your stupid father," he said suddenly,
then stopped at the shocked expression on her face.

"I'm sorry, Spirits Walking. I didn't mean that. So
hot out today, and I left my fan wavers behind. Makes
me irritable, I'm afraid. Forgive me, would you?"

She shook her head helplessly, not knowing what
to say. Somehow the morning had turned dark and
frightening. He had said too much, and what she had

so far ignored now lay between them like a swollen boil, waiting to be lanced.

And they both knew it, staring at each other. "Of course I do," she said smoothly, fighting for time to get her thoughts in order. She had him to herself, at least for a short time yet. When they returned up the cliff to the city, then he would slip beyond her grasp.

Her last chance . . .

"Broken Carver!" she said sharply. "Are you deaf? Can you not hear the High King? Surely we have fans, and slaves to wave them?"

Broken Carver scrambled to his feet, his flabby teats joggling, his eyes suddenly wide with terror. He said, "Yes . . . yes, of course, my Lady. Right away!" He turned and launched a ponderous kick at one of his servant's backsides. "Go . . . you fool. Can't you hear?"

Harvest Mountain watched all this with secret amusement, but it was a grave expression he turned on Spirits as a flock of barely dressed men, each bearing a tattered fan, came running toward them.

"Thank you, my Lady. You are too kind."

She inclined her head. Once again, her cheeks felt as if the sun had played on them for hours. "Perhaps we should start back?" she ventured.

He nodded, and offered his arm. "An excellent idea, Spirits. Would you join me for some porridge when I break my fast?"

And what will Green Water think of that? Spirits wondered. But she only smiled demurely, and said, "I would love that . . . Harvest Mountain."

IV

On the slow stroll back up the cliffs, this time accompanied by the earnest efforts of a small army of fan wavers, who managed only to assault them with

turgid breezes at least as hot as the ambient air, Spirits
tried once again to order her thoughts.

She knew something had happened down below,
perhaps something important, but she wasn't sure
what it was, or if she could weave it into her own
plots. And as she thought this, it suddenly came to
her what the youth at her side must undergo. He was
the High King, and as such, the center of all plots, the
object of desire for all his subjects, from the highest
to the lowest. Even she thought of him not primarily
as a boy, a fellow being, but as something to be ma-
neuvered, captured, *used*. A wave of disgust swept
over her, and worse, pity. The pity was unforgivable;
for it put her on a pedestal above him, looking down,
and he was the High King. She wondered if he had
any idea . . .

But of course he did. He must have. She knew what
her own upbringing had been like, the hard lessons
her mother had whispered, her stubby fingers weaving
incomprehensible patterns in the air: Spirits, be careful. Always be watchful. You are who you are, not
just a girl, but a princess, the daughter of your blood,
a target always . . .

This, for a babe no more than six summers old,
listening to her mother's voice. No doubt Harvest
Mountain, named from birth his father's successor,
had been taught lessons even more unforgiving. And
with good reason, she knew: was she not herself plotting against him?

Was she any better than Green Water or Sky Wind
Warrior? No, she was not, she decided. For who was
to say her own goals were, in the end, any better
than theirs?

She wished she could talk openly with him about
these things, but she stayed her first impulse to speak.
She feared she'd already made a botch of things. Such
openness could only make things worse.

"Your sister wants to marry me, I think," Harvest

Mountain murmured into her ear. A wicked grin made his sharp, hard features seem to dance. "What do you think about that, Spirits?" He still held her hand, and as he spoke, he tightened his grip, turning her slightly toward him.

"My Lord—" She glanced at the nearest of the fan wavers, a limber creature, one of the High Race, his face carefully blank as he waved his ragged implement.

But Harvest Mountain seemed not to notice. "She came to me last night, you know," he went on, that devilish grin widening. "It was . . . pleasant."

Suddenly Spirits feared for her life. She saw in his expression a test, but one she couldn't understand. Nevertheless, if the moment standing next to his stone had been important, this was even more so. Down below, with one irritated outburst, he'd as much as admitted he knew about her father's plots. Now he was asking her opinion on matters she should not even have been aware of, let alone had thoughts on. What to do?

She settled on the one thing about herself she trusted, the thing that had seen her through much in her short life. Honesty.

"I think my sister would be a wonderful wife for you," she said. "She is very beautiful. And, as you say, pleasant."

He chuckled softly. "What do you know of pleasure, Spirits?"

She shrugged. "Well, of course, I personally know very little. I am still young," she want on practically. "But Green Water has told me things."

"I can imagine," Harvest Mountain said. "But, tell me—do you think that is what a High King should look for in his wife? Remember, she will not be a consort or a concubine. She will be Queen."

The question was such a surprise that Spirits actually stopped, her features suddenly screwed up in thought. Harvest Mountain's question had thrust to the very heart of her own long musings. What did a man want from a woman? More important, what did a man need from a wife? Was it only the pleasure? Was there something else?

A door seemed to have opened, one she had not expected to find. And with it, a chance. But she would have to be careful. If only, she realized suddenly, she didn't like this golden-skinned, hard-faced boy beside her. It was far easier to think of him as the High King, than as Harvest Mountain, now grinning quizzically at her.

She took a deep breath, and plunged in. "You have asked two questions, Harvest Mountain. One is about a wife. The other is about a queen."

He arched his dark eyebrows. "But in my case, aren't they the same thing?"

A ghost of memory touched her: he had been married already, and his queen was no longer with him—yet nobody in Holy Stone City knew the true story about it. Carefully, then . . .

"I don't see how, my Lord. As a wife she must serve you in one way. Your children, your home, your . . . pleasure. But as a queen, she must also help you to bear your burdens."

His eyebrows floated even higher. "Ah. And how might a *woman* do that?"

She bridled against the question, for in it was everything she rebelled against: how could a woman ever be anything but a poor imitation of a man, fit only for bearing children and cooking? Yet she knew it could be different. Did he?

"She could listen, Harvest Mountain. She could speak if she thought it right. She could be trustworthy, an advisor. Bound to you by blood, by children . . ."

"Yes," he nodded, his expression suddenly going bleak. "Her children . . ."

She didn't know what had changed him, but now was not the time to pursue it. "You know what I mean," she said finally, wincing at the weakness. "Don't you?"

His expression cleared, and, almost impulsively, he reached out, took her in his arms, and gave her a quick hug. "Why, yes, Spirits, I think I do. It might be possible . . ." He paused, while she blushed furiously at his embrace, then finished: "if *you* were my wife."

She didn't speak another word all the way back to the top, where of course, like a bad dream, Green Water Woman and her entourage waited like a flock of brightly colored—though enraged—vultures.

V

"I ordered that a new stone be drawn from the quarries," Harvest Mountain said to Skull Breaker.

"Your image, your holy stone," Skull Breaker said. "I heard. It is all over the city."

"Hm. And what else have you heard, Lord Big Ears?" Harvest Mountain asked tartly. Sometimes, Skull Breaker's air of calm omniscience annoyed his master.

Skull Breaker, oblivious to Harvest Mountain's crotchets, as only an ancient, trusted, and *necessary* retainer could be, said, "Many things, Lord. It is said that you will marry the elder sister, because she gave you great pleasure."

"Hah! Evidently even here the servants have sharp ears."

"Servants have sharp ears everywhere, Lord. You might do better to remember that."

"Oh, Skull Breaker, quit preaching to me. You sound like my father sometimes."

"I should. I learned these lessons *from* your father. As did you, if you haven't forgotten all of them."

"Careful, Lord General. You overstep yourself."

"Ah, yes, Lord. My apologies." He didn't sound

apologetic at all. "At any rate, the tale of your, um, pleasure is also all over the city. And, finally, the fact that you cannot seem to take your eyes off the younger sister's childish breasts, even while you tell the whole world you think her father is stupid." He shook his head. "All in all, a fine performance for one day, my Lord."

"I kept my voice down," Harvest Mountain said petulantly.

"Better you should keep it silent," Skull Breaker said with some asperity. "If you must speak, let your cock do your talking. At least that isn't likely to inspire open rebellion . . ."

Harvest Mountain found this greatly humorous. "Ah, but Skull Breaker, you are the one who always tells me not to let that part of my body lead me around."

Skull Breaker grunted. "Better a one-eyed snake than a man entirely blind." He paused, sighed. "So. Are you going to marry the she-devil?"

"How do you know she's a devil?"

"She has a reputation that precedes both you and her," Skull Breaker said dryly. "If you know who to ask."

"Oh? And who might that be?"

Skull Breaker stared at him. "Anybody in Holy Stone City with a prick between his legs."

"Skull Breaker, are you trying to tell me that the eldest royal daughter of my loyal subject, Sky Wind Warrior, is a slut?"

"Yes, Lord."

"Ah. Do you believe that disqualifies her from becoming my queen?"

Now Skull Breaker's sagging features wrinkled into a radiant smile. "Of course not, Lord. Why would you ever think that?"

They both broke into laughter; Harvest Mountain slapped the older man on the back as they walked off,

still chuckling over the joke. Neither of them noticed
the girl with clear, dark eyes watching them, a faint
frown wrinkling her smooth forehead.

VI

Dripping with sweat, dizzy with exertion, drained
and exhausted, Harvest Mountain Lord felt his penis
shrinking, shrinking, until it fell out of Green Water
Woman with a soft, popping sound. She jerked at the
movement, sighed, and relaxed, stretching beneath
him like a great cat, sated.

On his back, a set of fresh scratches tingled sharply
against the damp night air. High and thin, the femi-
nine shriek of some hunting forest beast quavered in
the stillness. He shivered.

"Ahhh . . . Lord," Green Water muttered, her voice
thick with the dregs of lust. She stretched out her
hands, and in the glimmering dark he imagined he
could see bloody bits of his own flesh caught beneath
those hungry nails. And in the gloom, her teeth
flashed like the fangs of some dark jungle cat. Once
again he thought of the Lord Jaguar . . . though how
that mighty one could possess a *woman* . . .

He shook his head. She stretched again, this time
moving her body so the distant, reflected light of
torches flickered on the wetness that outlined her
breasts, her belly, her secret place.

"Mmmm . . ." Half moan, half summons.

His breath ratcheted in his throat. He licked his lips.
She was a terror, but he couldn't help himself. She
was a goddess, a sex goddess, untamed and untame-
able. Slowly, he sank down upon her fevered flesh,
hating himself, hating *her,* because he was helpless in
her endless spell . . .

Not a wife, though. She had not yet made him that
crazed, and he thanked the Nameless One for that.

"Oh, Lord . . ." he groaned as he thrust himself inside her once again.

She licked his ear and laughed.

VII

The whole city was aware of the change, almost as soon as Harvest Mountain formally requested a high audience with their lord, Sky Wind Warrior.

In the villages, where the bets had grown even more hysterical over the preceding two days, men wagered their women, their crops, even their thatched huts, but by the end there were no more wagers available.

Would the Great King take a wife from Holy Stone City? If the gamblers were to be believed, he would. And so there was more than passing interest amongst the villages and even the servants when Harvest Mountain Lord, wearing every feathered, beaded piece of his royal regalia, his round breast plate made of jade and polished to a mirror shine gleaming on his chest, strode slowly up the length of the Long Court toward the great table throne where King Sky Wind Warrior sat, awaiting him.

There was no disrespect in this, for everyone knew that Harvest Mountain, on this day at least, approached their lord not as High King, but as a suppliant. Lord General Skull Breaker, looking dour in a fantastic robe of yellow parrot feathers, a chain of skulls dangling from a belt around his waist, escorted him, his old features gray and heavy with disapproval.

Crowds packed the spaces along the tops of the Long Court, watching the pageantry approach from their vantage points between the royal mounds that lined the way. Would the High King take his wife from the city? Many faces concealed hidden smiles, and many thick fingers rubbed together in anticipation. Green Water Woman's skills had worked their magic again. Even a High King, it seemed, was not proof against them, and there would be much new riches in the villages this night.

Two fan wavers beat the air before Harvest Mountain. His herald, a bull-voiced soldier of the Jaguar Cult, preceded him as well, stopping directly before the table throne and throwing his head back.

"The High King Harvest Mountain Lord, Ruler of the City of Great Heads, leader of all the cities of the inner plains and forests, begs leave to approach the King Sky Wind Warrior on a matter of great importance!"

Spirits Walking Woman, standing with her mother and sister at the right hand of Sky Wind Warrior, directly in front of the throne, glanced between the approaching King and her father, who sat stone-faced in robes at least the equal of the man who approached, his own fan wavers gently moving the air above his head.

In his rawhide darkness, his one good eye shining like a beacon in a face of old mahogany, he looked every inch a king, and once again, Spirits was reminded how much she loved him, despite his foolishness.

And that brought a pang—for she had failed. She needed no one to tell her so. It was written in every line, every muscle, every sly poke of triumph from her sister standing next to her.

"I'm going to Great Head City," she'd hissed earlier. "The King chose me!"

And, indeed, Spirits did see how the High King's gaze swept over them as they stood there, seeking Green Water. But now, as he drew close to the throne itself, and his herald shouted his official request, he turned his eyes back, and up, to Sky Wind Warrior.

Spirits sighed. What would be, would be. She would just have to find another way. Perhaps she could go with her sister, as a handmaid or some other menial thing. At least she would be close to the seat of power, and perhaps, in time, she could exert some kind of

influence—though when she thought of trying to convince Green Water to let her come along, her inner
vision of the future reeled somewhat.

Harvest Mountain approached almost to the front
edge of the table throne and stopped, his head tilted
back so that he looked directly into Sky Wind Warrior's eyes, up above him. Spirits watched, wondering
if Harvest Mountain had ever stood in such an inferior
position before. Then she realized; of course he had.
He must have approached his own father in this manner a thousand times. But Sky Wind Warrior wasn't
his father.

The moment held for a beat, two: Sky Wind Warrior looking down, his face a carved chunk of burned
wood, Harvest Mountain staring up, a faint smile playing on his lips.

"I come to you, oh King, to beg a great gift," Harvest Mountain began.

Sky Wind waved his right hand languidly. *He's enjoying this,* Spirits thought. *He imagines himself like
this always . . . the fool.*

All the more so for making his pleasure so obvious.

But Harvest Mountain seemed not to notice. His
faint smile never wavered as he mouthed his way
through the formal passages of the request.

Spirits knew the words as well as she knew her own
thoughts; the plea to the father for marriage was as
ancient as the peoples themselves. Some said the ritual
was even older than the Old Ones, and had been pre-
scribed by the Nameless One itself . . .

As Harvest Mountain reached the end of the ritual
plea, Spirits realized that every muscle in her body
had tensed: her palms hurt, and when she uncurled
her fingers and looked down, she saw small bloody
half-moons, where her nails had dug into flesh.

"I come before you a man seeking a woman," Harvest Mountain said, his voice perfectly clear in the
vast hush that covered the Long Courtyard. Spirits

saw every face turned and still, focused on the scene before the throne.

"And so I beg you, Lord King, for your daughter in marriage. Fulfill the binding I seek, and give her to me, your precious daughter . . ."

The sound of breath indrawn was like a soft, shuddering breeze across the vast amphitheater.

Harvest Mountain's gaze flickered toward her. His smile widened.

"Spirits Walking Woman," he said.

The roar of the crowd frightened even the birds from the trees, and they rose up, a black cloud of surprise, the sound of their wings like sudden thunder.

CHAPTER FOUR

I

The heat of the afternoon struck along the top of the cliffs like a hammer, crushing the city. Harvest Mountain Lord, the barely crusted scabs on his back itching furiously, sweat slicking his skin, his head throbbing, sank back on his bed. He'd been planning on sleeping away the fiercest part of the day, but the commotion in his outer room, beyond the woven hangings that concealed his bed, brought him up to his elbows. The missing tooth showed black in his wide smile as he waited for her to shriek her way past his personal guards. He tracked her progress by the increasing frenzy of her approach, heavy grunts, muffled screechings, and once the sharp sound of palm meeting flesh. A true devil, that one . . .

She erupted into his chamber in the arms of a burly soldier, twisting like a trapped animal, her hair in serpents around her distorted features. Her eyes were slits of dark fire.

"Let me *go*, son of a pig," she hissed. "I'll *kill* you . . ."

Harvest Mountain laughed. He waved one hand. "Let her go, Flint Spear," he said.

The soldier, his massive arms covered with red stripes from her voracious nails, complied happily,

dumping her to the ground like a bag of maize flour.
She landed with a thud and paused, momentarily
stunned, shaking her head. Her sweat-matted hair
hung down in her face like twisted snakes. Her breathing was a harsh rattle.

Flint Spear bowed and backed out of the room, obviously relieved to be free of this clawing, spitting she-
cat. Harvest Mountain raised himself to a full sitting
position and crossed his arms across his chest. "Welcome, Green Water Woman. Have you come to con-
gratulate me on my marriage?"

With the wall hangings lowered for his afternoon
sleep, the interior of the small pavilion was murky; a
pair of torch stakes, set into the earth at the corners of
the enclosure, flickered and sputtered, tendrils of aromatic smoke drifting away. In the gloom he couldn't
precisely see her eyes, but sensed them, caught in the
shadows of her face: wide, staring, netting the glint of
the torches in dark, fire-crazed mirrors.

She lunged at him with the ferocity of a cornered
jaguar, fangs and nails foremost; a choked hiss
coughed from her throat, a sound he'd heard before,
hunting in the jungles . . .

He barely had time to get his arms up to protect
his face when she landed on him, her teeth snapping
like a turtle's, a rattle of sharp ivory clicks.

One knee caught him in the balls and doubled him
up like a worm in the rain. The bulk of her weight
slammed into his chest and knocked the breath out of
him. Something sharp raked down his cheek, barely
skirting his eye. He fought down the surge of pain and
nausea boiling from his testicles, gasped for breath,
and fought back.

It was like trying to stuff a maddened jaguar into a
sack with his bare hands. She was all writhing muscle
and fang and claw; her breath was a rank fire in his
face. She grunted with the effort of murdering him,
but never slowed for an instant. Finally, gasping, he

pushed her far enough away to land a solid blow with his right fist. His knuckles caught the point of her chin; her teeth slammed together with a sharp clack and she went limp all at once. He fell back, panting, her weight slack across his belly, his muscles grinding between stones of fear.

"Uhgg . . . get *off* . . ." He pushed her away in a spasm of knees and elbows and then collapsed, his chest heaving, his balls sharp knots of agony.

There was a rustle at the doorway. Flint Spear's face appeared, carefully expressionless. "My Lord? Is everything all right here?"

"No . . . yes. Get out of here, Flint Spear."

The guard bobbed his head once and vanished.

He lay several moments longer, waiting for the paralyzing talon in his crotch to loose its hold on him. After a time he was able to stretch out, and his chest relaxed enough for him to suck in great whoops of damp, hot air. But those spastic gasps tasted as cool as mountain spring water, and he uttered a silent prayer of thanks to his master, the Jaguar God, for preserving him.

His eyes were wide and shocked as he finally rolled over and stared at her, his expression caught somewhere between fear and admiration. "By the Gods," he murmured. "You would have killed me . . ."

Slowly, he reached across, took her shoulder, and began to shake her roughly. Her head banged back and forth on the flaccid stalk of her neck. After a time she moaned, and he flung himself on her, his erection stronger and more urgent than he'd ever imagined it could be.

She was possessed, yes, but oh . . . what a possession.

II

"I hate you," she said.

All the strength seemed to have melted from her body. She lay next to him, covered with sweat and streaked with his blood, her eyes flat and vacant. Sated. Once again she reminded him of the jaguar, after the kill, after the feeding, sleek and limp and full. The memory of their coupling still filled him; there was no doubt about it, she was like one of those priestly herbs that made you want more and more . . .

Until you died.

"You would have killed me," he said.

She eyed him dully. "Yes. I still want to."

He spoke into the supercharged silence. "Do you know why I didn't ask for you?" he said at last.

At first she didn't respond. Then she turned to stare at him, her black eyes leaden and filmy, her face streaked with sweat and blood and tears. "No . . ."

He held her eyes. He wanted her to understand. "It was when I met your sister. Spirits Walking Woman."

Her eyes flickered. "I should have strangled that bitch when she was born." She paused. "I thought about it later."

He shuddered. He knew she meant every word. "I need a wife, a Queen . . ." he said.

Her voice was harsh. "I would have been a great Queen," she said.

He shook his head. "You don't see it, do you?"

A fire was rekindling in her eyes now. "See what?"

He laughed softly. "You're a slut, not a Queen. Spirits is a Queen. You—I can have *you* any time I want . . ."

Her teeth and claws raked out again, but this time he was ready for her. In more ways than one.

Later, after the second time, he put his lips against her ear and whispered, "But you can follow me to Great Head City. If you want to . . ."

III

Spirits still felt the gauzy mist of shock muffling her thoughts when Queen Blue Parrot gathered her into her soft, reassuring embrace, whispered, "Come with me, dear," and led her away from the Long Courtyard to the dim and soothing confines of the women's pavilion.

Blue Parrot, by virtue of her status, had a series of rooms all to herself; a place for sleeping, another where she prepared, with her own hands, private meals for herself and her husband, another where she entertained women of suitable rank. She led Spirits gently into her bedroom, the most secluded of these rooms, and sat her down on the pile of fragrant grasses, covered by mats and furs, that was her royal bed. She moved about for a moment, pushing up the woven curtains that otherwise shielded the room, letting in the sunlight like green-tinged honey.

"Look at me, Spirits." She waited until Spirits was able to focus her dazed eyes on her familiar wrinkled face. She sat very close, her minty breath—she loved to chew various herbs, and that was one of Spirits's earliest memories, the sweet aroma of her exhalations—washing across Spirits's face.

"Are you all right, daughter?" she asked.

Spirits nodded slowly. "I . . . yes, Mother, I think so. It's such a shock."

Her mother nodded. "And not just to you, dear. If I were you, I'd try to stay away from your sister for a while."

Spirits thought about that. "She must be very angry . . ."

Her mother's tone was dry. "More than that, I'd say. Just keep away from her. You know she doesn't listen to me."

"Or me, either, mother," Spirits said. "She frightens me."

She frightened Blue Parrot, too, but the Queen didn't see fit to mention it. She would take her own precautions, however, to make sure her youngest avoided the worst of Green Water's rage. For in her

own mind, though still somewhat stunned by the shock
of Harvest Mountain's choice, she had already begun
to see the possibilities. The question was, did Spirits
also see them? And that was what this was all about—
the first time she'd ever discussed her own schemes
with another—any other. It was a delicate moment,
and she proceeded carefully.

"It is a surprise, Spirits, but not an altogether un-
welcome one. To me, at least."

Her breath was like the smallest of warm breezes,
caressing the fine hair of Spirits's cheeks. This close,
the god marks that obscured her mother's vision were
plainly visible, tiny white islands floating in darkness.

"You wanted Green Water to marry the High King,"
Spirits said, her voice soft, but still somehow accusing.

Blue Parrot drew back. "Well, of course I did. It
seemed to me this family needed *some* one of us to
marry him, and your sister's . . . abilities seemed best
suited to the task."

Spirits's mouth dropped open. There was a tone of
tart asperity in her mother's voice, a naked practicality
she'd never heard before. Nor had she ever entertained a vision of her mother in this way—hardheaded, cold-eyed, more than aware of the world
around her, and the potential of her place in it. In a
way, this sudden expansion was frightening; in another, exhilarating.

"Mother . . ."

"Does it shock you, dear, that I would know such
things?" Blue Parrot smiled faintly, and tapped her
temple, next to her eyes. "I may not see so well any
more, but I'm not blind, daughter. I cannot afford to
be. My ears and my head still work fine—better than
ever, actually—and a careful woman can always find
other pairs of trusted eyes."

Spirits reached over and took Blue Parrot's hands
in her own. She squeezed softly, and ventured, "I
didn't know . . ."

"Really? I thought you did, daughter. Was I wrong?"

The conversation was even more unsettling than her chat with Harvest Mountain Lord—and how had that turned out the way it did?—but Spirits tried to encompass it. For this was her mother, though she was slowly beginning to understand that her mother was a far different person than she'd heretofore suspected.

Everything was so different now . . .

Blue Parrot continued with a new and brisk brittleness in her tone. "What do you know of your father's plans?" she said.

"You mean his plots? His schemes to overthrow my soon-to-be husband?" she said, not without a little bitterness.

"Oh, my. I have made a mistake. Forgive me, daughter. I underestimated you."

"Yes, Mother, you did."

"Um. How did you discover these plots?"

"As you did, I suppose, Mother. The blind, the children, the women, it's all the same. No man notices us, no man pays attention. We might as well not be here at all. And men talk . . . why fear us? Why even notice us?" She paused, her soft lips set, serious. "It is a great advantage, you know."

Blue Parrot rocked back and forth, each unsuspected new depth in her youngest daughter a revelation, a thrill. "I owe you my apologies, my dear. And I think I owe you a great deal more."

"Tell me," Spirits said.

Blue Parrot did. Spirits listened carefully, interrupting a few times for clarification. It was a long talk, and when she had finished, she took Spirits in her arms again. This time her embrace was even more intimate, for it sprang from a shared understanding.

"You understand, don't you, Spirits? Even though your path now is very hard, you do understand?"

Spirits nodded slowly, wishing that this embrace

could last forever, that she didn't have to grow up, that she could somehow shift the responsibility to other shoulders. But she could not. The Nameless One had chosen her. If the Gods cared about such things . . .

"Never forget, Spirits, that your husband is a man. He may be a boy now, he may be a High King, but he is a man. And you are a woman. *That* is the great river you—all of us—must forever try to cross. And in the end, you will fail. But you must try, anyway. For us, but most important, for yourself." She shook her head. "I wish the world was different, but it isn't. You see, the Gods have cursed us. Cursed all women."

The bleakness in these final words shivered Spirits to her core, but the defiance in them uplifted her, too. A double-edged gift, a path of pain and joy . . .

"I understand, Mother."

Blue Parrot's soft words took on an almost formal tone, exhortatory, measured: "Then I send you on your journey, daughter. I would not have given you this burden, but it was not my choice. You hold our future, our lives and the life of our city in your hands. I wish it was otherwise, but it is not. And so take with you my blessing, and my love. It is little enough, but it is all I have to give . . ."

Spirits felt tears spring to her eyes, and saw them answered in the dim orbs across from her. And for one final moment she was a child again, seeking only the solace of her mother's arms. She threw herself forward.

"I love you, Mother. I love you."

"Yes, dear, yes, yes. I love you too. Come, daughter, let us make you ready."

They rose together, mother and daughter, and went out arm in arm to face the uncertainty shared by all women, to survive in a world made by men, and the Gods men worshipped.

"Wipe away your tears, daughter. Don't let them see you weep."

"No, Mother, I won't. Not ever again."

But even as she spoke these words, Spirits realized she'd held something back. The thing, the place hidden deep inside her, where the unknown, the unknowable, lay curled like an unsprouted seed.

IV

On the morning of the wedding, a servant named Twisted Nose was the first to feel her mistress's wrath; shortly after the sun had begun to burn off the high mist along the top of the cliff wall, but before the heavenly fire had penetrated the thick, white blanket that still covered the forests below, she carefully began to apply finger-wide strokes of bright red paint to Green Water Woman's jawbone. She had seen a purple streak of shadow along the ridge of bone there, and had taken care, but not enough.

The backhanded slap caught her looking the other way, turned her head halfway around with its force, and knocked her to the ground.

"You stupid bitch!" Green Water drew back her fist for another blow, and then, visibly, forced herself to relax. She exhaled a ragged breath. "Get up," she snarled.

Twisted Nose, her eyes wide with fear, slowly did so. "Go on," Green Water said. "Finish it. Careful . . ."

Twisted Nose's fingertips trembled as she dipped again into the wooden trough of paint. Tears leaked from her eyes, and ran down over the flaming, palm-shaped blotch on her right cheek.

"Stop your sniveling," Green Water said brusquely.

She held her head steady, wincing only slightly this time when Twisted Nose's fingertips once again brushed across the bruised area.

Her eyes flashed, but she made no further movement, though behind her eyes a riot of bloody imagery danced; Twisted Nose on the dusty earth, writhing,

screaming, her innards flayed out in crimson strips,
hot coals falling into the leaking cavity, sizzling and
searing.

She shuddered at the sick rush of joy she felt. But it
wasn't enough, this vision of burned meat and tortured
slave. No, it wasn't Twisted Nose's eyes she wanted to
see screaming as her tongue was torn from her throat.

Him. Him and *her.*

With murder in her heart, she made herself ready
for the wedding.

V

"Quite a surprise, my Lord," Skull Breaker remarked as he held up a beautifully polished onyx
breastplate worth the ransom of three or four villages
for Harvest Mountain's inspection.

"Yes, that one. Let Sky Wind feast his one ugly
eye on real workmanship," Harvest Mountain said.
"Surprise? You think so?"

Skull Breaker shrugged. "I thought you were going
to take the she-devil, which was surprise enough. Then
you claimed the other one, and . . ." He grinned.
"Forgive my curiosity, but I would love to know why
you made your choice in that manner."

"Oh, you would, would you? Old snoop, you're
worse than a woman. Spy to your toenails. Well, I
don't mind telling you. I imagine you've already fig-
ured out most of it, anyway."

Skull Breaker put down the mirrored breastplate
and picked up one of three brilliant feathered robes
laid out for the King's delectation. "Yes, Lord, but
one always wants to know for sure."

"Skull Breaker, why are you playing at being a serving man? I must have a ten hands of servants and
slaves out there, any one of whom can shake out a
fine robe better than you."

Skull Breaker grinned. "It keeps me humble, Lord."

Harvest Mountain snorted. "She saw the difference at once, Skull Breaker. Between being a wife and being a queen. She saw the . . . possibilities, almost as if she'd been considering them for a long time."

"Yes, Lord. You walked down to the quarries by yourself, and so I don't know what you said to each other. But when you came back, there were servants, and I know every word that was spoken." He paused. "A remarkable girl, for one so young. Remarkable, indeed."

"Is there anything you don't know, Lord General?"

Skull Breaker's sensitive antennae picked up the prickly undertone in his master's words. He bowed his head quickly, and said, "Forgive me, Lord. But it is for your own safety. You must know that."

Harvest Mountain turned to let Skull Breaker slip the gorgeous robe around his shoulders. "Yes, Skull Breaker, I know. It is why I don't turn you over to your own torturers."

Skull Breaker felt a faint chill, as if a shadow had passed over him. He said nothing.

"I have many enemies here, my General. Guard me well."

"Yes, Lord."

Harvest Mountain paused. "And keep an eye on the she-devil."

Skull Breaker nodded. "I will, Lord."

Harvest Mountain spread his eyes wide. The great cloak fell in soft, shimmering waves from his well-formed shoulders. "I look like a king, eh? Like a High King?"

Skull Breaker smiled at him. "You *are* the High King, Lord."

VI

"Oh, Mother . . ." Spirits breathed.

"Yes," Blue Parrot said. "My women and I have

worked on it for two full seasons, ever since I knew
the High King would be stopping here." She stepped
aside and gestured for the two serving women to
spread the great cloak even wider.

A thousand tiny beads of perfectly polished serpentine had been strung together, then sewn in long
strands from the collar to the hem of the robe. In
between these softly glowing filaments thousands of
multicolored feathers—brown hawk, black eagle, parrot in every color of the rainbow—had been attached
one by one into a panoply of riotous hues. The final
touch was strips of rabbit and ocelot fur, and long,
smooth lengths of ocelot tail, brown and yellow and
white, so that the entire assemblage shimmered and
glittered and glowed almost as if it were a living thing.
It was truly a robe fit for a queen.

"Mine . . ." she said softly, stroking the amazing
thing with her fingertips.

"Yours," Blue Parrot agreed. "Oh, Spirits, you'll be
so beautiful." She began to weep softly.

Spirits came closer and brushed the moisture from
her mother's raddled cheeks. "You said not to cry,
Mama."

Blue Parrot sniffed, and smiled through her tears.
"Tears of happiness, daughter. They are different."

"Yes," Spirits whispered. "They are."

Without another word, she bent her shoulders, and
let the woman slip the fantastic garment onto her
back. It was the happiest moment of her life.

VII

The noonday sun blazed a hole in the lapis sky,
trailing necklaces of lofty white cirrus on strings of
yellow fire. Shadows once long on dew-glimmered
grass now puddled at the feet of the gathered throng;
the majestic swath of the Long Courtyard vibrated
with movement, with the hum of countless voices.

Drums thumped and flutes wailed; many of those near the throne, close to the musicians, began to clap and shout along with the infectious rhythms.

A low sigh rose from the multitudes. King Sky Wind Warrior appeared behind his throne, resplendent in a crimson cape made of feathers plucked from coveys of spoonbills and scarlet macaws. On his head rested a huge crown shaped like a helmet, but covered with hundreds of tiny, highly polished stone disks. With his every movement the fantastic headgear flashed wildly in dazzling splinters of reflected light.

A cheer rose up. He climbed the wooden steps concealed behind his table throne with preternatural dignity, so smoothly that it seemed he floated slowly up into the air. In his right hand he grasped an intricately carved wooden staff. He held his left palm out and forward, a gesture of power. Rings glittered on his long fingers.

As he took his solitary stand on top of the throne and looked out over his people, the priests of the temples began their own procession from the opposite end of the Long Courtyard; first, the white-garbed followers of the Nameless All, that two-faced Creator who ruled on high; then, treading with measured grace, those who served the Four Gods; the Lord Jaguar, the Lord Morningstar, the Dark Lord, and the Trickster Lord. These priests advanced with slow, ponderous dignity, in single file, toward the throne.

After the priests came the rest of the royal family, and finally Blue Parrot and Green Water Woman, splendid in ceremonial robes so encrusted with beads and feathers and furs they resembled dreamlike beings, goddesses stepping down from night to walk in light, if only for a short time.

The High King made his way down the center of the Long Court at the head of his own procession, his young face set and chill, his eyes aflame, carrying himself with a terrible, kingly dignity. The crowd grew quiet as he passed by, a moving pocket of silence.

Spirits Walking Woman, escorted by a covey of servants and slaves, appeared last, a tiny figure almost lost beneath a tall headdress and a robe like a heavenly garden. The throng marked her passage as well, but not with silence. Instead, it surged as she glided by, so that from a high place the mass of people resembled a great patchwork rug heaving in the breeze.

There was little of remark in the rituals and ceremonies themselves: like all such things, they were long, hot, loud, and given over to the Gods.

After much of a grueling afternoon, which left even the most enthusiastic watchers limp with longing for the regular hours of their afternoon naps, the Gods finally offered their blessings. Then King Sky Wind Warrior stepped down from his High Throne, took Spirits's hand in his, and led her to his new son-in-law.

"Let the celebration begin . . . my son," Sky Wind Warrior said, his one good eye rolling.

"Indeed . . . Father," replied Harvest Mountain Lord.

VIII

The evening was hot and full of stars, touched by humid breezes and smelling of the river, when her mother's maids brought her to the High King's pavilion. Now Spirits wore only a shapeless garment of white cloth, simple sandals, and a white ribbon tied around her hair, as she stepped hesitantly toward her first night in a bed other than her own.

As she entered the outer reach of Harvest Mountain's encampment, though she was but a softly moving shadow among a host of shadows, she felt her passage marked by a hundred curious eyes. She kept her own gaze on the ground, and wondered if it would always be this way. Surely not—today she was the new

High Queen. But a season from now, what would her life be like?

As for the rest, Blue Parrot's predictions had been matter of fact, her descriptions explicit, and her instructions simple: "Just ignore the pain, Spirits. It will pass; at least, most of it will. And the part that doesn't will be in your thoughts, not between your legs . . ." A quick glance, and a final question—"You aren't bleeding now, are you?"

Spirits shook her head.

"Good. It would be a terrible way to begin things." And that was Blue Parrot's parting valediction, as she sent her youngest daughter away from her forever.

Spirits stepped as carefully as she could through the strangers who peered at her curiously, and tried to focus her mind on the man who waited beyond the pair of torches marking a half-opened flap of cloth. And so she never saw the serpent-tongued flicker of the knife from the shadows, striking for her heart.

CHAPTER FIVE

I

Spirits felt a stinging sensation, and then a warm gush across her breasts. At first she didn't understand what had happened; in the smoky murk, all she could see was a sudden scramble of shadowy forms, and one dim figure, quicker then the rest, leaping away and vanishing into the confusion.

Reflexively she touched her chest and felt warmth and stickiness. Her muddled thoughts were confused: did I spill something on myself?

Then everything began to spin. A heavy body crashed into her back and knocked her over. Somebody shouted, then somebody else. The last thing she remembered was Harvest Mountain, his face limned in torchlight, stepping out of his rooms, his dark eyes wide with curiosity.

II

"Who was it?" Harvest Mountain said grimly.

Skull Breaker knew better than to shrug. He spoke gravely: "We don't know, Lord. I was several steps behind her, and the pavilion was dark and crowded. Everybody wanted to see her. And it happened so quickly . . ."

Harvest Mountain and his general were standing in

the emptied outer room of his pavilion, a few paces from the door to the inner chamber, where the two men could hear the hushed tones of Queen Blue Parrot, her serving women, and some of the healing priests.

The enclosure was now brightly lit: Skull Breaker had ordered many torches brought within, although, as he muttered to himself, he was closing the hedge after the dogs had escaped.

Harvest Mountain was as angry as he'd ever seen him, and Skull Breaker understood why. The attack had taken place only steps from his own royal bed. If an assassin could penetrate so closely . . .

"My Lord . . ."

Harvest Mountain whirled on him. "Did you watch the she-devil, as I told you?" he spat through clenched teeth.

Skull Breaker paused, considering. He finally decided on the truth: "No, Lord, not personally. I had two of my best men watching her, but I felt my highest duty was to protect your new bride." He exhaled heavily. "Perhaps wrongly, but I was able to deflect the assailant's second blow."

Unconsciously, Harvest Mountain's fingers crept to his sharp chin and began to pinch. "What do you think, Skull Breaker? Man or woman?"

"It was very dark and confused, Lord."

"Don't evade me! You touched the killer, didn't you?"

Skull Breaker closed his eyes, trying to remember. Finally he said, "A small man, or a muscular woman, Lord. Very fast, very determined."

Harvest Mountain nodded, recalling the she-cat with whom he'd wrestled such a short time before. But surely Green Water wasn't addled enough to try . . . ?

"Those two you called your best men," he said abruptly. "Who watched over the sister. Question them."

Skull Breaker nodded, sighing inside. It would be a waste of two good servants, but—better them than him. "Right away, Lord."

Then Harvest Mountain fell silent, and turned to stare at the closed door flap to his inner chamber. The sounds in there had quieted somewhat. One of the serving women was weeping softly.

"You saw the wound?" he said at last.

Skull Breaker nodded. "A deep scratch, nothing more," he said. "The girl bled quite a lot, of course, but if the Gods don't send fever demons into her flesh, she should be fine."

"But scarred," Harvest Mountain noted. "No longer perfect."

Skull Breaker shook his head. "No, Lord. No longer perfect."

"After you've questioned your men, begin to make ready our departure. My wife will need a litter—I don't want her walking."

"Yes, Lord."

"The sooner I'm out of this pit of snakes, these murderers and traitors who call themselves a royal family, the happier I'll be." He turned away, and when he spoke again, just before ducking into his private chamber, he said, "It's time I went home, anyway."

This time Skull Breaker bowed formally, a tentative joy creeping into his thoughts. His master sounded different, more determined somehow. If it had required a scratch on the girl's chest and the death of two of his best men to achieve that, he would gladly pay the cost.

"Yes, my Lord, indeed it is."

Harvest Mountain raked him with one jaundiced glance, then vanished into his chamber. He didn't come out again until his slaves dismantled it around him, and gently lifted Spirits onto her litter for the journey.

III

The litter was little more than a thick blanket stretched between a pair of long poles, padded with a mattress of ocelot fur and covered with another cloth. Four bearers, short, stolid, heavily muscled servants, men typical of the Old Race, carried this contraption. Harvest Mountain Lord walked alongside, his right hand resting gently on Spirits's shoulder.

"Now, are you sure you feel well enough for this?" he murmured as their procession moved slowly toward the opening in the top of the cliff wall. Two days had passed since the attack; Spirits's cheeks were mildly flushed, but her gaze was clear and calm as she looked up into his face.

"I'm fine, Lord. You are too good to me."

He smiled and shook his head. "You are the High Queen," he said, as if that explained everything. He sighed, and turned to sweep the crowds gathered along the trail to the wall. This time they were held well back by many spearmen, his own and King Sky Wind Warrior's. There would be no repeat of the murderous attempt to mark their departure.

Standing next to the gate itself, Sky Wind and the rest of his family stood in formal array. As they approached, Harvest Mountain, flanked by two huge soldiers, broke away from the procession and approached the mountain King. As he came up, Sky Wind, Blue Parrot, and Green Water sank to their knees.

"Arise, my brother," Harvest Mountain said. "I thank you, both for your hospitality, and for the gift of your daughter."

Sky Wind Warrior came to his feet smoothly, and nodded. "Go with my blessings, brother. May your journey to Great Head City be swift and sure. And safe." He didn't look at Green Water as he said this.

But Harvest Mountain did—and found eyes like burning pits glaring back at him. There would be no proof, of course, and perhaps that was a good thing. The situation was too delicate, and Harvest Mountain was glad he didn't have to force the issue. Not yet, at least.

"Farewell, Lord," Green Water said brusquely, her gaze never leaving his face.

"Yes, farewell, Green Water. It was . . . pleasant getting to know you better. And now we are relatives."

"Yes, wonderful," she replied. Then, deliberately, she turned her head aside and spat into the dust.

Blue Parrot bustled forward, searching in her near-sighted way; "I wish to say farewell to my daughter, Lord," she whispered.

"Of course."

She pushed past him and came to Spirits's litter. "How do you feel?" she asked.

"Sore," Spirits said. "But I'll be all right. The herbs and unguents the priests applied, they seem to help. But they do itch," she added with a smile.

Blue Parrot patted her on the shoulder. "Make sure your serving women change the poultices every day."

"Yes, Mother."

A moment of silence. Then, "Oh, Spirits, I will *miss* you."

"I'll miss you, too, Mama."

The two women stared at each other. "Spirits? Did you see who it was? Who attacked you?"

Spirits stared at her for a long time, then turned her face away. "No, Mama."

Blue Parrot sighed. "As I feared, then. I'll try to keep her here, but I don't know if I can."

Spirits shook her head tiredly. "Don't worry, Mama. She'll do whatever she wants to, you know that. But if she does come, would you send somebody ahead? With a warning?"

"Yes, dear. If I have the time."

"That's all I can ask, I suppose. Mama?"

"What?"

"Sometimes I feel like I'm cursed. Like we're all cursed, our whole family . . ."

Blue Parrot stared at her blindly for what seemed like a long time. Then she shook her head, patted her again, and sighed. "Be well, Spirits. I'll do what I can."

Spirits smiled at that. "What a strange beginning to the rest of my life. I should be frightened, I suppose."

"Do what *you* can, dearest. It's all we can do, I guess. All the Gods allow us."

Spirits felt tears begin to sting her eyes. "Farewell, Mama."

Blue Parrot straightened. "Goodbye, Spirits. We will come visit after the short rainy season, if we can."

They both knew what she meant.

Blue Parrot bent low and kissed her daughter's cheek. Then, tears glittering in her own blurred eyes, she straightened up again, turned, and marched back to her husband.

"Take care of my daughter," she said to Harvest Mountain.

He nodded. "I will, Lady."

Then, with a final glance at Sky Wind Warrior's carefully passive features, and a quick cut toward Green Water's smoldering expression, he turned and walked back to Spirits.

The pipers and the drummers began their farewell racket as they passed through the gates. Overhead, a single black crow suddenly flapped low, squawking: but only for an instant, before a great hawk plunged from the sky.

An explosion of claws and feathers, then nothing but the predator's single cry of triumph as it rose and vanished into the turquoise morning, prey clutched in cruel talons, a cloud of black, blood-spattered fluff drifting softly down.

Harvest Mountain shivered, and went on.

IV

The Long Courtyard was thirty paces wide and a hundred fifty long. It was bordered on each side by mounds twice the height of a man, constructed of thousands of loads of stone and clay, each load moved by the strong backs and arms of men. It had taken many, many full wheels of seasons to do this; the work had begun with Sky Wind Warrior's thrice great-grandfather, and continued to this day. Along the top of these artificial mounds were broad stone platforms, constructed of great slabs of basalt cut from the mines at the bottom of the cliff wall and then dragged to the top and set in place. On these stone floors had been constructed the light, airy pavilions made of posts, covered with tall thatch roofs, and divided by panels of brightly colored cloth.

At the north end of the Long Court was a small pyramid-shaped mound, rising to a flat top twice as high as the side mounds. In front of this high altar rested the table throne of the King of Holy Stone City. Behind the throne and to the side, surrounding the base of the pyramid were the many platforms used by the royal family. Matching them on the other side were similar platforms and pavilions, these used by the various priesthoods.

At the foot of the Long Court was the Jaguar Temple and the pavilions set aside for those priests only.

Today, while most of the city slept away the heat of the afternoon, Green Water Woman paced. She strode along with the electric repression of a caged jungle cat, all flashing eyes and nervous, clicking nails. If she'd had a tail, she would have whipped it stiffly back and forth.

Those few still awake and about gave her a wide berth. Finally, she found herself behind the throne, peering up at her father's public pavilion, the place where he carried on the business of the city, and received those supplicants who desired to speak to him.

Two guards, both half-drowsy beneath the relentless beat of the sun, stood on either side of the cloth door-flap. Father was awake, and inside there somewhere—most likely in his reception chamber. She swiped her fingers across her brow, took a breath, and began to climb the inlaid stone steps toward the guards. When they saw her coming, they straightened up; but neither of them looked at her, nor she at them, as she went through the door.

After she had passed through, one guard glanced at the other, then unobtrusively horned his fingers in the sign of warding.

Devil woman.

The other guard nodded.

V

She found her father, not in his audience chamber as she'd expected, but in a smaller room at the rear of the pavilion. He was alone, sitting cross-legged on a woven straw mat, wearing only a clout. A bright blue curtain had been drawn back to let in the afternoon light. He was turned away from the door, staring moodily out toward the bulk of the pyramid.

"Father?"

He started, then turned back to face her. His expression betrayed no welcome; it was stony and cold. His one good eye focused on her, then blinked.

"Daughter . . ."

"I want to talk to you."

He shrugged. "Sit down, then. Over there." He inclined his head toward another mat. She went over, folded her long legs beneath her, and sat.

He shifted himself about so he was facing her. Now he stared for several beats, until she began to squirm uneasily. "What's wrong?" she asked.

"Daughter, have demons stolen your mind?" he said finally. His bad eye, a scarred, wrinkled hole in his face, somehow also seemed to be watching her. Accusingly . . .

She looked down, a sullen expression pushing out her lips, and said nothing.

"I want an answer! What were you thinking of? This is my city, girl, and I know everything that goes on in it. Did you think I didn't know, you throwing yourself into his bed like a common slut?" He shook his head. "You made enough noise to draw crowds to his pavilion . . ."

She twisted her fingers together. "Well, what was I supposed to do? You wanted me to marry him, didn't you?"

He leaned back slightly and regarded her with dispassion. "Of course. But I gave you credit for having some idea of how to go about it. You're a woman. What else would a woman know, if not how to catch a man? But you couldn't see what was obvious to everybody else, could you? Why should he marry you? He already had possession of you."

Her face turned the color of a fired brick as she remembered what Harvest Mountain had said.

"Father, I—"

He waved his hand in dismissal. "I don't care. The damage is done. And I can't see any way to mend it." He paused. "I should have paid more attention to your sister. But who could have guessed . . ." He shook his head and sighed. "Go away, Green Water. I'm sick of you. Now I have to find a suitable husband for you—if there are any noble men in the other cities who are willing to plant the fields already plowed by the High King. You are a fool, daughter, and worse. Now you're a useless fool. At least to me."

She felt her rage leap into her throat, a hot ball of deadly curses, and she ground her teeth to keep from vomiting it up. Now was not the time.

"You want me to go, and I want to leave. I hate it here," she said.

"Oh? And where do you want to go?"

"Great Head City, of course."

He stared at her in astonishment, then laughed harshly. "To the High King? After he's already humiliated you, discarded you like a peasant's garbage?" He glared at her. "I can't believe you're of my blood . . ." he said softly. "Perhaps an evil spirit left you in my wife's belly."

She spat at him. "Or the scum from another man's snake, my Lord," she said coldly. "But it matters not where I came from. What matters is where I'm going. And I'm going to Great Head City."

Sky Wind Warrior stiffened at her words, and his expression went dark and angry. He spoke through clenched teeth: "Understand me, little fool. You will go where I send you, or not. You will do as I say, or not. In short, you will obey me in all things, or . . ."

She glowered at him, her eyes blazing slits. "Or what, Father?"

He moved his shoulders. "The temples are always hungry. A princess would make a fine sacrifice to the Gods. Perhaps such a thing would bring me luck."

Her jaw dropped open. She'd heard of such things. But she was so self-centered that she'd never thought—and her father! Something twisted and coiled in her gut. It took her a moment to realize what it was: fear. In the end, in his coldness, he was harder than her fire.

"Father . . ."

He waved his hand again. "Go on, Green Water. Get out. I'm done with you."

She started to rise, then suddenly wailed, *"But he wants me to come!"*

She was already out of the room, eyes blinded by tears, when she heard his voice: "What did you say? Green Water, come back here."

VI

That knot was even larger in her belly as she told him what Harvest Mountain had said to her: "But you can follow me to Great Head City . . . if you want to." It was a humiliating admission, for she had to explain to her father what the circumstances were when the High King spoke those words.

And Sky Wind Warrior, to make her degradation complete, only laughed when she finished explaining. "Called you a slut, did he? Well, he knew what he was dealing with, I'd say." He reached up and knuckled the scar hole where his eye had been. "Have to give the boy some credit. I thought he was only following his penis around. But it seems he knows a little more than to let the one-eyed snake do his thinking for him."

She hugged herself and wished she'd never come. The shame of it all burned her like hot coals, and for each searing invisible scar, she knew where to put the blame.

Spirits Walking Woman. Someday . . . she promised herself. Someday each one of those hurts would be paid for. In blood.

"Well, daughter, it seems there is good news after all. You will never be High Queen, but perhaps you can be something almost as good. You can be the High Slut." He chuckled at his evil joke, but Green Water was beginning to see some possibilities, and so she only nodded.

"I am very good at that kind of thing, Father," she said seriously. "Men like me."

He turned his head, cleared his throat, and looked back. "Hardly a thing of pride, daughter. But certainly a thing we can use. Do you understand me? A thing *I* can use."

She nodded. "In your plots."

His eyebrows rose. "What do you know of my plots?"

In truth, she knew very little, for her ravening focus on her own desires left small room for any other concern. But—tread carefully, now . . .

"I can help, Father. I can go to Great Head City and spy for you. If he wants me . . . and he does, I swear it . . . well. Men talk, you know. After they finish, sometimes they talk."

He nodded slowly. "If I could only be sure I can trust you."

"Oh, Father, you can. I swear you can. I'll swear on anything."

He rubbed his bony slab of a chin thoughtfully. "That won't be necessary, daughter. You'd forget your oath as soon as the next sun rose, anyway. But perhaps I can set things so you have reasons for what you do . . ."

He spent the next several moments explaining precisely what he had in mind. When he was done, he raised his eyebrows again and said, "If you agree to all that, then I will give my permission for you to go."

"Oh, Father. Yes. I agree." This was better than anything she'd expected, or even hoped for. Everything . . . except what she really wanted, of course, but it was too late for that. Thanks to Spirits.

He nodded. "Good, then. I will speak to your mother about this. In the meantime, make yourself ready."

VII

The young man was awed to find himself in the presence of Queen Blue Parrot. He was a gawky youth, the cousin of one of her serving women, but had rarely been out of his distant village. Certainly he was unknown in Holy Stone City, and that was exactly the way the dumpy, nearsighted old woman wanted it.

He seemed a likely lad, however. What little she could make out of him physically was good: he was of the New People, lean and limber, with a well-shaped oval skull, sharp, high cheekbones, the nose of an eagle, and white teeth behind slightly down-curving lips that gave him a curiously half-serious, half-jolly expression, and made him appear older than he actually was.

"What is your name, boy?" she said.

He was kneeling before her, in her private compartment. He'd been escorted there by two male soldiers, but she'd sent them away. She'd sent everybody away but the boy. What she had to say to him was private.

He kept his forehead firmly on the ground as he said, "Laughing Monkey, Great Queen." It was hard to tell, with her faded eyes, but he seemed to be shivering. No doubt he was terrified.

"Sit up, boy," she said, in the kindliest tones she could summon. She didn't want him so terrorized he would forget what she had to say.

Slowly, he complied.

"Come closer to me, so I can see you better," she continued, and patted a spot next to her on the mat. He seemed frozen, staring at her. "Well? Do as I say. Come here, boy."

When he finally moved, she could see where he'd gotten his name. He was a gawky tangle of arms and legs, bony knees, knobby ankles, and his features had a curious, rubbery mobility; eyebrows, eyes and lips in constant fluid motion. Like the monkey, his namesake.

"Now," she said, when he had settled himself next to her. "I want you to travel to Holy Stone City."

She felt him jump. No surprise there. It was an awesome task, for one who'd most likely never been more than a short walk from his home village.

"Don't worry, I will send someone with you, to show you the way. But afterwards, if you travel the path again, you will have to find your own way. Do you think you can learn to do that?"

After a moment, he said, "Yes, Great Queen."

She made a clucking sound. "Call me Blue Parrot, boy." She glanced at him as sharply as she was able. Up close, she could see his lips trembling. "And don't be frightened of me. If you do as you're told, you have nothing to fear. You understand me?"

He nodded, his dark brown eyes—odd, not black like most people's—wide as saucers.

"Good," she said. "When you reach Great Head City, you are to seek out my daughter, Spirits Walking Woman. She is the High Queen."

". . . Yes, Great—Blue Parrot."

She smiled at him. "That's right, boy. You'll do fine. And when you find her, you must say this: She is coming, with her father's permission, and will arrive by the time of the short rains." She stopped, waited a moment, then said, "Do you understand? Can you remember that?"

He gulped. "Yes."

"Good. Repeat it back to me."

Haltingly, he did so. His accent was thick and common, only that of a poor farmer, but clear enough.

"Yes, that's right," she told him. "And you must also tell my daughter that if she needs to send a message to me, she is to send you. You see what I mean? You will learn the path well."

He nodded again. "I will try to learn, Blue Parrot," he said, sounding impossibly serious for one so young.

Blue Parrot smiled. She felt a good feeling about this young man. Surely he could not be much older than Spirits herself—but she found herself willing to trust him. It was only an instinct, but she'd become able, over the years, to have faith in her instincts. He would do, she decided.

"I want you to leave before tomorrow's sunset," she told him. "Do what you have to do, to make your farewells." She paused, then said, "If my daughter has other tasks for you, obey her in every way. Do you understand that as well?"

"I will obey her," he said. He seemed to be calming somewhat.

"If you fulfill your tasks well, I will see that both you and your family are richly rewarded," she said.

He grinned suddenly. "I thank you, Great Queen."

"I said—oh, never mind. Get going, then. Go on, off with you."

She clapped her hands as he rose. At the door flap, he turned, and remembered to make his bow. With his rubber face and gangling limbs, he really did look like a monkey.

VIII

The party was a half day's march beyond the high door to Holy Stone City when Green Water Woman, reclining on a litter carried by four strong soldiers, called a halt. Overhead the sky had gradually shaded from lapis to azure to cobalt; now the evening star rode the night like an emerald torch. All around them the forest had suddenly gone silent. She heard it just before she signaled the stop: the coughing sigh of a hunting jaguar.

It was an omen. This nameless stretch of road, little more than a footpath, would be the place.

She raised her head. "Stop, stop here."

Her party was small; her bearers, two sets of four strong men, doubling as guards. A squirmy priest of the Jaguar Temple with a nasal voice and whining manner named Dog Eye. Two elderly courtiers, no doubt spies for her mother, whom she intended to send back as soon as she reached Great Head City; a few servants, including the one her eye found as soon as the small party meandered to a halt.

The bearers lowered her litter to the ground and helped her to her feet. She took a deep breath as she looked around. They were in marsh country now, the air thick with fetid stinks: the odor of dark mud, of rotting vegetation, of still, scummy water. Thick bushes crowded right to the edge of the path—no clearing or other space for what she had in mind. But this would do; night was nigh, and they were well beyond the local villages that paid homage to the King of Holy Stone City.

She turned to her guards. "Build a fire," she said.

The one she'd spoken to bowed; "Yes, Lady. It might take a while to find dry wood."

She nodded. "We'll wait. In the meantime, we can eat."

She called the servant girl she'd been watching over to her. "Twisted Nose, come here."

The girl, still frightened of the mistress who had knocked her to the ground only a few days before, came hesitantly forward.

"Yes, Lady?"

"Help the others prepare a meal. And tell the priest I wish to speak to him."

Twisted Nose bobbed a short bow, her relief plain. It seemed her mistress was in good sorts tonight. If she had known just what thoughts had put her Lady in such a good mood, she would have run screaming into the swamps. A certain death, no doubt, but cleaner than what awaited her, there in the middle of the path, in the middle of nowhere, in the gathering night.

IX

When the fire had burned down to coals, Green Water Woman directed her soldiers and her weasel of a priest; she'd been unsure of the God-cryer, but when she'd told him what she wanted, his eyes had suddenly glowed.

"The Jaguar Lord will be pleased, my Lady. Very pleased."

"Yes . . ." she said.

She used her own knife, which she had retrieved from her mother, its razored edge still dark with the blood of a High Queen. They took Twisted Nose alive and held her as Green Water Woman worked her dark will, mixing old blood and new for the glory of the God.

The smell of living, burning flesh rose into the night as Green Water Woman dedicated herself and her vengeance to the dark one, to the Jaguar Lord himself. And surely he must have been pleased . . . for as Twisted Nose's screams finally faded and her naked heart pumped its last, there came floating across the night a familiar coughing sigh.

Jaguar come a-hunting.

After that, Green Water Woman feasted.

CHAPTER SIX

I

Spirits knew she had grown up in a world far different than that of the villagers who surrounded Holy Stone City. Not for her the ramshackle, mud-floored huts, loosely thatched, open to the hot breezes and the endless moons of rain. Though her duties had included frequent visits to these places with her mother and the healing priests, she'd always returned to the high stone pavilions of the city itself. And so she knew the great gulf between her life and that of her father's subjects. Even so, she was unprepared for—and shocked by— her first sight of Great Head City.

On high religious days, when all the villagers gathered in the Long Court of Holy Stone City, the total number would not exceed a double hand of three hands of hands. And that would have seemed like all the people in the world were crowded there. Still, because of this, she'd thought herself a sophisticate, used to size and grandeur in her life.

The first hint she had that things might be different from what she'd known before was when their long column emerged onto roads that were wider and harder packed than the faint paths they'd traversed so far.

This was on the twentieth day of their journey,

which had been a strenuous one for her. Still weak from her wounds, she'd been carried along at a great, bumping pace. Her new husband rotated her bearers every hour, so that they were always fresh. But the joggling and bouncing had worn her down, along with the constant humidity, the clouds of humming mosquitoes, and the never ending glare of the sun. A few days into the journey her fever grew worse. At the end of each day she collapsed into her bed, alone but for her watchful serving women, barely able to swallow a thin gruel made of boiled maize with bits of turkey in it.

But she was lucky. The Gods saw fit not to dispatch demons to rot her flesh—or else the magics of her priests actually did what they were supposed to do. At any rate, by the third hand of days she was feeling much better, able to sit up in her litter and take note of her surrounding. Not that there was much to see. She was about midway in the caravan, well back from where Harvest Mountain and Skull Breaker marched. She found it odd, and interesting, that her husband preferred to walk, rather than be carried. If her own father had undertaken a similar journey, he would have ridden on the shoulders of his men. Yet here was an even greater king, who saw nothing demeaning in hiking along in the same manner as his lowest slave.

Harvest Mountain had been a perfect companion, coming back to walk with her several times a day, making light conversation. But even after she felt herself well recovered, and had begun to stay awake after the day's halt, he kept to his own tent. She slept in her bed alone.

In a way, this was fine. She was no innocent. She knew what men did with their one-eyed snake, and she knew what that opening between her thighs was for. Dogs and villagers and even her sister—she'd had a graphic education. But she still wondered, and worried, and even feared the night that must come soon.

Her mother had said there would be pain, but had not been specific—except that pain was a woman's duty.

Then she began to wonder—why *hadn't* he come? Was there something wrong with her? He'd shown no hesitation in bedding her sister. Did that mean he liked Green Water better? But if so, why had he chosen *her*? Oh, yes, he'd seemed to listen to her when she'd spoken of a wife, a partner, but surely that wasn't enough to make him reject her sister's talents?

It was all so confusing. The endless beat of the sun, the thickening damp rising off the swamps like an invisible blanket, and the way the unguents her priest carefully replaced on her wound each day made her head spin—all these made it so hard to think. She decided it certainly wasn't an auspicious beginning to the path her mother had set for her. And as for that, what could she do? The meeting between Harvest Mountain and her father had seemed quiet enough, even convivial. They'd called each other brother, and smiled a lot . . . though when she'd watched them together, their smiles had been on their lips, and never risen to their eyes.

Preoccupied with her thoughts and worried about both the present and the future, she hardly noticed how the path suddenly widened, and a few small villages began to appear. They looked not much different than those she was already familiar with—pitiful clusters of ragged huts, squalling, naked babies and a few starved-looking dogs, surrounded by small plots of beans and squash. But then her interest, and her anticipation, began to rise. No doubt these outlying hamlets signaled the onset of Great Head City. She even said as much to one of the bearers, but that stolid slave only looked up at her dumbly, and said, "Oh, no, Lady. Not yet."

His expression was so vacant she didn't pursue the question any further, assuming that he wasn't much more aware than the average slave—and slaves, except

for the best of them, were little more than animals.
Still, she began to keep a close watch toward the head
of the column, waiting to catch her first glimpse of the
gates to the fabled City of the Great Heads.

But the hours passed on by, as opaque as the murky
green wall of jungle separating each village from the
one they'd passed just before. Her attention fully en-
gaged now, she noticed that these intervals of fecund
growth were growing shorter, and the spaces of clean,
dry farmland rising above the swamps were becoming
larger. When they finally came to a halt and began to
set up camp in the largest village yet, she wondered
why they were stopping. Surely this huge settlement
must be the outskirts of Great Head City itself? But
it was not, and as she drifted off into sleep that night,
she wondered at what she'd been told. At least another full day's march lay ahead, before she would see
the splendors of her new home.

II

The following day was a procession of wonders.
With each passing hour the villages grew larger. By
late that afternoon there were no more stretches of
marsh between the farming areas. It was all one continuous stretch of farms, people, and thatched houses.
She'd never imagined so many people in one place.
And now, with the sun beginning to fall behind the
horizon to the west, she heard thin shouts from the
front of the column. The word was passed back along
the line and her bearers stopped, then set down her
litter.

She sat and waited. After a short time she saw Harvest Mountain and Skull Breaker walking toward her.

"My Lord," she said, when Harvest Mountain
reached her. "Are we coming to the city at last?"

He smiled down on her. He seemed lighthearted,

his face wreathed in a wide grin. "Almost, Spirits," he said. "How are you feeling?"

"I feel well, Lord." And she did. The fevers had subsided, and the scab of her wound had dried to a thin brown line.

He patted her cheek. "Good. Can you walk?"

"Yes, Lord."

He nodded, reached out, and helped her to her feet. "Come with me, then. I want us to enter the city together."

He led her to the front of the procession, and placed her between himself and Skull Breaker. When everything was ready, they began the last stage of the march. As she walked along, enjoying the mild exercise, she watched the scenery change.

Now even the fields shrank until they became small plots, obviously gardens kept for individual use. There were no more villages. This entire stretch was one huge village, and now the people of this village began to line the broad path they marched on.

Most just watched. She saw mothers with babies in their arms, and younger children clinging to their skirts. And men, some farmers, some obviously soldiers, standing straight, watching until the King drew close. Then they would cheer and wave their arms, and when they saw Spirits walking next to the King, they cheered even louder.

"Smile at them. Wave. You are their queen," Harvest Mountain whispered.

Hesitantly, she began to do so. And every time she waved, they waved and shouted back to her, showering her with happy greetings.

"High Queen," they roared. "Welcome to our High Queen!" The women held up their babies as if seeking blessings, and the children leaped and scrambled to see better. For the first time Spirits began to understand what an awesome responsibility she had assumed. She had known almost every face in her old

city and the villages that surrounded it. But here was
a horde, a vast throng of people. How would she ever
get to know them?

Nevertheless, their welcome thrilled her. "I am
High Queen," she whispered to herself in wonder. She
thought she hadn't spoken, but Harvest Mountain
took her hand and squeezed. "Yes, Spirits, you are.
These are your people now."

She felt tears start in her eyes. It was all so thrill-
ing—and so very, very strange.

The path became a wide road, lined with stones the
size of a man's head. She looked closer and saw that
each stone had pictures carved on it: kings, generals,
priests gently bearing the half-human Jaguar baby.
The road began to slope downward, and they came to
a wide, slow-moving river. A huge raft waited there,
attached to a rope which ran from heavy pilings on
either side of the water.

Harvest Mountain helped her aboard, and they
walked to the front, where a waist-high platform was
set. They mounted this platform, which had been covered with soft black furs, and seated themselves. Spirits ran her fingers in wonder across the pelts. Could
these be the furs of the sacred Jaguar himself? She
asked Harvest Mountain, and he nodded absently. It
was then that her changed life struck the hardest—for
only the High King and Queen might sit upon the
skins of the Lord Jaguar without fear.

The raft was so large it barely wobbled as others
climbed aboard. At some unseen signal the steersman
cast off, and began to haul the raft along the rope.
The river tugged sluggishly at the craft, but it never
wavered. Finally, with a soft bump, it grounded against
the far bank, and once again Harvest Mountain helped
her up and led her off the raft to the soft earth.

He paused after they were down, then turned to her
and said, "Welcome, High Queen, to the Sacred Island
of the Jaguar. Welcome to your new home."

She felt a shiver of joy run down her back. For a moment everything was perfect in the soft gloom of dusk. The sun was sinking up ahead, a huge red ball that plunged the middle distance into shadow, though she had the impression of gigantic shapes looming in the murk.

They waited until the nobles and courtiers had formed up behind them and then set off, Harvest Mountain and Spirits walking a few paces ahead. Harvest Mountain held her hand. In the red glare of the setting sun, his hard young features glowed as if lit by a divine fire.

Finally the dim shapes ahead began to resolve. They had turned to the north after leaving the river. Now they approached, on their right hand, a vast construction, a truncated platform three times the height of a man, its sides faced with cut basalt, broad stairs cut into the stone itself. Along the top she could make out other constructions. "What are those, my Lord?" she asked.

"The temples of the Jaguar Priests, and the barracks of the Jaguar Cult soldiers," he told her.

She nodded, not really understanding. Then, as they drew closer, she gasped: All along the top of this platform a necklace of light suddenly appeared. Many hands of men stepped forward, each holding a torch. Harvest Mountain brought them to a halt, and stood waiting.

A great sound rose up: a mighty song, accompanied by many drums and flutes. An even brighter cluster of light appeared, and a procession began to descend, carrying so many torches it looked as if a river of stars was pouring down the side.

The sound grew louder, the light brighter, until a fearsome apparition approached them: it was a man, or at least she thought it was, but he was completely covered by long black pelts, which had been decorated with many feathers and serpentine beads. Surmounting all was a headdress so large she wondered how he could hold his head up. The most astonishing thing was the mask which covered his features; it was made of bright green jade; the top part of it had the features of a man, but the bottom part was the jaw of a great snarling cat. In the flickering shadow, he looked like the Jaguar Lord himself, half human, half animal. She gasped, suddenly afraid.

This strange beast man halted a few paces away. The musicians reached a crescendo, then fell silent. The priest stretched out his arms.

"My brother," he said. "Welcome home."

Harvest Mountain stepped forward and embraced him as an equal. Then he turned to Spirits. "High Queen, this is Smoking Mirror, the High Priest of the Jaquar. Give him greetings."

Spirits, unsure of what she was supposed to do, stepped forward a pace. Then the priest was there, enfolding her in his arms. His scent was sharp and musky.

"Welcome, sister," he said. He squeezed her again, and this time she felt something more of a man, and less of a god, in his embrace. He held the greeting just one beat too long, then stepped back.

A lesser priest stepped up and handed him an ax carved also of jade. He gestured with it.

"Your people await you with joy, Lord," he called loudly. "Let us enter into your city!"

The musicians renewed their mighty racket, the torches dipped and then rose, and the whole huge procession set off again.

And so it was just as the sun dipped beneath the horizon, casting its last molten rays, that Spirits saw for the first time the great Pyramid of the Mother-Father-Sun rising endlessly before them, the huge polished stone mirror at its peak catching those glimmers and concentrating them in a perfect explosion of fire.

Thus did the High Queen Spirits Walking Woman

enter the City of the Great Heads, at the beginning of the years of the Dragon.

III

The rest of the evening was something of an anticlimax. They passed through a huge crowd, but since it was only dimly visible in the light of the torches, her impressions were vague and jumbled: many people, much shouting and cheering.

Nor did they pause. Harvest Mountain led her up to and then around the vast central pyramid, which with the full sunset had lost its lighted peak and become just one more huge, shadowy shape.

They passed around it—it took a good while—and then once again they came to a stone-faced platform, this one even taller and wider than that of the Jaguar priesthood.

Harvest Mountain flicked a glance at her. "Home at last," he said wryly. They approached a broad set of stone stairs, wide enough for thirty men to climb abreast. The courtiers of the city had been waiting here, ranged all up and down the steps, and Spirits's eyes widened at the number of them. Twenty hands at least ranged along the top step. They made their way through this glittering mob, with Harvest Mountain muttering names into her ear she knew she wouldn't remember. Everything had dissolved into a confusing muddle of faces and music and drums and shouts—she felt dizzy from it all.

At the top of the steps more wonders waited. Because full dark had now descended, details were even harder to make out, but here, in what Harvest Mountain told her was his palace area, things were much different than what she'd known in Holy Stone City. She'd thought things grand there—but this was beyond anything she'd ever imagined.

The stone platforms on which the houses rested

were similar, though larger, than what she'd known before. But instead of poles set into holes in the platform, with thatched roofs and cloth hangings, here were stone columns. Many, many hands of them. And resting on the tops of the columns, long beams of carved wood, with thick layers of palm on top. The columns were spaced to allow the entrance of the winds, but some of them had been filled in with stone blocks chinked with hardened mud. And in the firelight she saw that every inch of these structures had been carved and painted and incised, a fantastic panoply of leaping animals, men, priests, gods, kings . . .

It took her breath away.

Most of the courtiers fell away as they passed into an inner courtyard, open to the stars, where they paused. Many torches were set into holders carved in the columns, so that here it seemed almost bright as day.

"The women's pavilions are that way," Harvest Mountain said, pointing off to his right. She looked over and saw several women waiting there, obviously for her.

"Why don't you go on to bed, Spirits, and I will see you in the morning. I have many things to do yet tonight."

She nodded, for in truth she suddenly felt exhausted. What a day it had been! And no doubt more wonders waited for tomorrow.

"Yes, Lord," she said. He nodded, and she started to walk toward the women, who began to move forward to meet her. She paused. "My Lord?"

"Yes?"

"Thank you . . ."

He seemed to understand what she was trying to say, for he smiled suddenly, his teeth a white slash in his shadowy features.

"You're welcome, Spirits," he replied. "And welcome to my city . . . it's your city now, you know."

She couldn't put her mind around that thought, no, not yet, though she promised herself she would try—for her mother's sake, if nothing else. But at that moment the burden her mother had set on her was dim and far away. "Good night, Lord," she said.

Then her women were there, and they swept her away into a life entirely new and strange.

IV

"Hand me some of those blue feathers," Spirits said.

Purple Grackle, a serving woman of noble birth, only a year or so older than Spirits, rummaged in the bag she held in her lap. She was a sweet-faced girl whose principal feature was a pair of dark eyes so large and round and luminous that one hardly noticed that the rest of her face was rather plain. In her blood was intermingled both the Old Race and the Younger Race, and she had evidence of both. Of the elder blood she showed a broad, flat nose and thick, down-curved lips, but her luminous eyes, high cheekbones, and heart-shaped facial structure came of the younger blood.

In the short time she'd known the girl, Spirits had come to like her and rely on her far more than any of her other new companions. Purple Grackle smiled readily and giggled often, but her personality was much like Spirits's own. Plain, practical, blunt—but with a sharp awareness and a hidden streak of incisive humor. What Spirits liked best was that she didn't take herself seriously, and that she wasn't afraid to speak her mind.

The two girls had become friends very quickly, beginning on the first night, when Purple Grackle had helped her prepare for bed. She'd spread a light blanket over Spirits and paused, her eyes glowing with concern.

"May I?" she'd said, and at Spirits's nod, had run her fingertip lightly down the thin scab on Spirits's chest.

"How horrible," she breathed. "Weren't you frightened?"

"It happened so quickly, I didn't have a chance to be scared," Spirits admitted. "Then I fainted, and didn't think anything at all."

Purple Grackle nodded. "Yes, I suppose that would be the best way."

Her face and tone were so matter-of-fact that Spirits giggled involuntarily, and the other girl drew back. Then she giggled as well, and the beginnings of a new friendship were formed.

Now, Purple Grackle finished with her search and looked up. "No more blue feathers," she announced. "Would green ones do?"

Spirits looked down at the robe she'd been working on and pursed her lips doubtfully. "Well, no, not really. What do you think?" She held up the robe for Purple Grackle's inspection.

The other girl glanced over and quickly shook her head. "No, you need more blue if you want to keep on with that pattern. Well, that's good. It's time you got out of the Queen's House anyway. You've been stuck in here, hidden away, ever since you arrived. If I didn't know you better, I'd think you were terrified of showing your face outside."

Spirits stared at her solemnly. "But, Purple Grackle, I *am* terrified." And her voice was so full of exaggerated fear that both girls burst out laughing.

"No, seriously, Purple Grackle, you can't imagine. I'm just a poor country girl. And your city is so . . ."

"Big? Loud? Dirty? Busy? Overwhelming?"

"Yes," said Spirits.

"Well, all the more reason, then. You just need to get out and get used to things. I mean, the city isn't going to change, so you might as well."

Spirits sighed and set her work aside. "I suppose you're right. My goodness—I don't even know how I should do it."

"What do you mean?"

"Well, I'm the High Queen. Back home, when I was only a younger princess, my father wouldn't let me go about without a guard and a serving woman, unless I was with my mother. I imagine it can't be much different here."

Purple Grackle smothered another giggle. "Oh, dear, you really are from the country, aren't you?"

"Well, yes."

"Spirits Walking, if you leave this pavilion and set out into the city as High Queen, you will have at least four hands of courtiers, guards, bearers, musicians—a small army."

Spirits's features sank with dismay. "But I don't want all that. I just want to walk about and see things quietly, with you."

Purple Grackle nodded. "Then the answer is simple."

"And what is the simple answer?"

"The High Queen can't go out. But you can . . ."

V

The High King caught his Lord General's eye and inclined his head toward a spot several paces away near the stone wall that ringed the high platform of the Royal Mound. They strolled in that direction, leaving behind a small clot of brightly clad courtiers.

"A beautiful day, eh, my Lord?" Skull Breaker remarked as he leaned his elbows on the wall and gazed out on the city bustling below.

Harvest Mountain glanced up at the sky, which was as polished and empty as a fine turquoise bowl. "Another moon, and then the rains," he said.

Skull Breaker nodded, then perked up his ears as

Harvest Mountain said, "The short rainy season might be a good time to call on my brother-in-law."

Skull Breaker's heart skipped a beat. He had been trying to raise this subject for many moons, but Harvest Mountain, embroiled in his search for a queen, had not been interested. Now, suddenly, it seemed that he was.

"What do your spies tell you, General?"

Carefully Skull Breaker said, "His strength grows, Lord. He has gathered many more villages under his direct control, and taken their young men into his army. The malcontents are flocking to him. There are always malcontents. And of course it is the Old City, and what that all means."

Harvest Mountain moved up close and plucked his own elbows down. "My father was a great conqueror," he remarked. "Many slaves, much sacrifice, much wealth. He made our city greater than it has ever been."

Skull Breaker nodded.

"I know you don't think I am the man my father was," Harvest Mountain continued, "but you are wrong."

"My Lord, I never said . . ."

Harvest Mountain waved him off. "You didn't have to say anything, General. I could see it in your eyes."

Skull Breaker felt a shiver. "I am loyal to you, as I was to your father," he said.

"Oh, I know that. Otherwise I would have strung your guts from this very wall. But it served my purposes to appear weak and silly, Skull Breaker. Think on it. Look over there, at that tree."

Harvest Mountain pointed at a large mangrove, its twisted roots digging deep into a stream that meandered through the city. "See those parrots on the branch?"

Skull Breaker nodded. "I see them, Lord."

Harvest Mountain eyed him. "If you were to send

an arrow into that flock, Lord General, how many would you see then?"

Skull Breaker thought on it, "I would see none, Lord. They would be frightened, and fly away."

"Indeed. As would my enemies, if they thought me strong. My father died unexpectedly, Lord. I did not know who my enemies were—or, more important, my friends. But now the weak boy king sees them all, a tree full of traitors." He paused, then tapped Skull Breaker on his broad shoulder. "And those who could have plotted against a weak king but did not."

Skull Breaker felt a shudder of relief. "As I say, Lord, I have always been loyal to you."

"To my family, to my father, perhaps. Now I will give you reason to be loyal to me."

Skull Breaker stared at him. A ghostly vine of fear crept up his spine. He had been so disillusioned with this seemingly worthless son of a great father, and so close to investigating other, perhaps worthier, candidates for his loyalty . . . "I must confess, my Lord. You have surprised me."

Harvest Mountain nodded. "I thought I would."

VI

"Are you sure this is the proper thing?" Spirits asked.

Purple Grackle said, "Proper? Of course it's not proper. The High Queen wandering around the city like a servant woman, with only one guard? And dressed in rags, almost?"

She giggled. "Harvest Mountain would have a fit."

Spirits looked dismayed. "Then maybe I shouldn't."

"Oh, Spirits, all the noble women do it. Otherwise, we'd never get out of the royal pavilions."

Spirits eyed her dubiously. "But I don't want to do anything my husband wouldn't approve of."

"How will he ever find out? Just don't tell anybody

who you are. And keep that shawl wrapped up high, so part of your face is covered."

"Well . . ."

It was midmorning in the city, a good time of day. The mists from the swamps surrounding Jaquar Island—so named because it was more or less shaped like a crouching Jaguar—had burned off, but the worst heat of the sun was yet to come.

The two young women were standing at the base of the Pyramid of the Mother-Father-Sun, which Purple Grackle told her was more commonly called simply All-Sun Mountain. In the bright daylight the details of this mighty structure were bright and clear, unlike Spirits's first glimpse of it.

Sun Mountain towered over them to the heights of four hands of men. It was so huge that Spirits found it nearly impossible to believe it had been built by men, but Purple Grackle said it was so. That entire pile had been carried, handful by handful, from all the dry hillocks surrounding the city. Except for the rocks, which had been carried even farther, from the cliffs below Holy Stone City. Spirits tried to imagine the number of slaves involved, and the time the construction had taken, but she failed.

Now she stared up Sun Mountain's great flanks, not realizing her mouth had fallen open. It even *looked* like a real mountain, broad at its base, but tapering roundly to its pointed top. The only thing up there was the circle of polished hematite that stood as tall as a man, glittering and winking its mirrored surface in the bright sunlight.

"They call it the Eye of the All-Sun," Purple Grackle informed her. "It's magic—the priests of the All-Sun climb up there and light torches by holding them in front of the Eye. Then the Three-God sends down its fire and lights them."

She seemed unimpressed by this miracle, although Spirits caught her breath at such a tangible expression of the All-Sun God's power. "They climb those stairs, I suppose?" she asked.

Purple Grackle nodded. There were ten deep grooves carved into the side of the Sun Mountain, each groove about two paces wide, the insides faced with polished stone. Running up two of the grooves were wooden stairs set into holes in the rocky lining. Spirits thought it must look impossibly grand when the priests of the Sun made their way to the top.

"You don't have anything like that at Holy Stone City?" Purple Grackle asked.

"Oh, no, nothing. Nothing there is as grand as it is here," Spirits added fervently. "The royal pavilions must be ten times as big as ours. And you have so many more priests and temples."

Purple Grackle nodded. "The priests flock here. They always do. To where the power is."

Spirits was shocked by the cynicism of her friend's reply. The priests were . . . well, the priests: the direct representative of their Gods, and partook of that divinity themselves. Only the Kings, who were in some part priests as well, could match them in stature.

Some of this must have shown on her face, because Purple Grackle changed the subject. "What do you want to do? We could visit the stalls of the feather sellers . . . or if you'd rather, we could just walk around. Wouldn't you like to see your new city?"

"Yes," Spirits said. "I'd like that. Where shall we start?"

"Follow me," Purple Grackle said.

They strolled anonymously around the city for a couple of hours. Spirits was astonished that nobody seemed to give them a second glance. She even saw another, similar party; two women, plainly dressed, and a guard—but she thought she recognized one of the faces from the courtiers who flocked around her in the royal pavilions.

Finally she relaxed and began to enjoy her jaunt. Purple Grackle seemed to know something about everything, and Great Head City was truly an awesome sight for a country girl, even if that girl had been a princess.

They had begun their stroll by descending the wide steps that led from the royal pavilions, which brought them to a grassy plaza, bordered with stone blocks, between the pavilions and All-Sun Mountain. It was here that they'd paused, while Spirits dealt with her misgivings.

Now they ambled across the plaza and circled All-Sun Mountain, moving generally south. There were many mounds of stone-faced earth here, extending outward as far as Spirits could see.

"The noble houses," Purple Grackle explained. "They own the farmlands and the villages, but they live here in the city. Traders, too, with their servants and slaves."

Spirits nodded. Her own city had similar, though much smaller, neighborhoods. Some of those mounds were almost as large as her father's royal pavilion.

They came most of the way around Sun Mountain and reached a long, wide road that ran straight from the mountain, all the way to the other end of the island. She had walked up that road when she'd first entered the city, but it had been twilight, and she hadn't fully appreciated just what a spectacle had surrounded her. Now, from her somewhat elevated position above the head of this road, she could look out over the entire sprawl of Great Head City, south of the Sun Mountain.

Off to her left, pressed up against the southeast side of the mountain, were the high mounds of the royal pavilions, and directly on the north side, now out of her sight, was the enormous sprawl of the Temple of the All-Sun. But it was to the south that the real wonders lay: she shaded her eyes, the better to see the wonder of the Jaguar Temple in the distance, its glittering walled mounds now sharp and clear. It was easy to see that, other than Sun Mountain itself, this was the largest construction in the city. On the wide, flat top of the vast series of mounds were countless pavilions, temples, altar spaces, even a small ball court. Also flimsy barracks and hovels for, she presumed, soldiers and slaves.

What had someone said? The soldiers of the Jaguar Cult lived there, too? "Purple Grackle?"

"Yes, Lady?"

"What is the Jaguar Cult?"

The other girl's eyelids flickered, and where she had previously been so voluble, she now paused, then said, "Perhaps you should ask the High King."

"I see," Spirits replied carefully. Obviously, she'd made some kind of mistake, but since she didn't know what it was, there was no point in pursuing it.

"And there is the Feathered Serpent's temple," Purple Grackle said, changing the subject. She pointed at a smaller cluster of mounds on the right hand side of the main road.

"What do you call that road?" Spirits wondered.

"It is the Grand Concourse of the All-Sun," Purple Grackle said. "Used for all the great ceremonies. The old king—Harvest Mountain's father—used to parade captured slaves up and down there before sacrificing them."

Spirits nodded. Her husband's father had been famed throughout the entire land of the People for the splendor and ferocity of his gifts to the Gods. She could imagine that broad road running with blood, and repressed a shudder.

"Let's go down," she said finally. "I want to see it up close."

And so they did, and spent a pleasant hour or so, as Spirits began to feel she was soaking up a bit of the real flavor of Great Head City. The crowds were

far larger than she was used to, but they seemed to
pay her no attention. Priests moved about in packs,
ponderous, dignified, most of them of the Old Race.
Many had the typical pear-shaped skull that indicated
their heads had been bound at birth, which meant
they'd been destined for the priesthood from the
very beginning.

They paused at a stall where a merchant sold fruits
and vegetables, and had their guard trade a turquoise
bead for several fat, juicy mangoes whose blushing
skins showed them at the peak of ripeness. The juice
was sweeter than any Spirits had ever tasted.

So they were standing off the edge of the Grand
Concourse when another party of priests journeyed
past. Spirits noticed right away this group was different from the others she'd seen.

It was only a small group, five or six men, but what
made them stand out was that they didn't stand out:
there were no guards, no servants or slaves, only the
men. And their clothing was simple. White skirts, sandals, none of the feathered and beaded grandeur of
the other priests she'd seen.

In the center of the little group was a man taller
than the rest. It was obvious he was the leader. He
did wear a feather, a single bronze quetzal shaft,
braided into his hair. She could tell by the way the
others seemed to revolve around him, by the way they
reacted to his every gesture.

He had been looking away from her, but now, almost as if sensing her gaze on him, he turned. His
eyes caught hers and flashed.

She gasped. He was the most beautiful man she'd
ever seen.

He nodded faintly to her and passed on, still talking,
but after he had gone, she still found her heart fluttering a bit.

"Who was that?" she asked.

Purple Mountain eyed her knowingly. "It won't do

any good, you know. Even if you are High Queen. He's a priest, and sworn to the Feathered Serpent." She paused. "He is Lord White Serpent Hawk."

"Oh," said Spirits.

"You want to be careful of him," Purple Grackle said.

Spirits turned. "Oh?"

Purple Grackle nodded. "You want to be careful," she repeated.

CHAPTER SEVEN

I

Two days after her venture into the city with Purple Grackle, the day Spirits had anticipated and dreaded in equal measure finally arrived. When she woke in the morning, surrounded by many of her noble serving women, she could hear a low, roaring mutter in the air.

"What is that?" she asked Purple Grackle, who was closest to her.

"The people gathering in the Grand Concourse, Lady," Purple Grackle replied.

"What are they gathering for?"

Purple Grackle glanced at her. "You don't know?"

Spirits shook her head.

"Oh, dear," said Purple Grackle, who looked embarrassed at the news. "Send the rest of these women away," she whispered.

Spirits did so, eliciting several malicious glances in Purple Grackle's direction from the older women there. Spirits noted them, and understood. Even her own court was rife with politics, as the women jostled and schemed to gain the new queen's favor. Obviously Purple Grackle had done so, and it was already a scandal that one so young should have immediately been so successful. Spirits, from her experience in her father's court, could well imagine that the knives were already being sharpened for her new companion. But that was a problem that could wait a while.

When her chamber was empty of all but the two of them, she looked up. "Tell me," she said.

For the first time since she'd known her, Purple Grackle hesitated. "You really don't know?" she said finally.

Spirits felt a flicker of irritation. "No, Purple Grackle, I don't. So tell me, please."

The other girl took a deep breath. "Well, today—this afternoon, actually, when the priests say the omens are right—Harvest Mountain is going to take possession of you. In the middle of the Grand Concourse. In front of everybody."

Spirits stared at her blankly. "I don't understand."

Purple Grackle waved her hands. "What don't you understand? Surely the priests and the people demand the same thing in your own city? Your mother was the queen, wasn't she?"

"Well . . . yes, of course. But—" Spirits tried to imagine Blue Parrot, so soft and dumpy and kind, allowing such a thing to happen. Tried, and failed. Her own thoughts began to whirl. Color flushed her cheeks.

"I don't think she would have done that," she managed at last.

Purple Grackle shrugged. "You wouldn't have been there anyway. And perhaps it isn't necessary for lesser kings. I really don't know about that. But this is the High King, the chosen of the Gods, and there must be no doubt about his descendants. The priests demand it, and so do the people." She paused, then tapped her chin thoughtfully. "Tell me, Spirits, are you a virgin?"

Spirits felt her face grow even hotter. "I don't see why that's any business of—"

Purple Grackle chuckled. "My Lady, it is about to

be the business of everybody in Great Head City. Tell
me truthfully—I have a reason. Are you?"

Spirits sighed. "Yes."

"You're sure?"

Now Spirits laughed softly. "You'd think I would
know, if anybody would. But why is it so important
that *you* know?"

Purple Grackle smiled faintly. "They put a white
cloth on the marriage bed. If you are a virgin, when
the King penetrates you, you'll bleed. It's proof, you
see."

Still not understanding, Spirits said, "Yes? And
so?"

"Well, I'd have to go kill a turkey. For the blood.
I am closest to you, and I will be there with you.
So if your cloth wasn't red, well . . . it would be.
You see?"

This was Spirits's first lesson in the hard politics of
royalty and religion, and, practical to her core, she
did understand. She had grown up among those who
thought and schemed with just such stone-headed real-
ism, but this was the first time it had ever directly
affected her.

She laughed weakly. "Well, you surely don't hide
your words, do you?"

"Would you want me to?" Purple Grackle asked
bluntly.

"No." She sighed again, and sat up. "What do I
have to do to get ready?"

"That's my girl," Purple Grackle said.

II

As the day wore on, it grew much hotter. This was
the season before the short rains, the hottest of the
year. There were many springs on Jaguar Island, and
some of them had been caught in stone-lined pools,
which drained through stone aqueducts down to the

river. There was one such pool completely enclosed
by the royal pavilions, and Spirits went there to bathe
just before high noon, grateful for the cool water. A
flock of her women accompanied her, and for a while
they chatted companionably while Spirits splashed
around in her bath.

Purple Grackle joined her in the water, the better
to wash her hair and untangle it.

"You want to look pretty," she said. "This will be
the first time most of the people see you."

Once again Spirits tried to imagine the ceremony.
The idea of doing . . . *that thing* . . . right out in
the open, and in front of a curious mob, was almost
impossible for her to imagine. She'd seen her sister,
of course, but surely that sweaty, grunting tangle of
limbs would not be repeated for the crowd?

She pulled Purple Grackle closer and told her about
Green Water. Purple Grackle filled a clay vessel with
water and poured it over Spirits's head.

"Oh, no, it won't be anything like that. At least I
don't think so. You have to remember, I was two or
three turns of the seasons younger when Harvest
Mountain took his first wife. And I couldn't see very
well, as I wasn't a part of Night Talk Moon's court.
But I don't remember that it went on a long time. It
was over quickly, as I recall."

Spirits thought about it. She supposed she could en-
dure anything, but she wondered why nobody, not
even her mother, had warned her of what was in store.

Or perhaps she had. She had spoken of pain, and
pain, Spirits knew, could take many forms. Shame was
one of them. But should she feel ashamed by this?
Wasn't it just one of those things a queen might have
to undergo?

She pushed her hair out of her eyes and splashed a
little water at Purple Grackle. "Women . . ."

"What about us?"

"They don't care how we feel, do they? Men, I mean?"

Purple Grackle stared at her as if she'd lost her mind. "When did they ever care?"

Spirits couldn't argue with that. After a bit more time, Purple Grackle judged that she was properly bathed, and helped her out of the pool. Other women quickly covered her naked body with a bright robe, but Purple Grackle said, "No. Wait."

"What?"

"Take off the robe," she said.

The women paused, but Spirits, curious, said, "No, go ahead. Do what she says."

Purple Grackle pursed her lips and eyed her up and down. "You have a nice form. Hardly any breasts yet, but you will. Too bad about the scar, though it's pretty well faded." She nodded at the women. "Cover her back up," she said. "Our little present for the High King. He'll unwrap her soon enough."

III

"Are you ready, my Lady?" Purple Grackle asked gently.

They were alone in Spirits's inner chamber, while Purple Grackle made the final arrangements to a fantastic robe that draped from Spirits's shoulders. "There," she said. "I think that finishes it."

She stepped back. "You look wonderful, Spirits. The High King will be proud."

Underneath the robe Spirits was entirely naked. It was a kind of relief. The day had turned into a furnace, and the robe was thick and heavy, encrusted with turquoise beads, thick with feathers and strips of fur.

But the idea that soon the robe would vanish, leaving her in only her flesh to stand before the massed gaze of strangers, left her with a sick, shameful feeling in the pit of her stomach.

"I guess I'm ready," she said finally. "How much longer?"

The rest of her court had been preparing themselves all day, putting on their best robes, painting their faces, fixing their ornate head dressings. They would escort her from the Queen's chambers to the Grand Concourse, themselves flanked by a procession of priests. Purple Grackle had explained everything to her.

"Soon, I'd say," Purple Grackle replied. "You can hear Smoking Mirror beginning the sacrifices. Listen to how the crowd roars."

Spirits had been aware of the growing cacophony for some time. Drums and flutes, high, thin cries and answering rumbles from the mob. And on the air now floated the thick, porky scent of roasting flesh. Some of that smell actually did come from pigs, she knew. But some came from other flesh—slaves, captured warriors.

The Gods must be fed.

And in a way, was she not herself a sacrifice? Her own body placed on the altar of her husband's royalty? Unsettling thoughts, but she couldn't put them out of her mind. And it was all so hypocritical. Her husband had taken Green Water. What if the Gods then placed a baby—his child—in her belly? It would still be his child, even if it would not be his official heir.

No, the men had no worries; only their women had to prove chastity. Well, that was the way of the world, and she had no expectation of changing it. Yet she did intend to fight against it, if she could.

She would take that much away from this shameful day, and somehow, knowing this, she felt a little better. "Well, should we go outside now?" she asked.

"I think so, Lady. Here, let me hold up the ends of your robe."

And so Spirits Walking Woman, garbed in turquoise and feathers, stepped out to meet her fate. As always a woman, in the end naked beneath her ornaments, was naked in a world of men.

IV

Since the Grand Concourse itself was lower than any of pavilions that surrounded it, Spirits could see the vast crowds that filled it side to side and end to end as soon as she reached the edge of the royal enclosure and paused at the top of the wide stone steps.

The blazing sunlight crackled and sparkled from the glittering costumes of the court and the priests; even the villagers had put on their best finery and their brightest trinkets, and the whole sea of people seemed a heaving wave of light. She paused, her breath caught in her throat at the sight. But she was completely unprepared for the sound that greeted her appearance.

It began softly, as a few noticed her, but quickly spread into an all-encompassing thunder that seemed to shake the very stones on which she stood. It was, she was sure, meant to be a cry of welcome, perhaps even approval. But it frightened her. She could sense beneath the sound something deeper and more ferocious. The heartbeat of some great and uncontrollable beast, an animal that, for the moment, might love her, but as easily could change into an unstoppable engine of destruction, one capable of consuming kings—and queens—as easily as the lowliest of slaves. That hidden beast, she thought suddenly, was very like a God. Perhaps it even was a God.

She shivered at the thought, took a breath, swallowed, and forced herself to smile. Now soldiers began to push open a path from the foot of the steps through the crowd. The people gave way cheerfully, laughing and shouting, making room for their new High Queen.

Purple Grackle took her hand and led her down the steps. A contingent of glittering priests awaited her at their foot, and took her in hand. They led her slowly through the mob to the cleared stretch of the Way of the All-Sun. Later, Spirits would realize she hadn't really *seen* any individuals, and only retained an impression of teeth, bulging eyes, reaching arms, stamping feet. The beast heart of the thing. And she walked through the belly of it.

In the center of the Concourse was a huge wooden platform constructed of stout logs. One part of it had been covered with a thick layer of stone and earth, and it was here that the sacrificial fires smoked and sputtered. As she slowly climbed the steps, the smell of that burning was thick in her nose, and when she reached the top, she saw white bones protruding from the coals. She never forgot that sight, for in the center, a skeletal arm and hand, its bony fingers curled, seemed to gesture invitingly at her.

It was with this grisly vision clouding her thoughts that she looked away to see the High King, Harvest Mountain Lord, step toward her, his own hand outstretched. And somehow, for the rest of her life, those two images remained entwined.

Before the altar was another platform, this one about the height of her shoulders, with a narrow stairway leading to the top. Harvest Mountain led her up this, while the drums thundered as the crowd fell silent. Courtiers followed them up. The priests were already there, waiting, as if for the ultimate sacrifice.

In the center of the platform was a bed, piled high with clean straw and fur, covered with white cloths. Spirits saw this, and thought of Purple Grackle and her white sheet. Well, at least that wouldn't be necessary.

Still, up to this point, it had almost seemed like a

dream. But now it became shockingly, brutally real. Hands plucked her robe from her, and suddenly she was naked, standing alone and exposed before countless glittering, feverish eyes.

Her stomach gave a quick heave, and she staggered slightly. Harvest Mountain, himself now naked, took her hand. "It will be over soon," he whispered.

She glanced at him. She felt defenseless and exposed, but he didn't seem to feel that way. There was a naturalness to his exposure, as if he were offering a gift to the crowd. His lean body seemed to glow as if his skin had been burnished, and his eyes, unnaturally wide with their painted rings, sparked with pleasure.

He led her to the bed. "Lie down there, Spirits," he said. His voice was high and clear, and to her ears it sounded almost kindly.

She mounted the furs, lowered herself, and closed her eyes, waiting for she knew not what. After a moment the mound of furs moved, as he lowered his weight, and then she felt him on her, his skin smooth and unnaturally dry. She took his weight without protest, though she had no idea what she was supposed to do next.

It didn't matter. The drums began to pound even louder, and she heard a hot sizzle as another sacrifice landed on the burning coals. She felt his strong hands on her shoulders, forcing her back, and became aware of something new. Almost like a club, growing between them, trapped by their bellies.

His knee wedged itself between her thighs, opening her, and then a thick, dry roundness shoved against her, thrusting its way into her.

She screamed. The crowd answered with ecstatic shrieks of its own. The drums pounded and the priests chanted.

Her mother had not lied. It hurt.

Some nightmarish time later, they waved the bloody

cloth, and Spirits Walking Woman became the true High Queen of Great Head City.

"You'll live," Purple Grackle told her, when they'd returned to the royal pavilions.

"How do you know?" Spirits asked.

"Because you have to."

It was something she kept in mind, later that night, when Harvest Mountain came to her again. This time she didn't scream. But it still hurt, she couldn't hide that. And she couldn't be sure, but it almost seemed like Harvest Mountain had enjoyed it.

Hurting her.

V

"I'm glad I'm not you," Purple Grackle remarked the next day.

Spirits was still in bed, though it was almost noonday. The dull, throbbing ache in her groin was a weight she wasn't ready to bear.

"Why do you say that?"

"Oh, not you, but the High Queen. I'm glad I'm not the High Queen. What you had to go through yesterday." Purple Grackle gave a little shiver. "I couldn't have done it."

"I couldn't either. But I didn't have any choice," Spirits told her. And in her heart, in that moment, she understood the chains that the Gods placed on even the highest.

"Was it awful?"

Spirits closed her eyes. "It hurt a lot. It still does."

Purple Grackle nodded. "Would you like me to bring you a herb woman? You're the Queen, and maybe a healing priest would be better, but they're all men. A herb woman . . . well, she's a woman."

Spirits thought about it, but the prospect of exposing herself to even another woman was too much. "I'll wait," she said. "If I don't feel better tomorrow, maybe then." She paused, sighed. "I wish my mother were here."

"Why didn't she come?"

Spirits wanted to explain, but she was afraid to. She knew why Blue Parrot had stayed behind. To protect her. Somebody had to keep Green Water under control, and somebody had to do what was necessary to shift Sky Wind Warrior's schemes. Duty, Spirits supposed. Blue Parrot knew her duty. And she had better get on with learning hers as well.

But to explain all this, even to Purple Grackle, whom she trusted as much as she could anybody after such a short friendship, was too dangerous. To admit her father was plotting revolt against her husband? No, even thinking about it was risky.

"She had to stay with my father," she said finally.

"Why? Is he sick? I hadn't heard—"

"Oh, Purple Grackle, let's talk of something else. Have you been out in the market today? Talked with anybody?"

"You mean about yesterday?" Purple Grackle was busying herself arranging bags of materials for sewing. She put down a handful of iridescent green parrot feathers and dusted her hands.

"I was at the markets early. Everybody was talking, of course."

"And what did they say?"

"Oh, they love you. So young, they said. So beautiful. And of course you are beautiful, Lady."

"No, I'm not," Spirits said, thinking of Green Water. "But go on."

"The omens were wonderful. From the sacrifices. The priests were very pleased. So, I hear, was the High King."

Spirits brightened a bit. "He was? About the omens, you mean?"

Purple Grackle smiled. "That . . . and other things."

She waggled her eyebrows. It was plain what the other things were.

Spirits blushed. After the ceremony, back in the royal compound, her husband had stayed in her bed for hours. He had taken her twice again, the second time with greater vigor than the first, and though the pain was still with her, she felt a bit of pride. He liked her. She was a good wife—at least in that way, she was.

"Where do you hear such things?" she asked.

"Oh, you know men. They talk. Even men who are kings. Everybody knows, anyway. And old Grumpy Chicken—you know, that ancient old woman, the senior of your courtiers, she's giving everybody the exact details of last night, right down to the sound your husband makes when he spills his seed in you. That half-shout, half-grunt thing he does."

"How in the world does she know that?" Spirits was appalled.

"Why, she snooped, of course. Pretended to fall asleep right outside your door. Don't worry, there wasn't anybody else listening. Except for the guards, of course, and they don't count."

Spirits opened her mouth, closed it, opened it again. "Don't I have any privacy at all?"

Purple Grackle's eyebrows floated up again, this time in surprise. "Of course not, Lady. You're the High Queen."

Spirits digested this, and realized it was the truth. Thinking back, she could not recall a single time, waking or sleeping, that she'd been truly alone since her arrival in the city.

Another thing to keep in mind . . .

"You said the priests liked the omens. What were the omens, then?"

Purple Grackle retrieved her feathers and began to sort them with quick, effortless motions. Spirits noticed how agile her fingers were—and she'd already discovered that Purple Grackle's sewing was far better than her own.

"Your son. You will give the King an heir. Soon, too, they say."

Spirits tried to shift herself a bit, but the pain in her belly and groin flared up again, and she settled back and closed her eyes. An heir. She hadn't even given any thought to that, but of course . . .

And wasn't there something else? Yes, there was.

"Purple Grackle, did you know my husband's first Queen?"

"Night Talk Moon? No, Lady, I already told you. I was too young to be in her court."

"What was she like?"

"We don't talk about her," Purple Grackle replied.

"Oh."

As she was considering the flat finality of that statement, she heard a minor commotion beyond her room. So did Purple Grackle, who put her work aside and stood up. "I'll go see, Lady," she said.

She vanished, only to return a moment later. "It's a boy, Lady. He says he brings a message from your mother. Should I let him in?"

"What's his name?"

Purple Grackle grinned in spite of herself. "He's an ugly little thing who calls himself Laughing Monkey. He looks like one, too."

Spirits nodded. "I'll speak to him."

VI

The first white strings of cloud were trailing across the sky when Green Water Woman and her small entourage came down at last to the river before Jaguar Island. This was a bit past noonday, when the heat was still at its worst. As was the temper of the princess from Holy Stone City.

Her bearers brought her litter right to the edge of

the river, so close she could smell the water, and she raised her hand to shield her eyes from the glare. "Well, how do we get across?" she said finally.

Her priest, who had grown closer to her as the trip had progressed, recognized her tone and answered quickly. "I think there is a raft moored on the other side. Can you see it?"

She peered some more. "Yes. But it's not doing any good over there."

The priest, who was young, bowed his head quickly. "Yes, Lady. I'll have one of the guards swim across and fetch the boatmen."

She peered over the edge of her litter. "Perhaps one of our big strong guards may be able to shout loud enough for them to hear on the other side?" She smiled a glittering smile and he bobbed another hasty bow. He was, she was pleased to note, sweating a great deal. She enjoyed being the cause of sweat on a man's skin.

The priest, whose name was Dog Eye, and who served the Jaguar, soon had all the guards shouting and hallooing and, presently, a thin cry echoed in response. After a moment they saw figures leap down to the raft, and in a few more moments the raft itself began to thread its way along its guide rope.

Green Water would not allow her bearers to set down her litter and take a rest. Instead, she sat crosslegged above their shoulders, watching the raft approach, and drumming her long fingernails on her knee. She wore a light traveling robe made of embroidered cloth, a skirt, and several necklaces of large beads that hung from her neck and partially covered her heavy breasts. Her hair, as usual unbound, streamed down her back and gleamed in rippling waves as the hot breeze touched it. Her eyes were slitted and thoughtful—it was a clear day, and she could easily make out the fantastic structures of Great Head City on the other side of the river.

It was a time for taking stock. She had been the first to see the top of Sun Mountain poking above the horizon of the huge stretch of villages, and she'd wondered what it was. When Dog Eye told her it was no doubt the famous Mountain of the All-Sun, she found herself unable to imagine that something so huge had been made by men.

She'd even asked: "Are you sure the Gods didn't build it?"

But the priest had shaken his head. "No, Lady, it was built in the city long ago, by great Lords whose names are lost in the shadows of time."

It seemed a flowery answer to her, a typical bit of priestly doubletalk, but since the God-servers never passed up a chance to take credit for anything on behalf of their ruling divinities, the fact that Dog Eye admitted All-Sun Mountain was the work of men was probably the truth.

Nevertheless, it was an impressive truth, and though her innate egomania would never allow her to admit it, everything she'd seen so far of Great Head City had impressed her. Already, in just the outlying villages on this side of the river, she'd seen evidence of far greater riches than her father could ever have commanded from his own citadel. And that was just the outer reaches. Gods only knew what splendors of power lay on the far side of the river.

A cramp hit her almost unawares, twisting her gut, and she doubled over. It was thinking about the wonders of Great Head City that did it—she'd managed to keep the worst of it safely buried in her thoughts throughout most of the journey, but now the rat of jealousy opened its yellow fangs wide and gnawed a huge chunk out of the inside of her guts.

It could have been mine! It *should* have been mine!

And so she stared, glassy-eyed and blinded by envy, at what might have been but wasn't. Until her priest said, "Lady? The boat is here, my Lady."

"What? Oh. Yes."

Her bearers carried her aboard, where she finally allowed them to set her down. The raft did bob in the water a bit, and she had no intention of letting herself be spilled into the slow green murk of the river. She was a princess, and she intended to arrive in the city of her dreams looking like one.

"Will you be happy to see me, sister dear?" she murmured.

Dog Eye said, "What?"

She glanced at him. "Nothing," she replied.

He took one look at her face, nodded, and turned away.

VII

Green Water Woman came across the slow river, its turgid movement her namesake, and at last stepped down onto the sacred ground of the Jaguar Island. A thrill trembled through her, though she was hard. She stretched her hands out as she gazed at the Mountain of the Mother-Father-Sun, rose-flanked, the eye of the Three-God glittering at its peak, as if to gather it into herself.

Skull Breaker said, "Welcome, Lady."

She started. She had not seen him come up, though of course he had seen her. His spies had told him of her coming for many days of march, just as they had informed him of the small boy who had arrived three days before her, and been taken directly to the pavilion of the High Queen.

She turned on him and glared, but he only smiled. He was General to the High King, and she was nothing more than a princess from the hill country.

She was fine, though, he thought as he watched the sun glint off her hair. He could understand what his master wanted, at least some of it. But first she must learn her place.

"Take me to the High King," she demanded.

"No, Lady."

"What do you mean? Do you know who I am?"

"Yes, Lady. You are a murderess and a slut." He paused, waiting for the explosion, nor was he disappointed.

Finally, when he had grown tired of her shrieking, he stepped forward and struck her hard across the face. The force of his blow knocked her to the ground, where she sprawled in a weeping huddle at his feet. He waited for the obvious reaction, and so when she leaped up, a stained knife in her hand, he was ready. He twisted the blade away with a surprisingly quick motion, struck her down again, and examined the weapon.

"I suppose you used this when you attacked your sister?" He shrugged and tossed the knife down. She made no move to pick it up, and he nodded approvingly.

"Stand up, Princess, and let me tell you how things will be," he said. And in his thoughts he reminded himself to watch his back from now on.

Nevertheless, he enjoyed her humiliation. She had escaped him once. He would take his revenge for that now, and she would learn. The thought pleased him. He loved everything that had more than one purpose. And they would both be the better for it.

VIII

Laughing Monkey could not, of course, serve in the High Queen's inner chambers, for that was forbidden to men. But Spirits warmed to him almost as quickly as she had to Purple Grackle, and arranged quarters for him just outside her pavilion, where he could come quickly at her summons.

"He is a monkey," Purple Grackle said.

"Yes, but a loyal one, I think," Spirits replied. "Mother wouldn't have sent him if she thought otherwise." She sighed and put down her sewing for a moment. "What evil news he brought, though . . ."

Purple Grackle carefully made no reply. Spirits had sent her away, and received the boy's message in privacy. She'd even taken care to whisper only, so that even the sharpest ears outside her room had not been able to make out what was said. Evidently the High Queen learned quickly, though Purple Grackle almost regretted telling her the truth about snoops, for her ears had been straining as hard as anybody else's.

She felt Spirits's gaze on her, long and thoughtful. "Can I trust you, Purple Grackle?"

Purple Grackle looked up. "Yes," she said simply.

Spirits watched her for several more moments, and Purple Grackle did not drop her gaze, only waited for her mistress to make up her mind. Finally, Spirits nodded.

"Very well," she said. "Come close, so we may whisper, and let me tell you a story . . ."

When she had finished, Purple Grackle only sighed. "I know you think it of great moment, Lady, but it is a familiar story. A sad one, yes, but familiar."

"Oh?"

"Yes. All kings plot and scheme. I'm sure your husband is aware of what your father is about. His General, Skull Breaker, knows everything. His spies are everywhere."

Spirits thought of Skull Breaker, whom she had not paid much attention to. "Then why hasn't my husband done anything?"

Purple Grackle shrugged. "I can't say, Lady. The ways of kings are complicated and treacherous. But he married you anyway. Think of that."

Unfortunately, that was exactly what Spirits *was* considering, and the more she thought, the more dismay she felt. Webs within webs. Nothing was as it seemed.

"What should I do about my sister?" she said finally.

"I don't know. She must have a good reason for coming."

"Of course she does. She hates me. She tried to kill me—I can't prove that, but I know it."

"All the more reason to beware, Lady. The High King would not allow her onto the island if he didn't desire her presence. So we will have to wait, and see what he does when she arrives."

Spirits nodded at that. It was sensible advice. Later, though, it became a mystery, when many days passed, and Green Water was nowhere to be seen or heard of.

Skull Breaker had done his work well; Green Water, hidden away in a small pavilion far beyond the central city, had already been in the King's bed three times before Spirits finally discovered that her nemesis had found her again. And by that time her moon-blood had already ceased, and she knew the child of the High King was growing in her belly.

CHAPTER EIGHT

I

"I am the Dragon," said Harvest Mountain to Skull Breaker. "That is the truth."

Skull Breaker had escorted his Lord out into the city, accompanied by a small band of courtiers. The High King had things on his mind, and Skull Breaker had learned that Harvest Mountain often spoke his thoughts better outside the structured confines and stiff formality of the royal pavilions.

The King noted much new construction on the north end of the island, in the traders' quarter, and was pleased. "Our reach grows longer every day," he remarked. "The traders send their caravans in all directions, and carry the fruit of our Gods to the north and the south."

Skull Breaker nodded. Hidden in these words was a thorn. He decided to grasp it.

"But not to the west," he said. "Not to the lands of the Old City."

This was when Harvest Mountain spoke of the Dragon. Skull Breaker smiled. "Yes, Lord, you are the Dragon."

They came through the traders' quarter and down to the edge of the river. Harvest Mountain knelt and trailed his fingers in the water.

"The river is rising," he noted. "The rains have begun in the heartlands. Soon they will be here."

Both men glanced up at the sky. The weather had turned cooler of late, and the sky, which had once been as clear as the eye of an eagle, now was often gray and lowering. The last of the harvests from the fields along the river, and the dry lands in the swamps, had already been brought in. It had been a good one, and the storehouses of the city were full of maize. In the farm villages the men were finishing their tasks, and with the onset of the short rainy season, they would soon be idle.

Skull Breaker thought on this, while he waited for his Lord to continue his thoughts.

Harvest Mountain had been squatting near the water, and now he stood. "The Dragon is the eye and mouth and claw of the All-Sun. I stand between heaven and earth and the underworld, and this is my city."

"Yes, Lord, that is true."

Harvest Mountain glanced at him. "I want my city to be great," he said at last. "The Dragon bows to no other gods, not the Jaguar, or the Feathered Serpent, or any of the Old Gods. Nor should my city do so, either."

Skull Breaker felt his heart begin to thrum. "I have been training the young men for moons now. A little bit at a time, sending out the Jaguar Cult to teach them the ways of war—the spear, the war club, the atlatl and the bow. When the rains come, they will be ready. A fine tool for the claw of the Dragon."

Harvest Mountain stared down at his hands. He flexed his long fingers, then clenched them into fists. The veins stood out on the inside of his wrists. "My brother-in-law, Lord Night Thunder, who calls himself Shaker, mocks me. My traders are not allowed in the Three-City, and my priests are turned away."

"Yes, Lord, he is rebellious. Even more so than your father-in-law."

Harvest Mountain grinned at him. "What a family I have, eh, General? Traitors and murderers and thieves and rebels. And of my choice, it seems. I married into both of them."

Skull Breaker knew better than to mention Night Talk Moon, the sister of Night Thunder the Shaker, but he said, "Women are women, Lord, and men are men. Spirits Walking Woman is a fine High Queen."

Harvest Mountain chuckled softly. "And her sister is a fine slut. Gods, Skull Breaker, she is possessed! It is like mating with the Jaguar himself!"

"Perhaps she is . . ." he ventured.

The King's eyebrows rose. "You think so? That she might be some kind of shaman, a were-jaguar woman?"

Skull Breaker shrugged. The Lord Jaguar's possessions were His own, and none but the most skilled and holy of priests might know His mind. Nevertheless, this King before him was such a priest, for he was the Dragon, the High Priest of the All-Sun, and the mouth of the Creating Triad.

"It is hard to say, my Lord. You would know better than I."

Harvest Mountain turned and began to walk away from the water. "I have not told the High Queen that her sister is here, on the island. Keep her hidden, if you can."

Skull Breaker remembered Green Water as she lay on the ground before him, a trickle of blood leaking from her mouth as she shrieked curses at him. He smiled. "I will talk with her, Lord."

Harvest Mountain nodded. "I would have peace in my home. For a while, at least. It cannot go on, but I won't give her up. In the meantime, though . . ."

"Lord?"

"Yes?"

"What of the Shaker?"

The High King paused, then stretched out his arms, taut and lazy as a cat. "My city must be great, for I love my people. The time has come for the Dragon to stretch His wings."

"And?"

Harvest Mountain's dark eyes turned fierce and cold. "Before the short rains end, I will eat the Shaker's heart."

II

"My Lady, the Lord Skull Breaker said you must not go out."

"And are you, Dog Eye, to be the one to stop me?"

The little priest shrank back. He had come to know Green Water's moods all too well; they varied little, and were mostly evil. But when, as today, she seemed to swell up like a snake full of venom, ready to strike, he was most afraid of her.

He had watched silently when she'd come out of her private room into the main house, her maids fussing with her cloak and her hair as she strode about like a caged leopard. It was plain what she was about, and he'd offered his single objection only because he feared Skull Breaker a tiny bit more than he did her.

Like many small men—small in both size and spirit—his fondest wish was to be let alone. Unlike some, he had no wish for glory, or great deeds. As a youth, when his family had offered him to the Jaguar Temple in Holy Stone City, he had felt only relief that his offering was of service, and not some more terminal sacrifice. He was the fourth son of that line, and it wasn't uncommon for such extraneous offspring to be offered in whole to the altars of the Gods in order to secure the fortunes of the remaining siblings.

He'd been glad to spend his next few years in the iron fist of Temple discipline, learning the lesser secrets, and perfecting those few ritual arts allowed to him. That he'd been sent with Green Water to Great Head City, his first excursion beyond the walls of his own town, surprised no one more than himself. Nor was it a happy parting or meeting. His mistress scared him to death. He'd learned her better than he'd wanted to on the journey, and his fondest hope had been that when they arrived at their destination, she would send him back to the mountains and his once peaceful life.

But it was not to be. She felt some bond had been forged when he had presided over the sacrifice of the unfortunate Snake Nose. In her eyes he had become a kind of living record of her dedication to the Jaguar Lord. And then Skull Breaker had drawn him aside, after their party had been settled in a house hidden away on the outskirts of the trading quarter.

"Come with me," Skull Breaker had said, taking his arm in an iron grip.

The General had dragged him willy-nilly through the teeming streets and finally brought him to the awesome walls of the Jaguar Temple. Thoroughly cowed, he had clambered up those broad stone steps and found himself delivered into a small room where incense burned in clay pots, where torches guttered, and where it seemed that even at high noon the light did not penetrate.

There, on a huge carved stone throne table sat a monster, waiting for him. Thus, shaking so badly he thought his bones would break, he met for the first time Lord Smoking Mirror, the High Priest of the Jaguar God, the most powerful priest in the city.

Smoking Mirror had greeted him in the formal position of power: seated on the edge of the throne, legs crossed beneath him, one leg dangling down. His right hand clasped the ankle of his folded leg, and his left hand was raised into the air, signaling his mastery of the Three Worlds.

Dog Eye had just about knocked himself out, banging his forehead on the cool stone floor, until he heard Smoking Mirror's soft voice say, "Arise . . . priest."

The upshot of this terrifying introduction was that Dog Eye would not be returning to Holy Stone City, but instead would remain in Green Water's household as a spy and, hopefully, as a moderating influence.

The interview had been short, succinct, and extremely explicit. And now he found himself as a kernel of maize caught between two stones.

He subsided immediately before Green Water's violently hissed challenge. He lowered his head. "No, Lady, no. Of course not. I thought perhaps you'd forgotten . . ."

She glared at him another moment. "Pah. Get out of my way."

He realized he was standing between her and the front door flap of the house, and jerked aside. "Yes, Lady. Forgive me."

She stormed on past, then stopped. "Come with me," she ordered. "I'm a princess. I can't go about like a common drab." Then she eyed him critically. "Do you have another cloak? You look like a beggar in that one."

It was the only piece of clothing he had. He looked down at the floor and admitted the shameful fact.

"Well, it can't be helped. Come on, then." And with that she was out the door, and he, a moment later, followed her into the overcast day.

She took two guards, two serving maids—she'd already dispatched her mother's ancient courtiers back to Holy Stone City—and Dog Eye. It wasn't the escort she might have wished, but it would have to do. If that pig of a general thought she was going to stay locked up in her house forever, he had another think coming . . .

Green Water's mind was in a turmoil, and had been for some days now. The High King had already visited her bed many times, and she was happy enough with the way that was going. The King seemed to find a peculiar release in her. They coupled, she thought, like beasts, all claws and nails, and his energy seemed to grow with each visit.

In a way, she understood. She knew far more of the needs of men than her sister did. Especially men of power, which were the only kind who interested her. Their lives were lived as if they balanced on thin branches, ever ready to fall—or be pushed—from their perches. The fears and angers and hatreds this sort of existence brought forth had to be bled off somewhere. Each man had his own escape valve. She was only grateful that Harvest Mountain seemed to find his release in her bed. If she could make him dependent on her for that, then she would have the leverage to do other things.

In the meantime, she had decided it was time to learn something about the city she now claimed, at least in her own mind, as hers. So after she'd put her weasel priest in his place—and who was he reporting to? Skull Breaker? The High King? Someone else?— she stepped out into the gray overcast afternoon, her nostrils wide, looking very much like some hunting beast seeking after prey.

She squinted down the narrow lanes leading away from her house, and into the traders' quarter proper. Finally she turned to Dog Nose.

"Where is the Grand Concourse?" she said. "That's where I want to go."

Trembling, he nodded, and showed her the way.

III

The worst of the rains had not yet arrived, but a pattern was becoming clear. Spirits at first found it a pleasing novelty, as the climate of the mountainous Holy Stone City had been much drier. But after several days of arising to a dull, heavy drizzle that lessened around noon, then quickened into downpours that beat at the thatched roofs and spattered through the cloth walls, making everything sodden, she grew tired, and then even depressed by the continuous floods from the sky.

So, after a hand's worth of days when the rain never really stopped at all, to arise one morning and not hear the endless drumming of the rain was a relief to her, even a blessing.

She poked her nose out of her pavilion, looked up and saw clouds, but they were a smooth gray cover, not the boiling tempests she'd become used to. She inhaled sharply; the air was cool and smelled freshly washed; even the ubiquitous scents of the city were, for the moment, sluiced away. She felt a surge of energy and whirled back into her rooms, calling for Purple Grackle.

"Let's go out!" she almost sang, her eyes bright with expectation.

Purple Grackle, though much less affected by the rain, responded eagerly. She'd noted her mistress's growing sourness of temper, and was pleased to see a break in the emotional weather.

"Yes, let's!" she replied. The two of them made quick preparations, called together a small covey of courtiers, and quickly set forth.

Spirits had learned to ignore the crowd that was deemed a proper escort for the High Queen, and no longer felt the need to creep about as if she were a commoner. It was, in fact, reassuring to have a squad of spearmen at hand, for her face was becoming better known in the city, and people sometimes pressed at her, frightening her with their noisy pleas. But always, closest to her, she kept Purple Grackle and Laughing Monkey, the only two of her court she really trusted.

When they reached the Grand Concourse and began to stroll down the Way of the All-Sun, she was glad she'd decided to come out. There was a cool breeze blowing, but no sign of rain. Most of the traders' stalls had magically sprouted up, and several barrows from the village farms as well. She felt light, free, and realized how dreary life in the rainy season had become, and how much that dreariness had oppressed her.

She took a deep breath and looked around. Yes, this was just what she needed. What all of them needed. And now that she looked, she saw other members of her court, some accompanied by men of her husband's court, others in groups, all ambling aimlessly to and fro.

They came to a barrow tended by a farm family, a man, his son, and two women. The mangoes looked a bit shriveled, but suddenly the thought of biting into one of those juicy fruits was the most delightful prospect in the world. "There," she said to Purple Grackle, and led the party over.

As High Queen she could not stoop to handling the fruit herself, but Purple Grackle knew her tastes, and quickly began to rummage through the rosy mound. She held up one, then another of the ovoid shapes, and finally Spirits smiled. "Yes," she said. "That one."

"And an excellent choice it is, Spirits," Green Water Woman said.

Spirits just about jumped out of her skin. "Wha—?" she said, as she spun around. "You!"

But Green Water only smiled at her. "Come now, Spirits. Why so surprised? Surely you knew I had come to Great Head City? Our mother must have sent you word I was coming." Green Water's gaze slid aside and rested on Laughing Monkey, who was regarding her with wide eyes and open mouth.

Spirits wanted to tell him to close his mouth, he looked witless. Somehow his expression made her feel as if she were at a disadvantage. And in truth she did feel stunned. She'd known her sister was here, but in

the moon or so since Laughing Monkey had brought
his message, she had not seen her.

"Oh . . . sister," she said. "Yes, of course I knew
you were coming." And then, her reluctance plain,
"Why didn't you come to see me?"

The temporary merger of their two groups had
clogged up the passage along All-Sun Way, and now
people were beginning to pause and stare. Spirits felt
their eyes on her, and saw them on her beautiful sister.
She could imagine the thoughts behind the stares:
Who was the mystery woman? Why was the High
Queen talking to her? But since she'd always regarded
herself as the ugly little sister, Spirits could not know
that what the crowd murmured over was the startling
beauty the two shared. Nor would she have believed
it if she had known.

"Let's move off the Way," she said.

"Yes, perhaps we should," Green Water said, and
then did an astonishing thing. She stepped forward
and, as if it were the most natural thing in the world,
she took Spirits by her arm and led her to an open
space of lush green grass behind the barrows, as if
they were the oldest and closest of companions.

"I think it's time we became friends, Spirits," she
said. "Don't you?"

Spirits was so surprised she allowed herself to be
urged along without protest. Her mind whirled. This
was not what she'd expected, no, not at all. She saw
Purple Grackle staring at her, and the expression on
her face helped to bring her back to earth. With relief
she felt her native practicality reassert itself, and her
thoughts became more ordered. Her first thought was
that one had to be careful when grasping a snake . . .

Her servants spread out cloths for them to sit on.
Green Water sank down first, while Spirits was still
standing. Spirits watched, amazed, as her elder sister
gracefully knelt and pressed her forehead to the earth
in submission.

"Oh . . . Green Water. Get up. You're my sister. That isn't necessary."

Green Water rose with calm dignity. "Yes, Spirits, we are sisters. But you are the High Queen, and you deserve the tokens of my respect." This said, they both sat down, facing each other. Green Water gazed calmly into Spirits's wondering eyes.

"Let there be truth between us, Spirits," said Green Water at last. "I thought your husband should be mine, and I went mad when he humiliated me and chose you. I couldn't understand it. I was a woman, and I proved it to him." She paused, and smiled faintly. "I know you knew about *that*, so I break no secrets here."

"Yes," Spirits said. "I knew."

Green Water nodded. "Try to understand me, Spirits. You know what a temper I have. I have thought much on it, and it seems to me I am my own worst enemy. Have you ever felt that way?"

Spirits was growing more amazed by the instant. She'd never expected to hear such things from her elder sister. Could this be the same vixen who'd made her life miserable for so many years?

"Well, I wouldn't say . . . perhaps enemy is the wrong word . . ."

But Green Water only chuckled bitterly at that. "Spirits, you don't have to tread around it with gentle words, like a leopard toying with a hare. I know what I am, and so do you." She spread her hands. "You cannot have many good memories of me, I'm sure." She looked down. "I don't have many good memories . . ."

"Oh, Green Water—"

"No. I don't seek your pity, Spirits, and I don't deserve your forgiveness. But I want you to know what happened to me. When the High King rejected me, I tried to kill you. That was me, and this was the knife!"

And with that, she withdrew from beneath her cloak the stained stone blade and showed it. Two of Spirits's guards immediately moved forward, but before they could do anything, Green Water slashed down twice, quick as a striking serpent.

A pair of long red lines appeared across her bared breasts. Immediately, a sheet of blood burst forth, covering her belly and soaking her skirt with crimson. As she did this, her eyes never left those of her sister.

". . . There," she gasped. "A token of my penance." She dropped the knife between them. "Blood is between us, sister. Can you ever forgive me?"

Spirits, her face white as a sheet, lurched forward, her hands seeking her sister. "Purple Grackle, fetch a healing priest. Send Laughing Monkey. Now!"

All the color had drained from Green Water's face. But her slanted eyes, so full of fire, remained focused on Spirits. "I can learn to love you, sister. If you will let me . . ."

And with that she sighed and fainted.

Immediately, though her skin crawled with horror, Spirits came to her feet. "Guards! Shield us!" As she spoke, she yanked off her white cloak and began to tear it into strips. With these she made a pad and wiped away the blood from her sister's front. "Purple Grackle, help me!"

Green Water let out a soft moan. Her lips looked gray. Her closed eyelids began to flutter.

"Oh, Gods!" Spirits gasped as she knelt frantically over Green Water's prone body. "Can no one help me?"

A crowd of gawkers had gathered round the bizarre scene. Suddenly they sprang apart, as a tall man in white appeared. His strange eyes took in the scene in a single glance, and he knelt quickly next to Spirits.

"Let me . . ." he said. "I am a healing priest."

She saw his nimble fingers begin to work, cleaning,

pressing against the wound. He glanced aside at her, his face serious. "It's not too bad, perhaps."

"Who are you?" Spirits asked. She found herself staring into eyes the color of polished lapis, the blue of a mountain pond beneath a cloudy sky. The eyes of a God.

"I am White Serpent Hawk." He looked up from his work. "We need to get her away from here, into shelter. It might begin to rain. Shall we go to my temple or to your royal pavilion, High Queen?"

Spirits's heart was yammering in her ears. But somehow this priest's words soothed her, and her turbulent thoughts began to calm beneath the magic of his soothing voice.

"To my pavilion," she said. Her eyes found her guards. "Quickly!"

IV

As Spirits had ordered, things moved quickly. Her guards carefully lifted up Green Water and began to bear her toward the royal pavilions, the rest of the guards using their spears to force a way through the gathering crowds. With half her mind, Spirits heard a rising mutter, and knew the city would be in an uproar over this. But that didn't matter, not now. What did matter was Green Water.

Dimly, she understood that things had happened too quickly, and that she might be, as she'd thought before, lifting a snake to her bosom. But that warning faded to nothing before the moment, and she bent all her thoughts to helping the sister she'd despised as long as she could remember. For that was her nature too, to think as well of things as she could, and always look to forgive those who wronged her.

She couldn't get those words out of her mind: *There is blood between us,* for they had more meaning than

the one Green Water had meant. That blood was in
their veins, as well as on the earth.

After the first shock, when they were marching rapidly along, she looked at the white priest who'd come
to her rescue. All his attention was on Green Water.
He walked beside her with a fluid grace, his hands
still busy, holding pads of cloth against her wounds,
his gaze grave and concentrated. He was very tall, and,
miraculously, his dark hair, in the gray light, was shot
with strands of gold. He wore it long and plaited in a
single braid which he twisted over his shoulder. It
hung down the front of his chest, and was tied with
only a bit of white cloth. As before, a single quetzal
feather, almost matching the golden strands of his
hair, was plaited into the top of the braid, and looped
down past his ear.

He wore no bracelets or stone bands about his bi-
ceps, and his garb was simple: a clout held by a white
belt about his high waist, a plain cloak, and sandals
no better than any farmer might have possessed. On
another this dress might have looked shabby, but on
him, it only served to emphasize the beauty of his
form. His chest was high and round beneath broad
shoulders, his waist like that of a wasp, his legs well
shaped and muscular.

There was none of the Old Race in him, and only
the best of the New; his cheekbones were smooth, his
nose long, narrow, and straight, and his eyes and hair
belonged to no race she'd ever heard of, unless the
Gods had created a new one.

All this she noticed almost in passing, but despite
her worry about Green Water, she did notice. He was
the most impressive man she'd ever seen. There was
a kingliness about him, like and yet different from the
dignity of her husband. But the one part of his aspect
that penetrated her mind most deeply was something
no artist could draw. A great and knowing calm

seemed to emanate from him, so that merely by his presence he soothed and gentled all who came near.

She felt herself slipping under his spell, and was grateful for it. But before she could pursue this any further, they reached her quarters and set Green Water down. Immediately White Serpent knelt next to her. His long-fingered hand (Spirits noticed the perfect elegance of his finger bones) fluttered across Green Water's sweating forehead.

He turned. "Bring water," he said softly. And then, to one of his own priests, he issued further instructions that Spirits did not understand, for they were in a secret tongue such as all priests kept for their own temples. Two of his followers immediately raced away, and returned in short order, bearing the things he'd asked for.

He looked up at Spirits. "If you could leave us for a while, High Queen?"

"Oh . . . yes. Yes, of course. Come, ladies," Spirits said, and led them from the inner chamber. They gathered outside. From the inner room came the sounds of soft chanting, and then the odor of sweet incense.

Spirits turned to Purple Grackle, and stared at her, speechless.

Purple Grackle nodded, and patted her hand. "It will be all right," she said.

V

Green Water Woman came awake sneezing. She felt bands constricting her chest, and at first fought against them. Her mind felt clouded and woozy, her lips and mouth dry.

Soft hands pressed her down, and a melodious voice hummed in her ear. She couldn't quite make out the words, but something about the tones of it was so immensely soothing . . .

Gently, a hand lifted her head, and then cool water

touched her lips. She drank greedily, but only for a moment, before the water was taken away.

"Not too much," the voice whispered, and now she could make it out. "Later, you can have more."

Her eyes were still closed. She was almost afraid to open them, but after a moment she tried. A face swam blearily in her vision, smiled, retreated.

She closed her eyes again, frightened. Surely she must be dead and in the Water World beneath the Earth, for she had seen the face of a God. And she thought of what must be in store for her, after the life she had passed in the living world.

"Who are you?" she whispered, dreading the answer.

But he only smiled, and stroked her brow, and said, "Rest. You will be fine. Through me, the Gods have healed you."

Her hands stole to her breasts, but instead of flesh felt bandages and poultices. A sharp, unfamiliar odor rose to her nose. She stared up at his face, confused. "What . . . ?"

"Rest," he repeated. His eyes seemed to grow into beckoning pools. She fell into them, and the world spun away.

VI

"She will be fine," White Serpent said. "But she needs to be watched. Can you send somebody from your court to her house, Lady, when she goes back there? And I will dispatch a healing priest from my temple."

They were seated on mats in the outer room of Spirits's pavilion. Servants served tea sweetened with honey in beautifully carved wooden cups.

Spirits said, "I'll do better than that. I've already given instructions that her things be moved from her house to here, in my pavilion." She shook her head.

"I don't understand. She was living in little more than a hut. And she is my sister." And my sister was not accustomed to living in hovels, she wanted to add, but didn't. It was a puzzle she still needed to unravel for herself.

White Serpent bent over his own cup. Once again she was struck by his beauty, and even more strongly by the purity of his spirit. Something about him called to her, and touched places deeply hidden inside her. It made her nervous, and was at the same time immensely attracting. He seemed to sense this, for he looked up and smiled at her.

"Yes, that is the right thing to do. She will need watching for at least a hand of days. She will be weak at first, but the spells I cast were propitious. Can you tell me what happened?"

Purple Grackle had been serving them, but Spirits cut her eyes at her and she bowed and withdrew. Spirits sighed. "It is shameful, I think."

White Serpent regarded her with utmost understanding, his eyes blue and wide. "If it pains you, Lady, do not speak of it."

But she did want to speak, for her mind was in turmoil. She didn't know what to make of the day's events. Green Water had come begging forgiveness, but her actions in this were as wild as anything she'd ever done before. It seemed that her sister, even in remorse, was incapable of moderation—and this was so foreign to Spirits's nature she found it profoundly frightening.

Somehow, it was almost as if she were at fault. But her need to sort it out was so great, and White Serpent's understanding so apparent, that to her surprise she found herself unburdening her fears to him.

He sat and listened in silence, only nodding encouragement when she faltered. And when she was done, he eyed her gravely and said, "But, Lady, why do you fear? You have only sought the good, and even the Gods must love you for that."

She lowered her eyes. His words had so relieved
her that she couldn't bear to look at him, for fear he
would mistake what he saw for something else. But as
she looked down at her hands folded around her cup,
she realized that wasn't her fear at all. No, she feared
he would see the truth.

"Who are you?" she asked finally.

"Me? A priest, that is all. I am the Feathered
Serpent."

Now she did look up, because she thought she'd heard
mistakenly. "But the Feathered Serpent is a God."

But he only smiled that soft smile, and said, "Even
the Gods must serve the destiny of the Three Worlds."

She wanted to question him further, for his meaning
was slippery, but he rose to his feet and set his cup
aside. "I must go, High Queen. My temple calls. I will
return tomorrow and look in on your sister."

She came to her feet to meet him, and for a moment
the room seemed to her very crowded, even though
only the two of them were in it. She was aware of his
every movement, of the look of his eyes, the smell of
his skin, the way the gold glinted in his hair. He was
a priest, but he was a man, and she, a woman.

"Very well, White Serpent," she forced herself to
say. "I will look for you on the morrow—and, thank
you so much. I don't know what I would have done . . ."

He bowed slightly, more a lowering of his gaze than
any head movement, and said, "You would have done
fine without me, High Queen. You are a practical
woman, I think. I am just glad I was able to help."
He paused, and his enigmatic smile returned. "And to
meet you at last."

Then, once again, he bowed and, just as quickly,
was gone. She stood for several long moments and
watched the door flap flutter gently back and forth in
the wake of his passage, her gaze distant, as if lost in
a dream.

CHAPTER NINE

I

It should have been a minor matter, what with the preparations for war, but coupled with his recent discovery of Spirits's pregnancy, Harvest Mountain could not ignore it.

"I thought I told you to keep them apart—to keep *her* away. And now she is set up in the royal pavilions as if she were the High Queen."

Skull Breaker was worried. He'd thought he had the she-devil well in hand, and yet in a trice she'd somehow not only escaped him, but somehow managed to get herself moved into the pavilions on a permanent basis. He shook his head. It made no sense—but who could have guessed she would mutilate herself by her own hand?

She was beginning to frighten him, but it wouldn't do for his Lord to get the slightest whiff of *that*. He sought refuge in the Gods instead. "I did as I thought best, Lord. She had plenty of money, servants, a house . . . and you." He raised his eyebrows knowingly. Harvest Mountain glanced at him and grunted.

"It should have been enough," Skull Breaker added, knowing it sounded weak. But it *should* have been enough. Damn that she-devil. If he'd known the trouble she would cause, she would never have risen from the spot by the river where he'd first struck her down. Then, invoking the final mystery, he added, "Women. Who can know their minds? They aren't like us."

At that, Harvest Mountain chuckled. "Be glad of it, Skull Breaker." But the edge seemed to have gone off his anger. "At least I won't have to weigh the balance much longer. Another two hands of days and we will be off."

"Yes, Lord. Everything is almost in readiness. I have had hunters out and the women drying meat. The armorers have equipped everybody with one good spear and a knife. The Jaguar Cult have their war clubs, of course, and we have ten hands of bowmen. And a troop of atlatlan, with their throwing sticks . . . mostly backwoods boys from the most distant villages, deep in the swamps."

Harvest Mountain nodded at this enumeration. By his counting, he would set forth with an army of eight fingers times a hand of hands of men, a huge force. But it would have to be large, for what he had in mind: the Old City, the City of Three, would be no easy nut to crack. And the Lord Shaker was no fool, no matter how much he might despise his former brother-in-law. He was a seasoned warrior, and no doubt had already looked to the defense of his city.

Thank the Gods that the Shaker wasn't laid up in Holy Stone City. With his skill, he might lurk there in safety forever. But the Old City was not so blessed with natural protections. Taking it would be difficult, but not impossible.

"I have to see that Sky Wind Warrior keeps Holy Stone City out of it. If he goes over to the Shaker while I am on the march . . ."

Skull Breaker nodded. Harvest Mountain didn't have to elaborate further. But thinking on it, he saw a way to put a better face on his failure with Green Water Woman.

"Lord, have you considered what it may mean, that you have both his daughters with you in the pavilions?"

Harvest Mountain had been looking out over the trading quarter, fidgeting, and now he turned. "What of it?"

"That man is a schemer, not really a fighter. One of his daughters is High Queen, and surely his own spies must tell him the other is your concubine, if you will."

Harvest Mountain quirked his lips. "Yes, it does sound better than royal slut."

Skull Breaker nodded. "And now we have this unlooked-for reconciliation between the two sisters. A word in the right place might convince Sky Wind he would do better to wait—especially if he knows Spirits is pregnant—than try anything rash while you are prowling around with your army."

"Hm. Do you think he knows of the child in Spirits's belly?"

"If not already, I will make certain he does so soon."

"Good, then. See to it."

"Lord?"

"What?"

"If you should be defeated at the Triad City, Sky Wind will attack immediately."

Harvest Mountain's eyes went opaque. "Of course. But I won't be defeated." He looked away, back out over his domain. "I am the Dragon, and my destiny is before me."

II

Spirits was still wary, but recent events had done much to convince her of a real change in her sister's feeling for her.

As White Serpent had predicted, she had survived

her attempt at self-immolation without permanent harm, except for a pair of still-livid scratches the healing priests said would fade until they were no more noticeable than Spirits's own wounds.

But while the flesh might remain more or less the same, it seemed to Spirits that a woman she'd never known before woke up from the trance in which White Serpent had placed her. Green Water kept to her bed for two days before Spirits felt safe enough in moving her to her new quarters, a large chamber only a few paces from her own.

As the days of Green Water's convalescence wore on, Spirits began to come in the mornings to visit her. The rains had returned, and with them came restlessness and gloom; and even though Spirits was not yet reconciled in her own mind to her elder sister, she was surprised to find herself looking forward to these morning visits. A certain rhythm developed.

Spirits would arrive a few hours after dawn, with a servant bearing a tray of hot tea, or she might carry it herself. The people of the city were great carvers of wood, and potters as well. The High Queen discovered a treasure trove of beautiful things laid away for her bidding, and so began to choose different vessels each morning; one day cups made in the likeness of leaping jaguars, carved from dark mangrove root, polished with oil until they gleamed. Or on another occasion a beautiful pot spun by a master of clay, tall and round, with white god markings incised on an ebony background, and matching cups, delicate as egg shells, to serve alongside.

At first there was a distance between the two women, as if they had met for the first time. Green Water, pale of skin and slow of speech, groggy from the potions the priests gave her to drink, would reply with formal politeness to anything Spirits asked, but say nothing of her own. They might as well have been strangers, and at first it put Spirits off. But when she thought on it she began to understand. In a way it was as if they *were* meeting for the first time. Their stations had changed so much, one to the other, it was as if they were two different women—and also, as Green Water admitted, there was blood between them.

Nonetheless, as the days wore on and the rains drummed an endless dull silver song, they grew easier with each other, and their conversations grew more open and friendly.

On this morning Spirits woke to the chatter of spider monkeys. A gaudy, raucous troop of them had come across the river and invaded the thatched roofs of the royal pavilions. They were bright, quick little things, and when the King's archers came to slay them for target practice, Spirits forbade it. She liked their happy chittering cries as an anodyne to the ceaseless beat of the rain. Now, smiling at their noise, she carried a lovely tray carved of soft yellow cottonwood, on which she had arranged a set of cups and a tea bowl of golden orange glazed over a white background, marked with a pattern of graceful volutes about the rims.

"Good morning, sister," she said briskly as she brought this into the room. "How are you feeling today?"

Green Water had lost a bit of weight during her ordeal, but looked none the worse for it. In fact, to Spirits, she looked even more beautiful, for the gauntness emphasized the strong planes of her face, and set off her lovely slanting eyes.

As usual, Green Water was awake, sitting propped in her bed on a heap of pillows, a light cover thrown over her lower body, her chest and shoulders naked to catch the breeze. The short rainy season was the warm one—it would grow distinctly cooler with the advent of the long season, but that was several moons away yet.

Spirits set down the tray and busied herself with pouring. "Honey?" she asked.

Green Water nodded. "A lot, please. I crave the sweet."

"Yes, I've noticed lately. You didn't used to, though. When mother would put honey in your mouth you'd make faces and spit it out."

Green Water smiled. "Yes. Things change, don't they?"

Spirits raised her own cup and sipped. "Ah. Just right." She peered at her sister across the rim. "Your scratches are almost gone. But you look so pale now."

It was true. Green Water had always been an outdoor type, and the sun had burnished her to a red-hued darkness. But she had not left her room since Spirits had brought her there, and she had paled. Now she was creamy and golden, which made her black hair and eyes seem to vibrate against her skin. She had become the most striking woman Spirits had ever seen.

Green Water took her own cup. "Spirits, you've been so good to me, who least deserved it of you. But now I must go. I have intruded on your hospitality long enough. Father gave me enough money to maintain my little house. I am fully recovered. I should go back there now."

"Oh—no, sister."

Green Water sighed. "There is no reason to be polite, Spirits. I know you must hate me, and how can I blame you for that? But I don't want to cause you any more trouble." She sank back against her pillow and stared at the roof beams. "I'm even considering going back to the mountains."

Spirits sat up straight. "Look at me," she said. She waited until Green Water's tilted gaze was locked on hers. "Sister, as you say, things have changed. I believe we have changed. What you did—well, it shocked me. Upset me. I must confess, I had misgivings, but we have been together and talked as true sisters for the first time in our lives. I would like that to go on. I have none of my family here but you— and nobody I can fully trust. Tell me true, Green Water. Do you know what our father is?"

Green Water nodded slowly. "A traitor and a plotter. And a fool. He risks the life of Holy Stone City."

Spirits inhaled sharply. She had not expected so incisive a tally. "Yes, then. Do you see? I try to do what needs be, if I can, to protect the dear things of my childhood. I love my husband, but I love the old things, too. And you could be my ally in this, if you would."

Green Water set down her cup. "You have no reason to trust me, Spirits."

"But I do," Spirits replied. "Lord White Serpent says I must learn forgiveness."

Green Water's eyebrows rose. "That beautiful creature who rescued me?"

Spirits giggled. "Oh, Green Water, not you, too?"

They both laughed then, and in their shared understanding Spirits felt a bond was sealed. So, for a time, Green Water Woman came to stay in the royal pavilion of the High Queen.

III

In the city, unlike the pavilions of the royal women, there was no reconciliation. Beneath the deceptively placid surface of things, turmoil bubbled, for the Gods and their servants were becoming locked in secret battle. And so, as Skull Breaker dispatched the Jaguar Cult soldiers to and fro, readying the High King's army for the coming march, in the temple of the Jaguar, Smoking Mirror stretched out his hand and plotted.

Today he wore only a simple cotton cape, dyed red with an embroidered border of blue threads, and a

simple helmet crown denoting his position. Atop the
Jaguar Temple's great mound was a small pyramid,
one of the first built in the city and older even than
the Mountain of the All-Sun. Its rough stones were
blackened and cracked here and there, but it still possessed all its dark, brooding strength. To Smoking
Mirror it seemed as if it crouched over the earth, like
the Jaguar whose divine spirit it served. Hollowed out
inside this were both ancient public rooms, and others,
more secret. It was the heart of the Jaguar Temple in
the city, and Smoking Mirror preferred to spend most
of his time there, away from the sun. Like his heavenly
master he was a creature of the night, loving darkness,
and for light, fire rather than the sun.

Now he seated himself on a boulder only roughly
shaped, the crudeness of the incisions on it testifying
to its age. This seat, he suspected, was even older than
the pyramid that guarded it, and might even have been
the first token of the Jaguar to come to Great Head
City, in the lost days when the city was only a village
on the river. As for himself, Smoking Mirror thought
that was true, and that this stone was the heart of the
city, given by Jaguar Himself. Sometimes he would
come at night to rest his hands on it, and fancy he
could feel its stony beat . . .

He seated himself and gestured for his picture
scribes, who traced out the god marks onto thin strips
of wood with sharp flint knives made especially for
the purpose. It was the job of these scribes to make
a record that others might see, of the glory of the
Jaguar and His priest, Smoking Mirror. He had de-
signed his own picture mark, a graphic coupling of the
Lord and himself, with the picture for Light as their
offspring. This picture meant his name, Smoking Mirror, for all who saw it, though of course only the edu-
cated priests and aristocrats had the learning to
understand.

When all was ready, he nodded for his advisers to

approach. They did so, bowing, their shaved skulls gleaming in the light of many waxen candles. He waited till they finished their prostrations, then clapped his hands.

"Dark Eye Seer, what of the preparations for war?"

Dark Eye, who was Smoking Mirror's Chamberlain, and responsible for the everyday operations of the temple, stood up and moved closer. "The High King will leave in a hand of days. Skull Breaker is satisfied with the condition of the army. He says our Jaguar soldiers have done a good job of training the farmers."

Smoking Mirror nodded. The Lord General had already said as much, but it was good to have it confirmed through other sources. Skull Breaker's net of spies was legendary, but Smoking Mirror's own web was nearly as large, and much less known. He preferred it that way.

"Have we had any word from our brothers in the Old City?"

Dark Eye nodded. "A messenger arrived late yesterday."

"Mm. And is all in readiness there?"

Dark Eye spread his hands. He was a squat man, thick, heavy, soft-looking. He ate well. His belly bulged out beneath his cloak. Smoking Mirror knew these audiences were a trial for him, because he had to stand, and his knees were bad. He much preferred to sit upon his wooden stool, which was, of course, why Smoking Mirror insisted he remain upright in his presence.

Now he waddled even closer, and bent as much as he could to bring his thick lips close to Smoking Mirror's ear. "The omens for the Shaker will be terrible. And public. The people will tremble in fear when they see them."

Smoking Mirror nodded. The God was the God, but how the omens were read was the province of priests. Who were men, of course. He had made certain decisions long ago, for even then he'd seen something in the young man who was then only a prince. There was a spark in Harvest Mountain, and Smoking Mirror intended to fan it into an all-consuming flame, a fire upon which entire cities might be sacrificed to his Lord.

"Good," he said. "But make no reply at present. They will see their reply soon enough—and one cannot trust everyone to keep their mouths shut, even in the Temple."

Dark Eye nodded at this advice. "Their messenger, then?"

Smoking Mirror waved one hand gently. "Cut out his tongue. There is no need to kill him."

"You are merciful, Father."

Smoking Mirror gestured again to acknowledge the truth of this, and continued: "What do the Lords of the Jaguar Cult think of the campaign? We are well into the short rains now, and the journey is arduous through the swamps. Will they be successful before the sun returns to the sky?"

Dark Eye considered. The Lords of the Jaguar Cult, who were the permanent officers of those men whose lives were dedicated from birth to war in the name of their God, were tough and realistic war chiefs. And they were divided on the question. Some felt that the Old City would fall easily, that Night Thunder Shaker roared and threatened but was full of wind and would run at the first sign of the High King's army. Others weren't so sure, and pointed out that the Old City, being divided into three parts, might be difficult to take if the defenders were sturdy and well led. And of course there were questions, privately debated, about the High King himself: was he strong enough, brave enough to lead his men to victory?

Those who were uncertain of the answer to that— and there were several, for all soldiers knew the only proving of those things was in battle, not in talk—

those men placed their faith in Skull Breaker, who was, at least, a known and tested quantity.

Dark Eye related all this to Smoking Mirror, who grunted. "About what I expected," he said. "I don't know what it is about fighting men. Take them away from their spears and they turn into a bunch of old women. Tcha!"

He spat in disgust. A slave came forward to wipe up his spittle and save it, lest an enemy find it and use it for some malign spell.

"And . . . the one who calls himself the Feathered Serpent?"

Dark Eye sighed. "As always, Father, but more so. He preaches to the people every day now, both in the temple and out on the streets. Many listen to him. He grows more powerful every passing hour."

Smoking Mirror nodded. He had seen it for himself. The followers of the High Priest White Serpent Hawk were easy enough to spot, for they forswore grandeur and wore only plain white clothing of simple cut. And the farmers, whose dress was always simple, wore white ribbons tied around their heads to mark them as followers of the Feathered Serpent.

He settled back on his stone seat and gave himself over to thought. His subordinates were used to this, and seeing his eyelids drop and his gaze go unfocused, they relaxed and prepared to wait. Sometimes Smoking Mirror would keep them like this for an hour, awaiting some decision he wrestled with.

For he was a subtle and careful man, and knew his own strengths. One of those strengths was patience: He was willing to wait and let time itself help him to achieve his goals.

Now he thought on the one who styled himself the Feathered Serpent, whose name was White Serpent Hawk.

In a way it was frightening how quickly he had gathered power to himself. He had appeared out of the

west only two hands of years ago, a lone priest carrying a staff of plain wood, creeping into the city one
afternoon and announcing his presence in the most
simple of ways. He had walked up the center of All-
Sun way and begun to preach.

In a short time he had gathered a small crowd, who
listened to him attentively. From that modest beginning he had never looked back, and now he had his
own temple. It, too, was modest, but there were rumors he intended to build anew, for the space within
its walls was no longer large enough to contain those
who wished to worship there.

Which, if that had been all there was to it, Smoking
Mirror would not have given it a second thought. But
he was a subtle man, and understood the potential
danger, for White Serpent Hawk did not preach as
other priests did.

And without puffing himself up, he was glad that
he was High Priest when White Serpent Hawk came
to the city. Another might not have recognized the
danger, but he had scented it as soon as he first heard
the White Priest speak. Oh, yes, he had gone, and
without his robes or acolytes, but alone, dressed as
any other man. To this day he wasn't sure whether
White Serpent had recognized him. He had held well
back, and as far as he knew, the new priest had never
seen him before. Nevertheless, as White Serpent had
preached, his tones clear as the water bells, Smoking
Mirror had felt the younger man's gaze pause and
settle on him more than once. So perhaps he had
known, even then.

And Smoking Mirror knew that if he understood
anything at all, he understood the Three Worlds, and
the Gods who lived there. He served the Jaguar, who
was mighty in the three, as was the Dragon. The
Feathered Serpent was the brother of these two, but
always the lesser, though He also had the power to
move amongst Heaven, Earth, and the World Under

Water, the home of the dead. And there was a fourth God, the Trickster, and so all were brothers, born of the All-In-One, the Mother-Father who sat on the same throne and looked to the east and the west at the same time.

But Gods, though eternal, played their games with men. They stepped out of the Three Worlds to mold the earth into their own images, to impress their glory in human hearts. And always they demanded sacrifice, they demanded the blood. Thus is had always been, and there was a balance among them, the four Brothers.

The Dragon was first, and then the Jaguar, (though the Jaguar had claimed this city for his own, and the Dragon had not demurred) and after those two came the Trickster, whose dark face always looked down, toward the Underwater World, and finally and least the Feathered Serpent. Thus was the balance, and White Serpent Hawk never questioned it. In his preaching he said, in fact, nothing at all about strength or power, or how the Gods should rank themselves in the eyes of men.

Nevertheless, what he preached was as deadly as if he had counseled that his followers should overturn the altars of the Jaguar and burn the priests of the Dragon. For in the end, his teachings would destroy the balance just as surely as if he did holy murder with his own hands. For he preached love.

Yes, Smoking Mirror thought, it was a good thing he was here, for his eyes, at least, could see the deadly viper cloaked in that gentle skin.

The Gods craved blood, but White Serpent's God did not. He wanted fruits, and vegetables, and aromatic woods burned for him. He wanted songs sung and prayers, and the sound of drums and pipes. But he did not want the smell of burning flesh in his nostrils, or so White Serpent said—and in that simple thing lay the seeds of destruction not only for the Divine Balance, but for the temples and the city itself.

"Blood," Smoking Mirror murmured, not realizing he spoke aloud. "We are founded on blood, we float on it . . ."

"I beg your pardon, Father?" said Dark Eye, and Smoking Mirror started. "Eh? What—did I speak?"

Dark Eye nodded reverently. "You spoke of blood, Father. The holy blood . . ."

Smoking Mirror snorted inwardly. Yes, there was holy blood, and blood not so holy, and when mixed it was impossible to tell one from the other. That was also a lesson he had learned from his earliest days, and he would not forget it now. In the meantime, it was sufficient that he knew his enemy, and had made his plans. In the end they were all tools, and the Gods would decide. So be it.

"How go the preparations for the sacrifice?" he said. "I feel the Jaguar Father's thirst. It is terrible, and before the High King departs, it must be quenched."

"With blood," Dark Eye whispered reverently.

"With blood," Smoking Mirror agreed.

IV

Skull Breaker, along with some of the Lords of the Jaguar Cult, spent the day touring the city and the near villages to make sure the new army was fully supplied and ready to fight. He was pleased with what he found. "War is a strange business," he remarked to Fire Dead Walker, the highest of the Jaguar Chiefs, a man as tough and grizzled as Skull Breaker himself.

"War is a messy business, and in the laps of the Gods," Fire Dead replied. He wasn't much for philosophy, military or otherwise. He had been pledged to the Jaguar Cult at birth, and had known no other life but that of a warrior. Because of that, he was one of an extremely small minority in Great Head City, for most men toiled at some other work, and only rarely needed to take up arms against their fellows.

Or so things had been for many generations. But Skull Breaker had seen the breaking of that long mold in the reign of Harvest Mountain's father, the great King Tall Mountain, who had tipped the balance between the Old City and Great Head City by sheer force of arms.

War, Skull Breaker reflected, was as much a matter of the Gods as of men, for men were the arms of the Gods. When the Old City had ruled, it was because the favor of the Jaguar, the Dragon, the Trickster, even the Feathered Serpent, had fallen on that city. But with the rise of Tall Mountain in Great Head City, (which was called Jaguar Island City then, before he had brought many stone thrones, heads, and altars to his seat) the favor of the Gods had shifted, and he had taken on the mantle of the Dragon as a token of his power.

As Skull Breaker strode through the villages he found much that was pleasing, and some that was not. Today the rains had quieted to a steady light drizzle, and mists curled about the thatched pole houses where the farmers lived. And that was the key, of course: the farmers. The Jaguar Cult, the professional soldiers of the city, who spent their lives learning war and training for it, numbered no more than twice ten hands. They were the core, passing down the knowledge of arms from father to son. But to raise an army, the farmers must be turned for a time into soldiers.

This could happen only during the rainy seasons, when the fields lay fallow. Otherwise, farmers must farm, or the people of the city would starve. Which meant that there could be no such thing as an occupying army. No city could commit so many men to an army that they could waste their own farmers in physically occupying another city. Luckily, he reflected, as he paused before one cluster of houses, it wasn't necessary.

Five men came out of the huts, three young, their faces eager, and two older men, scarred, veterans he recognized from past campaigns.

"Ho, Limp Belly," he greeted the eldest, a man with one squinting eye and a caved-in chest that made his round gut look like a ball, "the claw of the Dragon stretches out again. It will be good to have you with me."

Limp Belly bobbed his head. His expression was plain, neither eager nor fearful. Soldiering was just a thing to do, if the Gods demanded it of him. And of course there would be loot, if the Dragon was victorious.

"Your sons, Limp Belly?" Skull Breaker inclined his head toward the younger ones. The middle of these stepped forward and bowed low, but he couldn't hide his grin.

Limp Belly said, "Leaping Fox, by my third wife."

Skull Breaker nodded and extended his hands. "Your spear, Leaping Fox."

The youth handed it over. Skull Breaker hefted it, held it closer to look at the point. Turned and showed it to the Jaguar men, who grunted approval.

It was a fine weapon, the shaft of tough wood, well balanced, about a head taller than young Leaping Fox. The point was a deadly shard of finely worked obsidian, a very valuable thing. When this campaign was over, the spear would be collected and taken for storage to the armories of the Jaguar Cult, kept safe behind the temple walls.

Skull Breaker was pleased. When he was a youth, Tall Mountain had begun his campaigns with soldiers armed only with pointed, fire-hardened stakes. That Great Head City could now afford to arm its soldiers with such weapons was proof of the wealth of the city, and proof of the love the Gods bore for it.

"And your knife?" he asked.

Leaping Fox dropped his hand to the belt that both held up his clout and circled his waist, his young face twisting with dismay. Skull Breaker laughed out loud. "You forgot, sprat? What a soldier you are!"

The Jaguar men grumbled behind him, but he paid no attention. "Where is it? In your house?"

Leaping Fox nodded.

"Well, go and get it. And next time—don't forget, understand?" He glanced at Limp Belly. "See to it, eh?"

They walked on. Here the land was mostly dry, the damp and dank of the swamps distant, a green darkness at the edge of vision. The mists sidled along the paths of the villages like lonely cats, rubbing against the houses. Here and there a fire sputtered, and the sound of the women grinding maize was a rough scrape in the background.

Fist Turtle, the highest of the Jaguar chiefs, said, "I wish we'd had a bit more time with them . . ."

"It will be enough. Those boys are rough, but they looked willing," Skull Breaker replied. "And my spies say that the Shaker has given stone-tipped spears to only a few. The rest have pointed sticks. He doesn't have the wealth we do."

Fist Turtle, ever the cautious soldier, said, "Well, let us hope so. Old City is a long way off if we have to run all the way home."

"Or feed their Gods' bellies," Skull Breaker added. He was a soldier, too. Then he slapped Fist Turtle on the back. "You and I, we're too old to run, eh? So I guess we'll just have to win, instead."

Both Fist Turtle and Fire Dead Walker chuckled heavily. They had been working with the farmers for two moons, readying them. The idea of running from their enemies appealed not at all, and it was not propitious for Skull Breaker even to mention such a thing. These hard men dealt in realities. The farmers were, as needs be, also hunters, skilled with the bow and the light spear. But it was a different thing to hunt the boar than to stick men, and like all generals, they would have their doubts until the battle was done and they stood victorious in the middle of the field.

Skull Breaker caught their mood immediately, and put his palm across his mouth. He thought: Enough of this, and dismissed the others.

As they made their way deeper into the villages, approaching the scattered patches of dry land that marked the limits of the city's immediate possession, Skull Breaker's brow began to lower. He mentioned what he saw, and Fire Dead scowled. "There are many of them. Many more than there used to be."

The old soldier spat in disgust. "Cowards and weaklings. Fools." He spat again.

Skull Breaker scratched his head. "How do they think the city lives? Does grain fall from the sky? Do the stones walk by themselves from the mountains? Yes, they are fools."

The objects of their scorn were all about. For some reason there seemed to be more of them out here in the boondocks, but he'd noticed them everywhere. Men and women wearing the white ribbon bound around their heads, followers of the upstart priest who claimed he was a God.

None of these bore spears, or greeted Skull Breaker and his chiefs. They listened to their White Priest instead, who told them that war was evil, and that the blood sacrifice was to be shunned. He preached that farming, growing things and planting, helping others, and sacrificing only the fruits of the earth, not the fruits of blood, was the way to please the God.

Sheer foolishness, of course, but people would believe anything. Skull Breaker knew that Smoking Mirror was becoming concerned about White Serpent Hawk, but his own master, Harvest Mountain, paid the young priest scant attention.

Harvest Mountain was admirably hardheaded, Skull Breaker thought, and prone to put more trust in the strength of his arm—and his army—than in any god. Though he did follow the sacrifices, as he should. But even this might be a weakness, for it blinded him to the power of men such as White Serpent Hawk. He, who did not fully believe did not understand the strength of those who did believe.

They passed a final cluster of houses, these barely huts, perched at the end of a grassy finger that extended deep into the circling swamps. Here birds flew, parrots and grackles, and in a clear pool beyond, a shining silver fish jumped, a spark of silver against the green and the gray.

From one of the huts a man peered out, then like a turtle pulled himself back in. Skull Breaker saw the scrap of white ribbon on his brow.

"Let us go back," he said to the others. "We are as ready as we're going to be."

CHAPTER TEN

I

Spirits found that as the time grew closer to her husband's departure, she saw less and less of him, not that their life together had ever been close. She had told Green Water that she loved him, but secretly thought she didn't, at least as she understood the word.

But she was a woman of her class, and hadn't expected otherwise. Men lived in their world, women in another, particularly among the nobility, who had wealth enough to provide separate rooms for the sexes. In the villages men and women lived together in the same room, and sometimes she thought she envied that. But at other times she saw the advantages of her own life, kept safe and pampered among women and not forced to bend every part of her life to a man's wishes.

Yet it was a conundrum, and worrisome to her. She hadn't solved it yet, and sometimes wondered if she ever would. Also, now that she was pregnant, she found strange thoughts drifting at times through her mind, so in a way it was a relief not to deal with Harvest Mountain. His visits to her bed, never frequent, had ceased entirely upon her pregnancy. Nor did she miss them, if truth be told. She had some learning from her mother, who had not been enamored of her own husband, beyond the duty of children. And since she'd borne him only girls, she was considered a failure. Sometimes, Spirits wondered if that accounted for her father's wild ambitions.

At any rate, Harvest Mountain had tried, she supposed, to be gentle. Yet his penis was so big that, no matter how much care he took, she still hurt and bled. Her mother had explained her duties: to serve her husband in all things, to be a good wife. But it was a relief not to serve him in this.

In the meantime, she began to understand that she was no longer happy. She'd known she must sacrifice much, to leave her home in order to try to save it, but she had always trusted herself. Now, as the long gray days crept past, and the rain beat on her disposition like numberless tiny silver hammers, she found herself growing lethargic. Not even the life quickening in her belly did much to assuage the vague sense of grief that marked her waking thoughts.

One morning she awoke to a particularly dismal day, so dark and misty that beyond her windows was only a formless, shapeless blanket, and found herself thinking about her own death, almost wishing for it. It was as if she had plunged to the bottom of a well. And in fact that precise image occupied her thoughts: the sacrifice of the infants, when the babes were tossed into the well of the Gods, to sink forever in the Underwater World. She envisioned herself sinking, sinking, growing colder, the eternal waters locking her in their chill embrace—

"Enough!" she murmured to herself, and threw off her covers.

"Purple Grackle!" she called. Her maid appeared quickly, rubbing sleep from her eyes.

"What is it, Lady?"

Spirits opened her mouth to speak, then shut it. Why had she called? What answer did she seek? And then she realized the solution had been there all along, woven in the tapestry of her past. So simple! Why hadn't she seen it before?

She was dying inside. The answer, then, was to go outside herself. And that she knew how to do.

"Purple Grackle, there are many poor people, many sick people in the villages, aren't there?"

Purple Grackle, still fuzzy with slumber, nodded slowly.

"I am their queen. I should be helping them."

Purple Grackle stared at her. "Lady . . . there are the priests. That is what they are for."

"No, Purple Grackle, that is what I am for. I am their mother, as the High King is their father. Get ready! Today, the mother will visit her children, and learn their ways. Summon a healing priest, and Laughing Monkey. It's time I did something useful with myself."

II

Several day passages later, while Spirits was responding to the healing desires of her own inner nature, Green Water Woman paced her rooms, half maddened by the tug of her own dual essence. For though she had made a truce with her younger sister, a part of her had never accepted it. Now, with Spirits gone, Green Water found herself alone (for she had no desire to go with Spirits, or mix with the filthy peasants of the villages). And left to her own devices, much that she had put aside began to return.

With the incessant rain weighing her down even more than it did her sister, she found herself almost unbearably irritable. Her skin seemed a tight bag, enclosing her, intolerable. And her mind itched with fire.

She had sent her women away. In fact, she had viciously slapped one of the youngest to the floor for slopping her morning porridge, and then, disgusted with her weeping, had ordered them all from her presence.

Now she stood near her window, tapping her fingers on the wall of stones there, gazing blankly at the rain. Why had she come here? She remembered the day she had first gone out onto the Concourse and seen Spirits for the first time. She could still remember the flash of rage that had taken her then, so strong she had gasped as if a snake had bitten her. But then a kind of lassitude had immediately followed, and darkness had coiled behind her eyes. Something had come upon her, called by her anger, and soothed it; taken it into itself, folded it up and left her empty. And in that emptiness it was as if she stood outside herself and looked in with cold, dispassionate eyes.

What she saw then was a series of images: herself locked in sweaty embrace with Harvest Mountain, drawing passion on his back with bloody fingernails while he sated himself in her. Herself the object of scorn, her own mother's lip curled at her as if she were nothing but trash. And worst of all, herself sprawled at Skull Breaker's feet, bleeding, while that old man looked down on her and laughed.

In the bright sunlight she had stood as if turned to stone, her eyes bright and empty, waiting for she knew not what. And it had come, a few words: *Go to her.*

And so she had, without the slightest idea of what she would do. When the stone murder knife had appeared in her hand, she had been as surprised as anyone. And what she had done—it was as if the God guided her hand.

Then the blood gushed out, and she had fainted. When she woke, her fires were banked, and she saw the priest with blue eyes. It was him, White Serpent Hawk, that she thought of now. But she knew that inside her another ruled.

Smokes from the morning fires mingled with the mist; the wind flapped her curtains listlessly. Spirits had taken her into her heart, but she didn't want to be there. What to do? Two struggled for her. And then, slowly, she remembered her journey, and the One to whom she had pledged herself, her arms wrist-deep in Twisted Nose's guts. Who, or what, had spoken to her in the sunlit silence of the Concourse?

Low through the mist, the sound like a distant summons, she heard the cry of a hunting cat. It was answer enough. She looked up at the leaden sky. Then she turned and called for her women, and when they were ready, she went out.

III

On the day before the army was to depart, Harvest Mountain made a final tour of the city and the villages with Skull Breaker and the chiefs of the Jaguar Cult. He returned to the royal pavilions satisfied that his generals had done all they could, and his army was prepared for what he asked of it. Then he retired alone to his inner rooms, and left an order that he be undisturbed. He would sacrifice to the Jaguar later in the evening, a fitting act, for even the Dragon should seek His dark brother in times of war.

First, though, he wanted some time with his own thoughts. Skull Breaker understood. His father had been like that too, an inward-seeming man, full of secrets. And his son was in the same mold, even more so, for he had fooled Skull Breaker himself with his play at the fool.

Sometimes, Skull Breaker thought such men must speak directly with the Gods, without even the road of sacrifice to open the divine way. Tall Mountain had done this before battle, retreated into silence and solitude, and then returned refreshed. So the old general was pleased at this one more token of the son's likeness to the father. For the father had been the greatest general of all, and had made the city rich. Now he would learn if Harvest Mountain Lord could make the city great.

But Harvest Mountain, once the courtiers and the generals had left, and his rooms had sunk into silence, did nothing but stand in the middle of the largest room, his face calm, staring at nothing. For long moments he stood like this, his fine chest rising and falling, and no other sign of life. It was gloomy here; candles had been lit, and their dancing shadows played on his face. Their bright flames guttered in his eyes. He was neither statue nor man, neither living nor dead, and had Skull Breaker seen him in those slow seconds, he would have thrown up his hands in the sign of the God.

Harvest Mountain, son of Tall Mountain, felt Him coming now. It was his great secret. He had learned it as a child, and told no others, for the God had whispered in his ear he should not. He was King, and by his birth, Dragon, the mouth and fist of the Sun. But he knew he was more. He had watched his father strike his way to greatness, and had learned all that Tall Mountain could teach, both of the good and the bad. But always inside, the God had waited, looking out of his eyes, whispering in his ear.

It was that voice that had counseled him to play the fool, and so to draw his enemies from their hidden holes. And it was those divine inner eyes that had seen them when they emerged. There had been a great burning then, though he had kept that secret from his wife, and even from the city. Yet in hidden places beneath All-Sun Mountain, his temple, men had screamed in fire for the glory of that God.

Out of the Sun, the Dragon, he was given the mastery of the Three Worlds. The Gods knew it. But men did not, and of the Middle World, the world of living men, he would have to take that for himself. Eventually he began to shake, as the power of the God burned through his veins, and when he finally came out of his room, he was covered with sweat.

His courtiers dried him and dressed him for the ceremonies of the night. The sacrifices for war would be made to the Jaguar, in his temple. Harvest Mountain went to do his duty without protest. He had already made his sacrifice to the Sun, and now nothing remained but for the Dragon to stretch out his claw.

IV

In the House of the Jaguar, Smoking Mirror also made his preparations. It was to his Lord that sacrifices would be made for the success of the coming war. Harvest Mountain, the Dragon priest, might make his own arrangements with his namesake, but the island and the city belonged to the Lord of Night. It was Jaguar who bestrode the Three Worlds like a thundercloud, who gave the rains to the people that their fields might grow rich and their bellies full, and who demanded a rain of blood to pay for the gifts from the sky.

Of late, the High Priest had much on his mind. So much, in fact, that he left his usual haunts inside the ancient stone pyramid and took much of his day inspecting the preparations for the great blood rituals to come.

The temple mound was square, a hundred paces on a side. It was a small city within a city, and contained, beside the barracks for the Jaguar Cult and its chiefs, a temple of many pavilions, including Smoking Mirror's own quarters; the ancient pyramid with its squared-off top, upon which rested an equally venerable altar, and in front of this, a great basalt-stone platform holding three brooding, fire-scarred altars of even larger size than that atop the pyramid. It was to these that Smoking Mirror made his way, accompanied by his Chamberlain and his chief priests.

The altars had been decked out in colored cloths and bright flags and banners. Piled around the altars were many faggots of wood, for the fires would be started early and would burn throughout the day and into the night.

Smoking Mirror picked up one of the sticks of wood and hefted it: fine, dry cottonwood, taken from stores of wood aged within the temple confines. Next to this was another stack of aromatic pine, full of pitch, that would send up smells pleasing to all the Gods.

"And the incense?" Smoking Mirror inquired.

The Chamberlain showed him brightly woven baskets upon which jaguars and dragons cavorted beneath a many-rayed sun, full to their wide brims with powders and sticks and barks; the High Priest raked his fingers through and sniffed his palm. He smiled. "Very fresh. The God will be pleased."

Then they showed him where the pipers would sit, and the drums, great hollowed logs covered with tightly stretched skins, tall tubes of stone which made a sound like windy bells, and great clay kettles whose sound was as low as thunder. Then they took him to see the new robes which had been made, which were so thick with stones and furs they could barely be lifted. Set off to themselves were also four new pectoral mirrors, round concave plates of hematite so perfectly cut and polished that Smoking Mirror could see the tiny red veins of his eyes in their reflecting surfaces.

All this took a good part of the afternoon, for Smoking Mirror wanted to check everything for himself; after all, the honor of the Jaguar—and the luck of the God—were at stake. He had never failed Tall Mountain, and he intended to give Harvest Mountain no reason for reproach either.

The final stop was beyond the temple, to the south and west, a part of the domain of the Jaguar Cult that was not much visited by outsiders. His party came down the broad steps of the mound slowly. As he descended, Smoking Mirror looked out over the city, and the crowds beginning to fill up the Grand Concourse to the north.

It was easy to spot the farmers who would be soldiers on the morrow, for they carried their tall spears, which sported bright ribbons tied around the shafts. They had come with their families and would sleep in the Concourse, from where they would form up and march out the next morning.

But whole villages had turned out, for the men of the army were the least part of the people there. Work did not cease entirely with the rain; the fields were planted and must be tended, though the work was less than during the dry seasons, when trees had to be cleared and grass burned off.

The people had been coming in all day; if he looked closely, he could still see them clustering beyond the river, while the great log raft lumbered back and forth like the back of a huge turtle. Cook fires had already been set up here and there, and many stalls and barrows; the smell of roasting pig and frying corncakes rose into the wet air, along with that particular throbbing mutter of a throng gathered in happy anticipation.

Smoking Mirror strolled along, shielded by his guard, raising his hand and bestowing blessings absentmindedly when some shouting face snagged his attention. Eventually they reached a wall of pointed stakes set into the earth, tied together with stout rope, pierced by a single woven gate. This stockade enclosed an elbow of the river; the waters, infested with snakes and alligators, served as the rearward walls of the place. His nose twitched as he approached. The stench from beyond was appalling, thick and heavy, and in a strange way reminiscent of the scent of bread baking. Smoking Mirror knew what it was. It was the smell of starvation.

Immediately he clapped his hands together. The Chamberlain, Dark Eye, waddled close. Smoking Mirror kept his voice low, but it didn't disguise his anger, and the fat priest began to tremble.

"Smell that? Eh, do you? It is the stink of dying men. Haven't you been down here?"

Dark Eye put his palms together and began to bob his head frantically. "Yes, Lord, of course, but I've been so busy—"

"Too busy to see the Gods are fed well?" Smoking Mirror glared at him. "Open the gate!"

"Lord—"

"Open it, I said!"

With quivering fingers Dark Eye gestured at one of the guards, who untied the gate cord and swung open the gate. Smoking Mirror walked on through, his head high, mouth tight and angry, and stopped just inside. It was as he feared, and he swung around on Dark Eye.

"You fool. Look at them. Sprawled in the mud, most of them too weak to stand. What have you been feeding them? Grass?"

He stared the Chamberlain in the eye. "I need a dozen for tonight, a dozen healthy men, pleasing in the eyes of the God. And what do I have? Sweepings, dregs, tangled bones in bags of yellowed skin. Well, Dark Eye Seer, I will have my dozen." He paused, swept the pathetic creatures lying about, and the few who stood staring hopelessly at him. "Maybe of these four or five will do." He pointed at the ones he meant. Then he turned back to Dark Eye.

"As for the rest, Chamberlain, as I say, I will have them. And I will have them from you. Starting with your second son, and the rest also from your personal household."

Quaking, the fat man sank to his knees, tears streaming down his cheeks. "Lord, I beg you—"

But Smoking Mirror only smiled. "From your per-

sonal house, Dark Eye Seer." His smile grew wider.
"Be glad I don't take your miserable fat hide as well."

Then he walked away. Eventually, the wails of his
Chamberlain faded behind him, lost in the sigh of the
wind and the crowds.

V

His manservant called him from his inner room with
a tiny bell, which he rang at the door. It really wasn't
necessary. Unlike the Temple of the Dark Jaguar,
there was nothing heavy or ponderous in the Temple
of the Feathered Serpent. The poles on the pavilions
were sunk into lush grass, and garlanded with wide
cloths of red and gold and azure that fluttered before
every drifting breeze. Birds flew beneath the tall
thatched roofs, and monkeys played in the flowering
trees that grew everywhere. Even dogs wandered
about freely, not cringing or fearful, for inside the confines of this temple, all life was sacred to the God.

So when White Serpent Hawk was summoned to
the afternoon services before the low altar in the main
courtyard, it was with a bell, and no other pomp. The
manservant came in and helped him with his white
cotton cloak, and fastened about his brow a broad
white ribbon, which set off his mane of chocolate and
gold hair. His eyes glowed like sapphires, and his
cheeks, dusted also with gold, held a tinge of rose.

He went out into the courtyard, where he found a
larger crowd than usual; no surprise, for his ears had
been full of distant murmurs, the mutter of the ingath-
ering of all the people, and the preparation for war.

He walked slowly to his accustomed place before
the altar; again, nothing impressive, only a grassy
mound a little higher than the rest, so that he could
look out and see every face. As he mounted, he felt
a little thrill: it was always so, when he looked out

over those who had come, not out of fear, but from trust and hope, and, perhaps, love.

He presented himself as a simple man, but he was not. There were times when, preaching to them, he felt as if he were filled with a clear, cool, light, and knew his true nature was making itself known to him. He wondered if they could see it. Perhaps they could—they seemed to sense something, and would stare at him with mouths open and wide, wondering eyes.

It was a great burden. White Serpent Hawk could remember nothing of his childhood. As far as he knew, he had sprung into the Middle World a youth in a fishing village by the sea. Of course that must be wrong; his parents often spoke of his childhood, but he could remember nothing of that. It was as if, on that day, he had awakened from a dreamless sleep, and found himself in a strong young body. He could still recall how he'd wandered about, not knowing himself or anybody else, until some had thought the Gods had robbed him of his wits. He'd learned silence then, and how to watch and learn, for it was himself he observed, and his nature that he discovered.

According to the reckoning of his parents, he was in his fifteenth year when he left the village. His father had been a fisherman, and his mother a great weaver, whose delicate fingers danced on her looms, urging brilliantly colored cloth from the clacking sticks.

After his awakening, he had gone out in his father's boat, and had taken to the lines and the nets as if they were extensions of his own hands. His father had wondered, for before that he had possessed no great skills in that direction. But he had known it was in him, and that one day his catch would be men instead of fish. This was in his thirteenth year.

For two years after that, before his fated departure from the sea, he learned about himself, and about the Middle World as if he had just come into it. He saw things with fresh eyes; the village shaman said he was a see-er, a seer, and desired him to become his apprentice, but he refused, though his family wished it.

His family did not understand his reluctance, for the position was one of high honor; nor could he explain that he could not serve the Gods, his destiny was higher than that. To speak such things would have been blasphemy for any but a God, and though White Serpent Hawk knew even then he could have spoken anyway, he didn't. For by then he was coming to know his destiny.

On the day of his fifteenth birthday, at the beginning of the short dry season, it finally all came clear. Though he had not apprenticed himself to the Shaman, he had learned from him, and so he understood many of the secret rituals which opened channels between men and Gods, and paved the road into all of the Three Worlds.

Because this was his birthday, his parents beseeched the Shaman to help them make a sacrifice to the Jaguar, the Lord of the Land, in the name of their son, and it was agreed. And there would be a feast after the omens were read, to celebrate the happy event.

The sacrifice, which was a fine, fat black dog, was prepared before the sun rose, for the ritual would begin just before dawn. Even earlier, the Shaman had begun his own preparations; in his pipe made of precious serpentine, he tamped huge quantities of the yoyu leaf, lit and smoked it. He did this many times, until he could barely suck in more of the holy smoke, and his eyes, veined with red so they looked as if tears of blood shimmered there, bulged in his skull. Then he took tabac leaves and ground them into a fine powder. This he put on another implement, a flat spoon made of coral from the sea, and placed it beneath his nose and inhaled sharply. Three times he did this, and let out a moan like a stifled scream. He was ready then, drunk on the breath of the Gods, and they brought him to the sacrifice, staggering in divine intoxication.

The small altar was ready, the dog led up with a rope around its neck. A helper stoked the fire, so that clouds of snapping sparks rose into the still dark before dawn. The Shaman took the dog and flipped it over on its back, then with a single stroke plunged his knife into its round belly.

White Serpent Hawk turned away from this, his belly griping and his gorge rising in his throat. The sacrifice was to do the God—and himself—honor, but he found no joy in it, even if the God did. The dog made a short, squeaking bark and died, its entrails steaming in the chill sea air.

The Shaman plunged in his hands and brought them up dripping, and read the omens; White Serpent Hawk listened carefully. Nothing new or special there. The God wished him well, his future would be full of happiness. He felt disappointed; it seemed so little for the death of a fine animal. Killing for food, he could understand, but this . . .

The Shaman placed the remains of the dog on the altar, and the fire did its work; first the stink of burning hair, then the richer smell of roasting flesh, mingling with the smell of other dogs, and a pig, already broiling in deep pits dug into the sandy beach. The sky beyond, out over the ocean, had turned from dark into pearly gray when the God took the Shaman. He uttered a loud shriek, and suddenly sprang into a series of three backflips, and when he came up the third time, the God was in him, and he was a Jaguar.

His mouth worked as if his lips could not encompass the white fangs growing there. He turned his eyes on White Serpent Hawk, and in a voice that was half coughing roar, half snarling purr, he said: "How do I find you now in the Middle World, Brother? Why have you left your high seat beyond the stars?"

And with that, the Shaman's hand, covered with the

paw of a Jaguar, rose and pointed directly at White
Serpent Hawk. Slowly he stood, for he knew the God
was here, before him. And just as he rose, so did the
sun's first rays lance above the watery distance, as a
great light piercing from the Third World into the Second. Then White Serpent Hawk looked up and saw
the emerald of the Morning Star burning above the
horizon, its glimmer hard and clear in the first light
of dawn.

White Serpent felt that light shine through him as
if he were a polished piece of amber, and with the
light, power. It was then he knew his destiny.

He bowed toward the Jaguar before him, and said,
"I come to fulfill what is told in the ears of the Gods,
as you know well, Brother. And I know why you have
come, but your time is not yet."

All those who heard this gasped, all except the Jaguar, whose head tilted on His shoulders as if curious.
"Do you know, then, what you do, Brother?"

And White Serpent said, "I know my destiny—
and yours."

The Jaguar held his vessel a moment longer, then
left it, as the sun roared above the horizon. The Shaman collapsed as the essence of the God departed,
and would not wake for hours. When he did, he said
to White Serpent, "Through me the God made a
mighty prophesy. What did it mean?"

But White Serpent would not tell him. Three days
later he left the village, and would not return until the
destiny he knew was fulfilled.

All this he remembered as he stood on his speaking
mound before his temple in Great Head City, and
preached to his followers while the smokes of the sacrificial fires beyond rose into the air.

One thing caught his eye. At the back of the crowd,
surrounded by her women, stood the Princess, Green
Water Woman. Around her head was bound a white
ribbon, and her slanted gaze never left his face.

He said nothing to her. She was a part of destiny, too.

But as he watched her, he thought to himself, with fear and terrible joy: Now it begins.

VI

On the day, and far into the evening, the great festival and sacrifice proceeded. The people gathered close around the altars, spilling down the wide steps of the Jaguar Temple, cheering as the omens were taken—they were all good—and cheering even louder as the captives and slaves were led up for sacrifice.

Smoking Mirror stretched out the first offering himself, on the altar atop the Black Pyramid, and as the sun set in a blaze of crimson that banished, for a time, the clouds, he plunged in the sacred knife.

Down below, at his signal, the sacrifices on the Three Altars were equally dispatched; hardly anybody noticed that the Chamberlain, Dark Eye Seer, wept as he disemboweled his son. In the end, Smoking Mirror had relented somewhat, and allowed Dark Eye to administer a sleeping potion, so that the boy went off unknowing.

This was the mystery on that memorable day: the Gods left their perches and mingled among men, and their pawns and tools, who were kings and queens and high priests, danced for joy amid the smoke and fire. At the end, the clouds rolled back over the stars, but even this was considered a good omen, that the Gods were pleased and rain would continue to fall from the sky.

It seemed that the island was abubble with Gods, fizzing with destiny, great and green and silent in the river that led to the sea.

With the dawn came drizzle, and the fires of the altars finally sputtered out, leaving behind only a dank stench, and smears of blood and cracked bones.

Skull Breaker formed up his men. The drums began
to beat. Then the High King, Harvest Mountain Lord,
who carried his long spear in his right hand, and his
sharp axe at his belt, came to the front and led them
across the river.

Everything else came after.

CHAPTER ELEVEN

Spirits, along with Laughing Monkey, Purple Grackle, a healing priest from the All-Sun temple, and a few servants, was soothing a mother who'd just given birth to a fine boy, when she heard the shouting and raised her head questioningly.

"Laughing Monkey . . . ?"

The boy bounced up from where he'd been squatting. "I'll go see, High Queen." Spirits watched him run off, a faint smile curving her lips. He was so lively, sometimes just watching him made her feel more cheerful.

Which was not a bad thing. The birth sickness had been griping her of late; she'd vomited up her breakfast porridge three times in the last six days. She turned back to her charge, a heavy woman, a farmer's wife whose husband had gone off to war. Her husband's absence had made the birth harder, Spirits thought.

"There," she soothed, wiping the woman's sweating brow with a soft white cloth. "He's a fine, beautiful boy."

The infant had been wrapped in cloths and placed on the woman's breasts, but the birth had been difficult, and she still seemed dazed from the pain. Spirits turned to the healing priest and asked if he had a potion to help with that. He did; this wasn't his first trip into the villages with the Queen, and though he didn't understand her concern for these peasants, he was coming to the idea that Spirits was a queen unlike any other he'd ever heard of. A good woman first, and then a queen. In fact, in the villages, she was called the Good Queen, and the priest had discovered of late he enjoyed going out with her.

He went into his bag, then went off with the herb woman. After a while he returned and handed her a gourd full of dark brown tea, which he assured her would help the new mother's pain, though it would likely make her even more sleepy for a while.

"That's fine," Spirits said absently. "She needs rest."

A sharp cry interrupted her. Laughing Monkey came bounding up, a huge grin on his face. "They're back!" he shouted. "The High King is back victorious!"

Spirits rose from the side of her charge and smiled at Leaping Monkey. "Then we should go to meet him, shouldn't we?"

They were beyond the river from the city, though still in the nearer villages. The cries had come from farther out, as the van of the returning army made its way toward the river raft. She gave final instructions to a village root woman who had accompanied her to the new mother's house, then led her party out from the village to the road, where she stopped to wait.

Dawn had come up as usual for these days, misty and brooding, with sudden squalls of rain. Now the rains had stopped and the ground mist drifted away, and they would have a few hours of gray clouds before the heavy rains of the afternoon came down.

It was the best part of the day, as far as Spirits was concerned; the air was almost crystalline in its purity, though heavy and damp. Sounds carried for miles, or echoed strangely. As she stood waiting, she could clearly hear water dripping from the broad leaves of the *coyol* palms, and the harsh cries of kingfishers diving for their shining, slippery meals in the river. Now, over all of this sounded the deep thrum of male voices, singing.

She listened expectantly; it was a song of triumph, rising and falling, and it sent shivers leaping up and down her spine. Her party stood facing toward the outer villages. Here the road was wide and well kept, but a hundred paces or so farther down it made a sharp turn and vanished into a screen of woods. Suddenly, the road which had been empty was full of a horde of small boys, bouncing and shouting, waving palm fronds like flags of triumph.

"Coyo! Coyo!" they shouted. "Coo Coo Roo!" They ran on past, aping the sound of the songs; then she saw a familiar form turn round the corner. He saw her immediately. She could tell, because his eyebrows rose in surprise. Then he smiled as he marched forward. For a moment it was just him, the High King, walking along, and she felt her heart stutter with gladness. She hadn't realized how worried she had been. But he was home, and unharmed. Her child would have his father.

As she began to raise her hand in greeting, the road behind him was suddenly choked with men. And all around her, the villagers began to throng as the word spread. Old men and boys, women crying with joy, the farmers who had stayed behind, yet sent brothers, fathers, uncles off to war. The noise grew.

Skull Breaker and the Jaguar chiefs raised their hands to acknowledge the waves of cheers. She could see their teeth, gleaming in grins so wide it looked as if their faces might split. And then more soldiers, spears held high, red, blue, and green ribbons fluttering to their pace.

She stepped out into the road just before he reached her, and bowed to him. He brought up his hand. The column halted. He stepped forward, took both her hands in his own, and raised her up. His fingers felt dry and strong, like rope left out in the sun.

"Oh, husband," she told him, gazing up into his shining eyes. "I am so glad you have come back to me."

He looked at her and smiled. "I come in triumph, Spirits," he said. "Now I am truly the Great King."

She hadn't known until that moment he had ever doubted it.

II

Spirits wanted to walk with him, but he shook his head and told her it wasn't fitting that a woman should walk with warriors. There was a distance about him as he spoke, and watching him, she understood there had been a change. Something had happened since she'd seen him last, something she didn't yet know, though it showed in his face, in his eyes, even in the way he stood: tall, powerful, somehow seeming larger than he had before.

She bowed her head in acquiescence and stood aside with her small party.

"After we have gone past, return quickly to the royal pavilions," he told her. "I will see you then."

"Yes, husband," she said softly.

He nodded, raised his hand, and the long column pressed forward again. She stepped farther back, allowing her small party to mask her identity from the passing troops, though Skull Breaker caught her eye, grinned, and nodded. Then he was gone, followed by a small group of Jaguar chiefs and a few of their fighters, tough, hard-looking men who didn't smile, but kept their watchful eyes on their commanders.

Behind them came the captives. Their hands were bound behind them. They shuffled along, watched by a few soldiers, but she saw that a guard wasn't really necessary. Their heads were bowed. All the fight had gone out of them, all the pride, even, almost, their humanity. They stumbled forward like animals, their eyes dull and empty, their shoulders slumped. The cheers of the people had no effect on them. It was as if they'd already gone beyond, into a different world. The world of the dead.

It was the first time she'd seen men—and women, too, she now noted—as spoils of war. And she was surprised at what she felt. She'd never seen anything like this, but she had heard of it. Her husband's father had subdued many distant villages, and his power had been whispered in Holy Stone City as long as she could remember.

But Tall Mountain had never come in war to her home, though she dimly remembered some triumphant visit in her early childhood. That had been when her father had sworn loyalty to him. Her father, too, had sent out soldiers, but they only brought back a few for the altars, a handful, and she had seen their passing from a distance. Their faces had been unknown to her, and their hearts.

It was not the case here. These shambling hulks, empty of all hope, made her skin crawl; because they were still human, and it was possible to see what they had once been. And from that was only a short mental step to imagining her mother, Queen Blue Parrot, ropes tied around her chubby wrists, lurching before these soldiers, her blind eyes blank with the knowledge of certain death.

Still, as she watched, her mind warred within itself; the Gods had to be served, did they not? The Gods were everywhere, in everything, and all of the Three Worlds was Theirs to dispose of as They wished. And since time out of mind, the favorite dish of the Gods had been a trencher heaped with human flesh.

Laughing Monkey squirmed against her. She looked down. Without realizing it, she had put her arm around the boy's shoulders, and now, in his excitement, he wanted away, but was obviously afraid to push his mistress's arm off. She smiled faintly, released him, and said, "Go on, Laughing Monkey."

He shot her a wide smile and bounced off, his cheers mingling with the rest. He obviously had no reservations about this dolorous procession. A soft voice behind her said, "It's not their fault. They don't know. But this stinks in the nostrils of the God."

She turned and found herself looking up into the blue eyes of the priest, White Serpent Hawk. This close, his gaze was like a slap in the face, demanding attention.

"The God?" she murmured softly.

He nodded. "The Feathered Serpent," he replied. "I have seen you in the villages, with the people," he continued. "Whether you know it or not, you serve Him." He gestured toward the string of captives bound for sacrifice. "You serve Him, but not . . . this."

She followed his gesture. Yes, still they came, now children, yoked together with ropes tied around their little necks, some crying, some simply dazed. Whenever one stumbled, one of the soldiers would yank on the rope. To her horror, she saw that one child was dead, his neck broken; he was being carried along by the others like a chunk of meat in a grisly necklace. She turned away, and as if by the most natural of things, buried her face on White Serpent's chest.

He held her a moment. "It's a great evil," he told her. "And it is my destiny to end it, and save the people."

She stared up at him, and he nodded. His expression was so certain, so serene, that she found herself unable to gainsay him. All that was left, then, was belief.

And the beginning of something else. But that was destiny, too.

III

On the following day there was a great victory sacrifice. Those captives who were healthy played the ball game against the Jaguar Cult warriors, and lost, and died. The rest, bound hand and foot, were taken to the altars. There priests beat them to death with clubs, then spilled their brains and entrails upon the fires, for the glory of the Jaguar.

Smoking Mirror led the sacrifices, and took the omens, which were all good. Toward the end, when the blood lust of the people was fully sated, he allowed himself a moment of quiet triumph as he gazed out over the throng. Not a single white ribbon was in evidence, or the White Priest himself. His enemy had chosen to express his displeasure by staying away, and Smoking Mirror, taking the temper of the crowd, thought that was a mistake.

People loved victory, and now they associated the Jaguar with it. White Serpent Hawk could perhaps be portrayed as something other than he was, possibly even a traitor. Yet he served a God, too. It was a thorny question. Smoking Mirror decided to think on it further. There was, for instance, the interesting conversation he'd recently had with Green Water Woman, sister to the High Queen.

Possibilities there. He would consider those as well. Especially since he'd seen the Queen withdraw from the sacrifice, holding her belly. Perhaps it was her pregnancy. Or perhaps not.

He knew about her visits to the villages; White Serpent also went there. Perhaps there was something more . . . ?

IV

The object of Smoking Mirror's ruminations, White Serpent Hawk, had spent the sacrificial day in the villages, far from the stinking smell of burning flesh.

Many of the farmers had returned from battle wounded, and he spent most of his time leading his healing priests from house to house, offering what succor he could.

Which, he thought, was not to be despised. His hands brought rest, and surcease from pain. He knew from whence that power came, and blessed it. It was one more sign of his destiny, and so was both a joy and a sorrow. But for the while it was very useful.

As he worked, he kept looking about for Spirits Walking. Of course it was ridiculous. She was the High Queen. Her place would be with her husband, at the sacrificial altars. Yet he hoped. He had taken her mettle, and thought he knew her, perhaps even better than she knew herself.

He sighed at that thought as he rose from the bed of a young man whose left hand was gone at the wrist. It had been bound in a dirty rag, bleeding and crusted. He had cleaned the wound with fresh water, and then, while his priests held the youth down, he had applied fire. The boy screamed, of course, for though the fire would seal the wound and help it heal, in the short term it was agony.

Much like life, he told himself. The healing is painful at first, and men will fight against it. And fire might burn both ways.

She was a strange one, Spirits was. There was something hidden inside her that he couldn't penetrate, something beyond even the powers of the God. What could it be?

He supposed he would learn it eventually. All destinies played out in the end. Even those of the Highest.

A muffled roar from across the river turned his head. In his mind's eye he could see the spectacle. He wasn't a fool. The people there loved the fires and their smoking contents. And why not? It was all they'd ever been told, all they'd ever known. From the Gods

came their very lives: food, rain, health, sons, victory.
But there was another way, a better way.

"I will teach it to them, if they will listen," he
murmured.

The priest with him looked up, an expression of
adoration on his face. "Yes, Master, you will," the
priest said.

White Serpent Hawk smiled, and nodded, and they
went on.

V

Harvest Mountain came to Spirits's rooms late in
the evening, after the sacrifices were done. He found
her in bed, drowsy, and so he seated himself on the
edge of the straw mattress, trying not to disturb her.

"Husband . . ." she murmured, turning toward him.

He smiled and patted her hand. "I'm sorry, Spirits.
I know it was hard for you at the altars. But it was
necessary the people see us, the two of us together."
He paused, then grinned. "The three of us, actually.
Smoking Mirror tells me he has taken the omens, and
the God promises me a boy child."

"Yes, Lord, while you were gone he cast the bones
again to be sure. The result was the same. A boy."

He nodded, musing. "A son. My first wife never
gave me that," he said.

At these words her mind cleared and sharpened
suddenly. He had never spoken to her of Night Talk
Moon. Nobody had. She waited in case he should continue, but he only sighed and shook his head, his expression growing darker. Then he brightened.

"But you will, wife, and for that I owe you much."
He glanced at her covers, and the way her belly
mounded slightly beneath them.

"You were sick at the sacrifice," he said. "I'm sorry.
I asked one of the Jaguar's healing priests about it,
and he said it wasn't uncommon for a woman in your

condition. The smell of the fires probably set it off. How are you feeling otherwise?"

"My Lord is kind to ask. I am well, except sometimes I get sick in the morning. But the priests—and the women—say that is natural, and nothing to worry about."

He patted her hand again. His fingers felt warm atop her. The room, lit by a few lamps, seemed small and cozy, despite the soft prattle of the night rain. "It was a great victory," he said at last. "Would you like to hear of it?"

"Yes, Harvest Mountain."

He nodded. "We came upon them at dark. My brother-in-law turned out to be different than I'd expected, neither a coward nor a mighty war leader. We had the surprise of it. Skull Breaker led a part of the men, and I another, and we took them from two directions just after dusk."

She watched his dark gaze grow shadowed as he remembered it. "Night Thunder—he'd taken the name Shaker, which was a lie, as it turned out—had gathered men from faraway villages, places my father had taken. My father set up the God in those places, and those who could not bear the God left them and went to Night Thunder. So he had many men."

He sighed. "But he didn't have Skull Breaker, or the Jaguar Cult soldiers and chiefs, and so his army was little more than a mob. They broke when we struck them, and ran away. Or died.

"All but Night Thunder. When he saw everything was lost, he still fought me. He made his stand in front of his throne, and fought me with his spear. He was a big man, larger than me, but I am very quick.

"I killed him with my ax. He fought well. But I pulled down his throne. The God was with me, and stronger than his God. Now his people know."

Spirits listened carefully, trying to imagine what it

must have been like, from these few quiet words. I
killed him with my ax . . .

"Husband, I am so glad you returned. It must have
been terrible. I prayed for you to the God."

"Yes, the Jaguar protected me, as did the Dragon."

She nodded, and, not thinking, said, "I asked the
Feathered Serpent to watch over you, too."

He glanced at her. "Oh?"

She was so drowsy she didn't hear the way his
voice changed.

"Oh, yes, Lord. White Serpent Hawk himself took
my offering. It was a basket of mangoes," she said
artlessly.

"Mangoes."

"Yes, husband."

"Hardly the sacrifice for a warrior . . ."

"White Serpent Hawk says that the God doesn't
wish blood. He says it is a stink in the divine nostrils,
and that fruits, vegetables, fine cloths and other things
men have made are better, for they come from the
earth, as we do, and are proof of the love of the God."

His hand crept from hers. "I see," he said. "This
priest, White Serpent Hawk. Do you know him well?"

Even then she didn't hear the edge concealed in his
words. It was almost as if her ears had been muffled.
She would wonder about that later.

"Oh, no, Lord. I see him sometimes when he is in
the villages, preaching or healing."

"You go to the villages?"

"Yes, Lord."

There was a long silence. Her eyelids began to
droop. He touched her shoulder, then her cheek. "Ah,
well, we will speak of it another time. Get your rest,
Spirits. Give me a fine son."

"Yes, Lord," she murmured.

He left her then, but did not return to his quarters.
A few paces away was another chamber. He entered.

"Welcome back, Lord," Green Water Woman said. "I've missed you, these many days."

He sank into her bed. "That time is over," he told her.

CHAPTER TWELVE

I

"Y ou are the High King's . . ." Smoking Mirror let his words trail off, though his meaning was plain enough in his eyes, and in the way his lips curled at one corner.

"I am the High Queen's sister," Green Water Woman interposed smoothly. "And a princess, the first daughter of a king."

Smoking Mirror heard this and said nothing, though the expression of distaste on his face grew more pronounced. They were seated in his dark inner room, their faces lit only by bowls of oil in which lighted wicks guttered. He had taken a stool, and she likewise. They sat in front of the throne. It was not a formal audience. All their servants had been left beyond the heavily draped door, with instructions not to disturb them.

"I keep many things in mind . . . Princess," he said at last. "My question now is, why do you seek me out?"

She nodded. Fair enough. "Because, Father, I am pledged to the God."

"To the God? My God?"

"Yes," she said. "To the Jaguar."

He thought about it. "Ah. You were pledged in Holy Stone City, then."

"No. The God took me later, on my road here." Then she told him about the sacrifice of Twisted Nose, and how the Jaguar had coughed in the jungle, and accepted her gift.

At this his face changed. His gaze grew more concentrated, and he leaned forward.

"The God has chosen a woman? But . . . how extraordinary."

She shrugged. "The Gods answer only to Themselves. Do you deny the omen, or the choosing?"

He leaned back and folded his hands across his lean belly. Other priests might become fat, but often the Jaguar would take his body, and when this happened, he would curl into leaps and hoops and somersaults, and he must keep it ready for such times.

He already had news of the incident on the trail, for he'd spoken to her tame priest Dog Eye not long after her arrival in the city, and that man was still in her household, reporting regularly to him. Not that there had been much to report of late.

At the time he'd wondered if she had understood what had happened in the sacrifice. But he'd made no move toward her, preferring to let the God work His will as He would. Now the God brought her to him. What did it mean?

"No, I don't deny it. The God has put his claw in you, and you are His. But to what purpose? Have you any idea?"

She shifted on her low stool and arranged her cloak around herself more securely. It was cool in this hidden room of dank stone. And she sensed in the man across from her an interest that was more than religious. Well, perhaps not surprising. The priests of the Jaguar were not sworn to Him alone, but could take women if they desired.

Yet this was no slobbering lackwit, to be led by his snake and a woman's hand. She had learned much in her time in the city, and one of her discoveries was

that the men of power here were far stronger and
cleverer—and colder—than those she'd been able to
manipulate in her home city. Her father was a fool if
he thought he could plot his way past men such as this.

"I am not sure," she said finally. "I was hoping you
might have some guidance to offer."

"Ah."

She stared at him, waiting. He closed his eyes. She
could smell him, an odor mixed of sweat, herbs,
smoke, and . . . something else. Something frightening.
Finally he leaned toward her once again, and this time
she felt an opening, almost a welcome in his renewed attentions.

"I am the mouth, the eye, and the claw of the God,"
he said. "I am His fang. Do you understand what
that means?"

She nodded. She'd been ready for this. "Yes. The
God may have chosen me, but it is for you, who
speaks for the God, to tell me the will of the God."

His eyes widened. There had been no hesitation on
her part, and what she said was not only well spoken,
it betrayed an understanding deeper than he'd expected. Especially from a woman who was, by reports,
little more than a half-mad slut.

Perhaps the reports were wrong?

"Sister," he said, "listen to me."

She heard the change in his address quite clearly,
and responded by leaning forward herself, so that their
heads were almost together.

His voice was low. "The God has chosen you. But
you are not the only one He has chosen. His mark is
on the High King, too. Perhaps you were sent to help
him in the tasks appointed for him."

She nodded. She had wondered about that herself;
surely no one could do for Harvest Mountain what
she could. Certainly not her sister. And with that
thought, the rage that had been bottled up inside her
burst forth. She had feared her own anger, for she

had learned how it could harm her. But here, in the darkness beneath the ancient pyramid, she felt safe. Here, in this place, anger seemed right. No, necessary.

"I hate her," she said in a low, intense tone. "She took my place, the place that should have been mine. Next to him. I would have helped him. She is weak. She will drag him down. I know, I have seen it."

Her vehemence seemed to have no effect on him at all. He merely nodded, and did not draw away. "What have you seen?" he asked.

She told him of Spirits's habit of visiting the villages, and offering succor to the people. Of the way Spirits's eyes would crinkle at their corners, showing her pleasure in this weakling work; how even after the triumphant return of the King, Spirits had shown no joy, only sorrow over the wounded. And, finally, she told of things even she didn't comprehend; of the silent bond that seemed to have sprung up between White Serpent Hawk and her sister. Was it only accident that their paths now crossed so often beyond the river?

When she had finished, she saw Smoking Mirror staring openly at her, his dark eyes alert and probing. "White Serpent Hawk? They are close?"

The way he pronounced the last word, it could have meant anything. She looked at him. "Are the two of you enemies?"

But he didn't answer, not right away. She listened to his soft breathing, wondering if she'd put herself wrong. Then he raised his head. "It is said that men go mad for you."

It was an unexpected turn. And it brought back evil memories of both Harvest Mountain and Skull Breaker.

"What lies have you heard?" She straightened and tossed her head proudly. Her waves of black hair caught the torchlight and made it ripple. He stared at her flashing eyes.

"The God speaks only the truth," he said finally.

He regarded her further. "Have you met White Serpent Hawk?"

"No," she replied. "But I could."

II

On the day the rains ended, Smoking Mirror took thought of all he had learned, and all he now planned. He stood next to the parapet of his temple, his fingers unconsciously caressing the streaked stones.

The sun had risen in a pink bowl of clouds, but the sky peeped through them like the eyes of a cat, sharp and blue. The air swirled with smells: wood smoke, wet earth, the deep river still at the top of its banks and moving fast; and the slanting light caught the great heads that lined the Concourse, and turned them to gold. Atop All-Sun mountain, the Eye of the Gods winked at the morning.

He felt rested and at peace as he stared at all of this, musing. Skull Breaker had told him of Harvest Mountain's bravery: "It was as if the God possessed him, and filled his arms with strength, and guided his deadly blows," the general had said.

There was much to do, and done quickly, too. The idea of actually occupying the Three Cities never entered his mind. Who could waste valuable farmers to do nothing but stand guard? Yet it wasn't necessary, for Harvest Mountain had pulled down the thrones of the Old City, and scarred the heads that proclaimed the strength of the now-dead Night Thunder, who Shook no more.

The people understood. Though that war had been fought by men, it had been ordered by Gods, and of those the stronger had won. It was plain to see, even among the vanquished. And so a garrison was unnecessary, for the Gods themselves stood guard there. And everybody knew it.

In the meantime, the trade routes there, which

Night Thunder had closed, were now open. So the traders, everybody from the single men who carried their meager goods on their back, to the caravans of the great trading families, fifteen or twenty strong, were now free to bring their wares to the subservient buyers in the heartland.

And was this not another proof of the power of his God? He gave his people wealth, and they brought it to those who lacked it, proclaiming to all where the divine power now rested. Smoking Mirror considered this, and made a mental note to tell the Jaguar chiefs to add a few new soldiers to their cult. The larger traders would be renting some for the guards on their caravans, no little source of income for the temple.

He rocked back on his heels and clasped his hands behind his back. In a single stroke Harvest Mountain had vanquished his most powerful enemy, proved the strength of his Gods, and opened up a great market that had been closed to the city's traders. It was all very good, but much remained to be done.

The old king, Tall Mountain, had begun to stretch out the reach of his city, and even supplanted the Old City in power. But all about the heartland, clear to the western sea told of by the traders, north to the mountains and south along the eastern sea were villages that knew nothing of the power of Great Head City. They might worship the Gods, but they had never submitted to the paw of the Jaguar, as He lived in this city.

He turned his gaze north and west, and saw the ramshackle collection of rude pavilions that marked White Serpent Hawk's temple. The neat squares of gardens surrounding it gleamed with thick greenery and sparked with bright flowers. As he shaded his eyes for a better look, Smoking Mirror could see the typical white garb of many followers gathering there. The sun was up only a little; no doubt the White Priest would be preaching soon to his flock.

Spirits Walking Woman. Somehow she lay at the heart of many things. Her father controlled the Holy Stones, without which the Gods could not be worshipped. A potential enemy. And now she spent her days among the people, if not openly serving the Feathered Serpent, at least doing his work. And her sister thought there might be a stronger connection between the priest and the Queen. Another enemy—or an opportunity?

He glanced down at his hands, and for a moment it seemed as if many long strings, invisible to lesser men, stretched out from his fingertips, forming a net. In the net they were all caught; kings and queens, priests and people. But it was the net of the God, and it moved from his hands.

He raised his voice. "Find the General, Skull Breaker, and ask him to come to me."

In the sky, the sun turned white and hard, and burnished the heavens into a shiny blue glaze. Truly, the rains were over.

III

Spirits woke with a griping in her belly, and made a dash for the pot set at the foot of her bed. As she crouched over it, she heard footsteps and, a moment later, Purple Grackle's soft voice.

"Lady, raise your head. I have a cool cloth for your brow."

Gentle fingers wiped her face and her lips. "Oh, Purple Grackle, this is so annoying. The midwives say it is the usual thing, but—"

Purple Grackle led her back to her bed and laid her down. "It will pass, Lady. I've seen it before, and so have you. Are you hungry?"

Spirits shook her head. The morning sickness had been growing worse of late, and though she had seen similar things, the knowledge didn't help. Her stomach still rebelled. Carrying a baby was no easy thing.

"You should eat, Lady. For yourself, and for the child."

"I'm just not hungry, Purple Grackle. Maybe later."

"Has it begun to kick yet?"

Spirits placed her hands across the growing mound of her belly. "I don't think so," she said. "What does it feel like?"

Purple Grackle laughed. "You'll have to ask somebody besides me. I don't know any more about it than Laughing Monkey."

"Ah. Well . . ."

A breath of wind ruffled through the room, rattling the thatch and making the window cloths shimmer with color. A net of interlaced shadow and gold, like the spots of a leopard, danced across the bed, and Spirits looked up. "It's stopped raining," she said.

Purple Grackle was leaving with the chamber pot. The Queen's spew must be properly disposed of, lest malign spirits somehow make use of it—particularly now that she was pregnant. She turned. "Yes, Lady. It's a beautiful day."

Suddenly Spirits hated her recalcitrant body and the sickness that plagued her. Between it and the perpetually dismal skies, her moods had been so low she'd hardly left this room in a hand of days. Suddenly it seemed as constricting as a tomb, and she realized that no matter what it cost, she wanted out of it.

"Can you bring me some thin gruel? Perhaps I can keep it down. Some tea, as well. Then get Laughing Monkey and the others. I want to go out into the villages today."

Purple Grackle eyed her doubtfully. "Is that a good idea, Lady? You haven't been well, after all."

"It's only my spirits that are low," she replied. "Seeing the Lord Sun ride high in the sky will fix me up. I know it will."

Purple Grackle nodded. "As you say, Lady."

Spirits felt her heart beat faster. The rains were gone.

Joy!

IV

The crowds had been growing larger lately, White Serpent noted. Today they filled the entire courtyard of the temple, and they were a pleasing mix. At the beginning, when he'd first begun to preach in the streets of the city, with no temple at all and only his pack to lay his head on, most of those who'd listened to him had been women, and older ones at that. The ancient, twisted aunts and grannies who were too weak to work in the fields, who sat at home and minded the children while they wove and gossiped.

These women were still with him, in fact even more faithful, for they had seen much of war and had learned to hate it. But now there were men, sturdy farmers, even a few from the traders' quarter, cynical men who weighed and measured everything in their lives, and found most wanting.

He had never wavered in his faith, for he had seen his destiny, but it was a pleasure to see it now beginning to unfold as he'd known it must. For a moment his thoughts turned to the gardens around his temple. The Jaguar, his brother, gave gifts that were like himself; dark, powerful, bloody. But he had his own gifts to bestow, different from those of his black brother, and today he had seen a particularly wonderful thing. After he had finished here, he would show them the new maize that grew in one of his gardens. The ears on it were fully a third larger than what they had known all their lives. One-third more food from the same plot of ground! Was that not a better gift than bloody triumph?

He stepped forward and climbed his little mound.

As always, the clear light of the God filled him, so that he felt himself transparent in the radiance of the sun. He raised his arms and began to speak.

V

The High King had a great room constructed of stone, with high windows and a tall thatched roof strung with banners, where he conducted much of his business. Today, the stones were swept clean but the room seemed almost empty, with only himself and Skull Breaker seated at the foot of his Inner Throne, on squat wooden stools. Skull Breaker's heavy belly bulged between his thighs as he squatted, and Harvest Mountain laughed.

"You look like my wife," he chuckled. "What is about to pop from your belly? A full-grown boar pig?"

Skull Breaker slapped his gut and laughed out loud. He knew he was fat, and didn't care. His arm was still strong. He had slain many in the battle at the Old City. That was all that mattered in the end, wasn't it?

"At least one, Lord," he roared. "Maybe even two."

They both laughed over this. Then Harvest Mountain began to speak of what was on his mind.

"It was well begun," he said. "Night Thunder was a brave man, but not a very good soldier, and he is dead now. It went easier than I'd expected."

Skull Breaker nodded. He was getting older, and his body ached often of a morning, but he was still a soldier, and the triumph had been a great one. He wondered if Harvest Mountain had thought of the next step. That had been one of his father's few failings, at least in the general's eyes: that he took each victory as a single event, not connected to any larger plan. No doubt his son had learned from him, but had he learned anything more?

Harvest Mountain wasted no time in dispelling these worries. "We cannot raise an army for several moons. The long dry season is on us, and all the farmers will be in the fields. And I'm building six new villages, farther down the river, for new fields. The city is growing, and we need more food."

Skull Breaker nodded. It was true; there had been some small influx from the Old City, sharp-eyed men who understood which way the wind now blew, and wanted to be where the new power lay. Also more traders coming down from the north and out of the west to establish outposts in the city. "That is well, Lord," he replied.

"Smoking Mirror is adding to the Jaguar Cult. I think it is a good idea."

This was something Skull Breaker didn't know, and he should have. A little nugget of fear began to tick in his head. Why had he not been told? He was in fact a member of the Jaguar, had risen to chief, and then, under Tall Mountain, had gone beyond. But he was still pledged to the Cult, and somebody should have told him.

Harvest Mountain looked at him and said, "It isn't like that, Skull Breaker. He told me just this morning. He thought of it today."

"Oh." But what surprised him was that the King seemed to know his thoughts. The boy he'd known a short time ago would not have done that. Or would he? Had he ever known this man who sat across from him? One more unsettling thought on so fine a day.

"We have never had many permanent soldiers. Only the farmers. Which used to be good enough, but it isn't any longer. Not for what I want, or what the God wants."

Which God, Skull Breaker wondered.

Harvest Mountain sighed. "I want to bring our Gods to all these villages. It won't take many men, not if they are good soldiers. The Cult will be fine for that, if it grows larger. We can send out small parties to take these little villages, and establish altars there for the Gods. Fear will be enough to hold them, I think. And we can take a few hostages."

Skull Breaker nodded. It all meant more work for him, but what else did he have to do? It did give Smoking Mirror a lot of new power, though.

He mentioned this to Harvest Mountain, who nodded. "Yes. But Smoking Mirror is loyal to me." He grinned mirthlessly. "As long as he thinks I'm loyal to him. To the Jaguar."

Once again the general felt a slow sense of awe. The King was well ahead of him. Almost reluctantly, he felt a sense of trust begin to grow. He had worried about propping up this boy, for his father's sake. Now it seemed the King might carry him instead.

"Lord, there is something you should know."

"Yes?" Ridges on that youthful brow, in the dappled golden light.

"The new priest, the one called White Serpent Hawk. He doesn't preach against you. But he preaches against what you do."

Harvest Mountain shrugged. "I know of him. He is a woman. He preaches against war, and sacrifice. But he doesn't understand. How else can the city grow great? It's to be expected, though. His God is weak."

"You don't understand, Lord."

"What is that?"

Skull Breaker took a breath. "He doesn't preach for his God. He said he *is* the God. And he grows stronger each day." He looked down at his big, scarred hands, as if he'd just discovered them. "My Lord, I fear his power reaches even into your pavilions."

"My pavilions? What are you talking about, Skull Breaker?"

"Spirits Walking Woman," Skull Breaker replied. "The High Queen."

Harvest Mountain's mouth fell slightly open. He was silent awhile. Then he said, "Perhaps it is time I saw this priest for myself. Summon him to me."

"Yes, Lord. If he will come."

Harvest Mountain snorted. "I am High King. He will come."

VI

"I feel much better," Spirits said. There was a slow heat in the air, which was still thick and humid, but noticeably drier than it had been. The whole world steamed. Clouds of bright mist drifting up from the sodden earth, shrouding the cottonwoods in gauzy light, in which their new leaves glowed like emeralds. Hidden moisture sparked in the creases of the palm leaves. Even the ever present odors of human and dog feces had a rich, clean tang to them, mixed in with the darker smell of newly turned earth. In the fields around the villages brightly colored figures bent and tilled, wavering in the heated air, dark lines of freshly plowed dirt running out behind them.

Purple Grackle would not allow her to do anything more than watch and supervise, and made sure that Laughing Monkey stayed close to his mistress in case a bout of dizziness took her. The boy did this with fierce seriousness, watching her as if she might fall over at any instant. It was so comical, it was all Spirits could do to keep from laughing.

They were gathered at the door of a house that stood open to the weather. As soon as it became certain the rains were truly over, many of the villagers took down their curtains, the better to catch the breezes. The day's heat was something different than it had even been the day before. Now it curled like a great, lazy cat, reaching out to grasp the unwary. Spirits wiped at her brow with her hand, felt the salty film there.

And in truth, even with the heat, she did feel better. It was almost as if the new sun was drying out not only the world, but her bones. She felt lighter. Her skin felt smoother, and the itch that had plagued her seemed almost gone.

On a mat in front of the house was a boy a few years younger than Laughing Monkey. There was a thick, yellow crust dried around both his eyes; he was very thin, his buttocks streaked with dried feces where his bowels had voided until he was empty. His face looked like a skull with only a thin, translucent covering of skin over it.

"He is very bad, Lady," the healing priest from the temple of the Dragon she had fetched along finally reported. He was a short, kindly looking man with a long scar on his right cheek and gray hair streaked with a few strands of black. His breath smelled of cinnamon and mango.

"Is there anything—"

He shook his head. "I have seen it before. He will die, Lady."

She shook her head. All too often her efforts ended against this wall. Death was no stranger to the people. Women lost two of every three children, many shortly after birth. If a child survived the first full turn of the seasons, its chances were better, but still, too many succumbed to malign spirits and were taken away.

The priest had whispered too loudly. Suddenly the boy's mother burst into a loud wail and began to beat her breasts. "Waiee, waiee!" she cried.

Immediately, Spirits moved to her, knelt, and put her arms around the weeping woman. "There . . ." she whispered. But it was all she could say. Women wailing over their dead. It was a story that never changed.

She sensed him before she actually saw him come striding out of a cloud of golden mist, dragonflies humming around his head like a halo. His skin was the same color as the mist, so that he seemed to congeal out of it yet still retain some of its evanescence. As always, he walked with an animal grace, catlike, though the cat was not his God.

"High Queen," he greeted her. "What are the troubles here?"

She kept her arms around the woman, and only motioned with her head at the dying boy on the mat.

"Ah," White Serpent Hawk said. He squatted down and put his hand on the boy's dry forehead. He paused a moment, his blue eyes slitted in thought, then shook his head. "Very bad," he said. "The fever demons are inside him. Feel how hot he is."

There seemed to be no answer for this, so Spirits only nodded and held the woman, who had begun to wail louder at White Serpent's words. He glanced at her, then spoke: "The Feathered Serpent is here, mother."

Her eyes found him, flickered, then steadied. It was as if she'd just noticed he was there. Spirits felt her heaving body calm in her grip, and relaxed a bit. The woman snuffled.

"What's your name, mother?"

"Long Leg," the woman whispered.

White Serpent examined her face closely, as if seeking something. As he did this, Spirits felt that unearthly sense of serenity envelop her; Long Leg relaxed even more, and settled herself like a trusting child. Whatever White Serpent Hawk searched for, it seemed he found it, for he smiled suddenly. The effect was as if the moon had suddenly leaped into a dark sky, white and perfect.

Then he turned back to the boy, placed both his hands flat on the scrawny chest, closed his eyes, and began to sing. He had a good voice, Spirits thought, middle-ranged, clear, and soft. Though it didn't seem as if he sang loudly, she saw in the corner of her eye other villagers, women mostly, stop, raise their heads, and turn in her direction. She thought of the way the wind swept a field of white flowers and bent them all in one direction. There was even a perfume that came wafting, warm and light and dry, and she wondered what it was; then she realized it was the scent of White Serpent's sweat. A fine film of moisture covered his face, and glistened on his wide shoulders. He was not moving at all, yet she felt the sensation of great—superhuman—effort.

Suddenly the boy coughed, and at the same time White Serpent let out a loud yell. He arched his back like a bow and yelled again. Through all this he didn't take his hands from the boy's body, and now Spirits saw something rise up, flow up White Serpent's arms, a dark glimmer; it hung over him for a moment, and then a vagrant breeze snatched it away.

Demon . . .

"Give me a cloth," he said, his voice faintly furred, as if his throat was raw. Purple Grackle took one from the straw bag of things she always carried on these trips, and handed it to him. Gently, he began to swab the crusts away from the boy's eyes. That was when Spirits realized those eyes were open, calm and clear.

Long Leg twisted in her arms and then was gone. She flung herself across the boy, weeping again.

For a moment they all looked at each other, as if sharing in something no one could voice. Then the Jaguar Cult soldier came up and said, "The High King wants to see you."

"Me?" Spirits asked.

"No, High Queen. The priest. White Serpent Hawk."

Her eyes found his. "I will come, too," she said.

CHAPTER THIRTEEN

I

She had been very conscious of White Serpent as they walked back from the villages; he'd taken her hand to help her up onto the raft, and she'd felt a tingle as his warm, dry fingers touched her own. Light had danced from whorls in the water as they floated across; insects made tiny dots on the green surface, and here and there a fish, attracted by the bugs, made a leaping splash of silver.

The Grand Concourse was crowded today; it seemed the whole city had turned out to celebrate the change in the weather. As they passed up the Way, with the Mountain looming over them, and the Eye glittering cheerfully far above, she thought there were many new barrows. From her regular visits she had learned most of the faces; now there were new ones.

"Where do they come from?" she asked.

"Everywhere," White Serpent replied. "Traders and travelers, from the far northlands, come to buy our stones, our beautiful pots, the things our people make with their skills and their hands." He smiled. "It is a good thing, Spirits. Our city is blessed by its Gods, and the whole world is learning of it."

They reached the wide stone steps before the royal pavilions, and passed on up; a crowd of boys, all knobby knees and spindly arms raced past, teeth flashing white in copper-gold faces. Their feet danced about a rubber ball, and they shouted happily, barely noticing that the High Queen was in their midst. Then they were gone, leaving their cries hanging in the air like the passing of a flock of birds.

White Serpent had gone quiet; she felt a sudden watchfulness about him, a determination. "What's wrong?" she asked. "Haven't you met my husband before?"

"No," he said. "Not yet."

She smiled. "There's nothing to fear. He is a good man. He's probably heard about how well your temple is doing, and wishes to know more of you."

He nodded. "Doubtless that is it. And just as well; I've been wanting to meet him, too."

Something about the way he spoke made her feel uneasy. She glanced at him, suddenly doubtful, but he was no longer looking at her. They'd reached the top of the stairs, and now turned toward the public part of the pavilions, where her husband kept his Inner Throne inside a great room. Together they went that way; a courtier she didn't know guarded the door. He bowed and admitted them, taking care to smile at Spirits. She noted he didn't smile at White Serpent, and wondered what that meant.

"Spirits, what are you doing here?" Harvest Mountain called.

He was at the far end, standing with Skull Breaker near the throne. Strangely, his usual crowd of courtiers was absent; the two men looked small and lonely inside the wide space.

This was the largest room in the royal pavilions; its floor was made of tightly fitted greenstone paving blocks, worked into the pattern of the Divine Tree. This was the work of ancient kings, and generations of passing feet had polished the stone until it resembled the surface of still water. In the amber light that flowed from the windows, the green shadows rose up until it seemed the room was beneath some wide green lake, and they were the fish swimming languidly about. The thatch that arched overhead smelled of damp; she glanced up, half expecting to see white roots dangling down, but there was nothing.

She didn't notice White Serpent had not accompanied her to the throne until she reached it and sank awkwardly into a bow.

"Oh, no, don't do that," Harvest Mountain whispered as he lifted her immediately to her feet. "Should you even be out of your bed, Spirits?"

His dark eyes, now anxious, dropped to her belly. "Where have you been? Out in the villages again?"

"Yes, husband," she replied. The bow had been a mistake. She felt slightly dizzy, and a little flushed. "It is so boring to stay in my rooms all day, and the weather was good. Finally."

He nodded. "I forget, you are from the mountains and not used to this. Well, it takes time." He looked over her shoulder, and she saw his expression change. "Were you with the priest?"

"White Serpent?" Suddenly she felt as if she'd stepped into deep water, and had no idea why. "I didn't go with him, Lord. But he came and helped with a sick boy."

Then she related what had happened, and how White Serpent had sung the demon out of the child. Her husband's eyes flicked beyond her again, and his expression grew even more thoughtful. But he didn't explain himself, merely nodded and said, "Go back to your rooms, Spirits, and rest now. I think you've had enough for one day. And I would speak to your priest; I want to know him better. It seems he serves a very powerful God."

She stared into his eyes, again uneasy, though she had no idea why. "May I stay, Lord? He is a good man, and so are you. The two of you should be friends."

He thought a moment, glanced over at Skull Breaker, then back to her: "Very well. But you must let us do the talking. It is between us, King and High Priest. Do you understand?"

She nodded. Something very serious was going on. At times Harvest Mountain would come to her rooms just to talk; he seemed to value her opinion, and she took this with much gravity, remembering how she'd told him a wife could be more than a wife. On more than one occasion he'd said he valued her common sense, and although she knew there was much he didn't speak of to her, she tried to give him the best she had on those things he did discuss.

She bowed her head in assent. "I will be silent, Lord." Then she moved away from him, toward one of the walls.

Harvest Mountain raised his voice. "Bring the High Queen a stool."

Immediately, a servant appeared, and Spirits settled herself gratefully. She did feel tired, after all.

White Serpent Hawk still waited just inside the wide doorway, his white cloak draped around his broad shoulders, his expression alert; there was nothing subservient about him, though she didn't detect the unconscious arrogance in him she thought she saw in the Jaguar Priest, who seemed to strut even when he stood still.

Harvest Mountain stared at him a long moment, then inclined his head slightly and said, "Come to the throne . . . priest."

At that, White Serpent walked slowly across the room, with no more ceremony than he would use to enter the meanest hut in the smallest village. He moved lithely, and when he came up to the King, it was easy to see how much taller than Harvest Mountain he was. Nor did he bow; not strange in itself, for he was a High Priest, but there was no feeling of subservience about him at all. He might simply have been greeting some friend along the Way.

"Good morning, High King," he said.

"You are insolent," Skull Breaker replied, but Harvest Mountain raised one hand to silence him.

"Greetings, White Serpent Hawk. You see, I do know your name."

White Serpent smiled at him. "I thought you did. And I know yours, too, Harvest Mountain Lord."

Skull Breaker's hiss of outrage at this was audible throughout the whole room, but once again Harvest Mountain only shook his head for silence.

"Brother—and I call you this for it is true; we are both High Priests to our Gods—I greet you. How is it we haven't met before?"

"You haven't summoned me, Brother."

Harvest Mountain eyed him. "It is the duty of the temples to come to the High King," he said. "I serve the All-Sun, the Highest."

White Serpent nodded. "It is true that the Two-In-One, the Mother-Father, and Their child the Sun, rule over us all. But it is not for the masters to bow to the servants, and even the High Priests only *serve* their Gods."

"What? But you are a High Priest. As you say, you only . . . *serve*."

White Serpent said nothing for several moments, as if debating with himself. It was a shocking breach of manners, and the King could not ignore it.

"Well, priest?" he said. "You are the High Priest, aren't you?"

Still White Serpent didn't reply. The moment stretched out; Spirits saw Skull Breaker scowl and begin to drum his blunt fingers on his thigh. Then White Serpent sighed.

"Let us say, King, that I bring the word of the God. Let us just say that."

Now irritation was plain on Harvest Mountain's face. Spirits saw that he was trying to hold himself in, but it was hard. White Serpent was openly defying him, and she didn't understand that at all. She felt a flutter of dismay. Why couldn't they get on better? And it seemed to be mostly White Serpent's doing that they didn't.

Now Harvest Mountain took his time replying. When he spoke, scorn colored his words. "What, exactly, is that supposed to mean?"

White Serpent shrugged. "Whatever you like it to mean, King."

Skull Breaker broke in, his voice thick and guttural. "You overstep yourself, priest. This is the High King, not some stinking peasant."

White Serpent turned to him and smiled. "All men are men. All men serve the Gods."

"Yourself, too," Skull Breaker said, and then spat on the floor.

Harvest Mountain had drawn himself up. His straight body seemed to quiver, like a strung bow ready to launch arrows. He was still shorter than White Serpent, but he radiated power. And he was obviously angry. Spirits's dismay grew even stronger. She wanted to go to both of them and tell them to stop their silliness, that if they would just give themselves a chance, they would like each other. But this was man's business, and she was afraid she would only make things worse.

"It is said that you preach you are not just a priest, but that you are the God Himself. The Feathered Serpent. Is that true?"

"I bring His revelation, yes," White Serpent said mildly.

"Which means? Yes or no, priest, do you claim to be the God?"

But White Serpent only repeated what he'd just said.

Harvest Mountain's fingers sought his narrow chin and began to squeeze. It was not a good omen, Spirits thought.

"You are a slippery one, aren't you? Very well. It is also said that you preach against me. Is that true?"

For the first time Spirits saw a reaction in White Serpent. An expression of shock washed across his features, before he caught himself. "Oh, no, King. You are the High King, the lawful leader of our people. I don't preach against you."

"Yes, you do," Skull Breaker grated.

White Serpent addressed him. "I know your spies are everywhere, General. But have you, or they, ever heard me say a word against Harvest Mountain Lord?"

The questions knocked the general back a bit. He paused, then said, "You preach against our sacrifices. You preach against war."

White Serpent nodded. "Oh, yes. But Harvest Mountain is not a sacrifice. He is not war. He is a man, a king."

Spirits noted in which order he had put the last. Man first. King later. Oh, dear.

Harvest Mountain noticed as well. His eyes began to glitter dangerously. Spirits thought that any other man faced with him now would have stepped back in fear. But White Serpent only turned to him and spread his hands. "You do understand, don't you, King? I don't preach against you."

"You preach against what I do. What is the difference?"

"A deed is a deed, King. And once a deed is done, it cannot be changed. But a man is a man, and can change what he does. I bring a new revelation, though it is very old. It has been forgotten in this city, but I come to teach it again. Turn away from your murderous altars. Put down your weapons and cease to make war. If you do this, the city will prosper and grow greater than it is. Greater than it has ever been. That is the gift I bring to you."

Harvest Mountain stepped toward him, both his fists balled. There was so much contained violence in his movement that Spirits put her hand over her mouth and gasped, "No . . ."

But White Serpent didn't budge at all, merely stood waiting. Harvest Mountain pressed close to him, realized he had to look up to see into the priest's eyes, and stepped back. "You are a fool, priest," he said. "The city needed more trade. I took war to the Old City and got it. The city needs protection from its enemies. My soldiers defend it. The city needs more land. My father took it with war. And the Gods smile on us because we feed Them. How can the Sun ride across the sky in His fire boat, unless we send Him blood? How will the Jaguar shake the clouds for rain unless we feed Him blood?"

He paused, breathing hard. "If you say otherwise, priest, then you are not a God, and not even a priest. You are a fool, as I say."

White Serpent's eyes focused on him. His expression remained calm and mild. Spirits could feel that unearthly serenity radiating from him like heat from embers, but Harvest Mountain seemed unaffected. The King radiated his own heat, harsher, more dangerous.

How had it come to this?

"I am not a fool," White Serpent said. "If you would learn more, I will teach you."

Harvest Mountain glared at him, then turned his back. "Get out of my sight," he said.

White Serpent began to say something else, then looked at Skull Breaker, who took a step toward him.

"We don't have to be enemies," White Serpent said finally.

But Harvest Mountain only gave a violent shake of

his head. "I said leave me," he replied without turning. "Skull Breaker?"

With that the general did come up to White Serpent, reaching for his arm. But somehow, without seeming to make any effort to do so, the priest smoothly slipped from his grasp. Before Skull Breaker could do anything further, White Serpent reached the doorway. There he turned.

"Think on what I say, King," White Serpent said with great dignity. As always, his soft voice seemed to fill the emptiness, no matter how large. The King twitched as if he'd been struck. But he ignored White Serpent's plea, and so the battle was joined.

II

A ragtag remnant of a squall blew through just before dusk, scrubbing the palm leaves and rattling the thatch; the sun sank west into a lingering rainbow beyond the shadowing green forests. With nightfall a cricket began a solitary song, in a moment answered by a thundering chorus of frantically scraping wings. The river, receding now, left a coat of flotsam on its banks, and a damp, rotting odor in the air. Dusky brown moths flashed into torches and burned; their deaths made small snapping sounds.

The High King and High Queen took their night meal at a banquet in the great hall. Spirits tried to engage Harvest Mountain in conversation, but he seemed upset and preoccupied. After a while she gave up; the meeting with White Serpent Hawk had been a disaster. She couldn't rid herself of the idea that, somehow, she had contributed to it. When she'd tried to talk to Harvest Mountain immediately after, he'd sent her to her rooms. She couldn't tell if his anger then had been for the priest or her. Or somehow, for both of them.

Giving up for the moment, she turned to her left,

where Green Water Woman sat cross-legged on a mat before the low table which had been set up for the feast. The table creaked beneath its load of food: mounds of flat bread, delicately carved trays piled high with mangoes and lemons and palm hearts, squashes, huge smoking haunches of pig that smelled of pepper and sage, pale, carefully garnished cuts of tender dog, and in front of the king, a heavy trencher of venison, rich with fat and a sauce made of purple plums.

Servants moved about, replenishing as needed, and keeping clay cups full of pulque. The mood of the evening was uncertain; already, news of the High King's confrontation with the White Priest had passed through the court. On top of that upset, the King himself seemed tense and quick to anger. Twice he snapped at servants, and one he struck for fumbling with the venison. Also, he drained his cup almost as soon as it was filled, and gestured immediately for more.

"I just don't understand it," Spirits said to Green Water. "It was like a cat and a dog. Harvest Mountain seemed to hate him on sight, and White Serpent did nothing to heal the breach. If anything, he made it worse." She paused, and shook her head. "Men. Must they fight about everything?"

Green Water plunged her fingers into a platter of dog and brought a toothsome morsel daintily to her lips. Her knuckles glistened with grease. "Men are men, sister. Haven't you learned that yet?"

Spirits sighed. No doubt Green Water was right—in some ways, there was no doubting the superiority of her knowledge on the subject—but it was all so frustrating.

"Do you think it's just that?" Spirits asked. "Somehow it's hard to think of White Serpent as . . ."

"Just a man?" Green Water chewed, swallowed, and licked her lips. Her eyes were wide in the dim light; chips of red fire from the torches danced in their shining depths. "Believe me, sister, priest or king or slave, underneath it all they are still what they are."

Spirits, thinking of Smoking Mirror, nodded slowly. "I guess so."

"Your priest is no exception, believe me," Green Water added, not maliciously, just as a statement of fact.

"Oh, do you know him?"

"Not at all, sister. But I've heard of him, and would like to meet him for myself. It is said he has the eyes of a God."

"Well, you should see him, then. Would you like to come with me tomorrow when I go to the villages? I would have asked before, but I didn't think you were interested."

Green Water glanced over, wondering how much honesty was called for. Half and half, probably.

"I've changed somewhat, sister, but I still have no interest in those filthy peasants. I can't imagine what you see in them. But I would like to meet your priest, and so I will put up with your good works, if that's what is necessary."

Since this fitted precisely everything Spirits felt she understood about her sister, she found nothing amiss and readily agreed. She might wish Green Water could show a little more compassion for those who were beneath her, but that was probably asking a bit much; a leopard couldn't change its spots overnight, after all. And Green Water was so much improved in so many ways it still seemed a miracle. For that, Spirits was willing to overlook the rest.

"Wonderful," she said. "Don't worry, I won't make you do anything. You can stand back and watch." She paused. "I can't promise we'll see him. Sometimes he has other things to do."

Green Water shrugged. "A bit of those mangoes, sister? They look delicious."

She watched a rosy flush bloom in Spirits's cheeks,

and decided that things were about to get interesting. She glanced up and, by chance, saw Smoking Mirror staring at her. Slowly, she tilted her head to the side, and smiled.

III

Green Water, accompanied only by a pair of nameless slaves, surveyed her surroundings with interest. It had taken three boring visits to the villages with her sister before the White Priest happened to join them and she had gotten her introduction. Now she looked into those same startling blue eyes as White Serpent led her across the courtyard of his ramshackle temple toward the inner pavilions.

Her head swiveled slowly back and forth as she walked. It was interesting. The pavilions weren't large, and there was a good bit of space between them, mostly hard-packed brown earth scraped clean of grass by the passage of countless feet. The edges of the pavilions were grassy, not paved with stone as the other temples were. She wondered; was the temple poor, or did White Serpent simply not care about ostentation?

She smelled herbs boiling somewhere; aromatic smoke twisted in a nearly invisible line straight up from a fire in the distance, beyond the precisely arranged gardens behind the pavilions. Everywhere she looked were people, humbly dressed, walking or squatting or sitting, all absorbed in some task or another. Two men laughed softly as their nimble fingers danced on cones of wet clay, forming and shaping the graceful shapes of pitchers. Beyond them, gathered around a low wooden table, another group of men hunched over their work; she thought she saw the flash of serpentine, the cool green glow of jade.

Inside the main pavilion, somebody began to chant,

a thin, high, wavering sound. White Serpent turned and smiled. "What would you like to see?"

Green Water stared up at him. He was close enough to touch, and involuntarily she reached toward him, caught herself, and paused, frozen in midgesture. His blue eyes seemed to bore in on her, grow larger. It took her an almost physical effort to look away.

"Everything," she said, and tried to make the word mean what she felt—and as she did so, she was astonished to find she really meant it, that she *wanted* everything this man could show her or give her. That in him was freedom from herself, freedom from the dark God who held her. The revelation was so sudden, so overwhelming that she staggered, and put one hand over her mouth, as if she could take it back. Her black eyes widened.

"I can't," he said softly.

It was only an instant. Slowly, like a dazed bird fluttering to rest, her hand fell, the lips behind it now set in a hard, thin line. A line of terrible bravery and purity, the expression of a woman facing a fate she'd always feared, but now looked on as certain. After years of premonition, it would be true. And he knew it. He had heard her true question and answered it.

Her lips twitched, relaxed. "Yes," she said. "I see." And what she saw, though she didn't say it, was that same old sight: her inexorable destiny unfolding, the lash of rejection stretching out for ever and ever. Old scars, new scars. Still scars, and even the Gods, it seemed, didn't care. She felt an overwhelming lassitude, a sudden desire to sleep, to close her eyes and let the darkness come. But she knew that oblivion of old, and one more time dredged up the cure: the bright, clean fire of hate.

And perhaps at least one God did care. Not this blue-eyed one, though. He offered no salvation, even in the moment she would have accepted it. But he couldn't save her. And he would pay for that. They would all pay. She would see to it.

She moved forward. "Then show me what you want me to see," she said. "The rest doesn't matter anymore."

IV

"I worry about your sister," White Serpent said to Spirits a few days later. Spirits had come to the temple of the Feathered Serpent, something she found herself doing more often these days. Her husband was deep in hushed conversations with Skull Breaker and the Jaguar Cult generals, and had little time for her. Her belly now bulged and her breasts were heavy. Thankfully, her morning sickness had passed, but this just left her with more time on her hands. Because of her pregnancy, it was hard for her to go into the villages; the heat made her dizzy. But here, in the shade of the temple pavilions, she felt cool and at peace.

"Why is that?" she asked.

They both sat cross-legged on straw mats, back in the shade of the thatched eaves. A soft breeze brought the smells of meat smoking in wood coals, of slow-moving green water. The wind lifted her sweaty hair from the nape of her neck, and the moisture on her skin evaporated in a sudden tickle. Everything beyond the pavilion was outlined in enameled blue sky; there was a silence in the world, vast and breathless, in which the sounds of men were distanced. They might have been on an island, slowly receding from everything else. It was very comfortable, and at the same time, vaguely frightening.

White Serpent said, "There is a darkness about her. I felt it when she visited me here."

Spirits looked at him. His face, as usual, seemed utterly calm, his eyes focused on something just a bit beyond the normal. He was a hard man to know, she told herself. Then she wondered why she wanted that knowing, but flinched away from the answer to that, too.

"She is unhappy," White Serpent continued. He shifted his blue gaze in her direction.

Spirits sighed. "Yes, I know she is. I've told you something of her past—of our past."

"Yes." He nodded. "She has always been unhappy, maybe." The skin at the corner of his eyes wrinkled. "You must be careful of her, Spirits." His voice whispered in her ears, soft and utterly clear. She wondered how he did that.

She shifted uncomfortably, trying to find a different position for her belly, which she now held in her lap like a huge, soft ball. The herb women and the midwives were certain it would be a boy—and a big one. If so, she thought he would be active, too. He seemed to kick constantly, as if he couldn't wait to come out into the world.

"She's my sister, White Serpent, and she's changed. Oh, she's still quick to anger, and sometimes she is sullen and nasty, but I don't feel the hatred from her I once did. I think you're wrong."

"Perhaps she has learned to hide her hate better?"

But the baby kicked just then, sharp as a fist beneath her heart, and she thought of other things. Later, she would remember, but by then it would be too late.

CHAPTER FOURTEEN

I

"Y ou saw him?" Smoking Mirror asked.

"Yes. I saw White Serpent. You are right. He is your enemy," Green Water replied.

They were in the dark room of the Jaguar Temple. The space was like an oven; sweat glistened on them like honey. A dry, baked smell drifted off the stone. A lone mosquito whined between them. Even the lamps seemed dimmed by the heat.

He nodded. "Did you do as I suggested?"

She stared at him. "Offer myself? Yes, in a way I suppose I did. He turned me down." Her voice was flat.

"Ah."

"It's what you expected, isn't it?"

He nodded. "He claims his purity as a badge of his godhood."

"Is he? The God, I mean?"

"You saw him. What do you think?"

She tilted her head, considering. "I think he is a man. Whether he knows it or not."

Smoking Mirror stood motionless a moment, then sighed. "How can you help me?" he said finally.

But she'd been thinking about it ever since her abortive meeting with White Serpent, the meeting that had underlined once and for all her fate. She could not escape what she was. He would not let her, they would not let her, even the Gods would not let her. And she hated them all for it.

Did all women feel this way?

She shook herself. "My sister is falling in love with him."

She heard Smoking Mirror's tiny intake of breath, though his expression remained opaque. "That surprises you?" she asked.

His dark eyes gleamed in the shadows. It made her think of a rat, peering up from a black burrow. And the way his nostrils seemed to twitch. "I never thought of it. But it presents certain . . . possibilities. If it's true."

Green Water smiled bitterly. "Oh, I don't think she even knows it yet. He might, though. But he's too pure to admit it, even to himself. In other words, they're both blind fools." She paused. "Of course, in the end, we're all fools, aren't we?"

"Not all of us," Smoking Mirror said. He was wearing only a white clout. His hard belly streamed sweat down into the cloth over his loins, making a dark shadow across his crotch. She stared at the shadow and licked her lips. He smiled.

"Your sister could be a problem to me if she is a worshipper at the White Serpent's altar. Harvest Mountain listens to her. Listens to a woman."

He said it as if he couldn't understand such a thing.

"I'm a woman," Green Water told him.

"Yes. And I'd rather have the High King listen to you than her. You belong to the God. What does she belong to?"

"A different God," Green Water said. But her heart leaped at Smoking Mirror's words. Yes, the High King should listen to her! Yes, she should have been High Queen! And, with the help of this sweating priest, was such a thing entirely impossible? What if . . . ?

He seemed to hear her thoughts. "The High Queen will bear the King an heir. When that happens, nothing will be able to shake her."

Green Water raised her eyebrows. "It will be a boy? That is certain?"

"Yes. I myself went into the Upper World. I saw the child's life string, held it in my two hands."

"Better you had snapped it, then."

But Smoking Mirror shook his head. "No. A dead baby is only a dead baby. There are other ways."

Green Water found herself pacing. This was all going nowhere. She could sense the priest's lust, like a barely banked fire, baking off him. Men took themselves so seriously, and yet a woman could put her claws into them and never let go.

"What are you talking about?" she asked.

"The Gods may choose to send a message, and send it right out of a woman's belly." He went to his throne. On it was a small wooden tray, which held a round pot. There was a wooden cork in the neck of the pot. He picked it up and carried it gently to her.

"You and the High Queen drink tea together, don't you?"

She watched the pot in his hands as if it were a small, dangerous animal. "Is that tea?" she asked.

He smiled faintly. "A tea from the God," he agreed.

Her lips curled up. "Fit for a High Queen, then."

"We understand each other, I think."

II

Dawn felt like a hot, gray dream; Spirits opened her eyes and found her head pounding, and her vision filled with floating brown spots. She blinked; the spots changed to tiny bright sparks.

"Ohh . . ." She tried to roll onto her side, and for a moment couldn't understand what was blocking her. Some huge, soft mound. She flopped onto her back again, and the mound came with her, rocking back and forth until it settled precisely in her middle. Blindly, she put her hands on it.

Baby.

Dregs of ghost dreams shuffled through her mind, ragtags of dread. Her lips moved silently. "No."

She lay there and listened to sounds: the tick-tick of a raven pecking at the eaves, the sudden flap of wings, a burst of distant, childish laughter. Sweat rolled down her cheek and pooled between her swollen breasts.

The lingering shreds of night began to fade, leaving her, at last, with only one thing: the two faces, terrible in their set purity, and their single throne. But it had been a terrible dream; she had seen them lean forward and fix her with their awful eyes. Just before she'd wakened, she'd thought they would speak. The terror of that was what woke her.

A wad of bile bubbled in her throat; she swallowed weakly, then licked her dry lips. "Purple Grackle?" she whispered.

"She's not here, sister. I sent her away. Look. Open your eyes. I've brought you some tea. Drink it. It will make you feel better."

Spirits opened her eyes. Green Water was smiling down on her, holding a cup of steaming herb tea in her hands.

"Oh, Green Water . . . you're so kind."

Green Water kneeled down. "I worry about you, Spirits," she said as she brought the rim of the cup to her sister's lips. "Be careful," she said. "It's hot."

III

Long-limbed spider monkeys flung themselves in screeching arcs across the dark green canopy overhead. Sunlight sparkled through layer upon layer of leaves, dappling the stretch of stagnant, green-coated water before them. Beyond the water, on a low hummock, a raccoon dipped its prey and watched them with bright black eyes. A cloud of gnats whirled just beyond the bank of the slough, then slowly moved deeper into the swamp, finally vanishing within a curtain of hanging gray moss.

Harvest Mountain, clad only in a sweat-soaked clout, raised his hand and brought the small hunting party to a halt. He wiped moisture off his brow, looked around, and said, "We might as well rest here a while."

Skull Breaker, his belly bulging out over the top of his clout, uttered a long sigh of relief as he collapsed to the soft earth and arranged himself cross-legged. He looked over at Smoking Mirror, who had remained standing.

"Can't you intercede with the God? A few clouds would be wonderful just now," he said.

Smoking Mirror eyed him. "If you weren't so fat . . ."

Skull Breaker laughed. "But I am, priest, and nothing is going to change it."

Harvest Mountain gestured to one of the slaves, who ran up and placed a mat on the earth behind him. The King settled himself carefully, then folded his hands in this lap. "I should have brought the fan wavers," he observed.

Skull Breaker sighed. "The hunting is terrible today."

Smoking Mirror, a dour expression on his face, seated himself across from the two of them and swiped idly at a fly buzzing near his ear. He fixed his gaze on Harvest Mountain.

"High King," he said, "what do you plan for the next rainy season? The long one?" He paused. "I've added four hands of men to the Jaguar Cult."

Skull Breaker said, "I'm beginning to wonder if that wasn't a mistake."

"Why so?" Harvest Mountain asked.

"The new men came from the villages. Their families are angry. It will be harder for them to work the farms now, while the sun is bright in the sky." He drummed thick fingers on his kneecap, his eyes thoughtful. "The White Priest is telling the people you are wrong to do it. He has some of them stirred up."

Harvest Mountain let out a short bark of exasperation. "The people are fools, then. Don't they understand what makes our city great? How long do they think they will survive without my soldiers to protect them?"

Skull Breaker glanced at Smoking Mirror. "High King, of course that's true, but this priest is becoming a real problem. He teaches that safety comes from peace and learning, and practicing the old ways. He says that war and the sacrifice of captives is evil."

"Yes, brother," Smoking Mirror broke in. "You must be careful of this priest. He's a dangerous man. Skull Breaker's right. The people do listen to him. And if they listen to him, then they oppose you."

Harvest Mountain glanced back and forth between the two of them, then rocked back on his seat. "I talked to him. You were there, Skull Breaker."

The General nodded. "Yes, Lord. He defied you."

Smoking Mirror agreed: "Brother, if you don't squash this upstart, I promise you that he will hurt you."

Harvest Mountain stared at him. "What? Hurt me? How can he do that, Smoking Mirror? Does he have cult soldiers, like your Jaguar Cult? Does he command many spearmen? If what you say is true, then he teaches his followers to lie down for the leopard like helpless deer." He paused. "Maybe I should send his priests to the cities of my enemies." He quirked a smile. "I'd like the people of Holy Stone City to practice the ways of peace. Which reminds me, General. Have you heard anything from my father-in-law?"

Skull Breaker glanced around, then waved one brawny arm. "Off with you. Leave us be in privacy." He waited until the startled servants and guards stepped away, then bent forward and spoke in a lowered voice, almost a whisper.

"I *have* heard certain things, Lord."

"Your spies," Harvest Mountain agreed. "Go on."

"King Sky Wind Warrior fears you now, since you conquered the Old City. He won't oppose you openly."

Harvest Mountain nodded with satisfaction. "Good news, then."

"Remember what you said about the birds in the tree, Lord? How you could see them if they weren't afraid to sit on the limbs? Well, he's flown from his perch, and now he hides in the leaves, where he thinks you can't see him. But I can see him."

Harvest Mountain sighed. "He still plots. Is that it?"

"Lord, a few moons ago, when the short rains were still with us, we sent a party of workers to Holy Stone City to bring back a small stone. The carvers at the quarries there had roughed out the shape: a jaguar, for the God's temple. The party left the mountains as they planned, but somewhere between the quarries and the river they were ambushed."

Smoking Mirror sucked in a sharp breath. "I had wondered . . ."

Skull Breaker raised one hand and bade him pause. "In a moment, High Priest. King Sky Wind sent messengers to me saying that the stone was lost. That he'd sent out his own soldiers, but they found only the slaughtered bodies. He said he thought it was some band of roving marauders, and asked that I send a troop of the Jaguar Cult to protect any new shipments."

"And did you do that?" Smoking Mirror asked.

"No," Harvest Mountain said. "Of course he didn't. We would have known, wouldn't we?"

Skull Breaker bowed his head in assent. "You understand why, Lord."

Harvest Mountain fluttered one hand in irritation. "Of course. There were no marauders. And if we sent a small troop of Jaguar soldiers, they would most likely fall to the same fate. If Sky Wind knows they are coming, he can set an ambush."

"Indeed, Lord."

"The answer's simple, then," Smoking Mirror said. "Say nothing, and send all the Jaguar Cult. Bring this King's head back to spike before the Jaguar Temple."

"Brother, you are a great High Priest. But you are not a warrior. There is no way to sneak up the path to Holy Stone City. It is true, the Cult might outnumber the soldiers of King Sky Wind, but if they tried to breach the gates, he would kill them all. No, it will take a full army to defeat him. Why do you think I went to the Old City first?" He snorted. "It was by far the easiest target. The wise man saves his toughest nuts for last, and does what he can to weaken their shells beforehand."

Smoking Mirror glowered. "The God will strengthen our hand."

"Quite frankly, brother, I'd rather have many hands, all of them holding spears. And that won't be possible until the fields are planted and the rains come again. In the meantime, do you understand what my father-in-law is trying to do?"

Smoking Mirror spread his hands and shrugged.

"He's going to cut off the supply of holy stone."

Smoking Mirror's eyes widened. Slowly, his mouth fell open. "But that's—"

"Exactly," Harvest Mountain nodded. "The evidence of the God's favor for us and our city. I have a throne and a great head being prepared. How am I to bring down the God's favor on us unless I have the stones?"

"This King blasphemes, Lord. The Gods themselves will strike him down."

"Well, perhaps. Have your spies seen any of that, though, Skull Breaker?"

Skull Breaker shook his head. "None, Lord. King Sky Wind rules from his mountain throne even as we sit here talking to each other."

The King turned to Smoking Mirror. "You see? And now you give me word of this rebellious priest. Perhaps the Gods *are* angry with me. Could that be true, brother?" And for the first time, there was the barest hint of uncertainty in his voice.

Smoked Mirror heard it, and straightened sharply. "No, Lord! The Gods love you! Has anything you've undertaken been unsuccessful?"

"My first Queen . . ."

"That was your father's sin, Lord. I thought you understood that." Smoking Mirror's voice took on a breathy, urgent tone. "Brother, the Gods are with you. As long as you are with them. You are a High Priest. The Dragon gives you strength. The Jaguar gives you blood and water. The Trickster brings you wit."

Harvest Mountain raised one eyebrow. "And the Feathered Serpent . . . ?"

"Is the weakest of the four, brother. His forked tongue lights the storm sky, but only to make way for His brother, the Jaguar." Smoking Mirror looked down and realized his fists were clenched in his lap, the knuckles standing out like round, white stones.

"Crush this priest," Smoking Mirror said. "Do it now, while he is still weak."

Harvest Mountain moved his shoulders up, let them fall. "It's not that easy," he said. "I will talk to him again. I lost my temper the first time, and didn't explain to him. Surely he can't believe he actually is the God. And any fool must see the city cannot survive unless its army is strong and its sacrifices many."

Smoking Mirror stared at him, then looked away. Not any fool, brother, he thought. You are just one fool.

But he said no more, and waited on events.

IV

"Welcome to my temple, High King," White Serpent said. He offered a wide white smile in greeting, and once again Harvest Mountain was struck by the priest's sheer physical presence. What a man this was! Perhaps there *was* something of his God in him. And if that were true, what a team they would make!

He had left his guards and courtiers behind, milling about in the temple courtyard, and accompanied White Serpent into the shaded interior of the main pavilion. Across this room was a large altar, made not of stone but of intricately carved wood from the *trementina* tree, a common source of hardwood in the region. Harvest Mountain stared at it, thinking it too humble for the worship of a God, but he didn't say anything.

White Serpent followed his glance and, with that disconcerting perception he seemed always to have about him, said, "The Feathered Serpent is satisfied with lowly things. Plants, flowers, harmless lizards, prayers. He does not feed on the blood of His people."

Harvest Mountain nodded. "Brother, I lost my temper with you when we first met. I apologize for that now."

White Serpent tilted his head; small wrinkles of laughter appeared at the corner of his blue eyes. "Brother, I thank you. A High King need never apologize. That you can do so speaks to your strength, not to weakness." He fluttered one hand vaguely. "And I was, perhaps, less courteous than I should have been. I offer you my apology as well."

Harvest Mountain had the feeling he'd just participated in some intricate but nebulous dance he didn't quite understand. He felt a momentary flare of irritation and took a breath.

"Yes," he said. "Well. Do you know why I've come to you, White Serpent?"

The priest gestured toward a rough wooden bench, nothing more than a crude board sitting atop a pair of tree trunks. "I think so," he said. "Let's sit down and talk about it, as the brothers we might perhaps become."

Harvest Mountain's eyelids flickered. At least *that* message was plain enough. He followed White Serpent over, seated himself, and looked around.

The pavilion had a ramshackle, rambling feel to it. The posts set into the ground were taller than usual, which raised the high roof and let the breezes flow through easily. Curtains flapped with the vagrant winds; suddenly, silent except for the beat of wings, a white bird darted beneath the roof beams, arrowed on through, and vanished out the other side. The dry odor of dust rose from the plain dirt floor. Here were no mosaic stone offerings set into the earth. They might be buried, of course, but Harvest Mountain didn't think so. There was little air of anything hallowed here; except for the size, it might have been the shrine to some nameless jungle spirit.

Yet it was the temple of a priest whom his advisers assured him was rapidly becoming the second most powerful man in Great Head City—and whom his sister-in-law whispered was stealing the heart of his wife and Queen. Green Water was uncertain whether the theft was conscious on either side . . . but what difference did it make? It was still theft.

He leaned back against a pole behind the bench. "How many followers do you have these days, brother?"

White Serpent, seated next to him but an arm's length away, bonelessly sprawled, his legs poking out in front of him, shrugged. "I don't count those who seek the mercy of the God," he said finally.

"But many," Harvest Mountain persisted. "Many followers. And more every day?"

"Perhaps."

"Your temple is becoming powerful in this city,

brother. And with that power must come certain responsibilities. For the good of the city, of the people in it. Not just your own temple, brother, but something larger."

White Serpent raised his hands and examined their backs. He flexed his long fingers and said, "What could be larger than the will of the God? The destiny . . ."

Once again Harvest Mountain felt that warning flare of anger, and to cover it he looked away. Without turning, he said, "You have spoken of destiny. Could you tell me what destiny you do perceive?"

"You are asking for my story, is that it, brother?"

Harvest Mountain's lips twitched. "Yes, brother. I would like to know your story."

After a long pause, in which a dog began to bark loudly in a distant part of the compound, White Serpent nodded to himself. "Very well," he said.

"In the beginning was the darkness, and the Mother-Father sat on their single throne on top of Empty Mountain. Their first creation was the sun, and after that the Four Gods; the Trickster, the Jaguar, the Dragon of war, and me—the Feathered Serpent."

Harvest Mountain glanced at him in surprise as he said these things, but lowered his eyelids and remained silent. Sometimes priests took the name of their God. Perhaps one of White Serpent's secret names *was* Feathered Serpent . . .

The priest felt his slight movement and nodded as if to himself. "Then began the long cycles of the years," he continued. "The first cycle of the Sun, called Four-Tiger, lasted 676 years, and ended with the beginning of mortal man and women. The second cycle, called Four-Wind, lasted 364 years, and was destroyed by wind. The third cycle was Four-Rain and endured 312 years before perishing in fire. Then came the fourth cycle, Four-Water, lasting 676 years before water drowned the people."

White Serpent paused, licked his lips, and took a

long breath. "We live in the fifth cycle, called Four-Movement. In our time the Sun moves, and we live on corn. But the teachings of the ancients say this age, too, will end, in the quaking of the earth and terrible hunger. This is the Sun of the Feathered Serpent, brother, and this is how my time will end."

Harvest Mountain sat very still. White Serpent, too, remained silent. The interior of the pavilion seemed to crawl with shadows. The King felt a rill of sweat trickle down his spine. *His* time? This priest did not just take the name of the God, he believed he *was* the God. And such was the power of his presence that for this short time Harvest Mountain found himself believing it too. In the dimness, it seemed as if a soft white light emanated from White Serpent's golden skin. The King shivered. That glow was soft, but very pure, as if it might be dangerous to touch the High Priest's flesh.

White Serpent began to speak again; Harvest Mountain realized that the priest was almost whispering, yet the sound of his voice filled the King's ears with the power of thunder.

"Do you want me to go on, High King?" The words were formal; Harvest Mountain thought they were spoken with the same portent used to pronounce a doom, and he had to stop and think a moment before he said, "Yes. I want to hear the rest."

"Very well." White Serpent nodded and continued on, his soft voice speaking with the clarity of single pebbles falling, one by one, into a still pool.

"When it came time to remake the World at the beginning of the fifth age, I, the Feathered Serpent, spoke with my brothers the Trickster, the Dragon, and the Jaguar, before the single throne of our Mother-Father, with the Sun at their feet."

A faint, but steady breeze began to blow through the curtains, moving them all gently, like the bending of flowers.

"I said I would go to the Land of the Dead, the Underwater World, and bring back the bones of man and woman. I did so, and breathed on them, and watered their bones with my blood, and they lived again. But mortal man and woman must eat, so I went to the Food Mountain and brought them back ears of the sacred maize, and fed them. All my brothers helped me do this."

Harvest Mountain stared at him, caught in some gentle but inexorable stasis; the shadows drifted green among the fluttering curtains; he thought this must be like death, like the Underwater World.

White Serpent Hawk sighed; the sound was lost in the murmur of the breeze, where the cloths flapped like silent tongues.

"This is my age, King; and I am its destiny."

He fell silent and they sat, the two of them, staring at each other for a long time. Then, suddenly, animation flowed back into Harvest Mountain's face like water into a jug. He leaned forward and slapped his palms on the top of his knees. A feverish exhilaration swabbed his cheekbones red and convulsed his muscles. He came to his feet all at once, breathing hard, eyes flashing. For in that time he knew he was in the presence of a God.

"Yes," he said. "Yes, yes. I see it, White Serpent Hawk. We must drink on it! Have you no pulque to quench our thirst? Come, send for your servants and bring us drink. We must celebrate our meeting, our alliance!"

White Serpent's deep blue eyes, calm and still as the morning sky, fixed him: "As what I am, I cannot drink of that which will take away my mortal senses." Then he relented, and clapped his hands together, a sharp sound in the velvet gloom. "But you may, King."

A servant came rushing up. "Bring pulque for the High King," White Serpent said.

Harvest Mountain barely noticed when the boy returned and offered him a bowl brimming over with pulque. He lowered his face and drank greedily. The potent liquor made his eyes water. It was like pouring oil on burning coals.

Then Harvest Mountain drained the bowl and thrust it at the servant for more. It was as if he'd drunk the blood of Gods; a fire ran hot and bright in his veins. His tongue broke from the moorings of thought, and he began to shout.

"Oh, High Priest! Your tale is a divine mystery, and you are the noblest of holy men. Ah, together, we will make our city the greatest between the two seas!"

White Serpent bowed his head. "Great Head City will indeed be mighty."

"Yes! Yes! You and I, priest. You and I! Come, drink with me to seal our pact . . ."

Finally White Serpent stood from his rude bench. Next to the febrile animation of the King, he seemed a tower of coolness and calm. "I cannot make such a pact with you, King. Or with any other earthly ruler." He shook his head sadly, for this was not just his own destiny he now saw before him. "I come to teach the Middle World of light and wisdom. I do not bring the way of war, or the blood of mortal sacrifice."

Harvest Mountain heard his words, but in his ecstasy at first didn't understand them. He shook his head, much as the way a sacrificial pig might do, just after the mallet struck its forehead.

"But . . . what do you mean? Can't you see? Between us, we can be great. Our city can be great."

"I don't seek greatness," White Serpent replied. "I bring wisdom and truth. That is the way of greatness. Not war, High King. Your way is not mine, and never will be."

Harvest Mountain raised his chin. His neck was as stiff as if White Serpent had slapped him across the face.

"You reject me," he said, a terrible flatness in his voice.

"No, King."

"I call you brother, and you spit on me."

"I don't spit on you."

Harvest Mountain turned aside, his lips working furiously. Suddenly his throat convulsed, and a gleaming wad of spit exploded from his mouth. White Serpent looked down at the viscous blot on the top of his foot.

"I spit on you," Harvest Mountain said. "False priest. Deluded fool."

"High King, this need not be. You must listen to me. It's not too late—"

But Harvest Mountain was no longer listening. He was already halfway across the pavilion, his feet kicking up tiny puffs of brown dust. He glared over his shoulder without stopping. "That was your last chance, fool. I am High King. Did you think me a peasant?"

And with that, he passed beyond the curtains, and was gone. White Serpent stared at the door for a long time. Then he looked down, bent over, and wiped away Harvest Mountain's spit.

Finally he straightened again and walked over to the altar. He ran his fingers across the polished surface. The wood smelled of mango juice, of flower petals. White Serpent sighed.

"No, King, you will give me yet another choice," he said, his tone hushed and sad. "And that is the one I dread most of all."

Then he stood by his altar, silent and unmoving, until the afternoon shadows deepened into dusk, and it was time to go into the world again.

CHAPTER FIFTEEN

I

Green Water Woman came awake and sat bolt upright in her bed, confused at first by what had awakened her. In the darkness, only the horned gleam of a quarter moon cast a faint illumination on the shadowy forms in her room. Then she heard it again.

A low, choked-off scream, like all such night sounds seeming to come from everywhere and nowhere at once. She blinked as the slap of naked feet rushed past her closed curtains; once, then again. The hurriers breathed heavily. A vague sense of tension began to settle in the muscles of her chest.

The strange, muted cry came again, but now, fully awake, she understood. Spirits. Her time had come! She flung aside the woven coverlet and pulled herself out of the bed. It was only the work of moments to find a robe and fling it about her shoulders. After a moment's thought she found a strip of cloth and cinched it about her narrow waist for a belt. Then, like the unknown passersby of a few moments before, she set out barefooted to witness the event whose outcome was awaited by her, by priests, by men, and even, presumably, by Gods.

A warm thrill quickened in her veins, and made the fine hairs on the upper part of her forearms stand up as she moved quickly through the shadows. Now she saw the torches gathering ahead, more and more of them like sparks converging on a fire. A fierce sense of expectancy seized her; once again she heard that agonized cry, and this time she answered, her voice tight with dreadful, joyous anticipation:

"Spirits! Not yet! Wait for me, sister, I'm coming!"

For she wanted to see this passage from the womb into the light with her own eyes. Wanted to see it more than anything else in the world. The baby was coming in the night. What a wonderful, terrible omen.

For the first time in days, the night wind held a taste of coolness as it trembled among the torches and candles in Spirits's room: the light was red and gold, and it glimmered softly in the eyes turned toward the bed where she lay. The air was thick with the smell of sweat and pain and effort.

Spirits lay on her back, her eyelids half open, her eyes rolled back in her head till only the whites gleamed like bits of polished shell. She grunted harshly as the contractions, now almost continuous, shook her like a boneless rag.

Purple Grackle, confident in the midwifery she'd learned on her many trips to the village, knelt between Spirits's legs, her hands cupped together to catch the baby when it appeared. An ancient herb woman, veteran of a thousand such scenes, wiped Spirits's slick forehead with a wet cloth. Both women hummed soothing, meaningless sounds as Spirits bucked between them.

Green Water kept her place near the back of the circling crowd. She was tall enough to see over the straining female heads beneath her, and that was all she wanted: to see if the God had granted her wish, the one consecrated with only a small pot of tea.

The close atmosphere tightened and quickened: in the top of the V of Spirits's straining thighs, a white spot, impossibly large, appeared. Almost all of the women here had gone through this: now, a collective gasp of sympathy murmured in the candlelit gloom.

The three women on the bed seemed to thrash as one. Then Spirits uttered an explosive whoop, shuddered convulsively, and lay still.

Purple Grackle, her face shiny, raised the bloody handful, still moored by a twisted, glistening thread, into the stuttering light, the expectant silence.

A slap of palm on flesh, an answering whine, high and thin, of outrage.

Then Purple Grackle looked at the newborn boy. She held it up, so they could see. Her face was a white page of fear and grief. Almost as one, the women began to wail. And Green Water Woman felt herself rising on the clouds of a terrible joy, buoyed up in her own song of revenge and hate.

II

After that awful night Spirits hid herself in her room, allowing no one entry but Purple Grackle and Green Water Woman. She put the tiny bundle of flesh to her swollen breasts and held him there, his tiny hands, their six fingers caressing like blind spiders the tender skin around her nipples. Her skin remained pale beneath gold, like a layer of paint over bone; she feared the sunlight, because she thought it revealed her shame.

"You must eat," Purple Grackle urged her, bringing rich, thick soups clotted with cornmeal and broth, the tenderest cuts of birds, bits of boiled fish that flaked in her fingers. And she tried, because of those gentle urgings, feeling in herself only deeper guilt at her failure. She forced down the food, though it all tasted like ashes and dust; she had to, for the baby's sake.

The baby.

Everything about the poor, crippled thing she

clutched to her breasts, his tiny lips moving aimlessly against her flesh, reproached her. Yet he was of her flesh, and she loved him because she couldn't do anything else. His left foot was nothing more than a pink, gnarled turnip; he would never walk right. His right foot was perfect but for the sixth toe, sticking out from the end like a stiffened grub. Similar deformities marked each hand, benefices of some hateful God. And that was what she thought of as she pushed his tiny body closer, offering him warmth and milk, offering him her heart. The Gods, and whatever it was that hid at her core, cold and pitiless. In her something waited, but for what she didn't know. Or was afraid to know. Was this her punishment for containing such a thing?

Names swirled through her thoughts like drifts of rain, quick and silvery. Morning Star. Star Mountain. One Star. Always the names contained a star, the emblem of Gods—and it was all for nothing. Her child was no God, only a poor, wretched thing touched and ruined by them. Oh, yes, her child had been marked by Gods, irretrievably so.

Harvest Mountain did not come. Most of the time she floated in a daze, her only connection to the waking world the soft weight on her breasts, the occasional whine of hunger, quickly sated. But now and then she would wake, as if from tangled dreams, and see the world cold and hard, and then she knew: her husband, the boy's father, had not come.

She wondered what it meant, but was afraid even to ask Purple Grackle, who these days was mostly silent and kept her face down. Green Water Woman was more talkative, filled with the chatter of the court when she visited, but she had nothing to say of Harvest Mountain either. And in her Spirits felt a kind of fever, a hidden burning that made her uneasy. Yet Green Water remained kind, and would even hold the baby, joggling it and cooing into its perfect little ear.

Still, though, Spirits never asked, and it was finally for Purple Grackle to tell her the truth.

"High Queen, we must talk," she said, a catch in her voice, the faint stutter taking more of Spirits's attention than an outright shout.

Reflexively, Spirits squeezed her son tighter, as if to protect him, or herself. He let out a soft, burping sound, and squirmed at the pressure. She looked down at the top of his head: faint wisps of dark hair, translucent skin over still malleable bone. Tiny veins, pulsing.

"Talk about what, Purple Grackle?" She said it in her most reasonable tones, as if chatting about the weather. But she knew.

Purple Grackle had not brought a tray this time. Her visits had dwindled to little more than short appearances with food, tasks performed quickly and in silence. But now, her bright features shadowed and sad, she sat on the bed next to Spirits and regarded her steadily. After a moment she put out one hand and stroked the baby's head with her fingertips.

"You know," she said finally.

Spirits looked away from her, not wanting to face this. Not yet. "No . . ." she said, but the word was half-swallowed, and came out as a smothered cough that sounded more like shame than denial.

"Spirits . . . we have to do something. Do you know what is happening. Outside?"

Spirits blinked. A red wash had floated up, obscuring her vision, tinting the interior of the room a pale crimson. The sound of her heart thundered in her ears. The weight of her son was like a stone at her breast. "No," she whispered.

Purple Grackle folded her hands in her lap, then looked down at them as if she'd never seen them before. "I have to tell you a story," she said. Then she nodded, as if confirming permission upon herself. Her tongue peeped out, pink on her lips, moving. She inhaled softly, then exhaled. Waiting for whatever it was to come to her.

"Your baby is not the first one," she said finally. "Queen Night Talks Moon had one too. Also a boy."

Spirits moved her head slowly, a gesture of negation. Her hair was lank and pasted by sweat to her skull. "I don't want to hear," she said.

Purple Grackle's eyes were red, as if she'd been crying. Now the faintest rim of clear moisture trembled at their rims, hung, and spilled over onto her cheeks.

"I was too young to understand then. I heard the talk and didn't know what it meant. Later, I did, but it was all over then."

"No . . . please."

But now that Purple Grackle had got herself going, she found she couldn't stop. She'd been nerving herself to this for days, and now the dam had broken. She reached out and placed one hand on Spirits's shoulder. Gently, as if she were stroking a butterfly.

"The old king was still High King, and Harvest Mountain not much more than a boy. Tall Mountain picked Night Talks Moon for him, to be his wife, did you know that?"

No answer. Spirits's shoulder trembled slightly. That was all.

Purple Grackle's nostrils widened. An odor had begun to rise from Spirits, rank and sour, like spoiled fish; something rotten, sweating from her pores.

"When the old king died, Night Talks Moon . . . disappared. There were rumors. I was older then, and I heard. It was said that the old king had done something. Committed a terrible sin with his son's wife. And the Gods punished her, and marked her with her child. And then she was just gone." Reflexively, Purple Grackle patted Spirits's shoulder, a meaningless movement, motion for the sake of motion. Spirits remained turned away, but Purple Grackle felt her watchfulness like a smoldering fire.

"Spirits. Look at your child. Look at his eyes."

Now Spirits moved. It was like the sudden clutching of a starfish, all limbs in, then out, so sudden and sharp that Purple Grackle jumped back and put her hand across her mouth.

"No!" Spirits screamed. "No!"

But both women heard it, heard the word "yes," heard the acknowledgment buried beneath the negation. Saw the eyes of the child, only now, faintly, beginning to take their true colors: one dark, the other light. And blue.

"Spirits," Purple Grackle whispered miserably. "We have to decide what to do. You have to decide. Before somebody else does. You understand what I mean?

"You have to *decide*."

III

In his private chamber in another part of the royal pavilions, Harvest Mountain raised his head at the sound of a distant cry; at first he thought it some kind of forest animal caught by a greater predator, dying in agony. Then he realized it was human, and he shuddered.

The morning was still sleepy, and spectral with snakes of mist twining about the island, dissolving slowly beneath the weak, pale light of the sun. The smokes of a thousand cookfires mingled with the mist: the nutty odor of maize cakes frying, the richer greasy tang of meat and fish and burning wood.

He hadn't slept well, had tossed and turned for several nights, in fact. Self-examination was not his strong suit, for it brought him face to face with himself and his past. Out of the crucible of that past he'd forged himself anew, and he hated to return to it. He'd rather look forward, to the glories of the future, and the new man he'd made of himself. But he couldn't. Despite all his efforts he still dragged, like a bloody chain from the past, his own history. His family. In particular, the monster who had been his father.

Why won't you stay dead, old man? Nobody knew what had gone on between the two of them, and if it remained in his power, no one ever would know. How could he explain what that booming, jovial warrior, that man who slapped backs and slaughtered enemies with equally joyous vigor, had done to his only son?

And of course Harvest Mountain didn't need to explain to anyone else; he was still trying to explain to himself. He had ten fingers and thumbs, and could tick off an outrage for each of them, and each one still as plain in his memory as if it had happened yesterday. Or was still happening, or was about to happen. Sometimes he woke in the night sweating so cold he would shake and his teeth chatter like gourd rattles, and would hear a voice: *No, Father, no!* Then he would realize the voice was his own, and would look about to see if anybody had heard.

No one had. No one, for that matter, *ever* had. And that was why, though he'd buried the old monster with all the proper ritual, and then had performed other, darker rituals of exorcism and atonement to make sure the monster stayed buried, High King Tall Mountain still lived as he would have wanted to live: in the body and life of his son. Two kings, one body, one endless horror.

Oh, Father, let me count the ways, he thought to himself, staring blankly out his windows at clumps of fluttering greenery, at the blue flash of a morning bird leaping into the sky. He watched as the arrowing jay dwindled and vanished, heard its final gaunt cry, and saw the years roll away . . .

Her name was Night Talks Moon, and she was a guest. That was what his father called her; a guest, visiting from the Old City; a royal guest, the sister of

King Night Thunder Shaker. And Harvest Mountain, still a prince, thought she was the most beautiful girl he'd ever seen.

She was small, slender, and perfectly formed, her breasts just beginning to bud, her eyes, shaded with dark paint, the most mysterious and beckoning pools he could imagine. At first, when she'd arrived with a small party from the Old City, Harvest Mountain had caught only glimpses; she'd been taken almost immediately to a guarded pavilion in the women's quarters, and had not come out at all.

Guest. Harvest Mountain mused on that, as he worked through his days, taken up with military training, training for the priesthood of the Temple of the Dragon, and the more practical education any boy who would some day be High King must undergo.

Tall Mountain, his broad, bony features slashed by a pair of long scars, his left arm twisted but still functional, gave him lessons:

"Keep your snake in your clout, boy!" he roared. "That girl isn't for you." And as if he couldn't let any opportunity pass for a chance to humiliate his only son, he added, with a greasy, scornful smile: "Not that I worry that much, boy. Far as I know, you don't even know what that thing between your legs is for. No balls, understand what I mean?" He shook his head. "Well, that's fine. Just play with it. But keep your eyes off that little girl. She's not a guest: she's a hostage!"

All this was delivered with his usual jocular condescension on a burning morning in the royal courts, with a crowd of generals and courtiers chuckling behind their hands at his humiliation.

It had been a difficult time. Harvest Mountain had no idea why his father hated him so much. Once, when he'd protested the way the old man debased him at every turn, his father had merely sneered at him and growled: "This is what I mean, boy. You have to be tough. If you can't even take a few jokes among men, how will you be strong enough to hold your place when you follow me? Jokes aren't spears, boy, and it's spears you'll have to face when your time comes."

But Harvest Mountain had known they weren't jokes. If anything, he was the joke; he'd bowed his head and swallowed his shame and continued on. And he kept a careful secret book of memories, whose pages were inscribed with every disgrace, every slight . . . and the names of all those who had witnessed them.

So things had gone until one day after a particularly humiliating session with his father. He'd been forced to strip in front of drunken soldiers while the old man pointed out how small and scrawny he was, how little his penis was, all the while laughing his red-faced scorn. And when that was over, his face pale and set as stone, he'd walked with as much dignity as he could muster from the court and then dashed blindly through the royal compound, tears streaking down his cheeks. Some dusky green bower caught his eye: he flung himself into it and curled into a ball and then, in blessed secrecy, let the sobs shake him like the fist of a God. He hated himself when he wept like that; it confirmed in his own mind every despicable thing his father accused him of. Weakness, womanishness, lack of manhood. So he always hid himself, and never let anybody see him cry. But he still cried, and still hated himself for it.

This was all swirling in his mind as he tried to keep the noise he was making down to a racking series of choked gasps. The smell of crushed leaves was in his nose, and spindly bushes scratched at his skin. He'd thought himself alone, otherwise he could never have allowed himself even this much release.

Something gentle brushed his shoulder. A soft voice said, "What's the matter, boy? Why do you weep?"

He'd jerked violently and flung himself over; she stood above him, dressed in a simple white cloak, her gaze soft with concern. Her hand was still out-stretched. In that moment she was the most beautiful girl he'd ever seen, and all he could think was that he wanted to die because she'd seen him like this.

His humiliation was complete.

At first he was surprised and grateful that she didn't seem to recognize him, but then he thought what he must look like; wearing only the clout from which he'd just been stripped, roughly tied around his thin waist; his hair tangled and matted from his roll in the green-ery, his eyes puffy and red with tears. And she was never allowed out of her pavilion and its surrounding grounds, so there was no reason for her to know him, especially in his very un-prince-like condition.

"I'm sorry . . ." he said. "Forgive me, I didn't . . ."

She put her fingers to her lips. "Shhh . . . I'm not allowed to have visitors. If my guards find you, they'll beat you." She glanced around, a sudden merry glitter in her gaze, then squatted to her knees. He was trans-fixed by the grace of this movement.

"Tell me what's wrong. Why are you crying like this? Did your master beat you? What's your name?"

So many questions! And each one spoken in a voice that reminded him of the soft buzzing of bees, of the sweetness of their honey.

"What's the matter?" she murmured, bending over him. "Can't you speak?"

Her golden skin was flawless. Her faint scent, light and woody, filled his nostrils. He saw the gentle curve of her breasts pressing against the fabric of her cloak, saw the way the light rippled in the waves of her black hair as it fell across her face.

"No . . ." he whispered. "I mean yes. I mean . . . I don't know *what* I mean."

Her eyes found his as he stammered, and her lips, when he had finished, quivered deliciously. Then she burst into laughter, which she quickly choked off with a hand across her mouth. "We have to be *still*," she warned him again. "So you can talk. Can you stay and talk with me?" She paused, glancing around. "I don't get to speak with anybody." Her expression darkened faintly, as if remembering something unpleasant. "Well, anybody except . . ." Then she shook her head.

"Are you a slave?" she asked.

Something about the way she spoke wakened an echo in him. She seemed cheerful enough, but with his own experience he saw her unhappiness as clearly as he did his own. Poor little thing—hidden away, kept behind her women, far from her own home and family.

He wanted to rise up, take her in his arms and carry her away. Instead, he squirmed his way into a sitting position and folded his arms across his chest. Somehow, in that stance, he felt more in control of himself.

"No, I'm not a slave," he said. "Just a . . . boy. My father is in the court," he added, as if to assure her of his gentility.

"Oh. Do you ever get to see the High King?"

"Oh, yes. On feast days, and at the great rituals," he lied glibly. She didn't know who he was. To her, he was just another boy. He found he rather liked that idea. No, he liked it a *lot*.

She sighed happily and settled neatly into a cross-legged seated position in front of him, as artless as a child. Once again she put her finger to her lips, and her eyes gleamed with mischief.

"My guards are around the corner, sneaking drinks of pulque. They don't watch me as they should. So if we are very, very quiet, they'll never know." She glanced at him, and he nodded. He felt a smile trembling on his own lips.

"Good," she said. "You look happier now. So we can talk." She paused, as if she were about to dip her fingers into some unlimited tray of delicacies. "You say you go into the courts. What can you tell me. Please, I want to hear everything!"

He was caught up in her, in her innocence, in her insatiable curiosity about the court, about the city—though, curiously, she had no questions about the High King himself.

Slowly, then with increasing confidence, he began to answer her questions, and the air of delight—in him, in the day, in the world—began to grow. He basked in the aura of her happiness with him. Yet how could she be happy, locked away as she was? He still felt the shadow.

It was a puzzle. Just one of the things he suddenly realized that he loved about her. Love. What a strange idea, for a prince who had never known anything like it.

That was how it began.

He came to her almost every day, caught up in the complicity of attraction; he looked into things, and made sure that the flow of pulque her lazy guards so enjoyed never ceased. Sometimes he thought they must grow suspicious at how easily they were able to obtain their favorite beverage, even while on duty. But he knew pulque dulled the wits, and these men must have been stupid even when sober. Besides, he knew no soldier ever looked at such things carefully, only accepted them with a passing bow of gratitude toward the Gods.

So that summer went on, slow and dreamy, while they met in their hidden bower to examine the tidbits of court gossip he brought to her as a lover bestowing gifts. And she took them gladly, giggling over the silly things, looking properly wide-eyed about the larger tales of intrigue and treachery. She never, as far as he could tell, suspected him for what he was. Instead, she took him as he presented himself, just a boy of the court whose eyes were sharp and whose ears listened well.

He found that tremendously liberating; his disguise

freed him from himself and his life. These hidden meetings were their great secret, and in them he found the key to a world beyond the monstrosity his father created for him every day.

In Tall Mountain's world he was a failure, a pathetic joke, the butt of all men. But in this bower, fixed by her admiring gaze, he was stronger, wiser, braver than he'd ever imagined.

She would chuckle softly at some tale he'd brought, then lean forward and tap him on one knee: "Oh, that's a *good* one, Little Leopard," she would say, and he would smile at the way her lips caressed the name he'd made for himself. With her he was Little Leopard, the boy who knew everything, her eyes onto the wider world. And in that disguise he began to learn about the other boy, Harvest Mountain. The boy he saw reflected in her eyes was no pathetic coward; he was strong and brave. He was no lackwit; he was funny and knowing. And, best of all, he wasn't something less than a man; he could feel the new thing glowing between them, felt it in his belly and groin whenever she moved—just so—and he would catch a glimpse of honeyed thigh, of softly swelling breasts.

He wondered if she felt it too. Sometimes the urge to declare himself was overpowering, almost as strong as the other urge which he would relieve, by himself, after their trysts. But he was caught in a trap of his own making, and couldn't see a way out of it. He had lied to her, and so the boy she liked so much was made out of lies; he was afraid of what might happen if he finally revealed the truth. Would she hate him? Despise him for tricking her? Part of him longed to know the answer; but another part feared to take the chance, for she was the only good thing in his life.

He had no one to discuss his dilemma with; his father was out of the question, and his mother could hardly talk at all. She stayed in her own pavilion, with its curtains drawn against the light, and drank pulque all day. The last time he'd visited her, the air had been dank and stale, reeking of her sweat, of the strong liquor she drank, of bitter smoke from the herbs she smoked in an ancient stone pipe. Her teeth were stained yellow; her breath like vomit; and she had not known who he was.

So he had nobody but himself, and somehow he had managed to split even that into two parts. And one of them was a lie. His father knew nothing of his rendezvous with Night Talks, and she had no idea who he really was. Nor could he reveal any of it. Sometimes he thought the only answer was to take her hand and carry her from the city to someplace no one would ever find them. But that was crazy. And in the meantime, he would not give up his happiness . . . or his hope.

Of course, it could not go on forever.

As the long dry season of summer drifted toward the oncoming rains, Harvest Mountain began to feel as if something must break. On the one hand, his happiness in his guise as Little Leopard was almost complete. Now when he visited their bower, Night Talks sat next to him, leaning against his side, her head nestled on his shoulder. There was an artlessness to the way she accepted physical contact, and offered it, as if no price need ever be paid, or even considered. She was one of those rare girls who was secure inside her own skin.

Her weight was comfortable, familiar, and at the same time it inflamed him to the point he was afraid he would give himself away. Sometimes he had to cross his legs to hide his arousal. And sometimes, he thought she wasn't ignorant of it at all. But whenever he would put his arm around her she would tense slightly, and he would sense that darkness that lay beneath her sunny disposition. What was it? The idea that it might be him was more than he could bear.

And it left him even more snared in his own traps: he could not offer her the only thing he had to give—himself—because he had lied to her about what he was.

But one bright afternoon, when the flowers growing around the pavilions exuded a perfume so sweet it dizzied his senses, when thin lines of clouds marched like fish scales across the sky, the thing he'd lusted and dreaded finally occurred.

She was settled against him, her shoulder set into the hollow of his arm. He had brought her a carved bead of serpentine so perfectly worked that it was like a tiny world within itself. She held it in her fingertips, her head bent over it, her hair tumbling across her face—and he looked down into the shadow of her cloak, which had fallen open.

Something began to buzz in his ears; a pink flush clouded his vision; he was aware of her closeness, of her scent filling his nose, of her long eyelashes caressing the soft down of her cheeks.

Sweat ran down his wrists and pooled in his palms. Heat roared suddenly through him, and with a low groan he turned toward her and let his hand fall into her robe, to touch the flesh hidden there like a mystery.

And when she didn't turn away, but instead cupped herself closer against him, the joy that rushed through his skull was like thunder and lighting. It filled him up; he wrapped her in his arms as her face turned up toward him. Her lips tasted faintly salty; her teeth were like pearls, scraping his tongue.

And then she put her hand on his chest—her palm a distinct hardness, her fingers stiff and trembling—and she pushed him away. It wasn't much of a push; but his emotions, lashed by need into raw sensitivity, made it feel as if she'd slapped him across the face. It was a small, weak shove; it was rejection. It might as well have been a club.

"No," she said. Her voice was so thick he could hardly make out the words. Something inside was choking her. "I can't do this. I have been defiled enough already."

The sun had crawled higher, trickling in golden spangles through the leaves of their hideaway. He sat with his arm around her and listened as she poured out her tale: of course, in the end, it came down to one thing, one man, and the name burned in his mind with a sickly, throbbing flame. Father. Tall Mountain.

Her voice grew steadier as she told him of his visits; of the way she'd come to fear the night, because it brought him to her. She gave no details, nor did Harvest Mountain need any. He knew what it was to be humiliated and terrorized by his father.

"I . . . can't," she said at last. "You understand what he's done to me? I am an abomination in the eyes of the Gods. He made me that, made me unclean. I would kill myself, but I'm afraid. The punishment of the Gods is long, and their hands stretch into the Underwater World. Death would be only a release, not an escape."

She expelled a long, shaky breath. Tears still leaked down her cheeks. She seemed not to notice. "You are the best thing in my life, Little Leopard, but even you can't help me against the King. And now that you know, you must hate me too."

She said it as a statement of fact, but he heard the plea in it as well. And because he knew how to answer, he also knew what to do. His father would not destroy this part of him, too. But would she understand? Would the truth make her hate him, as she did his father?

He took a deep breath. There was only one way out of this. If she would allow it. If she could forgive him, and find a way to love him as he did her.

He squeezed her tighter, and reached up with his

right hand to brush away her tears. His fingertips traced a soft path down her cheeks, across her lips . . .

"Night Talks," he began. "I beg your forgiveness, because I have lied to you. But if you can forgive me, you must understand I only did it because I love you."

He felt her face move, turn up toward him, but he wouldn't look at her. His shame and his need were too strong, and he knew they were etched on his own features.

"My name isn't Little Leopard," he said. "It is Harvest Mountain—and I am the High Prince of Great Head City . . ."

Like many of the hardest answers, the solution to many problems was a simple one, though it would take every ounce of his courage, and hers. He contemplated that, wondering if his father really was right about him, or if the strength he sensed in himself as Little Leopard was also a part of Harvest Mountain. He felt a sense of dislocation about all that: his experience with her, as Little Leopard, was so far different from his "real" life, that it was almost like having two people in his skin. And which one of them was the real one?

He thought about this as he finished his tale and finally fell silent. She said nothing, but he felt her watchfulness in the tension of her body, and, frightened, answered it with his own. "Do you hate me?" he asked.

She shook her head, but said nothing.

"Well?" he asked.

Her breath came out in a long, ragged gasp. "There isn't anybody I can trust, is there? I trusted you, Little Leopard, but Little Leopard doesn't exist, does he? The boy I trusted is someone else, a liar."

Her words tore at him. They were no more than he'd expected, no more than he deserved, surely, but just the same, he felt something inside him darken,

and begin to disappear. Something that had been
bright, till its fire was touched by his father's filthy,
ruinous hands. Ah, how they both had been damaged
by that monstrous touch.

"I lied out of love," he whispered.

"You lied," she replied.

But then he noticed she hadn't moved away from
him. Her words opened a chasm, but her body said
something else.

"Do you love me?" he asked her.

"I loved Little Leopard."

And that was like a great wall of black clouds rolling back to let in a great wash of sunlight. Suddenly,
his ears, which had been tuned only to the sound of
her voice, now heard birds singing in the trees above
them. Heard the screech of monkeys. He smelled her
hair, a faint tangle of sweat and musky desire. His?
Hers? Who knew?

"Little Leopard loved you, too, Night Talks. But
Little Leopard wasn't a lie, not wholly. He is also
Harvest Mountain, and Harvest Mountain wants to
marry you. If you will have the two of us. Will you?"

He had never before, and would never after, wait
any longer for anything of this world, though she only
paused a few moments; a few heartbeats.

"Yes," she said. "If I love the one, I can learn to
love the other. Can't I?"

He stroked her hair. "You must. It's the only way
we both can live."

Harvest Mountain told his father that same day. He
had expected Tall Mountain to explode, but the old
man had only smiled evilly, shot him one twisted
glance, and said, "Eh? The hostage bitch? You're welcome to her." He'd paused, then added, "Your wife,
my fine little puppy, will still be a hostage."

It had been a strange marriage, the ritual hurried,
the prayers to the Gods brief and almost perfunctory.

Only a few slaves had been sacrificed to assure the happiness of the new couple, and even the omens had been divided, neither good nor bad.

The High King had not allowed a public bedding, as was customary for a marriage in the royal line. He had good reason, as Harvest Mountain discovered shortly.

He had gone to her on the night after the wedding ceremony, and this time she had welcomed him happily, with smiles and kisses. But there was still that darkness about her, and when he discovered the reason for it, his heart cracked like a dropped egg.

"I'm pregnant," she told him. "I told you I was defiled."

Harvest Mountain's half brother was born with no eyes and a deformed right arm eight months later. By that time the Old King was dying of some hideous demon that turned his skin hard and black. When that was over, the new High King ordered his father's chambers cleared. Then he spat in the dead, ruined face. A face as dead and ruined as the idea that Harvest Mountain would ever be free of him, or would ever know love again.

Night Talks Moon vanished shortly thereafter; her child had never been seen at all, except by the midwives. Sadly, these all died as well, of diseases that some murmured were not true illnesses at all.

The High King Harvest Mountain spent two years drinking and whoring and playing the fool. Then he went looking for a new wife.

By then he understood all about women, wives, enemies, and hostages. He swore to himself he would never again be gulled.

And his first child by his second wife had a blue eye. But there was only one man in all of Great Head City who had that particular mark . . .

CHAPTER SIXTEEN

I

Spirits felt as if she were imprisoned in some night-mare from which she could only watch, helpless and horrified, as the real world came crashing down around her.

Outside her window, water trickled from a covered cistern, liquid and echoing. In the distance, hawkers shouted raucous greetings as they set up their barrows for the day. The pale sunlight grew stronger, sharpening the shadows.

"He would kill me?" she asked finally, still not believing the terrible story which Purple Grackle had told her.

Purple Grackle said, "I told you we don't talk about Night Talks Moon. This is why. It's all rumor—all the old women who knew the truth are dead. But I believe he murdered her, yes. He is a terrible man when the Gods move him to be."

Spirits chewed her lip as she nodded slowly. Yes, if this was true, her husband was a monster. But still she felt pity for him; if he was a monster, something—or someone—had made him so. And if it had been the doings of a God, that was even more to be pitied. She wondered if there was a way out, one that would protect both her and her child.

"And he killed the baby, too?"

Purple Grackle nodded. "So the rumors say."

"It must have been terrible . . ."

"Do you see your choice, High Queen? It is terrible, too, and even that may not be enough."

But Spirits had already rejected one half of the choice, and what was left was no choice at all. "I will not murder my own child," she said softly. "That is a sin in the eyes of all the Gods. Even to save myself. If my baby is marked by the Gods, then there must be a reason."

Purple Grackle sighed. "It is marked with a blue eye, Lady. Whether from the Gods, or . . . who knows?" She paused. "And he bears the marks of a great sin." She stared frankly at her mistress.

"Don't you believe me, either? Do you think White Serpent is the father of my child?" Suddenly, anger thickened her voice. "Would that he was! At least I would not have to murder this innocent baby to save myself from him."

Her tension, and the sudden noise, awakened the child at her breast. He began to squall, his tiny face red, his eyes twisted shut. Spirits joggled him. "There, baby. Shhh. It will be all right." She pulled him to her teat; after a few moments his cries lessened, then ceased. A beatific smile appeared on Spirits's face.

"Oh, Purple Grackle, he's mine. Kill him even to save myself? No. I won't do it."

"Perhaps, then, mistress, you both will die." She said it in flat, bald tones, hoping to convince Spirits of the real danger of her situation. The story she'd told her, based on darkly whispered rumors, was too easy to ignore. But she had done what she could. Anything else was out of her hands, and in the power of the young woman on the bed.

"What will you do, then?" she finally asked.

"I will trust in the Gods," Spirits said. "And I will wait. I am married to the High King, Purple Grackle.

I *know* him. I simply can't believe things are as bad as you say. He isn't the easiest of men, but he isn't a monster, either."

II

The object of all this speculation turned away from his window, his brain on fire with memories that burned and seared. Things he'd thought safely hidden, even from himself, now rose from the dead past—*and in almost the same way*. It was as if his father, like some malign curse, kept tormenting him over and over again from the Underwater World. Now, just as before, he was faced with the evidence of betrayal—and Spirits had not even the excuse of helplessness, as Night Talks Woman had. No one had forced Spirits, but the message of the Gods was the same: a sin is a sin, and We will put Our mark on the fruit of the sin. And so They had, on a twisted, wretched, many-fingered abomination with one blue eye to name the sin for all the world to see.

Well, the mark was plain enough. So now what? Was there any way he could restore his honor, wipe away the sin, and perhaps, accomplish something else as well?

It was said that White Serpent Hawk was so purely a priest that he was beyond the gifts of mortal men, that he craved nothing of the earth. But the Gods had shown what he craved, though he must have thought to hide it.

The more he thought about it, the more he saw its beauty, its elegance. Indeed, it was a perfect solution!

Now he felt happier, more animated, as if he'd just had a pot of fine pulque. Which was an excellent idea in itself, wasn't it?

He clapped his hands. Servants appeared. "Bring me breakfast, and bring me drink," he commanded. While he waited for this, he gestured at a messenger.

"Summon White Serpent Hawk and Smoking Mirror. Bring the Jaguar priest first."

The sun was well up, almost noon high, when Smoking Mirror came striding into the court. Harvest Mountain was already half-drunk. He waved at the priest and gestured him to a stool. The heat of the sun had turned the day into a furnace; even the birds and monkeys had stilled, and the priest was drenched with sweat. He took his seat gratefully, then noticed the danger signs: the High King's eyes were slitted, his face puffy and reddened, and his breath was rancid with pulque.

Go carefully, Smoking Mirror reminded himself. "You called for me, High King?" he said.

Harvest Mountain's bony chin waggled loosely as he pinched it between his fingers. "I've been thinking about my blue-eyed son," he said.

Smoking Mirror felt a wave of tension tighten all his muscles at once. "Oh?" he said.

"You seem remarkably quiet, brother. Don't you have anything to say?"

"What would you have me say, High King?" Smoking Mirror had assessed the situation as well as he could. Wary circumspection seemed by far the best course. He knew more about Harvest Mountain's past than he would ever admit.

Harvest Mountain worked his lips loosely, then spat. "I know what you're thinking."

"King, you should send the servants away."

Blinking, Harvest Mountain stared at him, then nodded. A measure of alertness came into his gaze. "Ah. Yes, you are right, of course." He cleared the room with a few brisk commands. "Now. Is there something you wish to say for my ears only?"

Smoking Mirror bowed his head slightly. "I thought perhaps you might wish to say something to me, Lord. You said you have been thinking. Have you reached any conclusions?"

"About the God-accursed monster my dog-bitch wife has borne me? Yes, I have. Let me tell you what they are."

When he finished, the High Priest rocked back on his chair. The King might be drunk, but there was nothing wrong with his mind. Once again Smoking Mirror reminded himself not to underestimate the man before him. He might become an obstacle in the future to the will of the Jaguar, but at the moment Smoking Mirror had to admit he could not have done any better himself.

He allowed himself a slow smile. "In the short term it is brilliant, brother. No one could fault you. And you would kill many birds with a single arrow. Have you thought about the future as well?"

Harvest Mountain lifted another bowl, drained it, and belched. A pinched, sly expression crossed his features. "Rumors might be started, rumors that would not destroy White Serpent, of course, but might weaken him for a stronger blow later. I suppose you could help with that?"

Smoking Mirror laughed out loud. "Yes, he is my enemy, too." He clapped his hands in delight.

"When, Lord?"

"Today," Harvest Mountain replied. "Now."

III

Purple Grackle came running into Spirits's chamber. "Lady, we must hurry. The High King has summoned you to the court. Right away. And you are to bring the baby, too."

Spirits had been drowsing in the leaf-filtered sunlight that lay across her bed. She came awake at once, her features slack with surprise and fear. "What? Oh, dear! What does it mean?"

Purple Grackle was already shaking out a fresh robe, this one a beautiful thing of bright red feathers and pale pink coral beads. Spirits's usual simple white cloak would not do for a formal court appearance. And she would have to find something better than a diaper for the child. "I don't know, Lady, but we have to hurry. The messenger said to come right away, and there are two guards with him."

Guards? Spirits wondered. What do we need with guards?

Carefully, she set the baby down on the bed and climbed out. It was still very hot, though the worst of the afternoon heat had lessened a bit. She ran fingers through her hair. It felt lank and sweaty. "You'll have to comb my hair, Purple Grackle. I wish I had time for a bath."

Her legs felt weak, and now bile gurgled in her chest, just beneath her throat. She'd eaten little today, and when she stood, dizziness spun the room about her. She staggered a bit, before Purple Grackle noticed and caught her.

"Lady, are you all right?"

"I'm . . . I'll be fine. Just give me a moment. Is that the robe? Good, help me with it."

Quickly, Spirits stripped out of her bedclothes and allowed Purple Grackle to drape the feathered finery about her shoulders. Then she sat on a stool while her handmaid ran a wooden comb through her hair. It was badly matted, and Purple Grackle didn't have the time to be gentle.

"Ouch!"

"I'm sorry, Lady, but . . ."

"I know. Go on, don't mind me."

The baby began to cry. Both women looked over. A ripe smell arose from the bed.

"Oh, no," Purple Grackle said.

IV

The summons had reached White Serpent while he was behind his temple, out in the gardens where his farmers were showing him the seedlings from the newest plantings of maize. They had followed his instruction the previous season carefully, and the results were plain to see: it was the best crop yet. The ears were a good finger's length longer that anything that had ever been known before. It meant much more usable cornmeal from the same number of fields. And these plots, so carefully tended, seemed to be less damaged by the bugs that were such a problem elsewhere.

So he was moderately annoyed at yet another demand from a man with whom he'd already had two fruitless confrontations, and he dallied a good amount of time before leaving: most of the afternoon, in fact. Nevertheless, he told his people he would return, and departed with the armed guards—armed guards!—the High King had sent to fetch him.

What was it this time? he wondered as he walked toward the royal pavilions. Surely the King must by now understand he could not compromise himself. A thought struck him; perhaps the High King had suffered a change of heart, coming at last to understand the wisdom of the old ways, and was now willing to accept the way of peace that was offered to him. From what he knew, it seemed unlikely, but the ways of destiny were often strange to behold.

It would be a wonderful thing, though, wouldn't it? And so that happy thought filled White Serpent Hawk's mind as he approached his third, and last, confrontation with the High King Harvest Mountain Lord.

V

Harvest Mountain, though somewhat disordered by drink, had sense enough to bar everybody from the court whose tongue might wag. He kept only two servants, whom he trusted for a pair of reasons: the first, that they had proved their loyalty over the years. The second, that their tongues would not wag, for they lacked tongues at all.

One of these ushered in White Serpent Hawk, who seemed unaware of how long he'd kept them waiting. The second led Spirits and her unnamed child in from the women's pavilions. Harvest Mountain sat on his throne table in the position of power, one leg angling down over the edge. As soon as Spirits saw this, she clutched her child more tightly: for this was the stance of the High King, who passed judgement.

White Serpent seemed undisturbed by the display, however. He merely nodded to Smoking Mirror, who sat on a low stool at the High King's foot, and smiled at Spirits. She took some small reassurance from that smile, since everywhere else was only dourness and anger.

White Serpent, still smiling, said, "Greetings, my brothers. I have come as you asked, High King. How goes the day with you?"

Harvest Mountain fixed him with a harsh glare. He didn't look at Spirits, in fact made no acknowledgment of her presence at all. She felt a warning beat in the veins of her neck, and blood began to thrum in her ears.

"The day goes ill, as well you know . . . *brother*," Harvest Mountain replied.

White Serpent spread his hands and bobbed his head slightly, still smiling. "I'm sorry to hear that, brother. And from your expression, I'd say you think the illness has something to do with me. But I have done you no harm."

"You speak glibly, priest. Perhaps you think it is funny how the Gods have marked me—and *mine*." He drummed the fingers of his right hand on his knee-cap. "What does your God say, White Serpent, to that defilement?"

Spirits caught her breath. She had not left her quar-ters, or spoken to any outsider, since the birth of her baby. Nevertheless, some servants did know, and she doubted that the secret had been kept. But it was possible, she supposed, that White Serpent didn't know about her son with his one blue eye. She knew that even on his works of mercy in the villages, he refused to listen to harmful gossip. He would turn such away with a grin and the admonition that the Gods cared not for such, so why should men or women?

At the King's reply, White Serpent seemed for the first time to understand the gravity of the situation, and the smile left his face. "How so, King, that you are defiled, you or yours? I am High Priest. Surely, if my God knew of such, I would know also. But I do not. So tell me what you speak of."

Harvest Mountain seemed taken aback, and paused for a moment before speaking. Spirits noticed that he sipped from a pot of pulque, ready at his right hand, before he answered, and she thought: Oh, no.

Finally, Harvest Mountain looked over at her. His eyes sparkled wetly from the drink, but his face was dark and reddened. He pointed at her. "You, wife. Come forward. Show this . . . priest what I'm talking about."

She had wrapped her child in a blue cloth whose borders she had embroidered with crimson threads, during the long time of her pregnancy. Now the babe stirred, as if sensing he was the center of attention. She lifted him up and kissed his forehead; soft, smooth, warm. She felt a shudder of love pass through her so strongly she almost staggered.

"Well," Harvest Mountain snapped. "Are you deaf, wife? I said bring the monster into the light, so that everybody can see my shame."

"Lord . . ."

"Do it now, Spirits!"

She grasped the baby more firmly, and slowly came

up to the throne. She felt Smoking Mirror's hot eyes on her all the way. She didn't look up at the throne.

"Yes, there. Stop now. Unwrap it, show it to this High Priest whose God is so ignorant of what he's done."

Her thoughts already racketing at a fever pitch, Spirits understood these words could be taken two different ways; a nice bit of work, but not for her. Either way, the danger to her and her child remained constant. Her mind whirled, seeking an answer, a way out of the situation. She had come to this city hoping to save her family. Now she must save herself. Perhaps the Gods really did hate her.

"Lord," she whispered. "He is just a child, a harmless thing. Perhaps these are marks of favor . . ."

The King's laugh was like a dog barking. "Is that so, priest? Are these marks—I said *show him,* Spirits—are they the hand of a benevolent God? What does your God know of them?"

White Serpent had come closer as Spirits approached. His face was grave as he bent over the bundle she held. One tiny hand, bearing five fingers and a thumb, groped blindly up toward his face. The stunted left foot was plainly visible, where the concealing cloth had slipped away.

White Serpent stared at the babe for a long time. The child stared back at him vaguely, its one blue eye soft in the fading afternoon light. When White Serpent saw this, his own eyes flicked up to meet Spirits. He didn't smile, in fact his expression remained unchanged, but she suddenly felt an amazing rush of serenity, a calmness so perfect that all her worries fled. Somehow this would turn out all right.

The priest held her glance for one more beat, then sighed, turned, and faced the King again.

"You think I am the cause of this. Perhaps you are right."

Smoking Mirror gasped audibly, delight plain on his

saturnine features, and Harvest Mountain jerked backward as if he'd been struck. "You dare admit this to my face, priest?"

"I admit nothing, brother, that you can't see for yourself. I have blue eyes. This child has one blue eye. It is plain you think I am the father, that I have defiled you, my office, and my God, that I have stolen your woman and this poor baby is the mark of my sin. Is this not so?"

"Of course it is so! What else could it be?"

Now White Serpent, tall as a spear, grave as a stone, came right up to the High King's table and stared at him. He ignored Smoking Mirror as if he weren't there, and that priest had to lean back and crane his neck to look up at the White Priest.

"High King—though you are my brother, I will give you your earthly name—there is another answer. This is obviously the mark of a God, working in the flesh of your child. I repeat, King—*your* child, for it is not mine. I have kept to my vows. But consider what the mark is, the sign you think is damning. One blue eye. Why not two, Lord? If I have two, and the sin is mine, should not this child also have two blue eyes? But it does not. What does this mean, then?"

Harvest Mountain leaned forward as if to speak, but White Serpent showed him his palm to forestall him. "Let me finish, King. The one blue eye is a mark, no doubt of it. It is too plain not to be one, and it doubtless comes from the Gods. And I have blue eyes. Now think, King: what has gone on between the two of us? What great dispute have we? You speak of power, of war and sacrifice and spoils. And I teach of the old ways, the old wisdom and the new wisdom I bring. I speak of peace, and the greatness of our city. We each have our visions."

Smoking Mirror snorted. White Serpent glanced down at him, smiled faintly, then turned a solemn expression back to the King.

"The mark of the Gods is this," he said simply. "The blue eye on your child is as my blue eyes. It tells you who has the right of our disagreement. It is a sign that you should break your weapons of war, and turn to peace. That's what it is, and that's all it is." He turned, looked at Spirits, then looked back at the King. "Your child is crippled, Lord. Did you not know my temple is a shelter, and the God a protector of the halt and the maimed? In every way this infant warns you to the path of peace and goodness. It is truly a message from the Gods. What more proof do you need?"

With that, White Serpent bobbed his head a final time and smoothly stepped away from the throne, leaving a shocked silence in his wake.

A moment of faintness clouded Spirits's vision. The court seemed to darken, and she imagined she saw sheets of dark light ripple between the two men. And then she saw their eyes: Smoking Mirror's gaze was red as fire; White Serpent glowed with the blue of a still pool beneath the sun; and Harvest Mountain looked out with eyes of molten gold, the eyes of a cat hunting by night.

With a deep inner tolling, she felt that which was hidden inside her awaken, and she saw the Two on Their mountain throne, leaning forward as One. As if They were listening. Their perfect faces were cold and set. Never before had she been so afraid.

Harvest Mountain broke the stillness. His voice was low and quivered with barely controlled rage. "Priest," he said, "just as your master, the Snake, you twist portents and omens to suit yourself. Do you expect me to believe such a thing?"

White Serpent shrugged. "I care not what you believe, Lord, for what is destined by the Gods is your destiny as well. If you choose to ignore their message, it is on your own head. I have already offered you the way of greatness, for you and for your city. Now the

God sends you a message, too. Ignore it if you will—but the peril is not just for you, but for all the people."

Harvest Mountain raised his head. "And I suppose it is not your city as well?" Suddenly, all the anger drained from his features. He looked bereft. "Brother," he began again, softly this time, "I love my city. I would see it great. And I think you love it too. Can you not join me, so that together we can accomplish all that we will?" He took a sharp breath. "Look, then. I offer to you my greatest gift, and one I believe you can not resist. Spirits Walking Woman is my High Queen, the most beautiful flower I possess. But for my city I will give her to you as a token of our bond. Join with me, White Serpent, and together we will rule the world!"

Nausea boiled in Spirits's stomach, so strong she thought she would disgrace herself right there on the floor of the court. She held it back, though, for there was another thing, like a bolt of lightning, crackling through her mind: *Yes, White Serpent, say yes and take me, free me from this nightmare that is my life.*

She didn't realize she'd stopped breathing as she waited for the White Priest's reply. What the King had said to White Serpent seemed to have struck him dumb. For the first time his expression turned uncertain, and his eyes jumped back and forth between Spirits and the High King. Still on his stool, Smoking Mirror grinned like the edge of a knife, glittering and bloody and waiting.

Then White Serpent trembled just a bit, a small quaver but still noticeable, and took a breath.

"Your generosity is wonderful, King, but my answer must remain the same. For me to join in your cause would betray my destiny, and for me to take this good woman in the manner you speak of—and even your offer of her is a sin, for she has done nothing wrong—would be to utterly defile myself, worse even than you claim your own defilement is. But there is and will be no such defiling, brother; neither for me, for I must refuse your offer, nor for you. For all that has occurred is only a message, not a sin, and there is nobody on this earth to blame for it." He stopped for a moment, deep in thought. Then he went on. "You say we will conquer the world. Yet it is not the world we must conquer but ourselves. And if we seek greatness, we must look inside for it, because there is the only place it lives." Then he raised one hand, let it drop gently, and fell silent.

Smoking Mirror made a soft, choking noise deep in his throat, as if he were about to laugh. Then, slowly, he began to clap his hands together. The sound echoed strangely in the nearly empty confines of the court. "Very good, brother. You have all the arts a high priest should. And if you read the omens to suit yourself, what else can be expected?"

Now he stood and faced White Serpent. "You are a fool, brother. I will say it for the High King; if you expect us—or anybody—to believe your words, you are not as smart as I think you are. Listen to me! Take this offer, and take it now. Or you will face the wrath of all the Gods, and the High King, too. Do you hear what I'm saying to you?"

White Serpent looked at him for a long time. Finally, his face as still as any of the carved heads that gave the city its name, he nodded.

"I understand my destiny, brother, and that of this city, too. It is a pity you don't. In the end you will pay for it. As for the wrath of the Gods, I have faced all of them before."

His words were so full of prophecy that Spirits closed her eyes; she felt as if she'd just heard a great doom pronounced, and wondered why the others did not tremble. But they did not. Smoking Mirror laughed, then abruptly quieted.

Harvest Mountain said, "This was my final offer, priest. I have done all that can be expected, and you have reviled me in my own house. Get out of it, then, and know that it is war between us. Go on, get out of my sight."

White Serpent only said, "But I do not make war, brother. Not in the way you suppose." Then he turned and walked away.

When he was gone, Harvest Mountain looked over at Spirits. His features were contorted with disgust and loathing.

"And you, wife, you get out, too. Go back to your rooms. I can't stand to look at you any longer." He paused. "And never again bring that monster before me." Bitterness and self-scorn seared his next words. "That mark of the Gods your false priest so values. Well, now you know how much he truly values it—or values you, either. Are you happy with your treachery?"

"My Lord . . ."

"Go on, get out. I'll decide what to do with you another day."

From that day on, Spirits was High Queen in name only. Her rooms became a prison, and her life was filled with fear. But she loved her child anyway, because she did believe what White Serpent had said. Her child was a token of the way of the Gods. And so she named him Shining Star Spirit, as a token of what he was to her. And what the dread thing hidden inside her whispered he might become, in the fullness of time and destiny.

VI

Great Head City, though it was the largest of the Middle World, was still small enough that its citizens were at least able to nod at most everybody else, and certainly to gossip with them, especially in the Grand Concourse, along the High Road where the barrows and the peddlers and jugglers and singers made their livings. And it was to this place that servants and slaves came from the royal pavilions to shop for the courts and for themselves, even the pair of slaves who served the inner court, and who had no tongues. Which did not stop those who knew them from understanding the rude language of hand signs they had developed.

So everybody knew something terrible had occurred with the High Queen and her newborn child—and some had knowledge of specific details. It had not been so long before that another mystery involving the royal wife had occupied tongues and thoughts in this place, and so it was again. Even more so, for Spirits, from her works of mercy and kindness in the villages, had become known to even the meanest of the peasants, and was very well liked.

But for those who knew, the mark the Gods had placed on the newborn child was unsettling, for it was a frightening omen, if interpreted as a judgment on sin. Slowly, the city began to split into two factions, depending on where one stood as to the meaning of the omen. Did it favor White Serpent Hawk and his rapidly growing temple? Or was it a portent of the rightness of the High King's way, which was supported by all the other major temples, most importantly that of the city's guardian, the Jaguar?

Nor was the split healed by the news that rippled up and down the Way a few days after the rumored confrontation in the inner court: that the High Queen had been ejected from the royal pavilions by her husband, who said he knew her no longer. Now it was said that she lived as a priestess in the Temple of the Feathered Serpent with her child, and was High Queen no longer. But there was a lot of disagreement on how this had happened, even whether it was true or not. For no one had seen Spirits Walking, and there had been no formal announcement. Wise old heads, standing around the barrow where caged parrots, trained to speak, were sold, doubted there would ever be any official word. There had been none about Night Talks Moon's fate. And at least the former High Queen had not simply vanished, as had Night Talks. Some who served in the Temple of the Feathered Serpent said they had seen Spirits, with her handmaid Purple Grackle, making a place for themselves in an inner room of the temple.

Some wags, with more tongue than wit, said this was proof of the rumors about White Serpent himself; but others, more temperate, were content to wait and see what further omens might appear. In the meantime the city roiled uneasily, abuzz with tales of every stripe, and here and there fistfights broke out, between followers of White Serpent and those of the High King. These sorts of ruckuses continued as the long dry season waned and the crops began to be brought in.

The harvest brought yet another point of contention for those disposed to discuss the rift between the King and the White Priest, for it looked to be the best in all the years anyone could remember. Some said this was proof that the Gods had smiled on White Serpent and his works, for it was the farms of those who followed his new teachings that yielded the most. Others preferred the view that the fine crop came from all the Gods, and was an affirmation of the High King, who had made the city even greater than his father had. These opposing points of view led to further tension, and more brawling, at a time when some felt there should have been general celebration at their good luck—for the city was at peace, and the people had full bellies, even the poorest. It was plain enough that some Gods smiled on the city. The biggest question was which ones. And why.

Then, as the first thin clouds, harbingers of the coming rains, began to drift across the periwinkle skies, the habitués of the Way had a new topic to chatter about: without any warning, the Temple of the Jaguar had begun to expand the Jaguar Cult. Lord Skull Breaker was seen much about, and ten hands of men from the villages had been brought into the city and now trained every day on the grounds near the river the Cult used for that purpose.

This would not have been of much moment, except for the number of men taken—fifty was a very large number, and brought the Cult to a strength it had never possessed before; and also, the secrecy about why it had been done. But the gossips didn't have to wait long for an answer to this. Even while the new recruits were training, squads of hardened veterans, armed with clubs and spears, began to patrol the streets of the city. Mostly they broke up fights, sometimes brutally. And if the followers of White Serpent Hawk often got the worst of these confrontations, who was to say the reason? But men wondered, and the worry was a stain on the glory of the city.

Soon would come the Harvest Festival. Perhaps things would be made clearer then, they told themselves. Many went to the daily rituals at the Temple of the Jaguar, or of the Dragon, where the King was High Priest. But many also went to the Temple of the Feathered Serpent, and so the split grew. And some of the wisest old men began to talk of destiny, and of what the Gods had prepared for Great Head City.

While all this transpired, the Jaguar Cult began going out into the villages, and the squad leaders to mark likely men. But they didn't tell those they singled out, only kept a tally in their own minds, for later.

VII

For her part, Spirits sank into a kind of numbness, in which her feelings became vague and fuzzy. She kept to the room White Serpent had given her, and nursed Shining Star even when unnoticed tears ran down her cheeks.

Purple Grackle tended her. She had come willingly
with her mistress, for she loved her, though it meant
she was herself exiled from the courts that had been
her life. But she kept in communication with a few
people, whom she would meet when she went to the
market, and so she was able to keep abreast of the
gossip and rumor of the royal pavilions, which was
somewhat more accurate than what reached the small
knots of men standing along the Way.

But she didn't speak of what she heard to Spirits,
rightly guessing this would only make matters worse,
for what she heard were frightening tales of treachery
and malice. She knew, for instance, that Green Water
Woman had moved into the High Queen's chambers,
and had set herself up as the consort in everything
but name. And Harvest Mountain Lord came to her
rooms almost every night; the slaves reported there
was always a great ruckus, with much groaning and
shrieking, and often they had to change the bed covers
the next day, for they were streaked with blood and
other fluids less mentionable.

"It sounds like two cats mating," one young girl
reported in tones of fascinated awe. "It doesn't sound
like people making love. More like two beasts tearing
at each other. But they seem to like it."

Purple Grackle had never wholly believed in Green
Water Woman's sudden friendship with her mistress;
she'd sensed even at the beginning a dark ambiva-
lence, as if Green Water herself was unsure of the
truth of her feelings. But she'd kept her own counsel,
being herself undecided as to the best course. Her
own experience had taught her that in such situations,
sometimes doing nothing was the only thing to do.

Now she faced a dilemma; her mistress had been
humbled in the most devastating way, and Purple
Grackle feared for her wits, if not for her life. And
there were things Spirits needed to know, if she
needed to protect herself; yet she was so broken down

with shock and grief Purple Grackle was afraid anything more might be the end of her. In fact, it had become plain enough that Spirits chose to live only for her son. Even White Serpent seemed unable to penetrate the fog that surrounded her like a tangible thing, a gloom that seemed to sweat from her pores. He would come and try to speak to her, but sometimes she would say nothing, as if he weren't there, and others she would answer in one word or two, her gaze drifting off behind his shoulder, or to some more distant place only she could see.

He kept on coming to her, but his visits grew fewer as he saw the hopelessness of his task. One day he put his hands on her forehead and she barely noticed him. She was humming to herself and holding the baby. He took Purple Grackle aside and said, "Keep watch on her. Do what you can. If you need anything, come to me right away. If the Gods mean to heal her in the fullness of time, They will. But I know of nothing else to do."

Yet Purple Grackle knew that what her mistress needed was not in this world. At least nothing in this world she could have, or that would give itself to her.

This continued as the time for the Harvest Festival grew closer. Now Purple Grackle found the Way always crowded with people: rough-dressed farmers from the villages, come to the city hoping for news; the old men who were always there, now arguing rumors at even greater length; traders and buyers from far places, speaking with others like themselves, or with the larger dealers along the road; and flocks of children moving in packs, shouting, tumbling, and sometimes fighting.

It was the children whom Purple Grackle noticed most; many of them wore white rags around their skulls, and these would fight with other groups that did not wear the white. She snagged one small boy as he scrambled past her, catching him by his ear and jerking him up short. He twisted in her grip till she slapped him into silence. He was not above seven summers, and small even for his age.

"Boy, why do you fight with the others?" she asked.

"Because, Lady, they have done a big sin."

She looked into his dark brown eyes—irises the color of nightmoth wings—and said, "What sin?"

"I don't know, but it is terrible."

"You don't wear one of those white headbands," she said. "Why not?"

He tried to run away, but she twisted his earlobe until he answered her, his face red with anger. "I am not a sinner. My father says we must kill all the sinners." Then, with a yank so strong he might have left part of his ear behind, he leaped from her grasp and ran away. She stood looking after him for a long time; the children had no idea what a perfect mirror they made, for their ignorance was without flaw. But in their reflection was visible that which was flawed: the dark fire now eating at the city's underbelly.

She shivered, finished her shopping, and went back to the temple. After she'd checked on her mistress, she went to find White Serpent Hawk, to tell him what she'd seen.

But when she found him with a group of lesser priests, talking quietly near the great wooden altar, she was afraid to break in, since their faces were so serious. He saw her just as she made up her mind to turn away, and smiled.

"Purple Grackle, wait," he called. "I'll be with you in just a moment."

He was as good as his word, and listened carefully to what she told him.

"Even the children, eh? This is a great sin that comes to us, that infants should take up quarrels even their parents ought not wage." He tipped his head to her. "How is Spirits Walking Woman?" He had not been to visit for several days.

"She is the same, Lord," Purple Grackle said. "But the baby is fine. If she has enough time, and nobody harms or shocks her, I think she will be better one of these days. What happened to her was terrible."

White Serpent's blue eyes flickered. Faint lines of merriment appeared at their corners. "You are a sturdy one, Purple Grackle. Do you think, then, that I let down your mistress when she was offered to me like a piece of meat?"

She covered her mouth with a hand and blushed furiously at such plain speaking, especially from a great lord like White Serpent, but he saw in her eyes that she believed at least some of what he said.

"Don't worry, dear, you don't offend me. Your loyalty to your mistress could never be offensive. And you should know—and you may tell her this, when you think the time is right—that if I ever would have broken my vows, it would have been in that moment. But my vows are stronger than my will, and they bind me. As they should, for they are chains of destiny. But I am a man also, and if I could have helped her more, I would have."

She bowed then and took her leave, her cheeks still flushed with pink. But as she returned to her quarters, she pondered what he'd said: that he was a man. She wondered if she was the first to hear that admission— and she wondered what her mistress would say when she heard it, too.

Any hope—even a false one—was something when all hope was lost.

CHAPTER SEVENTEEN

I

On a fine morning which she could not see, but could feel from the quality of the light that filtered through many colored cloths, Spirits awoke to herself, and her thoughts were once again clear and sharp.

There was in the air a deep, thrumming whisper, which she associated with the past—times of triumph and glory, when all the world was new, like a toy for her pleasure. But in her newfound clarity of mind, she knew those times were gone, and she lay in her bed staring blankly at the roof beams, sad beyond endurance. Yet there was a different quality to her grief; it was no longer heavy and all-encompassing, but sharp and specific. Her days of vagueness were gone. She could recall them only as a formless misery, a mental fog colored like a gray pearl.

The child in the crook of her arm stirred; she turned to him as if seeing him for the first time, suddenly knowing that this weight was all she'd kept close to her heart, even when her thoughts had fled far away.

"Shining Star . . ." she breathed. She put her hands beneath his chubby arms and lifted him up. His tiny fists waved; his mouth screwed into a rosebud of waking. Finally his translucent eyelids, marked by the tiniest of blue veins, like fine embroidery, lifted, and he stared at her with his black and blue gaze.

"Muhhh . . ." he grumbled, already wondering where his breakfast might be, and groping blindly for it.

She stared at him in wonder. Her last clear memory of him was as little more than a handful of flesh, but somehow he'd grown into a fine, strong babe, with a rounded belly and fine, fat limbs. And strong, too, if his hungry squirmings were any sign. If one didn't know, one would scarcely notice the extra fingers on his fisted hands; only the stunted left foot was still obvious, but it was too soon to tell if he would actually be crippled, or only limp.

"Yes, baby, mama is here," she cooed at him, noticing with delight how he responded to her voice. She pulled him to her breast, and that was how Purple Grackle found them when she came to see to her mistress's morning needs.

"Good morning to you, Purple Grackle," Spirits said cheerfully, when the girl came into the room. "It looks to be a fine day. Have you been about yet to see?"

Her handmaid's reaction told her everything she needed to know about what had gone before. "Lady, you are awake!" Purple Grackle cried, her face suddenly wreathed in a wide smile.

"Why, have I been asleep?" Spirits asked. "Yes, I suppose I have, haven't I? But I am back now."

"All Gods be praised!" Purple Grackle shot back, smiling even more broadly.

"Well, I suppose we must praise Them," Spirits said, feeling that her usual practicality had returned. "We are in the temple of one of Them, aren't we?"

Purple Grackle came over to the bed and sat on its side. She stared hard at Spirits's face. "Are you truly feeling better, Lady? I was so worried . . ."

"I am fine now, Purple Grackle. But my memories

are a bit cloudy. Can you help me? I'm sure you took notice of everything."

At this the younger girl's eyes sparkled. She had missed the long conversations she used to have with her mistress, where they rummaged through bits of gossip and rumor like children playing with bright trinkets. She put one hand on Spirits's shoulder. "Oh, yes, Lady. I have much to say. I wondered if I would ever get the chance."

And when she said that, Spirits understood for the first time just how deeply Purple Grackle loved her, and how strong her loyalty had been. Another pang of grief pierced her. "Oh, dearest, I am so sorry. You gave up everything, didn't you? And how can I repay you?"

"I gave up nothing worth keeping!" Purple Grackle shot back fiercely. "To leave a place of treachery and evil is a blessing, not a curse. I only wish we could have departed sooner."

Spirits took her hand and squeezed. "Dear heart, somehow I will make it up to you." She glanced around the room. "This is all we have, now, isn't it? Exiles in the Temple of the Feathered Serpent."

Purple Grackle took a deep breath. "Better the meanest room in a place of safety, than a grand chamber in a hall of death."

Spirits nodded. "Yes, I suppose so. You are right, of course. I don't remember everything. Was it really as bad as that?"

"The God is kind to you, Lady, if He has taken those memories away. Yes, it was as bad as that. For a time I feared your husband would kill both of us, and the baby, too. But instead he cast you out, and I brought you here. I think it was your sister's doing."

"Green Water? How so?"

"She lives in your old rooms in the courts, Lady. Some say the High King will marry her and make her his Queen."

Spirits sighed, and joggled Shining Star against her breast. He made a soft, bubbling sound, and soon got back to work.

"Well, then, I guess I owe her gratitude, too."

"How can you say that? It was her doing that he cast you out, and now she sits in your place. It's said she serves him in all ways, and that he's besotted with her. Shameful."

But Spirits shook her head. "Oh, no, Purple Grackle. Don't you see it? She saved my life. We are all of us only women, remember—and we have to use guile to reach our ends. The High King must have been ready to murder us all, but she saved us. She gave him another choice, one that let us live. It was all she could get. If she'd hated me, it would have been as easy to counsel murder, but she didn't do that."

Purple Grackle, who had felt the slant-eyed glare of Green Water Woman as she'd swept into the women's quarters and begun to order their departure, thought it might not have been kindness that motivated Spirits's sister. Rather the instinct of a cat to toy with its victim alive, the better to enjoy its terrible fate. But she didn't say this, only thought that her mistress was sometimes too generous and forgiving. Well, it was better than being too much the other way.

"I suppose you are right, Lady," she said. "I didn't think of it that way, I suppose."

"What is that low, roaring sound? It reminds me of the great crowds that gathered when my husband first brought me here."

Not wanting to dredge up those old memories, Purple Grackle answered quickly: "It is a crowd, Lady. The whole city is full, the Grand Concourse packed with people. Today is the beginning of the Harvest Festival. It will continue four days. Is it the same in your city, that it is the largest festival of the year?" But when she said that, it reminded her of other rumors she had heard of late, of which she was afraid to speak, and so she fell silent.

Spirits, with her newfound clearness of mind, heard the undertone in her words, and said, "What is it? Don't worry about me, Purple Grackle. My old home is beyond me now, at least for the moment, but I have good memories of it, and nothing has happened to make me regret them. It is something else, though?"

"I . . . I can't say, Lady. I don't know . . ."

"Come, dearest. Has something happened to Holy Stone City?" A thought suddenly struck her, and she drew in a sharp breath. "No word of my mother, is there? Is she well?"

"Oh, no, Spirits. Nothing I have heard. As far as I know, your family is fine. I still talk with a few who serve your sister, and they don't mention anything like that."

"Well, then, what is it? Tell me, won't you? Anything is better than not knowing."

"I have heard rumors," she finally said. "There is almost open war between the followers of the Feathered Serpent and those of the other Gods. And the High King has allied himself and the Temple of the Dragon with all the rest, because he hates White Serpent Hawk. Now the soldiers of the Jaguar Cult rule the city with an iron fist. And it is said the King plans a great new war, to make his place unshakable."

Spirits sighed heavily. "And the villages are still full of poor cripples from the last one. White Serpent is right. War is the greatest evil. Why can't men learn from him?"

Purple Grackle fervently agreed, but had less faith than her mistress in the ability of any woman to ever swerve a man from the death lust. "It is said the High King has already selected his next enemy, one he claims has been treacherous of old, whose treachery extends even to his children."

Spirits felt her heart skip a beat. "Oh, no . . . Is it Holy Stone City?"

Purple Grackle glanced away. "Except for your sister, Lady, I fear he hates every one of your line. Yes, that is the city I've heard named."

Spirits hugged Shining Star closer to her breasts. The baby had stopped suckling, and now dozed, but the movement awakened him. He burped softly and began to make a small humming sound. Spirits stroked his head as she gazed into the middle distance, her forehead crinkled in thought.

"Is that it, then? All the bad news? My benefactor opposed to my ex-husband, and Harvest Mountain planning to destroy my old home?"

"No other news, and even that isn't certain. But think about this, Lady: if Harvest Mountain succeeds, surely he will be so strong that even White Serpent can no longer oppose him. Then he might think of the last of your line, besides Green Water Woman. And the child is still an affront to him. He thinks it is the living mark of his shame, and your treachery."

"Yes. He would, I guess. What else should he think? Oh, dear, why have the Gods done these things? White Serpent says his God is good, and brings gifts to his people. But what sort of gift is this?"

"They are the Gods, Lady. What else can we say but that?"

Feeling she'd heard enough bad news for the morning, and wishing to get out of bed and stretch her flaccid limbs after so long a time, she said, "One good thing, at least. If I am no longer High Queen, I won't have to be so circumspect if I want to walk around and see the festival. What do you say, Purple Grackle? I could cover my face with a cloth, and nobody will recognize me. As if it matters now—and if they even remember me anymore."

"Are you sure, Lady?"

"Why not? I've been in bed too long. It's time I got myself out of it."

Purple Grackle stared searchingly at her; then, finally, like the silvered underside of a dry leaf flashed up by the wind, her old, impish grin appeared. "Yes, Lady, it is. Come, sit up and let me comb your hair."

II

Spirits had never taken the trip downriver to the sea, but the sound she heard as she and Purple Grackle made their way from the White Temple to the Grand Concourse was what she imagined the ocean waves would make as they pounded onto sandy beaches: a continuous, rolling roar, muted and then suddenly rising into a froth of cheers or shouting.

She went barefoot, for the day was fine; the well-beaten dust of the paths through the city puffed up warmly between her toes. Overhead the sun peeped from behind veils of feathery clouds, turned lemon-pale by the smoke from a thousand cookfires. The warm morning air was rich with scent: wood charring to hot, white coals, fat rabbits and dogs roasting slowly, trampled grasses now dry after the summer heat, the pungent odor of many people rubbing shoulders and sweating from their own heat. And over it all, the sharp, distinctive odor of the rare woods and herbs used to fuel the high altars for the sacrifices.

The narrow streets grew more choked the closer they got to the Concourse, as the entire city emptied into its own heart, continuously swelled by entire villages crossing from behind the river to take part in this greatest of days. She'd thought her own city had celebrated the Harvest Ritual in the grandest of manners, but compared to this, all the finery and festivity of Holy Stone City was little more than a farmer's backwoods celebration. Indeed, for a fleeting moment she could see the city as it saw itself: the center of the universe, the throbbing heart of all the people of the world. And with this feeling came sudden understanding of what the great men struggled over; how best to make it so, and keep this immensity of glory forever. Her ex-husband and her current benefactor both wanted the same thing. But their disagreement was how to reach the goal, and now that she understood the stakes, she saw how murderous that battle might become.

Spirits carried Shining Star in her arms, wrapped in a white cloth lest his deformities be noticed. For herself she had a similar plain cloth wrapped like a shawl around the lower part of her face and across her head, so that only her dark eyes were visible. It was not an unusual dress; she saw many other women in comparable garb, for the dust from thousands of moving feet choked the air with gold-flecked clouds, and many covered their mouths and noses against it.

As they were carried along by the close-packed throng, Spirits felt a sense of relief, as if for this day, at least, she could shed her burdens, or at least their dread power. Indeed, as she thought of all that had occurred, it was almost as if these things had happened to someone else.

It was with this joy in her restored faculties that she began to notice things she otherwise might not have seen: every place where the larger paths crossed stood a squad of four burly Jaguar soldiers, the long points of their tall spears glittering in the light. These men watched the crowds carefully, alert for . . . what? She'd never seen so many of them before, and wondered why they were there.

She began to watch more closely. Now she noticed that their dour expressions did change; whenever some groups of people crossed before them, their scowls would deepen, and some would pound their spear butts into the earth and mutter barely heard threats. It didn't take her long to see what aroused their anger;

only those who wore white ribbons tied around their heads got noticed.

"Are the people with the white headbands faithful to the Feathered Serpent, as used to be?" she asked Purple Grackle. "There are so many of them."

"Yes, Lady. Those who follow the way of the White Priest have grown great in numbers. His temple is without a doubt the largest in the city."

Spirits nodded. Purple Grackle might not see it, in fact might think this power was a token of their own safety, for they sheltered in the temple. But Spirits saw it for what it was: a deadly threat to the aims of the High King, and no doubt to the priests of the other temples. There had always been a balance of sorts between the Four, but now it was broken, one temple opposed by three. White Serpent Hawk might have grown powerful, but he faced an alliance that was even greater. She thought of a farmer building his house, and how he would pound down the poles until they were all even, paying particular attention to any which stood too high.

And worse than that, his power must frighten his opponents. She well knew that frightened men did things they would not do otherwise.

She had heard White Serpent Hawk speak of destiny. Now she understood just how terrible its stony grip could be.

"Cheer up, Spirits! You look as gloomy as an afternoon storm. Look, here is the Concourse at last. Where shall we go?" Purple Grackle raised one hand to shield her eyes, trying to see out over the huge gathering. "I think I see some open space . . . that way," she said, pointing.

The Grand Concourse occupied a slight declivity, which generations before had been scooped out of the earth to create a vast amphitheater, bounded on both sides by the courts, Sun Mountain, and the High Temples. She looked to her left, back the way she had

come, and saw that the crowds before the ramshackle
Temple of the Feathered Serpent all wore the white
band; in number they seemed nearly as great as all
the rest, spilling out to front the Temple of the
Dragon, and even that of the Trickster. Where the
edges of this crowd met others, she could make out
small pockets of agitation, and once in a while see
shining spears moving to quell them.

"Should we sit with White Serpent's followers?" she
wondered. "We don't have the white bands, though."

"I could get us some," Purple Grackle said.

"I don't know. I have the child. What if some violence broke out between the two factions?" She rose
on tiptoe, trying to find what she was looking for. "Is
there any place for people who haven't taken sides?
Surely some must still be neutral."

Purple Grackle joined her and finally pointed.
"There, where I saw the open spaces, over in front of
Sun Mountain. That ought to be safe enough. It's well
away from where the Jaguar followers rub against the
White Serpent."

Grasping Shining Star more tightly, Spirits nodded.
"Good, then. Let's go there."

III

As they tried to make their way across the Grand
Concourse, it was heavy going. People were packed
nearly shoulder to shoulder; some stood in little
groups, gabbling almost lip to ear, while others, families or neighbors, had spread out small banquets
around smoky cookfires, and one had to nearly climb
over them. But nobody seemed to mind, and when
she tripped over somebody's outstretched leg, another
hand reached out of the mob and swiftly set her
aright again.

The smoky haze grew thicker as they penetrated
deeper into the Concourse, but Spirits didn't mind. It

felt wonderful to be in command of all her senses again; the overwhelming numb roar of the crowd now broke down into individual voices: here a woman with a high, lilting voice urged her small son to eat some of the broiled dog she'd just fished from the coals; there a young man, his face shiny with sweat, sang a song to a girl who stared at him with dark eyes as wide as plates; a melon seller had built a pile of his wares, and when he split one open for a customer, the shocking pink-orange meat caught her eye like a sudden torch. The sweet smell of the juicy flesh made her mouth fill with saliva, and she licked her lips.

A mindless surge swept her away from the fruit vendor. He vanished like a knot of wood tossed into a swift river. Shining Star squirmed against her, kicking out with his little legs. She kissed the top of his head and whispered, "Soon, baby. Sweet baby."

Off in the distance, near the center of the Concourse, the altars had been built again, and the priests who tended the fires glittered like gods themselves, the sun breaking upon their gorgeous robes in explosions of shattered light. There were singers there, trained acolytes of the temples, and their sweetly massed voices floated over the general din like softly swooping birds. More impromptu songfests had sprung up here and there, and these voices also drifted up to mingle in the general din.

She bumped against a very fat man who should have been a pillow, but felt instead like a large sack of rocks. He turned, curious, and she saw a large black mole on his right cheek, just under his eye. Several shiny black hairs grew out of its center. He smiled at her; many of his teeth were gone, and the rest mostly black stubs, but his happiness was infectious. He bobbed his head and said, "Here, Lady, let me push a path for you."

He was as good as his word, putting down his huge head and shoving forward on legs like freshly cut logs.

Bellowing happily, he made her a path of fifteen or twenty strides before he fell away, still laughing and motioning her forward.

She lost track of the time, caught up in the gaiety and joyous abandon of the feast day, and was surprised to find herself suddenly in an open space, green and still untrampled, edged by the ragged, thinning fringes of the general mob. Purple Grackle came panting up behind her, struggling with the basket she'd prepared for their journey.

"Here, Spirits," she said quickly. "Let me spread a cloth for you to sit on."

She was as good as her word. A moment later, Spirits sank gratefully to the ground, surprised at how weak she felt. She'd always been a strong girl, and this unaccustomed debility convinced her she would have to start getting out and around. Maybe, when Shining Star was a bit older, she could start going about the villages again. She would no longer be queen, of course, but she could still help.

"Ahh . . ." she murmured, and turned her face up to the sun. The smell of the still green grass filled her nostrils, far darker and richer than the dry scent of summer-burnt straw that filled much of the open spaces of the city. Of course, the Grand Concourse was watered by stone drains built long ago, to channel water from the holy cisterns; these were the living proof of the love the Gods held for the city. The year-round greening of the Concourse was even known throughout the far lands, and people journeyed for many hands of days to seek it out, to see the wonder with their own unbelieving eyes and then return home with tales of the power of the Gods of Great Head City.

Purple Grackle joined her, and began to unpack the rest of the basket. She'd brought ripe fruits from the gardens of the temple. By virtue of the hand and mind of White Serpent, these melons and mangoes and squashes were far larger and tastier than those available in the general markets, although more and more farmers were beginning to take to the White Priest's teachings on agricultural matters. Ever practical, those who tilled the earth were more than willing to overlook theological disputes in favor of better yields from their fields.

Now Shining Star began to cry softly. She unwrapped him a bit; his face was red. He was probably hot from the trip across the Concourse, and most likely hungry as well. She lifted him up and wrinkled her nose, sniffing to see if he would need new wrappings. Normally, she would have carried him naked, as any other child of his age, but she was afraid someone would notice his hands or his foot.

She shifted her shoulders to let her cloak fall open, and brought him to her breast. He subsided immediately, and she relaxed, feeling his soft lips moving, sucking gently at her teat.

The first thin screams were so few and so distant she didn't notice them. Purple Grackle had split open a particularly juicy mango, and broken it into pieces. They both ate, the sweet juice running down their chins. Their first hint that anything might be amiss was the way those folks camped nearby began to crane their necks and turn their heads all in the same direction, like a flock of curious birds.

"What's going on, I wonder?" Spirits said. From her seated position she couldn't see anything, but she was so comfortable she had no intention of moving.

"They must be starting the rituals on the high altars," Purple Grackle said.

"No, I don't think so. Everybody's looking in the opposite direction. Toward the north, where the White Temple and the courts are."

Both women stared in that direction. They could sense without seeing that the crowds were energized; it was like watching the edges of a lake, when the water was disturbed in the center. And the noise of the throng had changed; they heard an undertone, a deep mutter beneath the general sounds. Purple Grackle raised her head suddenly.

"What's that?"

Spirits felt a growing sensation of dread, and a premonition of danger. She stood up, gathering Shining Star to her. She made sure he was so tightly wrapped it was hard to tell he was an infant.

"I think it's screaming," she said.

Both women stood frozen for a long moment, their eyes still, heads slightly cocked, listening. Indeed, in the distance there was a chorus now, high, thin, and wavering, but growing constant. A fog of terror.

"Let's get out of here," Spirits said suddenly. "Not toward the center. We'll go back this way, get beyond the Concourse to the outer city. It should be safe there."

Purple Grackle nodded as she stooped and began to gather up their things.

"No. Leave it. We don't have time, I think."

Together, they began to walk across the cleared space where they'd been sitting, away from the still unseen disturbances nearer the center. But as they walked, behind them the edges of the crowd suddenly surged. The disturbance had grown, and now was moving the entire mass of the crowd like waves lapping farther and farther up the beach. A few ragged tendrils overtook them, men with terror-widened eyes running blindly, looking back over their shoulders, women trailing cloaks, their breath harsh in their throats. And children, pale and no longer laughing, running to keep up with their parents.

"Hurry," Spirits said sharply. They'd been walking quickly. Now they broke into a jog, Spirits trying to keep Shining Star safe, though something of the atmosphere must have reached him, for he began to wail.

They thought they would make it, but as they ap-

proached the thin line of merrymakers, now beginning
to scatter in alarm, on the far side of the open space,
another force broke through.

People shrieked as heavy spear butts slashed and
pummeled a path for a squad of Jaguar soldiers, four
hands strong. The soldiers were large men; she saw
immediately they weren't from the new recruits, but
grizzled, battered veterans of both her husband's and
his father's wars. Their faces were set, their eyes glowing with dark battle lust, their teeth set in white snarls.
They clubbed everything in their way, viciously and
without mercy: men, women, even small children. She
saw a little boy fall, blood spurting from the front of
his face.

"Oh, no . . ." she breathed.

But much as she wanted to go to the child's aid, it
would put her directly in the path of the soldiers—
and her first goal was to keep Shining Star safe. She
began to run, dashing off at an angle to their path of
advance; she was dimly aware of Purple Grackle at
her side, panting like a dog in the sun, but she could
see they would make it all right. Then disaster overtook them.

The main mass of the crowd to their rear, in full
panic as whatever had happened in its center now
pushed outward to the edges, abruptly *heaved*. In a
moment they were engulfed by screaming, brawling
figures, and then the shock of the advancing Jaguar
troopers smashed in from the other side, and blood
began to flow in rivers onto the green grass.

A man fleeing for his life smashed into her back,
and they both went down in a tangle. Somehow she
kept Shining Star firmly against her chest, but at the
cost of taking the fall without her hands to cushion
the blow. White fire exploded in her left shoulder and
up the ladder of her ribs on that side where the man
had struck her.

She got to her knees, surrounded by a forest of

pistoning legs, and then, almost on top of her, she
felt the iron tread of the Jaguar soldiers, relentlessly
advancing on a wave of blood and screams. Their
spears were down now, the sharp points glittering no
longer, for they were dipped in crimson. Then she saw
a horrible thing; one of the troopers stood over a thin,
middle-aged man who had fallen, stunned; the soldier
looked down at him with no expression on his face,
then reversed his spear, raised the shaft high over his
head, and brought the stony point down with all his
force.

Thank the Gods her head was plain, with nothing
to mark her as part of one faction or the other. She
flung herself around, looking for Purple Grackle, but
could see her nowhere. Then another heavy blow took
her in the side, as a fat woman keening a continuous
wail of horror, tripped over her and fell like a bag of
rocks. Spirits felt herself fall again, and this time she
didn't try to get up. The woman who'd struck her was
evidently knocked senseless by the force of her tum-
ble, for she lay unmoving, pinning Spirits's lower body
to the ground. And there was no time left; the Jaguar
soldiers were wearing only clouts and hardened
leather breast plates; she could see one hairy leg only
a couple of paces away.

Mouthing a prayer to the White God, she folded
herself like a snail around Shining Star's tiny form,
closed her eyes, and waited to feel the spear thrust
that would end her life. A heavy foot tramped down,
and she smelled the sudden fragrance of amaranth, its
purple flowers crushed into the grass.

CHAPTER EIGHTEEN

I

White Serpent Hawk awakened that morning with a sense of happy anticipation. The day had dawned clear as the eye of a cat. Sunlight poured through his open curtains onto the foot of his simple bed. He lay stretching and yawning for a moment, then sat up and blinked away the remnants of sleep.

Beyond his windows, in a clump of gumbo-limbo trees, whose branches dripped a shower of small white flowers, a flock of parrots had taken rest; they flapped their wings and squawked at each other, an ever moving cloud of jeweled colors amongst the dark green, multilobed leaves.

Somebody was grilling corncakes nearby, and his mouth began to water. He stood up and draped himself in the simple white robe that lay across the bottom of his bed. He stretched one more time, as the last of his dreams faded into the warm light of the morning.

For once his sleep had not been much disturbed. The endless vistas of the First World, where the rules were different, the ages long, and the Two-In-One ruled eternally from Its silent mountain throne, were a constant ache to him. From there he had come, and to there he would one day return, when his destiny here was ended. Yet it was no help to return to that place in his dreams, for he sought understanding here, in the Middle World, and none of that was offered in his long home. It was why he'd left it. At least, that was what he thought. It was different, visiting the First World in dreams; everything that had been familiar was somehow separate, and he was locked away from it.

Today began the Harvest Festival; and in his dream he'd seen an omen. Today, perhaps, Spirits would wake from her own dream and return to the land of the living. He had seen her soul in the First World, wandering lost, a dim shadow, and had been amazed to find it there. But when he'd approached it, he'd felt the breath of the Two on his shoulders, a warning, and he'd turned away.

But what had the Two to do with Spirits Walking Woman? The mere fact he'd been given the vision had to mean something. He sighed heavily. It was hard being a man, and remembering having been a God.

He shook himself, ran long fingers through his copper-golden hair, and left his chamber. There was nothing to distinguish his own room from any of the other priests' cubbyholes; in his temple, all who served the God were equal in their earthly treasure. He had set it that way from the beginning, lest the priests themselves become corrupted by the lust for earthly wealth and pleasure. As had many in the temples of his brothers, sad to say.

He turned left and made his way out the back of the temple, to a large open area where many women were busy grinding corn between the *mano* stones they worked back and forth on the larger, flat surfaces called *metates*. These simple implements, made of the dark holy stone, had to be imported all the way from Holy Stone City, and were very valuable. And since even the poorest of farmers in the villages had to eat, sometimes they had to mortgage their children to the dealers in order to purchase what they needed. It was a practice he meant to change; as his temple grew richer, he intended to import the stones himself, and give them to his followers. It was an idea that would no doubt earn him even more enemies among the other temple priesthoods, some of whom made a great deal of wealth out of the trade.

In the meantime, he allowed those of his acolytes who didn't possess the stones to come here and grind their daily bread; their faces, shining with gratitude, watched him like sunflowers as he walked among them, greeting each woman and child by name. The sound of their happy contentment was a soft, pleasing buzz in his ears.

"Lord," one woman said, beaming up at him from where she rocked her *mano* tirelessly back and forth, her broad shoulders flexing in the sun, "today is the Festival of the Harvest. How should we sacrifice to the God?"

He smiled down at her. One of her children, a boy of four or five turnings of the seasons, squatted next to her, watching the shower of cornmeal that flew from her work.

"We have built our altar on the Concourse, near our temple," he said. "We have much fruit, good grain, fine fish. And lizards, too. The God will be pleased. I am certain of it."

But her broad forehead wrinkled. "You will not go on the Great Altar in the center of the Concourse, with the others?"

He shook his head. "They do not want me, mother," he said. "And I do not want them. Human flesh will smoke on their altars, and that is a sin in the eyes of the God. But we will be there, though apart. That way the Four will at least be present, if not together."

He could tell she was troubled by this. He preached to them that there must be a balance among the Four, and he knew that to her this arrangement seemed out of shape, somehow wrong. But he didn't wish to plague her with his own troubles, and so he patted her shoulder and said, "It will be a good time, mother. Don't worry."

She nodded, then broke into a crack-toothed smile. She trusted him; sometimes he felt the weight of their trust as an unbearable burden, for he knew the end of his destiny—and theirs. But what could he do? Only what he did, and pray to the Two that it would be enough. After the end of an age, another age always followed.

For some strange reason, as he moved away from the woman and deeper into the courtyard, he thought of Spirits again. She had been much on his mind of late, particularly since she'd sunk into a kind of malign stupor which, even though he'd exercised all his mortal powers, he'd been unable to relieve. He supposed it was the shock of all that had occurred to her; the High King had done great evil, but she had faced the consequences. Bravely, it seemed to him; nor was he blind to his own feelings. He was a man, and she a woman, and his manhood had been both a test and a fulfillment. He'd wanted to know why the children of the Middle World did as they did, defying the Gods or serving Them, but never constant either way. Now the itching in his loins told him one answer; this great act of life and love given by the Two to mortal men and women was both the greatest of pleasures and the most evil of curses.

He grimaced, then shook his head. Spirits Walking Woman was well named; her spirit did indeed, it seemed, go walking. Even unto the First World. What did it mean?

White Serpent put it out of his mind. He embarked on his usual morning tour of the temple grounds, speaking to the artisans, the potters hard at work, the weavers and the gardeners. He paused to watch one old man carefully drill out the center hole of a tiny serpentine bead no larger than a pea. He bent to look; the exquisite carving on the tiny thing winked back at him. He had taught this man how to do this sort of work. Others had learned as well; now the jewelry and pottery of Great Head City was famed throughout all the lands, from the dry highlands far to the north, to the impenetrable mountain jungles of the south.

Even as he smiled at the artist, a pang of grief smote him. Why couldn't they learn? Out of their own hands and their own fields could come wealth far greater than they could take by force of arms. But so many of them couldn't see that; they'd rather send out their brutal soldiers, and burn their captives on stinking altars, as if that would feed their children and make their city safe.

He stood up and looked around, and his grief lessened. Many did see the truth; some were here, and others scattered throughout the city and the villages beyond. Still a minority, but growing. Yet even that disturbed him; for now his followers brawled with those of the other Gods, and blood flowed on the streets and paths, and stained the dust. He taught against it, and told them to forswear violence, and convert by example. But how could he counsel a man to remain at peace when thugs and bullies attacked not only him but his family?

The balance was broken. That was what he'd hoped to avoid; one path to destiny maintained the balance among the Four, and though an age might still pass away, it would do so in peace and glory, and be the foundation stone for an even greater one to follow. This was what he'd hoped to foster, a rebuilding of the balance. Instead, it seemed he'd shattered it. Could he make good his mistake? He didn't know. That was hidden from him.

Thus White Serpent Hawk's thoughts were both cheerful and clouded as he led his priests down from the temple toward the temporary wooden altar they'd built on the green near the edge of the Concourse. There was no stone on it, but it was beautifully carved of fine dark wood, with a wide stairway leading up to a broad space on the top.

Escorted by his fellows, he ascended the stairway, the air around him filled with the appreciative murmurs—even some cheers—from those who followed his ways.

He looked out over them from his perch well above the top of their heads. Men, women, children, all of them in plain white robes, all wearing the white headband. He took a deep breath and felt his lungs fill with smoky air; already, the stench of that which should not burn was drifting in greasy clouds across the Concourse. His eyes burned from it. He tried to take comfort from the numbers of his followers; they were many, and were a testament to the success of his own teachings.

But when he shaded his eyes and looked beyond, to the length of the Concourse itself, he could see the white patch of his acolytes was only the smaller portion of the vastness of the crowd. Enough to break the balance, but not enough to restore it, certainly not by force of arms, even if he would sanction such a thing.

Overhead, the sun gleamed through the haze that rose up to it, smokefires of sacrifice, each in its own way a tribute to a God, and thanks for a good harvest to come. Now his followers were on their feet, singing and clapping. He shook his head slightly, as if coming out of a trance. One of his priests touched him gently on the elbow.

"We should begin, Lord," he whispered.

"Yes," White Serpent Hawk agreed. Piled about the altars were mounds of fruits and vegetables. Now, the other priests began to heap these onto smoking char pits burned into the top of the broad wooden altar. These fires had already been stoked; clouds of aro-

matic smoke immediately arose, to further cheers and
cries of joy.

It was a clean, fresh smell, unlike the abominations
that wafted up from the great altars in the center of
the Concourse. But cheers came from these, too, and
when he glanced over, he thought he saw the red wink
of fresh blood spurting.

He raised a fine lizard, one as long as his arm. It
squirmed energetically in his hands. The God must
have meat and blood, but not that from human bones.
Such was the old way, which the new priests, in their
passion for human blood, had forsaken.

He carried the beast to the altar and slit its throat
with a knife another priest held ready. Blood gushed
onto white coals; another gout of smoke rose up; he
nodded, and went on with the sacrifice, beginning the
great chants to the Feathered Serpent, that he bring
His holy lightnings, from which He took his name, to
water the fields just now planted.

The rituals were long and complicated; he breathed
deep of the pipe of dreams, and felt himself begin to
slip away, his mind already reeling into the First
World. Out of the corner of his eye, he saw a flash of
movement in the crowd, as if somebody had dropped
a large pebble into an already roiled pond. A moment
later, the screams began.

III

Her eyes screwed tightly shut, Spirits felt the earth
shake around her as the Jaguar soldiers trampled over
her. The fat woman grunted softly as a spear pierced
her side, and Spirits shuddered as the hot gush flooded
over her. Her nostrils quivered at the bitter copper
smell of fresh blood. Then the fighting was beyond
her, a line of death crunching its way toward the center of the crowd. She remained motionless for a time,
then slowly opened her eyes.

It took her several moments to push the dead woman off her. The woman's eyes were open, her mouth frozen in the death rictus. Slowly, she climbed to her knees. The air was thick with blinding smoke. She began to cough; her eyes watered and she wiped them on the hem of her cloak. Her one thought was to get her child away before some even more dreadful calamity overtook them.

For a moment her mind whirled. Then she remembered. They'd almost reached the edge of the Concourse, and safety. She staggered to her feet, ignoring Shining Star's frantic wails. The rise of the edge must be . . . that way. Gasping and grunting, she set off.

It seemed as if it took forever. Her legs were leaden beneath her, but finally the earth began to slope upward. She forced herself to climb, and moaned as she felt her strength begin to fail.

She made the last few strides on energy she never knew she had. When she reached the top, the air was clearer. The heavier smoke seemed to have filled the amphitheater of the Concourse like soup in a bowl. She turned and looked back; all that was visible now were shadowy figures heaving and trampling in the greasy fog. The sound of screams drowned out everything else.

The horror of the scene below froze her with terror. How many were dead or dying down there? As she stood, transfixed and staring, a wind began to come off the river, and sweep the smoke away. Now she saw the extent of the disaster. In the center of the concourse, the ground was empty around the High Altar. Glittering priests lined the edges of the platform, peering off toward the north. Around the base of the altar a squad of Jaguar soldiers, their spears pointed outward, guarded them from attack. But none was coming in their direction. The slaughter was far away, around the smaller altar of the Feathered Serpent.

White Serpent Hawk!

She had her hand shading her eyes, desperately trying to make out what was happening, when Purple Grackle appeared as if by magic beside her.

"Lady," she gasped. "Thank the Gods! I feared you were dead!"

"No, I'm all right." Spirits glanced down, saw that a large, purple bruise was spreading across the side of Purple Grackle's face, and blood leaked from the side of her mouth.

"Oh, dear, are you hurt? Here, let me look."

She shifted the baby into the crook of her left arm and gently touched the bruise. Purple Grackle winced. "Open your mouth," Spirits said.

"It's nothing," Purple Grackle told her. "Somebody shoved me down, and I bit my tongue. It hurts like a demon, but I'll be all right. Lady, we have to get out of here! Come, give me the baby, and we'll be able to run faster."

But Spirits had turned back. Now, squinting, she could pick out figures clad in white on the top of the Feathered Serpent's altar. The mobs around its base ebbed and flowed like water in a stream; but tighter knots of movement, and the flashing of spears, showed her where the Jaguar soldiers cut through those human streams like sharp rocks. Once that throng had been all in white. Now it was mixed like salt and pepper, as followers of the other Gods brawled their way through it. Then she gasped. The altar itself, though no doubt sturdy enough, had never been built to resist the forces now slamming into it like waves against the shore.

As she watched it began to weave back and forth. The tiny white figures on top staggered, grasping for support. One was thrown into a still smoking altar, and knocked it over. Tiny red flames immediately began to lick across the top. Then, to her horror, the entire structure gave a huge jerk, fell sideways, and began to disintegrate. The priests on top fell off like stones from a tilted table, and vanished into the thrashing mob below.

"White Serpent," she said again, her fist across her mouth.

"Lady," Purple Grackle said urgently, *"come! We can't stay here, it isn't safe!"*

But Spirits's eyes were riveted to the place where she'd seen White Serpent fall. She thrust Shining Star at Purple Grackle. "Take him back to the temple. I'll be along when I can."

And with that, she plunged down the grassy verge, her handmaid's despairing wail ringing in her ears. A moment later she vanished, swallowed by the day that history would forever remember as the Great Blasphemy, or the Day of Slaughter.

IV

White Serpent Hawk, his mortal senses addled by the smoke he'd taken to open the way to the First World, staggered about the top of the altar platform, stunned by the ferocity of the slaughter below. Jaguar soldiers with stone faces and bloody spears slew anything they could touch; those who escaped them had to face bloodthirsty bands of men with rude clubs, followers of other Gods. The part of him still rational understood this was no accident; these brutes had come prepared for battle, unlike his own followers. Whose hand was behind it? As if from a dream, Smoking Mirror's features filled his mind . . .

He saw not only men but women and children struck down. The trampled grass around the altar became dark and sticky with blood; it mixed with the dust into a gruesome brown mud that stuck to anything it touched.

He reeled to the edge of the platform and peered over. His stomach churned at the butchery below. A great rage seized him then; he'd been almost through to the First World when this had begun. The door remained open; it would be a small step to go on through, and return with his weapons. There was nothing here that could stand up to the bolts of the Feathered Serpent, no, not even if his brother, the Jaguar, took the field with his white claws and shining fangs.

But even as that thought seized him, his own destiny replied and slammed shut the door. He moaned. He had never expected his mortality to become such a burden as this. His own people, faithful worshippers of the Peaceful God, dying like helpless flies.

"Oh, Mother-Father," he prayed. But there was no answer. "Forgive them," he groaned, but there was no reply to that, either. Nothing but the killing below, and his own mortal helplessness above.

Suddenly the wooden platform shivered, then jerked. He turned; one of the priests nearby stumbled into a still burning altar and screamed as the flesh on his right arm came away seared black. In his extremity he kicked over the altar. Now fire began to spread among his panicked fellows. Still dazed from the holy smoke he'd taken, White Serpent raised his arms and tried to shout some order into the screaming chaos. But nobody listened to him, and before he could go any farther, the entire structure, weakened by the buffets it had taken, lurched far to one side and began to fall apart, like a raft foundering in a wild and churning river.

He had only a moment's thought. Then he, too, toppled into the abyss waiting below. The earth rose up and struck him a mighty blow. After that, nothing but darkness.

As he sank into it, he thought it was the mortal death, and was almost grateful. For only in the dark beyond the stars could he hide the shame at what he had wrought.

V

By the time Spirits reached the area around the collapsed altar of the Feathered Serpent it was all over. A group of six Jaguar soldiers passed her going the other way, their faces grim yet somehow joyous. She shivered as their eyes passed over her, but they didn't stop.

Part of the altar was still burning. Rags of smoke drifted about her as she picked her way through the carnage; death was everywhere, grinning up at her from bloody lips already turning blue and cold, watching her from eyes wide and blank and staring.

Her gorge rose as she stepped over a little girl whose entrails spilled out onto the ground; the dead child still clasped a doll made of straw in her chubby little arms.

Finally she came to the wreckage of the altar. A tangle of bodies, limbs twisted, lay piled to one side. Not all here were dead; she heard moans of agony. Arms and legs twitched or shuddered; one hand, fingers clawed, waved like a grisly flower.

She began to pull bodies aside, searching for what she feared above all else. Her mind was numb. She couldn't face this, but somehow she would have to. If he were dead . . .

Grunting with effort, she shoved one already waxen corpse aside, and saw the familiar bronze gold glint of his hair. At first she thought her worst nightmare had come to pass, but when she put his head in her lap, he groaned, and his eyes flickered open.

Relief as golden as morning light poured into her, filling her heart and mind. He still lived! And until that moment she had not understood, or acknowledged, just what that meant to her. Suddenly, in the midst of the charnel pits, she felt the peace that passed all understanding. Her fingers trembled as she used the hem of her robe to wipe away the blood that covered his features. For a moment his blue eyes glowed up at her, and without thinking at all, she bent forward and brushed his lips with hers. Something more powerful than love passed between them as she touched his flesh—a need so strong it was all she could do to tear herself from him.

He tried to smile. His lips moved faintly. Then he sighed and closed his eyes again. But he lived.

He lived!

VI

When White Serpent finally returned fully to the land of the living, the first thing he heard was the sound of parrots. He lay with his eyes closed; sun beat on his eyelids, shooting painful sparks into his brain. His thoughts were a hopeless welter; he could remember little of what had happened. The holy smoke had already begun to work on his mind when the terrible shock of the riot and ensuing fall had blasted everything into darkness.

Somebody was humming softly. The sound was infinitely soothing. He smiled at it; as soon as he did this, he felt a cool, wet sensation on his forehead.

"So you're awake at last, are you?" the soft voice said. "Are you thirsty?"

He remembered the voice—and remembered something else as well. And it was with that memory he opened his eyes and saw her face bending over him, smiling but creased with concern, as he remembered it before. But she had been closer then.

He stared at her, trying to recapture that moment, and then he felt a rush of ecstasy, and an understanding so poignant he wanted to laugh and cry at the same time. A great mystery had been lifted for him, and she had been the one to brush aside the veil.

So this was love?

"Here," she said, withdrawing. And when her face

passed out of his vision, he felt a loss so strong he would cheerfully have thrown down his godhood and his destiny to reclaim what she had given to him. But he couldn't. He was what he was. His lips moved.

"What?" she said, returning with a cup full of water, deliciously beaded with condensation on its dark sides.

"Hard to be a man . . ." he murmured.

"Well, I should think so," she replied. "It's hard to be a woman, too. Here, let me tilt your head up." Gently she lifted him, and brought the rim of the cup to his lips. He drank greedily; the cool water was the most delicious thing he'd ever tasted. His parched mouth and throat soaked it up so quickly it was as if he drank the morning air.

"There, that's enough," she said, and took the cup away. "How are you feeling? Does your head hurt?"

He stared at her as if he'd never seen her before. In fact, that was exactly what he felt. She had been an object of pity to him, a good woman trapped in a terrible situation, and he'd done what he could to help her and her child. But something had changed between them. He wanted to reach out and stroke her cheek. He wanted to taste her lips again. He wanted to . . .

No. That was forbidden. But what sweet agony.

He shook his head, negating . . . what? He didn't know. But with the movement he did indeed feel pain, a blinding lance of it striking through his skull, sending up showers of sparks behind his eyes.

He gasped.

"Don't move your head." Her voice had sharpened. "You've got a lump on it the size of a melon. And you hurt your left arm, too."

He listened to this and thought, No more than I deserve. I should have died. It would have been fitting. And it would have ended this charade.

Spirits sat on the edge of his bed, gazing at him. "You'll get well again, White Serpent. Many healers have been here, and I have stayed by your side. And I will remain here until you are fit to leave your bed. Do you understand me?"

He started to nod, his heart pinioned by her beauty. But he caught himself before he could light the fire of agony again. Somehow it was enough that she would be here. He couldn't find it in himself to send her away. If anything, he yearned to pull her closer, to smother her with kisses, to wrap her in his arms.

What a terrible sweet gift love was. The Gods did not know it. They watched it without understanding. It was what he'd shackled himself with divine destiny to learn. How could he know it would sear him more deeply than any bolt he could ever launch from the heavens?

The Two had created everything, so It must understand. And how It must be laughing at him now.

"It was all my fault," he whispered. "I have broken the balance."

She stroked his brow. "We'll see," she said.

VII

They didn't all come together until two days after the catastrophe of the Harvest Ritual, and when they did, they met in secret.

Harvest Mountain and Green Water Woman came to the inner room of the Jaguar Temple by themselves, clad only in simple robes. Smoking Mirror greeted them. He had set out stools before his throne; a servant brought them honey corncakes and diluted pulque. When this was done, he sent everyone away, and closed the heavy cloth that sealed the door.

In the flickering light of the oil lamps scattered about, their eyes looked hollow in their faces; their expressions fearsome and hungry. The room smelled of stale smoke and ancient, damp rock.

"Well," Smoking Mirror said. "It didn't work. He

still lives. But we hurt him, I think; his body, and his temple as well."

Harvest Mountain nodded. "Almost ten hands of his followers died, and three of his highest priests. Another twenty hands injured. Some of them will die as well."

Smoking Mirror smiled at that. "He is in seclusion. What does Skull Breaker tell you about that?" He already knew; but he wanted the High King to feel the pain and rage again; he was easier to manipulate that way. His father, under stress, had gone cold as stone; Harvest Mountain tended to bubble like a volcano.

Nor did he disappoint now. He said, his voice a choked hiss: "The bitch my former wife tends him. She does not leave his rooms. Maybe she sleeps with him. She keeps their child there as well."

Smoking Mirror nodded, his features perfectly blank, though he was laughing inside.

"Have you spoken with your sister, Green Water Woman?" he asked.

She shook her head. She seemed calmer than the High King; Smoking Mirror sensed a good portion of his own chill inside her. A formidable woman. But that was all right. He had plans for a formidable woman.

"No," she said. "As the King says, she keeps to White Serpent's room. Her handmaid gossips with my girls, though. I hear a few things. The White Priest is recovering; but the rumor is his spirit was badly wounded by what happened. It is said he blames himself." She smiled grimly at that.

"He is a fool, then," Smoking Mirror replied. "But we already knew that. Never mind, he still lives, and his followers, too. Far too many of them. And I am sad to report the result of the . . . incident at the Harvest Ritual may have had some unforeseen effects."

Harvest Mountain nodded then, a bit more briskly

now the subject had moved away from his own shame. "Yes, Skull Breaker spoke of it. The slaughter polarized things; many who'd been wavering in one direction or the other tilted all the way over. More on the Feathered Serpent's side than ours, it appears. It was something we didn't plan for, and should have. The Jaguar soldiers were overly brutal. They frightened too many people. And the destruction of the Harvest Festival was a dire omen. Some of the people blame us for it."

"We weren't trying to win the hearts of his followers. We were trying to kill White Serpent," Smoking Mirror reminded him sharply.

"And we failed," Harvest Mountain shot back, equally astringent. "So what now? The man seems to have the luck of the Gods."

Smoking Mirror shrugged. "Remember, he claims to *be* a God."

"But he is not. He is a man," Harvest Mountain said. "A man with a wandering penis, in fact. How can the people believe in him when the evidence of his sin is right in front of their faces?"

Green Water broke in, her dark eyes sparkling, her lips parted over white teeth: "Don't you see, that *is* the problem? Perhaps the Gods favored us by saving his life. What if we'd succeeded? Perhaps others would have taken his place, made even stronger by his martyrdom. No, what we have to do is discredit *him*."

Smoking Mirror stared at Harvest Mountain. "She may have something there, brother."

Harvest Mountain slid a sideways glance at Green Water. He had not expected this from her, had not even intended to bring her to this meeting, but Smoking Mirror had asked for her to be present. He had complied, as much to see what the priest was up to as to obey his wishes.

"You may, indeed, Green Water. What else do you have to say?"

"If you want to destroy not just him but the beliefs he teaches, all those 'old ways' he prattles about, then it is better he lives. At least for a time. We can't do anything to discredit a dead man, but while he lives there are always possibilities."

"Yes," Smoking Mirror said. "And do you have any suggestions what those possibilities might be?"

She leaned back on her chair, stretching like a cat. "He preaches of his own purity. That he never addles his mind with pulque, nor does he break the vows of chastity he has taken before his God. And his followers believe him. That's why they accepted his story about my sister's son. And as long as they believe in him, we will fail, even if we kill him."

"Yes, yes. That's plain enough. But what can we do?"

"My maids tell me that White Serpent's spirits are very low. He is saying that it is all his fault for what happened at the Harvest Festival. That he has caused the shattering of the balance among the Gods, and that he will preach no more in the streets or the temple."

Harvest Mountain inhaled sharply. "But that's exactly what we want. He is withdrawing. He will no longer oppose me. That's the best news I've heard yet!"

"Is it?" Smoking Mirror asked. "She is right, brother. As long as he lives, his people will remember his teachings and follow them. And they will oppose you. Remember, you take their husbands and sons for your army, and you tax them heavily to pay for it. Why wouldn't they want to oppose you? Your way is hard for them."

Harvest Mountain bristled. "Do you oppose me, too?"

"No, of course not."

"The people don't understand. What do you think protects this city, if not their spears? If the barbarians and nomads don't fear us, they will roll over us like the waves of the sea. And the Gods must be fed. If the sacrifices don't come from the captives my army takes, then where will they come from?" He shook his head. "The people are fools. They don't even understand what they must have for their own survival. It is why the Gods set Kings over them, to take care of them and lead them to glory."

Smoking Mirror nodded judiciously. "Of course, Lord. I agree with you. I just point out how some of the people must feel. And you need to understand that, if you are to lead them and destroy your enemies."

Harvest Mountain subsided. "Well, then." He turned back to Green Water Woman. "I'm sorry. Would you go on with what you were saying?"

"Smoking Mirror has the right of this, Lord. As long as White Serpent lives undefiled, or even dies that way, he is your potent enemy. But if we can show the people what he really is, in such a way they must believe their own eyes, then we can overthrow him—and his teachings—forever."

"Ah. And you have some thoughts on the matter?"

"Yes, Lords, I do. I have met one of the artists of White Serpent's temple. He is . . . attracted to me. He is also in charge of the decoration of the new buildings, and he is skilled in many other things. The making of fine robes, for instance. His name is Brush Weaver . . ."

VIII

"Where did you find him?" Spirits asked.

Purple Grackle, the bruise on her face turning a livid plum-yellow, leaned forward to whisper, "He was living wherever he could. Stealing food from the barrows. He looked very hungry."

Spirits stood just outside White Serpent's door. Purple Grackle thought she looked very tired; the lines in her face had not been there before. And no wonder; she had not slept since she and a straggling band of followers had carried the High Priest to his tiny room from the carnage on the Concourse. She glanced toward the door curtain and said, "How is . . . ?"

Spirits smiled. "He's better. He's awake now. But he needs a great deal of rest."

"Oh, that's wonderful!" Purple Grackle's dark eyes shone with relief. She'd been terribly worried that White Serpent would die, leaving no protection at all for either herself or her mistress.

"Yes," Spirits replied. "We must all pray to the Feathered Serpent." Then, as was her wont, turning coldly practical, she said, "Is he strong enough?"

"To make it through the jungle? Yes, Lady, I think so."

"Well, it's the best thing for him. You say he isn't willing to stay here in the temple, and there isn't anything else for him in the city. Best to send him home, and make him useful at the same time. Bring him to me."

Purple Grackle bobbed, turned around and walked away, only to return a short time later tugging a young boy along beside her.

"Laughing Monkey, thank you for coming to see me," Spirits said. She reached out and ruffled his dark hair. "You look hungry."

His mobile features convulsed in a spasm of delight. "Lady! I'm so glad—I'd heard rumors . . ."

"Yes, I'm sure you did. But I need you now. Do you remember what you promised my mother, the Queen? To do whatever I asked you to?"

He nodded his head eagerly. "Yes, Lady. Of course. What do you want me to do?"

"I want you to go back to Holy Stone City, and tell my mother what has happened. Let me explain it to you, so you have it right."

She pulled him aside and began to whisper rapidly in his ear. He listened intently, nodding once or twice. When they were done, he stepped away and dropped to his knees in a formal bow.

"Oh, get up. That's not necessary. I'm not a queen anymore."

"But you're still a princess," he reminded her, grinning.

She smiled in return at the truth of it. "Purple Grackle will see that you have food. Will you be all right?"

He nodded, suddenly serious. "Yes, Lady. Remember, I came that way once already."

"And so you did," she agreed. "Very well. Off with you, then. Go with Purple Grackle."

As she watched them vanish round a corner, she knew she'd done what she could. If Queen Blue Parrot received her warnings in time, perhaps something might yet be done. If nothing else, Harvest Mountain would not come on a city undefended and unprepared. She knew that even her husband feared the strength of Holy Stone City and its fastness in the high rocks.

"Spirits . . . ?"

The voice was low and weak, and to her ears, utterly irresistible. She turned. "Yes, White Serpent. I'm coming."

CHAPTER NINETEEN

I

Underneath everything he was terrified. She could tell from the way he twitched like a frightened rabbit when she wrapped her fingers around his snake. *That,* at least, was responding properly. It felt hot and hard in her palm, and jerked each time she stroked it.

But despite his terror, he was too ready. His body wasn't paying any attention to his mind. She had learned her craft well, and knew better than to let him spurt before she was ready. She'd discovered that what she did was almost like magic to some men. They were pigs, of course, used to plunging into any woman until their juice exploded. And the women took it, lying on their backs, as unmoving as a dead fish. So when such men found a woman like her, who actually knew how to arouse them, it was a revelation. Sometimes a dark revelation.

"Shhh . . ." she soothed. "Relax, just lie back and let me . . ."

His eyes, in the moonlight that flooded her chamber, glistened white in the dim glow of a single lamp. His teeth were bared, his breath rasping in his throat. She knew he wanted to stop himself; he understood who she was. Probably he imagined himself being disemboweled by the High King for trespassing on the royal prerogatives. But he couldn't help himself. He had tasted her fire and wanted more. Wanted it so badly he would do anything to have it, and have it again . . .

She stretched out the act for a long time, teasing him, bringing him right to a peak and then backing off, until she felt herself begin to respond. Then she used him with no more thought than she would have given to any slave, and when she was done, she slid away from him, disgusted at his naked, slobbering lust.

"Brush Weaver," she said, when his breathing had subsided, and the sweat on his skin had turned cold and slimy, "you are a great artist. Everybody says so."

After a moment of silence, he grunted softly. She could tell he wanted to get up, run away, before anybody discovered them together. His fear delighted her. What a sense of power!

"What?" she whispered, running her fingernails across his slickened chest. He jumped again, and she smiled a secret smile. Men were so easy, if you knew what to do with them.

"Yes . . ." The word was strangled, as if he had to choke it out.

"Do you love me?" She almost laughed out loud as she said it, but managed to keep her face straight. He had turned and was looking at her, his mouth half open, his eyes wide and fearful.

"Ye . . . yes . . ." he sputtered.

"Good. I want you to do something for me. Can you make me a robe, the finest robe anybody has ever seen? It can't be anything ordinary. Nothing that you could buy, or that my women could make. Are you good enough to do that?"

This challenge to his artistic skills broke through his fear and lust as nothing else could have. He hitched himself up on one elbow. "Of course I can. Is it for you?"

She scraped his chest again. "No, my darling, it is for someone else. A gift . . ."

He thought about it. "I will need many things. Expensive things."

"Certainly. Spend what is necessary. I will give you what you need before you leave tonight."

His eyes darted from hers. "How soon do you want this . . . gift?"

She considered. "Three hands of days should be sufficient. When the moon has grown horns."

He nodded.

She lay back. After a while she turned and touched him again. He was limp and wet. He didn't want to. But his body did. It wanted her more than anything in the world.

She smiled in the darkness, waiting.

II

As it turned out, Brush Weaver, chief artisan of the Temple of the Feathered Serpent, was as good as his word. Green Water Woman carried the heavy package carefully as she walked alone down the rear of the royal pavilions, skirted the base of Sun Mountain, and finally reached the precincts of the Jaguar Temple. The night was quiet; the horned moon, two sharp points thrust upwards, cast little light. It didn't matter. By now she knew the way.

Smoking Mirror awaited her in a secluded spot near the rear of the temple. He was alone. They both preferred it that way. Together they entered his throne room, as always a chamber of darkly dancing shadows from the many lamps and torches.

She unrolled the package. In the flickering light it was as if she'd opened the skin of a God. Smoking Mirror drew in his breath sharply.

"It's beautiful," he finally said. He reached out one hand and stroked it gently. "I've never seen anything like it."

Green Water nodded. She'd thought so, too, but was pleased to see Smoking Mirror shared her opinion. In a way, it was almost a shame this example of Brush Weaver's great artistry must be wasted on . . . But no matter. Perhaps later she could commission another such garment for herself. The squirming, sex-crazed little artisan had a deeper talent than she'd imagined.

"Well? Do you think it will work?" she said at last.

Smoking Mirror tugged thoughtfully on his lower lip. Finally he said, "If it won't, I can't imagine what will." He examined it another long moment, then gestured for her to roll it back up.

"It will be sufficient if the rest is properly prepared. And that we will see to tonight, sister. Are you ready?"

She had been studiously ignoring what was tied to the top of the altar throne at the end of the chamber. Now it began to writhe, though because of the gag cruelly tied in its mouth, the sacrifice could not speak. Later, she knew, they would take out the gag, for screams were always welcome in the ears of the Lord Jaguar.

The High Priest moved toward the altar and picked up a small pot. "I have brewed this using the secret skills. Mixed with pulque, he won't be able to taste it, but it will addle him immediately." He turned and showed her the pot.

She bent forward and sniffed it. There was no odor; it might have been faintly cloudy water. There was a faint oily sheen on the top of it. She nodded, then reached under her robe to withdraw a small clay bottle, stoppered with a bit of wood.

"I got this from one of the village root women,"

she said. Then she told him what she proposed to do with it.

His smile flashed in the gloom. "You are my priestess now, Green Water, sworn to the God. Do you remember it?"

"Yes."

"Very well. Then you must assist me. These potions of ours must be blessed by the God Himself. And He must find us pleasing. I have prepared a gift for Him to assure His aid in our quest."

The man on the altar throne strained against his bonds. To no avail. His eyes rolled like pale stones in the gloom. She felt warmth flower in her belly at the sight. There were more ways than one to make a man scream.

"Yes, brother," she whispered. "I will do my part."

Together, they turned toward the altar. And the sacrifice.

III

It had been nearly a moon since the disaster on the Grand Concourse. White Serpent's wounds were healed; only a few faded patches on his once golden face revealed where bruises had been. His left arm, badly sprained, now seemed as strong as his right. Physically, he had recovered, or as near to it as Spirits could tell. But he had not left his bed yet.

As was her usual habit, she woke him in the morning, bustling into the room with a sunny smile, though the day, well into the rainy season, was cool and overcast; the air smelled heavy and tingling, as if pregnant with storm. Only a single parrot sat in the branches beyond the window, and it was quiet, its head tucked under its wing. It looked forlorn; even its normally jewel-bright colors were dulled in the gloomy light.

As always, she found him awake. Sometimes she

wondered if he slept at all. He lay on his back, propped on a mound of pillows, covered with a white sheet. He wore only a clout; his broad chest, now pale instead of bronze, rose above the hem of the cloth. His arms and hands rested at his sides, unmoving. His face was silent, still, waxen; he gazed into the distance, looking at nothing she could see. The miasma of depression in the room was so thick she thought she could smell it: sharp, bitter, the odor of failure. The smell of death.

She kept her smile pasted on her lips, though sometimes it was all she could do to keep herself from bursting into tears. What she really wanted to do was climb into the bed with him, and offer him her warmth. She might even have tried to do so. But she knew what would happen.

"White Serpent?" she said softly. "I've brought you your morning porridge."

She settled the tray on his bed. The room was small; she'd had a plain wooden stool brought in, so she could sit with him. As he'd recovered from his physical injuries, she'd gradually dismissed those of his followers who wanted to serve him. She could sense what he wanted, and get it for him before he even asked. And he seemed aware of what she did; he would offer her a grateful smile every now and then, but little else.

What tore at her was not the little acts of practicality, of kindness, she gave him—yes, he wanted those, and she was happy to be able to offer them—but that she knew what he needed. And she couldn't give it to him, because he wouldn't take it.

She wondered how long this would go on. The temple was in evil straits now, drifting with no High Priest at the helm. And most of the other senior priests had perished in the holocaust of the altar on the day of the Harvest Ritual.

Some time he will have to awaken, she told herself.

His people need him, and he can't deny them forever.
It isn't in him. But he is still terribly injured inside,
and needs more healing. I can help him here. And
perhaps I can help his temple, too.

She settled herself on the stool and smoothed her
robe, as he absently raised the bowl of gruel to his
lips. He sipped, wrinkled his lips, and murmured,
"Ah. Good."

She waited until he had drained the bowl, then
swiftly whisked away the tray and set it outside the
door. "Lord," she said, her voice hesitant, "I'd like to
discuss something with you, if I may."

He winced, and seemed not to hear her. She waited
for him to reply, but he slowly turned his face away
from her, toward the wall. Her heart gave an aching
beat.

"It's about the temple. We have to do something."

His head didn't stir, but he raised his right hand,
then let it fall in a gesture of denial. Or despair.

"The temple?" he said finally. His voice was a
parched whisper, weak as a dry breeze. "What of it?"

She told him how things were, that the artisans were
downhearted, and worked less without him to guide
them. How the gardeners neglected putting down
straw and dung along their rows. How some of the
jewel makers had left the temple precincts to work
and sell their wares elsewhere. Some had even left the
city entirely. And, finally, how work on the renovation
of the temple had ground nearly to a halt. Only Brush
Weaver, the chief painter, still appeared to work on
his murals every day. And something was wrong with
him, too, a furtiveness she sensed but could not
decipher.

He heard her out, or at least didn't interrupt her.
At times it was hard to tell if he actually listened or
not. Sometimes it seemed that he only pulled farther
away from her, as if he were diminishing, growing
smaller right there in front of her eyes.

After she'd finished, she waited. He said nothing.

"Lord?" she ventured.

He sighed. "It's all over anyway," he said. "I ruined it. I broke the balance, and now all will pay the price for my sins. I thought to help. But all I brought was destruction."

She stared at him. Suddenly a sharp flame of anger flared up inside her. What was wrong with him? He was a good man; why was he doing this to himself? To her? To *everybody* who needed him, now more than ever.

Her lips tightened. Maybe there was still hope, if she could just hold everything together until whatever demons that gnawed at him finally had their fill and left him in peace. Sometimes she wondered if there would be anything left of him after that, but—no, better not to think that way. It was, for one thing, impractical. Hopelessness had never appealed to her, not where even the slightest hope remained.

"If you would give me leave, Lord, I could order things in the temple. I can't take your place, of course, but I can see to the everyday things . . ."

He made a sound. With his face turned away, it was hard to tell, but it might have been a sob. She yearned to go to him, to offer him greater comfort than he would take, but instead simply waited. She'd said what was needed. Now it was up to him.

Somehow he seemed to sense this, for he turned back and looked at her. His blue gaze had faded, and now it glistened with unshed tears.

"Spirits . . . my dearest."

How she thrilled to hear those words!

His smile was weak, but at least it was a smile. "I can't . . . I'm not . . ."

"Hush, Lord. I understand."

"Do you?"

She stared at him. "It isn't your fault, White Serpent. You are a good man."

He sighed. "That is the trouble, Spirits. That is my agony, that I am a man. It is so hard to be a man, did you know it?"

She nodded. She'd told him once it was hard to be a woman, too. But she didn't think this was precisely what he meant. He was talking about something beyond her understanding, wide and deep and dark. Like a black river he would have to find his own way across.

"Lord, you will be better soon. But your people need you, need your teachings. If you aren't strong enough for that right now, at least I can see that the temple is here for them."

His lips moved when she spoke of the people and their need for him, but nothing came out. Once again he raised his hand, then let it fall.

"You are better than I am, dearest," he said at last. "I name you my High Priestess. Go and do what is necessary. Help my people." He paused. "Someday I may return to you. But not yet."

She nodded. She had what she'd come for. Life could be awful, and love even worse. But she would do what she could, while she could and, beyond that, trust to hope and the Gods.

"Yes, Lord," she said. "And when you do come back, I will be here. Waiting for you."

He glanced at her, nodded, but said no more.

IV

It was raining when one of the temple acolytes found Spirits in the back courtyard and told her she had a visitor. With the onset of the rainy season, she had ordered that temporary shelters be erected for the women who wished to use the temple *metates* to grind their maize, and for the artisans who preferred to work out-of-doors.

"Oh, who is it?" she asked. The acolyte, a youth

barely into his manhood, blushed. "A great lady," he mumbled.

"Well, then. Where is she?"

"In the altar chamber," he said.

She nodded, wondering what great lady would visit her now. "Well, then. Let's go and greet her." With that, she strode briskly toward the main temple pavilion, leaving the boy behind.

As usual, the main chamber of the temple, being the crossroads of the central pavilion, was busy. Acolytes and priests hurried about, and a team of artists under Brush Weaver's direction was putting finishing touches on the new decorations for the great wooden altar.

At first she didn't see her. Then, standing in the corner, a plainly dressed woman called out, "Sister! Over here."

Green Water's hair was heavy with damp, and her cloak smelled of rain. Otherwise, she was just as Spirits remembered her, her head held proudly back, her eyes glittering.

"Sister!" Spirits cried. "I am so glad to see you!"

The two women hugged. Green Water pushed her away, then held her at arm's length, peering at her face. "You look fine, sister," she said. "Motherhood becomes you."

Spirits made a brushing motion. "I'm older, that's all. And I'm still glad to see you." She paused. "Is it all right . . . ?"

"For me to be here? I think so. You guessed that's why I didn't visit sooner?"

Spirits sighed. "Yes, of course I did. And I've wanted so much for a chance to thank you for what you did. Saving my life, and Shining Star's."

Green Water tilted her head. "How is he?"

"Oh, he's fine. Very healthy." She looked around. "Come, dear, let's go to my room. We'll have some tea. You look like you could use a bit of drying out."

"You knew what I did?"

"Oh, yes. Purple Grackle thought I should hate you for it, but I understood. How else could you save my life, except to do what you did?"

Green Water nodded, her eyes serious. "I wasn't sure I could do it. He wanted to kill you, just as he . . ." She shook her head. "We won't talk about that. I convinced him it was wiser to let you go."

"No, we won't talk about it, then. But we must have some pleasant things to discuss, don't you think? Come, let me serve you tea and some fresh honey cakes. The ones they make here are the best I've ever tasted."

"Yes," Green Water said, her smile broadening. "Let's do that."

Arm in arm, the two women walked away. Purple Grackle came into the main chamber just then and saw them leaving. A worried look on her face, she hurried to follow.

V

White Serpent dozed, lulled by the monotonous patter of rain on the thatch above his head. At first he didn't realize somebody had entered his chamber—somebody other than Spirits. But it was the unfamiliarity of the steps that woke him.

"Eh . . . what? Who . . . ?"

Smoking Mirror set down his burden and smiled. "Good day, brother. You're looking better than I expected to find you."

Smoking Mirror's heavy scent, redolent of arcane herbs and his own sharp body odor, filled the room. White Serpent, still groggy, pushed himself up on his elbows and wrinkled his nose. Smoking Mirror busied himself with the large package he was now unwrapping.

White Serpent shook his head. It seemed to help.

Suddenly his thoughts were clearer. And a heavy sense of dread made a slow drumbeat up his spine. He shivered.

"Brother . . . what brings you here?"

Smoking Mirror smiled broadly. "I've been worried about you, brother. You haven't been seen for many days. I heard strange rumors. I just wanted to see for myself. And it looks to be a good thing I came."

White Serpent stared at him. "I don't understand," he said softly. The room felt as if it were growing colder by the second. He pulled his thin cover up, like a child. But Smoking Mirror seemed unaffected.

"Brother, what's wrong with you? Is what I've heard true, then? Have you truly renounced your own God, and your temple? Your people wander in the streets. There is much fighting, I'm sorry to say—but who is to blame for it?"

White Serpent's heart began to flutter in his chest like a bird trying to fight its way out of a cage. Sweat started on his brow; he took deep breaths.

Smoking Mirror watched this, a faint smile still playing on his thick lips. "Don't you think it's been long enough, High Priest? You have a responsibility, you know. I do what I can, but only you can calm your people. It's time for you to leave your bed and take up your duty again. Aren't you the one who always prated of destiny?" He paused, his smile growing wider. "Well, then," he said again.

"Smoking Mirror, I—"

"No, I won't hear of it. You know where your duty is, surely. Or do you hate your people now?"

Numbly, White Serpent shook his head. His thoughts had become a hopeless swirl. He couldn't understand it. Something was clouding his mind, but he couldn't find a way through the fog. All he could see was Smoking Mirror's face, looming closer.

"I can see you are weak, brother," the High Priest said. "It's plain enough, and easy to understand. Your spirits are low from your illness. But I have just the thing for you! As I said, it's lucky I came today. It looks as if I'm just in time."

White Serpent pushed away his sheet and sat up straight. His skin was pale as a fish belly, and hung loosely on his bones. Smoking Mirror shook his head. "It's your spirit that needs healing," he announced. "Not your body. Come, get out of your bed and see what I have for you." He reached out, took White Serpent's hand, and tugged him unprotesting from his pillows.

Once the White Priest was on his feet, Smoking Mirror reached into the bundle he'd unwrapped and drew out a robe of incredible beauty. Everything about it shimmered and glowed—feathers, beads, tiny chips of coral, strands of fur like still-living pelts. He raised it to shoulder height and gave it a couple of shakes. Even in the overcast gloom it seemed to gleam with a light of its own.

Without thinking, White Serpent ran his fingers across it.

"Yes," Smoking Mirror said. "Isn't it beautiful? I have blessed it myself. Here, put it on. It will give you strength, brother. It will lift up your spirits like the clouds! I promise you, it is just what you need."

And before White Serpent could protest, Smoking Mirror draped the unbelievable garment across his shoulders and stepped away.

Amazingly, as the supple material arranged itself about him like a second skin, White Serpent felt the chill that had congealed in his bones vanish. A rising heat began to fill him. The robe touched his skin as sensually as a woman's fingers. And his thoughts suddenly seemed clear and sharp.

He looked at Smoking Mirror, who was watching him with a strangely worried expression on his face. But at the sight of the White Priest's slow smile, he grinned in return.

"I told you, didn't I? Just what you need. Don't you feel better now?"

Feeling as if his body was moving on its own, White Serpent felt himself nod. And he did feel better. Better than he'd felt since the . . . since the what? He couldn't remember.

In the dim inner recesses of his mind, he sensed two great, cold faces slowly turning, two pairs of distant, unblinking eyes begin to focus on him. But that sensation only lasted an instant. Now Smoking Mirror bent down to the bundle and came up with a round black gourd. A wooden cork stoppered its neck. "Here, brother," he said heartily. "Drink this. It will give you energy."

Some final barrier yet remained to him. He managed to say, "You know I don't drink pulque."

But Smoking Mirror plucked out the cork and waved the gourd under his nose. "It's only water, brother, with a little honey to sweeten it. See? Can you smell it?"

He thrust the gourd into White Serpent's hand. "Go on, drink. Your voice sounds parched and dry. This will help."

The eyes had found him now. They watched him with a terrible intensity. And in their bleak and endless gaze, he knew. He looked at the gourd in his hand and saw his destiny.

So soon? he thought.

It is time, came the hidden reply, in a roll of silent thunder.

His heart answered it. He lifted the gourd and drank it down. Then he threw it on the ground and faced Smoking Mirror, as the fires roared in his veins.

"What will be, will be," he whispered.

"Yes, brother, it will," Smoking Mirror replied. Then he could contain his glee no longer. He clouted White Serpent heavily on the back. "Go out into your temple, brother, and bring joy. Bring strength to your people! Lead them in song through the streets. It is a great day. The White Priest returns . . .

"Sing for joy!"

VI

A temple servant brought a stool to Spirits's room. She sat on it and bade her sister to take the bed. At the far end of it, little Shining Star lay sleeping, thumb in mouth, wrapped in a nest of sheets.

"Won't I wake the baby?" Green Water wondered.

"Oh, no, he sleeps like the rocks. You go ahead. The bed's much more comfortable, and anyway, I'm well used to sitting on this stool."

Green Water settled herself without protest; a few moments later the servant returned with hot water and the makings for tea. Spirits found herself humming softly as she put the herbs into the pot to brew for a while. Despite the unceasing gloom of the day, the visit from her sister had lightened her heart greatly.

She, better than her Lord, knew how bad things were, not only in this temple, but in the city, too. She had again taken up her practice of going out into the city and the villages to do whatever she might for the people. Now, more and more, she saw broken bodies, men, women, even children with terrible injuries. It seemed not a single day went past without vicious fighting between the factions in one part of the city or another—even in the farming villages now. Without White Serpent's calming voice, his followers ran mad with anger and terror. And those who worshipped solely at the temple of the Jaguar replied in kind; there was no voice of reason to be heard anywhere.

But the fact that her sister felt safe enough to come here to see her might mean that Harvest Mountain, at least, was subsiding in his anger against

White Serpent. If so, it was the best thing imaginable, for if there could be peace between those two men, all else, even Smoking Mirror, would eventually fall into place.

She was surprised at how these speculations soothed her sensible soul. And grateful above all for Green Water, who had no doubt risked much to come see her.

"Dearest," she said, after she set the tray on the floor to let the tea steep a bit, "give me your hands. Now, tell me everything you can."

Green Water immediately leaned forward and began to tell Spirits every bit of harmless gossip she could recall. She watched her sister closely as she spoke, waiting for her chance. But Spirits, so starved for any kind of companionship, kept her gaze riveted on Green Water's face, nodding and smiling, occasionally offering a meaningless interjection; but there, always there, never looking away even for an instant.

The tea sat forgotten at their feet, steaming. Green Water grew more nervous; surely she didn't have much time left, not if Smoking Mirror had been successful in his own tasks. And everything might hinge on her own success here.

Finally, when it seemed her throat would simply dry up and close, she rasped out a harsh cough. "Oh, dear, I'm sorry," she said.

But Spirits knew just what was needed. "Oh, we've forgotten our tea. Here, I'll put a lot of honey in it. That will soothe your throat."

Green Water, seeing her chance at last, waved one hand. "No," she croaked. "Do you have some water? Something cool . . . ?"

Spirits immediately leaped to her feet. "Give me just a moment. I'll be right back."

Green Water watched her duck out the door, and waited until the flap swung closed. Then she quickly reached under her robe and withdrew a tiny clay bottle. She unstoppered it and shook its contents into the pot of tea. She knew what it would do. It didn't matter to her whether she drank it or not. It wouldn't kill anybody. Not directly.

VII

"This way," Smoking Mirror said, swallowing a greasy chuckle as he led White Serpent in his glorious robe toward the altar chamber. He could hear a growing hubbub up ahead; excellent, the rest of the plan was right on schedule.

White Serpent staggered slightly. "Be careful, now, brother," Smoking Mirror said, grasping him by the elbow and straightening him up. "Don't fall. You must stand straight to give your followers your spirit. How do you feel?"

"Feel . . . dizzy."

"Oh, it will pass. Come, right this way."

They paused on the threshold of the great room, Smoking Mirror with a broad grin, almost a grimace, of delight. White Serpent swayed next to him. His flesh felt hot and dry beneath the Jaguar priest's fingers, as if a fire were blazing inside him. Well, it was, he thought happily. A fire that would bring White Serpent down in ashes.

He had thought merely to get White Serpent publicly drunk, and let him make a fool of himself in the finery he had so often scorned, and so discredit his reputation for purity. But Green Water Woman had shown him another way; if it succeeded, the White Priest would not only be shamed but ruined entirely.

Now, if it worked with Spirits Walking Woman as well . . .

The huge room before them was shuddering with exhibitions Smoking Mirror was quite certain had never been seen before in these hallowed chambers.

Two of his acolytes lumbered heavily through the wide front doors bearing a broad wooden tub. They set it down in the middle of the room, next to two more just like it. Another rushed up with a cloth bag, which he immediately opened. He began handing out rough hollow gourds—big ones—to the ever growing swarm of White Serpent's followers.

Smoking Mirror had proposed a drunken riot; it had taken Green Water to suggest an orgy. And the way to accomplish it. Each of the tubs brimmed over with frothing, golden pulque . . . and something else, something all the root women knew about but few spoke of.

Green Water assured him she had more than a sufficient supply, and from the look of things, she hadn't lied to him. He felt White Serpent stir woozily against his shoulder, and he laughed out loud as a very fat woman, her chaste white robe hiked up around her flabby waist, galloped past with a little man half her size in hot pursuit. Both brandished nearly full gourds, obviously not their first.

The noise level was rising as more and more followers of the Feathered Serpent flooded into the temple from all directions. And that was no accident either. Smoking Mirror had sent runners throughout the city and the nearer villages to shout the word that the White Priest had risen from his stupor and all was well in the White Temple again.

Somebody hauled a huge drum up to the altar and began to pound on it. The deep, heavy rhythm seemed to saturate the air; even Smoking Mirror felt it insinuating itself into his blood, his bones. Immediately the debauch ascended to a new level. One woman screamed, whether in terror or joy he couldn't tell, but the sound was quickly muffled. The drum pounded louder, and was soon joined by another. Some of those cavorting riotously around the room began to sing as they tore each other's robes and clouts off.

The great chamber began to overflow with grunting, sweating bodies. The smell of rut wafted gently into the suddenly heated air.

Smoking Mirror turned to White Serpent and smiled. "Your people seem glad to see you," he said. Then, his smile twisting into something else, he took White Serpent's unresisting arm and pushed him forward, into the abyss.

CHAPTER TWENTY

I

Spirits stared dumbly at the debauchery taking place before her. The noise was tremendous: drums, shouts, cries of pleasure, groans of ecstasy. Everything seemed in motion: men and women crawled, leaped, grappled with each other, fell in writhing piles that hardly looked human.

But for some reason what should have filled her with horror and shame only energized the hot ball of fire in her belly. That flame now spread even further, creeping into her chest, her arms, her thighs; her fingers began to twitch in rhythm with the incessant beat of the drums. Even her heart seemed to resonate with that throbbing pulse.

"Have to think . . ." she mumbled, staring numbly at the impossible orgy before her. But she must have spoken aloud. She felt fingers jerk at her arm, and turned. Green Water stood next to her, her face the color of freshly fired clay, burning with lurid eagerness.

"Don't think," Green Water hissed. "You know what you want. Go and take it." And with that, she gave Spirits a great shove forward. The last thing Spirits saw of her, she was stripping off her robe and clawing her way into a nameless, faceless pile, her slanted eyes wide and staring in a face that looked like a skull.

The heat in Spirits's groin became a vast itch, a need she couldn't comprehend, but couldn't resist, either. Every time she thought she'd regained the tiniest bit of control, the heavy thud of the drums would thunder into her head. Half-blind, she swiveled her head back and forth, trying to see through the pink haze that filled her vision.

Shapes and shadows leaped before her. A mad chorus of groans filled her ears. Her nostrils quivered at the stench of rut, of semen, urine, and vomit that clogged the air. The potent fumes of the pulque sickened her as she staggered along, buffeted by stray arms and legs.

A hand ripped at her cloak. The cloth tore and fell away, exposing her. She grabbed for the robe, but it vanished into the shrieking bacchanal, and she forgot about it.

The overheated atmosphere felt marginally cooler on her naked skin. Dimly, she understood something terrible was happening, but she was in the grip of it, and powerless to stop. Blindly she staggered forward, her hands outstretched, groping for—what?

You know what you want. Go and take it.

The words echoed in her mind like a demonic mantra. She tried to banish them, but they only grew stronger. Because they were true. She did know what she wanted. And in her unholy, fire-shot fog, she wanted it more than anything in her whole life. It *was* life. It was *destiny*.

She found both in front of the altar, where he stood as naked as she, his broad pale shoulders sheeted with sweat, his member like a spear before him, hot and pink, its point the color of dark blood.

"No," she whispered as he lifted her up onto the altar, then climbed on top of her. "No . . ."

But her treacherous body and her greedy heart said, *Yes! Now and forever, yes!*

Only the watchers, hidden in the deepest part of

her, remained cold and vigilant. But when he entered her, she forgot even them. His chest crushed her milk-swollen breasts, scraped already tender nipples. Somehow, in her drugged stupor, the pain became a hot, dark pleasure. And all she saw was *his* eyes: their bright blue fire.

She gave herself into the blaze.

II

The monstrosity created by Smoking Mirror and Green Water spilled from inside the White Temple out into the streets and became something else: a riot. It spread like a ravening cancer. Soon the entire city was locked in a rictus of death and destruction. The rain had become intermittent. Fires flared up, were extinguished, then roared into life again.

Unaffected residents stumbled on scenes of blasphemy. Struck with horror, they tried to stop the debauchery, only to ignite more violence. Throughout the lanes, paths, and streets of Great Head City, people fought and fucked like animals; sometimes simultaneously. The frenzy was contagious and in the end, deadly.

Harvest Mountain had called out Skull Breaker and all the Jaguar Cult as soon as he understood what was happening. This was the worst riot yet. But as he led his soldiers on a trail of butchery, he couldn't remain unaffected himself. Now he was drunk on blood, on death, on power.

He staggered through the pall of acrid smoke that hung over the island, the club heavy in his right hand dripping with the blood and brains of his victims. As he floundered to a halt, his lungs heaving with fire, two Jaguar soldiers rushed past, dragging a screaming woman by her hair. He watched them vanish in the noxious mists as if they were ghosts.

Sweat ran down his face. The whole city stank of

things that should not burn but were; for a fleeting moment he wondered how many houses and pavilions had been destroyed. The smoke seemed heaviest in the traders' quarters. He'd just come through the Grand Concourse. The Way had been deserted. Only a few overturned barrows remained of what had been a bustling, busy thoroughfare just a few hours before.

He took a deep breath and looked up, dazed with the enormity of the catastrophe. The thick haze shifted a bit, like a flimsy curtain drawn open, and he saw the courtyard of the White Temple before him. It was relatively quiet here. Most of the frenzy had burned itself out. Bodies lay quiescent and exhausted, clogging the open gate. He stared in disbelief. As he watched, he saw movement and raised his club reflexively.

A single naked figure shuffled through the opening and stood, staring in round-eyed disbelief at the wreckage. Harvest Mountain could hardly believe his eyes. The figure was smeared with smoke, streaked with sweat, but as pale underneath as a ghost. Only when White Serpent turned to face him did his blue eyes become visible. And when Harvest Mountain saw who stood before him, his rage, so long contained, boiled over at last.

"You," he choked out, his voice guttural with fumes and rage. "You, priest! This is all your doing, who claimed your purity over me. You've murdered my city, you monster! And now you'll pay for it, I swear by all the Gods!"

With that, the High King raised his club over his head and rushed forward.

White Serpent, moving like a man in a dream, slowly lifted his arms. "Ah, God," he moaned. "Why have you deserted me?"

He seemed not to see Harvest Mountain at all. On his handsome features was an expression of anguish so deep that he looked like he'd aged a hundred years in a few moments. Only in the last instant did he appear to recognize his assailant; and to Harvest Mountain's dismay, what transfigured his enemy's face then wasn't fear, or even hatred.

It was joy.

The sound of club meeting bone was thick and meaty. A spasm of pure pleasure tingled up Harvest Mountain's right arm as he felt the shock of the blow. The White Priest dropped like a stone.

Harvest Mountain straddled him and raised his club for another blow. But he never finished it, for beneath him White Serpent Hawk lay as one dead. He didn't move at all.

But the earth did.

III

Spirits blinked. At first she thought she was still dreaming, but the slow, rolling motion she felt was no nightmare; a dull, roaring thunder breathed in the rotten air, and in the distance another chorus of screams arose.

She shook her head. Something painful was jabbing her in the back, down low near her buttocks. She stifled a groan as she rolled away. She peered blearily back over her shoulder. The source of her discomfort was obvious: an elbow, sticking up, but attached to a naked man who was snoring noisily.

Naked man. The thought percolated sludgily through her mind. Comprehension was slow to come; she had a pounding headache, so bad that every time she drew a breath, white sparks exploded behind her eyes.

The rolling motion slowed, seemed to stop, then resumed with a final sharp jerk. It shook some of the cobwebs away, and she blinked again.

Naked . . . she was naked too. And cold. The light was gray and smoky, and the stench was unbearable. Weakly, she rolled over on her side and emptied her stomach. Then, gasping at the effort, she reached out and found herself grasping a dark, heavy shape. It felt solid; with much effort she levered himself to her feet.

Her mental fog was clearing rapidly now; but what came flowing in was impossible. Surely it was impossible? But no—it was all around her. In the gloom she could make out clots of supine human forms; hardly anybody was moving. Maybe they were all dead.

Maybe *she* was dead. She jumped as a ripping, cracking sound heralded the collapse of part of the roof. The earthquake—for that was what it was, she recognized it from her life in the mountains, where such things were more common—had weakened the posts which supported the roof beams. Gods—what if the whole structure came down? All these people . . .

She turned, staring wildly, and saw what she'd been leaning against. The high altar, its polished wooden surface now slick and sticky with spilled pulque, with vomit, with . . .

She groaned as the memories came flooding back. Then she turned and ran for the front door, pausing only to grab a discarded robe stained with awful fluids, and tie it about herself as best she could.

The building gave another lurch. She almost turned around and went back inside. Death by crushing seemed a far better thing than living with the memories of her degradation . . . and *his* fall.

IV

Harvest Mountain, cold sweat pouring down his chest and belly, staggered to his feet from where the quake had piled him on top of White Serpent's unmoving form. Terror greater than anything he'd ever imagined jittered and jigged in his muscles. He'd dropped his club when his fingers went lax of their own accord, and he couldn't seem to tighten them again.

It was all he could do to stand upright; but the stark horror had cleared his mind at last. What had been fire in his brain was now ashes, cold, bleak, dead. A strange, harsh sound rattled in his ears. It took him a moment to realize it was his own breath.

A final aftershock, not strong enough to unseat him, rumbled through the earth. He looked down. White Serpent lay between his legs, one arm thrown back. There was an immense lump on the side of his skull. The eye on that side bulged blankly; all the color had leached out of it. The other eye was closed.

The earth had cried out at his death. Harvest Mountain, a silent shriek bursting his throat, knew that as surely as he knew he had slain a God.

But it was the scream from within the courtyard, twin to the sound trapped in his voice box, that snapped his head around.

"You killed him! Oh, my Gods, you killed White Serpent Hawk!"

He didn't recognize the disheveled scarecrow of a woman who hurtled through the gate and flung herself, weeping hysterically, on the fallen High Priest. Her hair was a sodden, tangled mess; her rag of a cloak soaked with vomit and liquor. But when she rose from White Serpent's body, her hooked claws reaching for his face, her knew her.

Doom.

Gasping, he turned and ran as if all the dead of the Underwater World were after him. Behind him, he heard her death wail begin to cleave the afternoon like the sharpest of sacrificial knives. The dead weren't seeking him, not yet; but others would be, soon enough.

v

Harvest Mountain staggered and lurched through the shrouded streets of the city, making for the royal pavilions as quickly as he could, Spirits's accusing cries still ringing in his ears.

He was dazed and disoriented by the magnitude of the disaster. Half the city seemed to be in flames; he couldn't move very fast. Every time he began to run through the murk, he would end up stumbling over some prone figure crumpled in the mud, or detouring around the burning rubble of some house collapsed into the street.

Now the skies opened up again, this time with a fusillade of thunder; the Dragon roared, and the Feathered Serpent hurled his bolts as if the pair of Them would destroy the city entire. *And why not?* he thought in despair. *I've just killed a God.*

Somehow he knew that didn't make sense, not if the Feathered Serpent was still in the skies, howling and scattering His divine bolts as a farmer would toss corn to chickens. But nothing made any sense anymore. He couldn't understand what had happened. It was as if a spreading madness had seized not just him, but all his people. And now everything he'd planned and dreamed for was collapsing around his ears. And he couldn't seem to *think*!

He stumbled on, heedless of the growing mutter behind him. Had he looked, he would have seen the beginnings of yet another mob, shouting his name, baying for his blood. Not all of them wore the white band around their heads, either. The tale of White Serpent's murder had traveled almost as fast as the earthquake which had marked it. Many who'd been undecided about the White Priest before no longer were. And the blood price must be paid.

Harvest Mountain finally reached the courts. It took him a good while, because he'd been afraid to cut across the open space of the Grand Concourse, where he could be seen. Panting and shaking, he reeled past the waterworks. Their stone cisterns were overflowing, the bathing pools near to brimming over, and the stone aqueducts roaring with water.

The throne room was deserted. He threw back his head and shouted for servants, but there was no reply, only the dull pounding of the rain. It was dark in here. He searched helplessly for a light; the lamps were there, but he didn't know where the fires were kept; he was High King. He didn't know how to light the lamps.

Nor did he have much time to worry about it, for now the crowd that had been baying on his trail reached the royal pavilions and broke apart like a wave along a rocky shore. It shattered into rivulets of crazed, howling men and women, all of them intent on one thing only: vengeance.

Feeling as if his world were coming to an end, Harvest Mountain took flight again, racing wildly through the women's quarters—no sign of Green Water, either—and out beyond the pavilions entirely.

The houses in the back of the courts were fewer than those on the other side of the city. They seemed deserted as he galloped past, their window and door cloths tied securely against the rain. Only a few showed light; he saw no faces marking his passage.

Then he was beyond them and turning south, looking for safety along the riverbank. The waters were swollen; they churned past him like black honey, with a low, hissing sound. To fall in would be death.

Winded and exhausted, he sank to his knees, then crawled beneath a clump of squat, wide-leafed palms that arched out over the water. He curled himself into as small a shape as possible. Dusk was coming on now, and with the smoke and storm he knew he would be very hard to find.

He was cold and wet and frightened, but after a time, when the sound of the mob faded, he began to think for the first time he might live through this.

He hugged himself and thought of Skull Breaker,

and the Jaguar soldiers. White Serpent would pay for this!

But White Serpent was dead. And the city was half destroyed. Who was to blame for all that?

Could he have been *wrong*?

VI

Morning finally came with the dull rising of a silver sun. Beneath its weak, gray light, the city lay as if dead. Only a few fires still smoldered. Just as the fires in the hearts of men had died when the body's fuel was exhausted, so had the flames which scorched the city. Here and there, groups of women beat their breasts and wailed the death songs. Men, their eyes downcast, were still pulling charred corpses from the ruins. Beneath a sky the color of stone, the city on the sacred Island of the Jaguar lay wounded, and the stench of death filled the air.

Spirits staggered from the bone-deep weariness that weighed on her as heavily as that dreadful sky weighed on Great Head City, but she kept on finding one last reservoir of strength, and when that was drained, she found another.

What was left of the temple acolytes—some were dead, some injured, and some simply vanished—trudged slowly about, doing her bidding. Purple Grackle was with her, carrying messages, holding the baby, and constantly urging her mistress to go to bed, get some rest before she collapsed on her feet.

"No," Spirits said. There were great dark shadows beneath her eyes; they looked like bruises. "He is gone. I have a duty, too. I am His priestess."

Purple Grackle didn't miss the new emphasis. *His* priestess. Evidently *He* was now a God, at least in the mind of *His* High Priestess. Purple Grackle remembered nothing of the terrible events; she had slept through them, on Spirits's bed, holding the baby in her arms. Nothing had disturbed her. She wondered how that had been; perhaps some merciful God had shielded her and the child? But she didn't speak of this. Instead, she had brought Spirits a clean robe, and wiped away as much of the filth as she could. Spirits refused to take a proper bath. Her hair hung down across her face like a nest of greasy snakes.

"I will wear my shame," Spirits whispered. Her voice was almost gone, from the smoke, from constant use, from despair. She pointed at the last pathetic clump of bodies, piled in the corner of the front walls, four or five adults, and what appeared to be a child.

She directed a few of the acolytes to untangle the pitiful pile. If this was sacrifice, some horrid God must be well pleased with His night's work. The child—it was a boy—tumbled limply out. When she stopped to see his face, she gasped.

It was Laughing Monkey. "Oh . . . Purple Grackle. I sent him away. How is he here?"

But when she stooped closer, the answer was plain enough. There were knife marks on the boy's scrawny chest. His finger and toe nails had been ripped off. And livid burns scarred his belly and penis. He had been tortured. There would be no warnings going to Holy Stone City. Not from this child.

Only one man took pleasure in such vile doings. She knew his name. But how had Skull Breaker known? It must mean that he still spied on her—which meant also that he still feared her.

As she stood from the ruin of Laughing Monkey's pathetic corpse, she vowed that before this ended, the General would have reason to fear her again. She didn't know quite where this vow came from—it was a hard, cold thing. Then she realized. She had become hard and cold. Her armor was inside, and for the first time she was grateful for the thing she'd feared so long. Now she wanted it, and wished she knew how to summon it. The chill faces, the icy eyes. The hidden place. It wanted her, and she wanted It. At least Its power.

"Bury Laughing Monkey by himself. He deserves at least that much. Look how they tortured him. He must have resisted for a long time. He was loyal . . ."

She sighed, turned away, and went back into the altar room. The workers here had been busy. All the signs of the debauch had been cleared away. The high wooden altar was scrubbed clean, and heaped with fresh flowers from the temple gardens. In front of it a rude wooden box, open at the top, rested on the floor. More flowers were piled around its sides.

She walked slowly to it, stopped, and looked down. He rested comfortably, it appeared. She had closed the one bulging eye, and piled blossoms around his head, to conceal the terrible wound from Harvest Mountain's club.

"What will we do?" Purple Grackle whispered. She held Shining Star, who was sleeping soundly.

Spirits looked up at her from a face as waxen as that of the corpse reclining so peacefully below. "We will tell the people that the God who loved them is resting now, and they may come see what they have done to Him, if they wish."

She paused. "After that . . . I don't know. I just don't know." And with that she sighed and, gently as a flower closing its petals for the night, sank to the floor in a dead faint.

VII

"I was chased from my own courts," Harvest Mountain said bitterly. "I hid in the bushes like a common thief, while madmen hunted me as if I were an animal. Me. Their High King."

Harvest Mountain, Smoking Mirror, and Green Water Woman stood at the top of the Jaguar Temple's great stone staircase, ranged along the wall there, looking out over the still smoldering city. The temple proper bristled with armed Jaguar soldiers; the stairs themselves were guarded by a troop ranged along their foot, spears outward, denying all entrance.

Smoking Mirror nodded. "Why did you kill him?" he asked.

Harvest Mountain paused. "I . . . don't know," he said. "A madness was on me. His hatred of me destroyed my city." He thrust out an arm in a sweeping gesture. "Look at it! See what he's done!" He shook his head. "He deserved to die."

Green Water nodded. "And because of you, what we feared has come to pass. The people aren't blaming him, but you for the disaster."

He glared at her. "And for you, Lady? This was all your idea, wasn't it? But when it all fell apart, where *were* you?" He raised one hand to forestall her reply. "Don't answer. I know the truth. Skull Breaker tells me you were fucking in the White Priest's temple like the slut you are, and then hiding here, with your fellow plotter, my *brother,* the High Priest. Is it true you are now his High Priestess, as well? I see you have moved your things and servants out of the royal pavilions."

At his insult, two burning red patches suddenly glowed along Green Water's high cheekbones. "Slut? You fool. We had won. Our plot, as you call it, worked. White Serpent had fucked his own High Priestess on the very top of his holy altar. If you'd stayed your killing lust, all the city today would be spitting on his name. But you murdered him, and now all that is forgotten. Instead, he is more powerful than ever. Because the earth shook when you slew him, now even those who didn't follow him before are calling him a God. And blaming you, my foolish Lord, for the evil that has befallen them."

"How dare you . . . ! I am High King. You can't talk to me—"

Her golden eyes spat sparks at him. "High King?" she laughed. "Yes, you are that. For the moment."

He blanched. "You dare?"

"Not I, Lord. But the people are a great stack of dry wood, waiting for a spark. If the spark is your name, well . . ." She shrugged and turned away.

He lunged forward, but Smoking Mirror caught him and pushed him back. "She's right, brother. And strangling her won't change that."

Breathing heavily, Harvest Mountain relaxed. "Brother? I smell the stench of your fingertips, smeared with blood, in all this, *brother*. I know you envy me—and now the two of you are together. Your plot stinks, brother. Even I, the fool that she names me, can sniff it out."

Smoking Mirror shook his head and raised his hands. "Brother, calm yourself. Think what you are saying. You knew what we planned. You approved it yourself. Yes, things got out of hand, but if you'd stayed your war club, everything would be fine now. Don't blame us for your own errors."

Harvest Mountain subsided then, his eyes narrowing in thought. Finally, he heaved a great sigh. "You may be right," he said. "Well, then, what do we do now?"

Green Water, who had been facing away from them, her arms folded across her chest, her right foot tapping impatiently, now swung back to rejoin the conversation. "My sister has laid the White Priest in a wooden coffin, open so the people can see him. Even as we speak, the crowds are coming up from the farthest villages to worship at his corpse. And the rumor is that death doesn't corrupt him. He is surrounded with flowers, but not to conceal the stink of putrefaction. It is said he smells as sweet as the blossoms upon which he rests."

"That is . . . terrible." Harvest Mountain shuddered. "First the earth quaked when he died, and now this.

Perhaps he is what he claimed to be." His face had gone pale again.

But Smoking Mirror shook his head. "He was no God, Lord. I assure you of that. The Lord Jaguar Himself has told me so. You think he wouldn't know His own brother?"

Harvest Mountain felt absurdly grateful for this news. So grateful, in fact, that he suppressed his own knowledge as a High Priest—that sometimes, for Their own reasons, the Gods lied to those of the Middle World.

"All right, then. Half the population is kneeling at his bier. And I hold my own courts only by force of arms. So what do we do?"

Smoking Mirror and Green Water glanced at each other, sharing smiles of absolute complicity. "The people blame you," Smoking Mirror said.

"So we have to make them blame him," Green Water finished. "And here is how we will do it. Do you remember an artist named Brush Weaver . . . ?"

VIII

Purple Grackle was nearly frantic with worry. Spirits had refused to leave White Serpent's coffin, and had gradually sunk into a fever-wracked stupor. But whenever Purple Grackle had tried to move her, she had awakened and fought like a jungle cat, spitting and hissing. Purple Grackle feared that demons had truly stolen her mind, but what could she do? Even the baby, Shining Star, had no effect on her. And so, for three days, the babe's mother lay like a wilted bouquet next to the bier, with the eyes of the people on her in wonder as they passed by, silent and fearful. Some were already saying she was the avatar of the White Priest, sent by the Gods to guard his rest.

So when Purple Grackle came to her on the third morning, she had small hope of succeeding where all her earlier efforts had failed, but she came anyway, and gently shook her mistress's shoulder.

"What? Uh . . . Purple Grackle?"

Spirits stared up at the handmaid. Her eyes were sunken and red, and surrounded by bruises. Her hair resembled old, gnarled roots creeping across her face. Her cheeks were raddled, and her breath smelled of the grave. But she was awake, and Purple Grackle thought she detected the light of understanding in her gaze.

"Oh, mistress," she whispered, sinking down to join her. "You must get up. It's been three days . . . soon the people who come to see him will begin to gather. I hate it for them to see you like this."

Spirits moved her right hand weakly, then reached up and stroked Purple Grackle's cheek. "Dearest . . ." she said. "You are so good to me, but let me rest here a while longer. Don't be afraid. I won't leave you. He won't let me."

The sounds of doom whispered in her words so strongly that Purple Grackle had to turn away, lest she begin to weep. "But, Spirits . . ."

"No, just till the end of the day. The third day. Then I will go away, for my duty is not done." She licked her lips. "May I have a bit of water? I am so parched."

This request, the first Spirits had made, lit a small flame of hope in Purple Grackle's heart. Quickly she found a gourd, filled it, and brought it to her mistress, who drank a bit, then subsided.

"Mistress, the Jaguar Priest has summoned a great gathering. He says it is to cleanse the city of the demons summoned by White Serpent's death. I am afraid. What if the riots start again?"

Once more Spirits stroked Purple Grackle's cheek. "Don't worry, my old friend. Nothing will touch us here. And the whip that is used may turn on its user."

She let out a small breath. "In the meantime, let me abide here until it is finished."

Nodding, Purple Grackle slowly rose. Until *what* was finished? She didn't know. All she knew was that she was still terribly afraid. What had the world come to?

And what yet *would* it come to? She had no answer to that, so all she could do was as her mistress bade. She would wait.

IX

On that day the drums pounded from early in the morning onward, never stopping even for a moment. By noon the crowds had gathered beneath a windy sky. The sun came and went, came and went, as wads of gray clouds fled beneath it.

The slaves and servants of the Jaguar Temple had labored long to make ready the great altar and platform in the center of the Concourse. Now the mass of priests, with Smoking Mirror, the High King, and Green Water in front, stood ranged along its top. They gazed out over the throng, which was noticeably smaller than it had been on earlier days. Some were dead or injured, but many had fled the city entirely, saying it was cursed by the Gods.

Harvest Mountain said, "It might work."

"It will work, Lord," Smoking Mirror replied. "Everybody knows this artisan Brush Weaver." He glanced over his shoulder at the unconscious man who lay bound and gagged atop the altar.

"When the God reveals how this treacherous slug betrayed his own master and poisoned the water of the White Temple, who will disbelieve? And the blame will be shifted from you to him."

"What about your own acolytes and their tubs of brew?"

Smoking Mirror shrugged. "So the Jaguar wished to

feast his brother, the Feathered Serpent. What could be wrong with that?"

The High King glanced down at the Concourse, where the wave of people lapped uneasily at the bottom of the altar steps. A low wall of rocks freshly gathered from the river had been constructed there, and it held them back.

Strange, Harvest Mountain thought. We didn't need that before . . .

"As I say, it had better work . . ." He nodded meaningfully at his General, who stood with a large contingent of Jaguar soldiers ranged along the low wall below. At least I have them, Harvest Mountain thought to himself. In the end, brute force is the best ally, for it is more certain even than the wrath of Gods.

Of course, he didn't speak of this. But there was a confrontation coming between himself and this High Priest. Green Water had not returned to the royal courts. It was now plain to Harvest Mountain that she would not, and that told him something, too.

He pushed these thoughts away. They thought him weak. They would discover otherwise, when the time was right. But today he needed them. He stepped back. "Let us begin, then. Let's get it over with."

Smoking Mirror clapped his hands together sharply. Lesser priests rushed to him, bearing the sacred pipe. One held it to his lips, while another dropped a glowing coal into the cup-shaped bowl. Smoke rose immediately. The High Priest gulped in great gouts of the fumes, and after a while, his eyes rolled back in his head . . .

After that, Harvest Mountain lost track of things for a while. Even the side drafts of the potent smoke had a calming effect, and that was furthered by the muted thump of the drums, and the comforting sameness of rituals he'd learned as a boy priest and knew as well as he knew the sound of his own breathing.

Things proceeded. The crowd grew quiet, although there was a gasp or two when Smoking Mirror suddenly threw away the pipe, let out a great shout, and turned two somersaults in the air. When he landed on his feet after the second one, the Jaguar Himself looked out over the crowd.

And it was the God who explained, in a guttural, whining voice, about the treachery of Brush Weaver. That hapless victim missed out on his own condemnation, for the drugs he'd been given to keep him quiet were powerful.

Out of the side of his eye, Harvest Mountain watched as the Jaguar Lord, in the guise of His High Priest, mounted the final steps to the altar. He saw the great stone knife flash in the intermittent sunlight, watched the sudden gush of blood, smelled the stink of open entrails steaming in the air.

All that remained was the reading of the omens found in the hapless artisan's guts, and then it would be over. The people, appeased with blood, would return calmly to their homes and begin rebuilding.

His own dreams of conquest were gone for this season, but another season always followed. He'd been hurt, but not destroyed. And there would be time enough while he rebuilt his strength to decide what to do about the Jaguar Priest and his new handmaid. Yes, he thought, smiling softly, that would be a pleasure to think about.

So lulled by his own pleasant, if bloody, musings, High King Harvest Mountain Lord could not have been more shocked when the High Priest Smoking Mirror uttered a piercing shriek and, with one violent motion, shoved the gutted corpse of Brush Weaver off the altar. And before the High King could draw another breath, Smoking Mirror came down off the altar, somersaulting his way across the top of the platform, where he finally came to his feet at the very top of the stairs where Harvest Mountain stood.

"The Lord Jaguar rejects this sacrifice!" the High Priest screamed. The aspect of the Jaguar was so strongly on him that many in the crowd below covered their eyes. Some began to scream in terror.

Smoking Mirror paid no attention. "The Jaguar says He wants the blood of the criminal, the monster who slew His brother; He says He will destroy his city unless you feed Him."

Somebody in the crowd, someone with a deep, carrying voice, cried out then: "Who does the Lord Jaguar want?"

Dramatically, Smoking Mirror flung out his hand, its clawed fingers splayed, but pointing directly at Harvest Mountain's slack-jawed face.

"There!" he howled. *"That one, the false King! The abomination in the eyes of the mighty Lord Jaguar!"*

And with that, Green Water Woman stepped up behind Harvest Mountain and gave him a great shove, which tumbled him down the long stairs into the frenzied crowd below.

The High Priestess watched him fall, a smile twisting her lips. "Slut, am I?" she murmured.

Harvest Mountain Lord felt his ribs break as he tumbled, and his right knee gave with a sharp crack. He lay on the ground a moment, stunned, then looked up at Skull Breaker.

"Help me . . ." he gasped.

But the General only looked at him blankly, and then, with a hand signal, gave orders for the Jaguar soldiers to depart.

After that, Harvest Mountain discovered what the wall of stones was really for.

He didn't scream long at all.

CHAPTER TWENTY-ONE

I

Spirits had been drifting in and out all those three days she'd spent mourning White Serpent. She'd eaten nothing the whole time, and the only thing she'd drunk had been the small amount of water Purple Grackle gave her. That vague awakening soon slipped away. The taste of water was not yet dry on her lips when she fell back into the star-shot darkness where she'd drifted ever since preparing White Serpent Hawk's coffin.

It was a strange, black, brooding space. She had the sense she wasn't alone; an impression of huge shapes moving and jostling about, but she couldn't see them. Loud, booming sounds would occasionally erupt, roll like thunder, then subside.

Some fathomless time later she felt the dream begin; she felt as if she had begun to move.

With no warning at all, she found herself looking *down* on the coffin from above. Everything was perfectly clear. She saw White Serpent's face, surrounded by flowers, waxen and empty. And next to the coffin, a pathetic, huddled lump. It took her several long moments to realize the lump was herself—her body—yet there was no feeling of separation. Instead, she felt a gradually brightening joy—and something tugging at her, pulling her up. She resisted only a little and then, with a sigh, let herself go.

It was a slow sensation at first, merely the feeling that she, instead of invisible things around her, was moving. Gradually the impression of speed increased, felt as a nameless wind that tugged at her bones, not her flesh.

She rose, passing through the roof of the temple in an eye-blink of shadow; a rain squall, all spatters of lightning and silvery sheets of water, whipped through her in a wave of translucent light.

II

"The city is ours," Smoking Mirror said. "I will be High King. You will be my queen."

Green Water Woman stretched slowly, feeling his eyes on her. They were both naked, in the hidden chamber of the Jaguar Temple. She waited, bathed in his lust. Finally she said, "Take me, then."

He nodded, and moved toward her. Aromatic smokes filled the room, rare and exotic herbs. She felt herself grow drowsy, her mind thick with the languor of triumph.

He would rule the city, yes. But she knew how to rule him.

Just before his hands found her breasts, she stopped him.

"My sister," she said.

He paused. "She will be the final sacrifice."

"No. She will be mine."

"As you wish," he said.

They sank onto the dark altar, groaning.

III

"Wake up, Spirits. Come, awaken now."

She heard the voice. It seemed to summon her from some far place she could no longer remember. But the hand that stroked her cheek was gentle and warm.

She opened her eyes. White Serpent stood looking down on her, with eyes like the morning sky. She gazed up at him, transfixed. "You have come back to us, Lord," she whispered.

She vaguely recalled crying his name in her dream. After a long time she had heard him answer. And then, in the dim shadows of the Underwater World she had seen his bright form rising toward her, his hand outstretched. When his fingers had touched hers, a great calm had filled her.

"You have called me with a love greater than death," he told her. "I heard you, and I have come to you. Now you must show me the way back."

The joy she felt then filled her with light, so that she floated up from the shadows, the blaze of her joy lighting the way for both of them. But before she reached the end of her dream, it began to fade. Then she had slept deeply, wondering what it meant. Now she knew.

She did not know if he had been truly dead, or only lay in his coffin sleeping as if he were dead. She had heard of such things. But whatever had happened was a miracle. He had come back to her and to his people. That was enough.

In the distance, somebody shouted. Then another. She heard the sound of running feet. But all she could see was his eyes.

"You've come back to *me*."

He nodded. "For a time."

Around her, the sounds of joy began to fill the air, as his followers saw their Lord standing by the coffin from which he had risen.

But now Spirits could hear nothing. For her there was only silence. What greater doom could she own than to love a God? For only a God might escape the grasp of the Underwater World.

Yet as she stared up at him, she felt the throbbing in her heart, the endless beat of love in her throat like tiny wings. Her own secret soul lay open, the power of its stony guardians a flood; but she knew him, and so she took his hand and felt the mortal flesh, and was content.

IV

The second miracle that occurred was that the rain stopped. Nobody noticed it immediately, but as soon as White Serpent rose from his coffin, the clouds which had boiled over the city began to thin, and finally vanish. Sunlight, at first weak and watery, then growing into strength as a hesitant child into maturity, washed the bones of the city with merciless hands, revealing wounds not yet healed to scars.

But the people crept out as the word spread, blinking like prisoners released from deep caves, the women holding children in their arms, the men turning to each other with wide, wondering eyes. This was the heart of the rain moons—only a God could change that. And so one had, said the words eagerly whispered, then shouted, from increasingly joyous throats. The White Priest, who was dead, had returned to them. In ever growing hordes they crowded the streets and paths around the White Temple, finally spilling through the gates into the compound itself.

And there they waited, silent, expectant, for the God who'd once been a man to show himself.

V

The first thing Green Water Woman realized, when she heard the news, was that the royal pavilions were empty. Oh, not deserted, but there was no High King, or Queen. Courtiers of rank still lived there, and of course servants and slaves, but the heart had gone from the royal house. Harvest Mountain had left no heir. But, she realized suddenly, he had left a son. He had cast out his wife, the mother of that boy, but the blood was royal. And when she walked out herself to test the mood of the city, she discovered that Spirits Walking Woman, formerly the High Queen, was not reviled for her sins, nor was her child rejected as demon spawn, marked with sin.

In fact, what the city spoke of was what White Serpent Hawk had said in reply to the High King's wrath: that the boy's marks were of divine origin, meant to show Harvest Mountain Lord the will of the Gods. Harvest Mountain, with force, brutality, and trickery, had contrived to blunt that explanation and turn it into a shameful thing. But now Harvest Mountain Lord was dead, stoned at the hands of the very people he'd tried to convince. And Spirits Walking Woman's name flew through the city like a fire, for she had never wavered in her trust of the old ways.

The Gods, it seemed to those who thought about it—and that was nearly everybody—had made their will plain enough. The High King was dead. And White Serpent Hawk had returned from the dead, to teach once again the ways of their ancestors, and the paths of peace.

It was intolerable. She would have to do something about it. She walked through the crowded streets, not noticing how the women slid their glances at her like sharpened knives, or how the men quickly gave way before her, not from respect, but from revulsion and the fear of the unclean. She didn't even hear the whispers: "Slut . . . whore . . . demon bitch . . ." that followed her along like mongrel dogs seeking carrion. She'd never in her life paid much attention to the mumblings of the common folk, and was not the kind to change her habits now. Not when her own instincts had served her well, better than she'd expected.

"It is our city now," Smoking Mirror had said.

Well, it seemed that the Jaguar High Priest was as much a fool as any man. If something were to be done, she would have to do it. Nor did she quail from the task; hadn't she brought down the King, and destroyed the White Serpent? So he'd come back. He was hard to kill, evidently.

Still, he was a fool. The city was his, if he wished to take it. The people would pour themselves into his hands like water. But would he do what he should, and could? Would he smite his enemies and reward his friends?

No. Because whether he was a God or not, whether he had actually gone to the Underwater World and then returned, he would still be a fool. He would teach the old ways of peace, of labor, of learning and art. His hands were too clean for murder.

But hers were not.

VI

In the end, Purple Grackle had to cut off most of Spirits's hair, leaving behind only a short, smooth, shining helmet. The tangles from her days of mourning were too much of a rat's nest to redeem, though Purple Grackle did try. Finally, though, both women agreed, after an interminable session of hair pulling that brought tears to both their eyes, that there was no help for it, and Purple Grackle went to fetch a knife.

The sacrifice of her hair seemed to lighten her mood. Spirits felt a new buoyancy as she strolled through the compound, and that very day she resumed her visits to the poorer parts of the city, and the villages. She was needed; she found more than enough misery, after the recent disasters, to keep her busy. White Serpent accompanied her, as he had in past times. His cheerful countenance, his untiring labor, and the blessings of his hands seemed stronger than ever before. Sometimes merely his smile was enough to bring healing.

Born of travail, a new bond grew between them. It remained chaste, of course; Spirits remembered the awful thing she had done with him on the altar, but she didn't speak of it. In truth, she was terribly shamed by the memory, but some secret part of her cherished it as well. Yet by some benison of the Gods, the people had forgotten that awful day; now they cheered when the two of them came among them, and so many wanted to hear White Serpent's teachings that he was forced to move to the Grand Concourse, where there was enough room for the crowds to gather.

He taught as he always had of chastity and love, of the glory of honest labor, and the triumph of art and craft. Of the little things: how to plant and nurture, how to weave, how to carve fine stones and spin beautiful pots. In the White Temple itself, artisans repaired the damage done by rioting and earthquake, and finally the new temple was done; white and shining, it stood as testament to the gentle power of the White Priest.

And for many days, while all this was done, nothing was heard from Smoking Mirror or Green Water Woman. The royal courts stayed quiet, though the ones who'd tended to everyday administration kept at their tasks, as White Serpent counseled them to do. Granaries that Harvest Mountain had set aside for his warriors were opened, and food once more was plentiful. The people thanked White Serpent for this, and those of the Jaguar Temple did not demur, though some of the granaries were theirs, set aside for the Jaguar soldiers.

The soldiers vanished from the street corners and confined themselves to their own training grounds, and stopped recruiting in the villages. Gradually, the talk of war died down, and the tax collectors lightened their efforts. It seemed that all things returned to normal, or even better than normal. But Spirits wondered, for White Serpent said, "Rebuild the city until the sacrifice is pleasing in the eyes of heaven."

When she heard this, she sensed uneasily that this time of peace and plenty was only temporary; that White Serpent had returned from the Underwater World with purpose and destiny, and the time for that fulfillment had not yet come. But it was coming.

She put these thoughts aside as best she could, tending to her work and her baby. Shining Star was filling out, becoming as pink and chubby as any other child, and if one did not look closely to see his twisted foot or his extra fingers—or his eyes—it was easy to think of him as simply her son, to be loved and cared for and cherished. It never crossed her mind that Shining Star was something else, as well: the son of a High King. The only blood of that King yet living. To her he was only a baby, not a High Prince of the royal blood. Or, as was technically true, the High King—for there was no other.

She was suckling him at her breast one shining morning—the great rains seemed to have vanished entirely, though there would be late afternoon showers sufficient to water the fields where crops flourished as never before—when Purple Grackle peered hesitantly around the door flap and said, "Lady, you have a guest."

Something in Purple Grackle's tone brought Spirits's head up, a question on her lips. "Oh? Who is it?"

"Your sister, Lady. The High Priestess of the Jaguar Temple," she continued, naming the title Green Water Woman now proudly proclaimed.

Spirits stared at Purple Grackle for a long moment, and then shook her head. "I don't want to see her. I have forgiven enough. I don't hate her, but I cannot love her, either. Let there be an end to it."

VII

Those shining days, of a happiness greater than she'd ever known, remained with Spirits for the rest of her life. But even in the dappled sunlight she felt the first hints of the shadow. It had become her wont, at the end of the day when dusk crept across the green jungles and wreathed the city in soft shadows, to walk with White Serpent about the temple, and talk of many things as they passed among the artists still hard at work.

She remembered Brush Weaver, who was gone, and who had been treacherous. She remembered, but didn't speak of him. In fact, her words with the White Priest were as notable as much for what they didn't talk of as what they did.

She thought he seemed less careworn, as if death had renewed him. Perhaps it had; for if the people believed him a God, or at least the avatar of one, she knew he had returned fully as a man, too. A calm humanity, stronger than ever before, went with him always, and touched those who came close to him. He showed interest in even the smallest of doings, praising a boy who had come lately to the temple, who showed the makings of a fine weaver. Or he asked after the children of the women who came to grind their corn, knowing each of them by name, though there were many.

But most of all he talked with her, about what was to come.

"This age will pass in sunlight," he said one evening, when the birds in the trees had quieted their screeching and the monkeys hid in the shadowed branches. The breath of the river wafted about them, soft and still. They stood at the edge of the rear compound, where she could see a pair of artists using the last of the light to work on a great mural.

"Lord, surely this age will not pass. The sin has

departed. You are triumphant in the city. Your teachings are honored everywhere. Even Smoking Mirror has come to you, and blessed you for the ending of the strife."

His hand found her waist, and he pulled her close. His touch sent warm thrills through her, and she looked up at him, smiling.

"You have never wavered," he said. "I love you for that, but I will not hide the truth from you. I have come back for a purpose. My destiny is as it always was. My age is ending now. All that remains is to set things right, and when that is done, I will go to my long home."

A great sadness settled on her, and for a moment the fading of the sun seemed to speak of a greater fading.

"Must it be?" she whispered.

His grip strengthened; she felt his strength, and took it for her own. Such was his way; he always gave more than he received. "All things pass away," he said. "Such is the cycle of the years, as is ordained by the Two. Even I cannot forestall it, nor would I. But it is not a fearful thing."

"I fear it, Lord," she told him.

"I know you do. It is a hard thing. But I will be with you always. Remember that, when things seem darkest."

She wanted to ask him what he meant, but he reached up and touched her lips with his fingertips, and she remained silent. Perhaps, she thought, it is better not to know.

VIII

Three hands of days after his return, White Serpent proclaimed a day of feasting and celebration, and sacrifice to all the Gods in thanks for ending the trials of the city. One more time the altars were built in the

Grand Concourse, though this time they were not separate. The White Priest himself would make a sacrifice, and on this day even the Jaguar would demand nothing more than the smoke of grain and vegetables, and the blood of lizards and pigs.

At the appointed time he led her up the stairs to the top of the platform, where altars honoring each of the Four had been constructed. Smoking Mirror and Green Water Woman waited in front of the Jaguar's altar. The priests of the Dragon stood by His altar, though no one had yet replaced their High Priest, the fallen Harvest Mountain Lord. The High Priest of the Trickster guarded his place, and White Serpent and Spirits, the last to mount, stood in front of the Feathered Serpent's altar.

She looked out over the crowd; the miracle of the sunlight continued. The day had dawned as bright and warm as a breakfast cookfire. The shimmering air vibrated with the sound of laughter. Children played their games beneath the fondly tolerant eyes of their families while women turned juicy haunches of pig, or glittering slabs of river fish over the campfires whose flames wavered almost invisibly in the limpid light.

The crowd was smaller than it had been, Spirits noticed with a pang of sadness. Many had died, and many still lay sick and wounded. The scars left by angry Gods, if hidden somewhat, were still visible for those who could see.

Smoking Mirror walked over to them and bowed. "Brother, it is good to see us all gathered in one place again. I'm glad you have returned to us."

Spirits watched him carefully. He seemed as oily as ever, and as always, his words could be taken in many ways. But in the happy mood of the day, she was willing to take him at face value, and smiled at him in return, as did White Serpent.

"I've returned, though I never left," White Serpent

replied. "But as you say, I am glad to be here. The wounds must be healed before I depart."

Smoking Mirror's eyebrows rose. "Depart, brother? Why so? Your people need you here. We have much to do together yet before our city is restored."

Spirits wondered if she were the only one who detected the sudden leap of eagerness in Smoking Mirror's words. But White Serpent seemed not to notice anything amiss, and merely said, "When we are done with the sacrifices, I will speak to the people."

Smoking Mirror nodded and bowed again. "As you wish, brother." With that he returned to his altar to begin the holy rituals, for the Jaguar was still chief among the Gods of the city.

Spirits kept her place and spoke the proper words for the ceremony; everything went smoothly enough. Smoking Mirror seemed content with the sacrifice of fruit and grain, untroubled by the lack of human blood for his divine master. Even the Gods showed no displeasure, for the omens found in the entrails of fish and lizards and pigs were uniformly good. When they were done, White Serpent stepped away from his altar and walked slowly to the edge of the platform. He stood there, his arms raised, and waited until the great crowd slowly grew silent. Then, with the rays of the high noon sun crowning his head in a golden nimbus, he began to speak.

"People of the city," he said, his voice ringing out over them, "this is a time of happiness, and yet for me a time of sadness. As I have said to you, my destiny remains, and with it, yours. This is the last time I shall speak to you as a man, and a priest, for after this day I depart from you forever."

He spoke on at a good length, commending some for their faithfulness, and forgiving others for their lapses, but all Spirits really remembered was his first words, for they rang with the echoing timbre of doom. She felt them as the promise she'd ignored, the truth she'd put aside. But the doom remained, and now, at long last, it would come to fruition.

To her eyes, even the bright sun faded, and gleamed vacantly over desolation. When she looked down at the crowd, she saw a vast field of corpses, and in her ears she heard cries and lamentations. It was the hidden sight given her, to know these things, and in that moment she would have given almost anything to be spared the vision.

She glanced over her shoulder and saw Smoking Mirror trying hard to hide the jubilation that swelled his face. His great enemy was departing of his own accord. No doubt, she thought, he has his plans already, and words of warning for White Serpent floated through her thoughts.

But then she turned away. The White Priest was finishing his last teaching to his people. Now the cries were real, but he soothed them. "Much will pass away, but not everything. When a field is harvested, the farmer saves some grain to plant again. So it will be now. And I will be with you always, for you have taken me into your hearts."

He waited then, as their cries grew louder, and finally spoke his last words to them.

"Be not afraid, for I have loved you. And that gift can never be destroyed, even if all the worlds are changed forever. Even in the darkest night love remains, as it always has, as it always will."

He lowered his arms then, bowed his head, and turned away from them.

You can love them, Spirits thought. *Why can't you love me?*

As he passed her, he touched her shoulder and whispered. "But I do, Spirits, more than anything else, I do love you. I said it was a gift, and it is. Be sure that even a God may find it more precious than anything else."

The next morning, White Serpent Hawk, having already made everything ready, crossed over the river with a great portion of his followers, and left Great Head City forever. In the wake of his departure, the smoke of his burning temple rose into the sky as a black pillar, marking what had been, but was now vanished into the bright mist of destiny.

He didn't look back.

CHAPTER
TWENTY-TWO

～～

I

The great host of people journeyed toward the sea with White Serpent Hawk and Spirits Walking Woman, her child in her arms, leading them. Because they were so many, they went slowly, pausing along the way to hunt or fish, or simply to extend this last time they would all be together.

The eye of the sun lit their way; as they walked, they sang songs of joy, though even these, which frightened the birds and sent the monkeys to screeching madly in their hidden bowers, were tinged with sadness.

They followed the slow meander of the river, for they were bound for the village by the sea where White Serpent had been born of man and woman. During these long slow days of march, Spirits felt her moods swing wildly; at times, walking easily at White Serpent's side, her child nuzzling at her breast, she would be transported into a state of happiness so exquisite she wished to die in it; then, understanding that this ecstasy would soon end, her heart would darken with desolation, and once again she would think of death. She spoke of this to him, and he pointed at a bright quetzal winging from a tree.

"That bird lives and dies in the moment. It has no past, and it sees no future. Some would say it's a curse. What would you say?"

Since she knew he often taught in parables, she tried to grasp the kernel of truth in his question, and answered only after some considerable thought. "Perhaps it would be a curse for me," she said finally. "But not, I think, for the quetzal?"

He nodded. "The Two have given many gifts, but the gift of knowing is the greatest. All else springs from it. Without dreaming of the future, and remembering the past, we cannot learn as the Gods would have us do. The birds of the forest do not need it; but without it we are no different than they. And like all gifts, it is a knife with two edges. Sorrow and joy." He smiled down at her. "Without death, there is no life."

"Lord, the Gods do not die."

His face became grave. Gently, he stroked her cheek. "Nor do they love," he replied. "Except one, and He will die the human death. All great things bear a great price."

She lowered her eyes, understanding at last the payment he made knowingly, and said no more of it. But at night, sometimes she wept, whether for him, for herself, or for the Gods, she didn't know.

One day they stopped by a spring that trickled from the forest into the river. A single boulder stood from the earth, a very strange thing, for rocks such as this were never found in this part of the world. She wondered if it had come from elsewhere, but he said it had marked this place for ages.

The throng settled down to make camp; here the road along the river dwindled to a footpath, with thick brush pushing almost to the riverbank, and so their progress was very slow. After the evening meal—a fish, which she cooked for him over a fire he kindled with his own hands—he took her to the spring.

"Here," he said. "Even the stones will remember us." Then he took her hand and pressed it next to his own on the ancient stone. She felt a burst of warmth. When she took her hand away, the rock was marked with her print, and his. Ever after, the place was called the Place of the Handprints, and travelers left sacrifices of flowers and fruit by the spring.

He worked other such miracles as they went; he gazed into a motionless eddy of the river, bright as a polished mirror of stone, and saw his face. "I have grown old," he said, and she saw the lines in his face that had not been there when she first knew him. He picked up a handful of pebbles and tossed them at a tree. The small stones sank into the thick bark and remained there long after he had gone, and the tree was called the Tree of Old Age.

Finally, at the time of dusk, with the sky painted the color of darkening sapphire and dusted with powdery stars, they heard the roar of the sea, and came at last to the edge of the green world, where sands moved beneath the onrushing waves. All the great throng spread along the beaches. The small village where he had grown up could not contain them all or feed them. He sent out fishers, and with his blessings they came back with baskets overflowing with great silver fish.

His mother and father were gone, but the village had been busy. Set upon the beach just beyond the highest reach of the waves was a great pyre of aromatic wood. It must have been there for some time, for when Spirits touched these timbers they were dry as dead bones. She knew they would burn like the sun itself, and once again she trembled with the desolation of what must come.

All the people camped there for two days and two nights. On the second night, just as the sun slowly closed its crimson eye over the vast green jungle to the west, he came to her and walked with her along the edge of the water until they were alone.

They stood and watched the waves roll in, long white lines that slowly began to glow beneath the risen moon. She looked at him, and saw that the light came from him also, and that êven as the stars glittered above, so did the light from his eyes shine on her.

"I will go tomorrow, with the dawn, for the dawn is my house," he told her.

She felt moisture on her cheeks. They stood very close, facing each other. Gently she knelt and settled Shining Star on the sand. Then she stood and fiercely wrapped her arms about him and pressed her face against his chest. Her body shook with sobs, and though she hated herself for this weakness, she couldn't stop.

He held her until she calmed, then bent and kissed the top of her head. "I once told you it was hard to be a man and remember being a God."

She moved her head against him, feeling his warmth.

"I didn't tell you that because of you, it will be hard to be a God and remember being a man."

She looked up at him. "Truly?"

He nodded. "A new age begins, and perhaps even the Gods Themselves will change. But heaven will know love, where none was before. Such is your gift to me."

Then he drew her away and they walked in the whispering dark until the eastern sky showed the first pale streaks of dawn, and the morning star burned like an emerald torch in the sky.

II

So it is written in the holy books that the Lord Feathered Serpent, on the third day of his sojourn by the sea, mounted up onto his great pyre as the sun rose with the dawn.

All his people were gathered there, and as the rays of the sun first looked over the eastern water, his priests caught the holy light in shining mirrors and focused it onto the wood, so that the wood burned and sparks showered up in great curtains of fire.

It is also said that his mortal woman stood at the base of the fire, holding a child; and that his eyes met hers as the fire claimed him, and did not waver, even when she let out a great cry.

And finally it is written that her shout echoed over all the worlds, and summoned the great, ghostly fleet that came over the horizon, floating like glittering leaves above the waters, to bear him away.

So it is said, and so written. But in the later ages, her name is forgotten, and so nothing is said of what Spirits Walking Woman heard, as the ships ascended into the House of the Dawn, bearing the Feathered Serpent back to the stone hands of his long home.

"Fear not, for I will be with you on Sun Mountain," he said. "In the morning of the new age, you will come to Me."

It was the gift she'd hoped for. But at the end of the fire remained only ashes, and she wept.

III

The Lord General Skull Breaker had selected the six men himself and given them their mission. They were the cream of the Jaguar soldiers, hard-bitten men whose skill at killing was unquestioned. They moved through the jungle like spirits or demons, unseen and unheard, trailing the edge of the throng marching to the sea.

They did not see the ascension of White Serpent Hawk, keeping themselves well back and hidden in the dark forests, waiting. Their orders were specific.

Only after the saddened army of believers had begun to straggle dispiritedly back the way they'd come did they finally carry out their mission.

It was on the second night of the return, when the moon rode above a thin veil of clouds, that they entered the scattered encampment . . .

IV

Spirits sat holding Shining Star, her shoulder rubbing against Purple Grackle. Outside, a chill wind, a messenger from the sea, had begun to blow. It easily pierced the light cloth tent Purple Grackle had pitched for them, and the two women shivered.

The baby squirmed against Spirits's chest, balled up tiny fists, and began to cry.

Spirits sighed. "He is unhappy. I don't know what's the matter."

Purple Grackle snuggled closer. Outside, a single guard, a priest from the temple, whispered hoarsely: "Is everything all right, Lady?"

"It's just the baby," she called back. "He doesn't want to sleep."

"Poor thing," the man replied, and then fell silent.

Spirits lay down on her bedcloth, feeling the occasional small pebble poke against her spine. She shifted uncomfortably.

"I don't know what to do," she said finally to Purple Grackle. "I feel so alone."

Purple Grackle, half asleep, mumbled, "The God will provide."

"Will He?" Spirits wondered. His final words still echoed in her mind: "I will be with you on Sun Mountain." But what did it mean? She had no idea. All she could see was the future, bleak and desolate without him.

The baby wouldn't stop crying. She tried to soothe him, but nothing seemed to work. And then a griping seized her bowels, and strong cramps curdled her belly.

"Oh . . . Gods," she said.

"What's the matter?"

"I don't know. Something I ate, perhaps."

Purple Grackle stretched out her arms. "Give him to me. I'll hold him till you get back."

Wincing against the pain, Spirits passed Shining Star over to her handmaid. For some reason this seemed to quiet him. He stopped wriggling, popped one fat thumb into his pink mouth, and closed his eyes.

"Well," said Spirits, smiling. "It seems he prefers you tonight."

"Be careful," Purple Grackle whispered drowsily. "Hurry back."

Spirits rose up and wrapped her white robe tighter against the wind. She pushed aside the tent flap. "I'll just be a moment."

Purple Grackle nodded and lay back, the babe nestled at her breasts. For some reason Spirits paused just before she ducked out of the tent, and stared for a long moment at the tableau caught in the net of moonlight filtering through the walls of the tent. Then another spasm caught her and she hurried on her way.

V

The small band moved like shadows through the sleeping throng; they had marked the spot earlier, and now saw the single guardian leaning half asleep on his stout stave.

At the last instant one of the Jaguar soldiers stepped on a twig; the faint snapping sound brought the priest's head slowly around, eyes blinking. "What . . . ?"

The point of the flint knife took him in the throat. He fell with a faint, gurgling noise, and lay unmoving on the ground. In the moonlight his blood spread in the dust like black oil.

The first soldier made sure of him, while two more stooped and entered the tent. The sounds of struggle were brief and nearly silent. The rest of the party crouched down, watching nervously, but there was no alarm. After the muffled commotion in the tent had ceased, the invaders crawled out. One held a small bundle, wrapped in white, in his arms. The tiny burden cried softly, but the soldier had wrapped a bloody sheet around it to stifle the noise.

"This way . . ." the leader whispered. Moving like the jungle cat who was their namesake, they loped softly through the sleepers, and vanished into the shadowed jungle beyond. They were well out beyond the farthest reaches of the camp when they heard a single shriek pierce the silent night.

"Faster," the leader urged. They ran on.

VI

"Ugly little thing," Smoking Mirror remarked.

Green Water lifted the white cloth to reveal the sleeping baby's face. Behind her stood the child's nurse, a blunt-faced village woman whose child had died at birth, but whose heavy breasts were still swollen with milk.

"Be glad of it," Green Water advised shortly. She touched one tiny hand with her fingertip. "If he didn't have the god marks, we couldn't be sure it was really Harvest Mountain's child. And then where would we be?"

Smoking Mirror leaned against his altar throne, settling back on his elbows. "It's over, you know. Spirits is dead, and we have the child."

She glanced at him. "I told you I wanted her. That she was to be mine."

His teeth flashed. "It couldn't be done. Better the

deed happened far from the city. Fewer complications that way."

"I wanted to see her body."

The High Priest shrugged. "Her followers say they burned it. The soldiers I sent testify they killed her, and took the child from her arms as she died. Her blood was on the sheet they wrapped the baby in. As I say, it's over. A week from now we will carry this child to the top of the Sun Mountain and proclaim him High King. With you, his aunt, and myself, the first priest of the city, ruling as his guardians and regents. And he will take up his hereditary post as High Priest of the Dragon Temple as well." His smile flashed again. "With myself as acting High Priest, of course."

She nodded. "What about the followers of the White Priest?"

"The White Priest is dead. What choice will they have? They are weak and dispirited without him. Her, too. They have no leaders. We are the leaders now, you and I."

She eyed him. "Don't think you can pull the same tricks on me, priest. I am not a weak and kindly fool, like my sister."

He raised his hands. "I need you. You are the child's only blood. Your presence legitimizes our regency if there is any unrest."

"Will there be? Any unrest, I mean?"

He shook his head. "None whatsoever. In one week Great Head City will be ours completely."

She nodded and looked down. "I don't think he's ugly at all."

VII

She came out of the forest at the farthest edges of the villages, a small, shrunken figure wrapped in a bloody shroud. She assumed the blood was that of her child; it was all she'd found when she returned to the carnage of her tent.

She had known immediately what had happened. The knowledge seemed always to have been inside her. She knelt next to Purple Grackle's torn body, her tears falling on the ruined face, so battered it was no longer possible to say who it was. Then, silently, she rose, left the place of the murder, and vanished into the darkness beyond. Only as she entered the jungle itself did she stop, throw back her head, and utter one long cry of grief and terror.

For two hands of days she wandered, desolation pounding its endless dull beat in her heart. She didn't remember eating or sleeping; she had moved like a ghost through the ancient trees, and even the animals and birds had fallen silent at her passage.

Once, half mad, she paused before the great black shape of a leopard that barred her path. For long moments they stared at each other. Then, coughing low, the beast turned aside, cowed by a rage greater than its own.

Now she trudged through the villages, which were strangely deserted. Nobody greeted her, or even saw her as she passed on by. She sensed only a great stillness, an expectation, as if the world held its breath, waiting.

She barely noticed. She had long since ceased to think in any human way. All that drove her now was destiny. She didn't know what it might be, but she knew where.

She came to the river. In the distance, beneath roiling black clouds, a fire glittered atop Sun Mountain, its leaping dance reflected in the great mirror there. It winked like the eye of a devil. Or a God.

She stared at that blaze as she waited for the raft to carry her into Great Head City. Her narrow shoulders were stooped. She bore the end of an age on her back, and its weight was heavy.

VIII

Green Water Woman adjusted her glittering robe as she peered up at the sky. "It looks like a storm," she said. "Can't you smell the rain in the air?"

Smoking Mirror, arrayed in even greater finery than hers, glanced at her. "Obviously, with the passing of the White Serpent, the rains have returned. It is a sign of his blessing on this day." He paused, then flashed a knowing grin. "Or so I will say. Who knows? It may even be the truth. Is the baby all right?"

She joggled her small burden. Shining Star was wrapped in a blanket made of woven quetzal feathers and serpentine beads. His tiny face was almost lost in its shining folds. "He's fine," she reported. "Not squalling, for once." Green Water Woman, now well past the first flush of interest in her nephew, was only hoping the brat wouldn't pee on her fine robe. She'd decided she didn't have much in the way of maternal instincts, but no matter. That was what nurses were for.

"Are you ready?" Smoking Mirror asked. He exuded an even greater oiliness than usual. Triumph, Green Water decided, didn't particularly become him.

"Yes," she murmured. "Let's get this over with." Once again, she glanced up at the sky, feeling strangely uneasy.

Smoking Mirror raised his right hand, and the great procession from the steps of the Jaguar Temple to the foot of Sun Mountain began.

Beneath the dark, lowering skies, a chorus of pipes rang out, harsh and clear; now the drums began to pound, a muscular tempo that matched the slow, majestic tread of the procession. As Smoking Mirror took his first step, so did the priests from the other three temples; from the Dragon they came, and the house of the Trickster, and even a token procession from the ruins of the White Temple. For the sake of the balance, Smoking Mirror had recruited a few of the stragglers who'd returned from the sea, a mummery of piety, but one he deemed necessary.

Slowly, inexorably, these four separate rivers flowed toward the mountain, passing through the people of the city as through immutable banks of stone. The people watched, and waited, and held their breath. Fathers raised sons onto their shoulders, and mothers held up babies too young to have any idea what was happening. But a new High King came rarely; the thick air hummed with the gravity of the moment.

Smoking Mirror and his procession passed through a long line of Jaguar soldiers, who stood rigid, smartly turned out in polished stone breastplates, clean clouts, round leather helmets, and tall, cruel spears. Directly behind him marched another contingent of these guards, led by Skull Breaker, whose brutish features were set and still. Except for his eyes, which twitched to and fro incessantly, watching for enemies.

A cold wind blew up from the river; quick and sharp, it flapped robes and tousled hair. Some of the courtiers grabbed at their ornate headdresses. As the four columns approached the base of Sun Mountain, torches suddenly burst into flame, as the afternoon turned even darker beneath the clouds.

Green Water, holding the child, looked up toward the peak of the mountain as they halted at its base. It loomed over them, its peak filled with red, wind-tossed fire. On each side of it, long wooden stairways rose from the base to the top. Smoking Mirror gave another signal, and each of the temples, in perfect unison, began to climb the stairs.

She imagined, in the eye of her mind, what it must look like from a distance; long, glittering worms of torch-lit fire, wailing with the sound of flutes, treading with the beat of drums, slowly ascending. She imagined one of the peaks of her early home, when the earth shook and molten stone flowed from the earth.

Like that, but with the lava flowing upward to the glory of the Gods.

For it was from such a mountain that the Gods had first come to the land, at the beginning of this age. She couldn't help it. The awe of the moment swelled even her stony heart, and twisted her muscles tight as fists.

The climb seemed endless. The wind whipped ever more strongly at her. It was growing colder, and now she saw the first flickers of lightning, still trapped inside the bellies of the swollen clouds overhead.

The lightning of the Feathered Serpent. Was it an evil omen? She gritted her teeth, clutched the babe tighter, and climbed on. Only a little while yet, and then it would be over.

Nothing could go wrong now. So why, she wondered, did she feel so uneasy? There was nothing to be frightened of.

Nothing at all.

IX

The single boatman had ferried her across the wind-tossed river in utter silence. She had fixed him with her gaze and he had turned white.

"Take me to the city," she said.

"Lady . . . ?"

"Take me."

Without another word, he cast off. When he reached the other side, he waited until she stepped down to the grassy verge, and then, panic clattering in his teeth, returned the way he'd come. As soon as the raft bumped the earth he leaped off and ran until he vanished in the gathering gloom.

She walked alone. The hem of the great city was as empty as the villages around it. But she could see the high mount before her, though it was too far away to make out any details beyond the worms of fire which crawled slowly up its flanks.

Behind her, the wind was rising, slapping at her cheeks, crushing the bloody rag she wore against her wasted form. She could hear the drums now, and the whistling shriek of the pipers. A fleeting memory of her first sight of Sun Mountain ruffled the edge of her mind. She cast it away. With every step she took, she felt herself grow stronger.

The noise of the ceremony grew louder in her ears, but she ignored it, as she did the fringes of the crowd that parted before her, suddenly murmuring. Their whispers meant nothing to her. They were the whispers of the dead, but she would not tell them. They would know soon enough.

As she had done before, Spirits came up the Great Way, with the throng cleaving before her as flesh before a knife. Whether by chance or destiny, when she finally halted, she stood at the bottom of the long stairs upon which had already passed the small procession from the temple of the White Serpent.

Some of those here recognized her. She heard gasps and a few scattered shouts, but paid no attention. Her hollowed gaze looked up and saw only one thing; the fire at the top of the mountain, and the tiny figures caught in its winking glare.

The weight of what she bore was so great she wondered that she could even stand, let alone climb that endless ladder. But after a moment she put her foot on the first step. And then the second.

High above, a long, feathery serpent of lightning whip-cracked across the sky.

She remembered: *I will be with you on Sun Mountain.*

X

The winds had grown ferocious at the top of the mountain. There was only a flimsy wooden railing surrounding the small platform, and most of the space there was taken up by the great stone mirror and the round firepit. The flames, fed by wood stacked beneath the platform, snapped and hissed as the wind tore off rags of fire and tossed them into the sky. Green Water Woman braced herself against the gale, and eyed the railing nervously. It was impossible to hear anything; even the faint tootling of the pipers who'd followed them up the stairs had vanished, though she could see their faces, pale and frightened, as they blew futilely at their instruments.

She edged closer to Smoking Mirror. "Is it over? I don't like this . . ."

He glared at her and said something, but the words were whipped from his lips before she could hear them. The small knot of priests and courtiers surrounding him leaned closer. The rituals had to be obeyed, lest the Gods become angry, and mark the beginning of the new High King's reign with evil omens.

At her breast, the High King began to wail. Smoking Mirror stepped closer and gestured. She held the child out as the Jaguar priest poured a gourd of scented oil over his reddened forehead. This only sent the babe off into a new crescendo of squalling cries.

Quickly, Smoking Mirror rattled off the rest of the ceremony, then sank to his knees before the child. Green Water rather enjoyed that, and imagined that it was to her Smoking Mirror offered obeisance.

The end of the ritual came quickly, and it seemed to her with much relief all around. The weather was turning truly ugly; thunder rolled and lightning spat across the clouds. A few heavy splatters of rain suddenly marked the wooden floor, and popped loudly in the white-hot coals.

"Long live the High King!" shouted Smoking Mirror.

The others raised their fists. "Long live the High

King!" they replied. Smoking Mirror took out a long knife, reached down, and yanked the sacrifice up by his hair. It was a young man unlucky enough to have been captured raiding one of the outlying villages. With a single quick stroke the High Priest cut his throat, dropped him, and bathed his hands in the gushing blood. Two acolytes then picked up the dying man and tossed him onto the fire. Green Water Woman was momentarily grateful for the wind; it swept away the characteristic stench of charred grease, which she hated.

Smoking Mirror placed his hands on Shining Star, marking him with the blood. He nodded. "Now it is over," he said.

The hurricane around them suddenly rose to a deafening volume, and then, just as suddenly, died. For a moment they all just looked at each other. The silence grew oppressive. Overhead, the clouds had turned the color of rotting meat, fat and bulging. Somewhere behind them hid the sun. But it had grown dark as night.

Green Water Woman pulled the child tight against herself, and looked around, a wild thrill of fear snaking up her spine. The hair on her arms stood up.

"What . . . ?" she said.

I have come for my child!

It was a woman's voice, far away, but as clear and cold as the wind itself. A terrible, wracking sound, torn by agony and tolling with the promise of doom. Green Water Woman peered over the edge of the railing. Her heart slammed in her chest, over and over again.

Down below, a tiny figure, almost invisible in the growing murk. Tiny, but moving, a stooped white shape in the gloom. Climbing the stairs, step by slow step, coming closer.

I have come for my son!

Green Water shuddered. "It's her," she said. She

glanced at Smoking Mirror, whose face had gone stretched and pale in the shadows. "She's returned from the dead. My sister. Spirits Walking Woman."

Then the clouds burst like rotten eggs, and the wrath of heaven belched forth upon the peak of Sun Mountain.

XI

Step by step, Spirits climbed the stair of Sun Mountain. When she put her foot on the first step, she heard a deep, bell-like sound that echoed in her bones. On the second step, a pocket of silence enveloped her; her ears popped, and she shook her head.

With each new step she took, some different phenomenon assailed her. She saw a flash of fire. She smelled the stench of the Underwater World. Once she glimpsed a great bowl of forest, but this time silent. No birds sang, and the dull sky was without a sun. On the spike in the heart of the worlds, two thrones stood uncrumbled but empty.

She glimpsed a turtle greater than the worlds, swimming in an empty night, its vast shell a sheen of polished jewels. She felt once again the nearness of giant, invisible shapes, and shuddered at their dark passage.

Still she climbed. Now each stair shifted and changed beneath her feet; one was a knife, the next a flowing stream; when she put her foot down again, Harvest Mountain Lord's torn body quivered beneath her; his mouth was open and gaped up at her like a fish.

She climbed on, a vast weight crushing her shoulders. Yet another mass grew in her belly, equally as heavy as the first. She was pregnant, bursting with cataclysm. The rain fell about her in blinding torrents; the dark trembled with thunder.

On her robe, the dried blood loosened, liquefied, flowed; in her vision it ran down into puddles at her feet, spreading like a flooding stream. She ignored it and trudged on.

Up above, she heard a baby crying.

XII

On the top of Sun Mountain, half-blinded by rain, they felt Spirits's slow approach as an ever growing sense of dread. Green Water turned to Smoking Mirror, a question on her lips, but he had taken a spirit pipe from one of the acolytes and, rudely shielded, was puffing on it as hard as he could. His eyes were small, hard pits; his skin seemed to have curdled, and was the color of a fish belly.

"What . . . ?" Green Water gasped. She turned to the others. "Kill her! Somebody has to . . ."

But none of them were armed. She shifted Shining Star into the crook of one elbow, then snatched the sacrificial knife from Smoking Mirror's hand. He didn't seem to notice. His eyes had rolled up into his head; what remained stared blankly out. His body began to tremble, the beginning of the divine paroxysm of transformation.

Green Water went back to the railing and looked down. Spirits was very close now, only a few hands of steps away, still coming. Her head was hooded. Green Water couldn't see her face, but her inevitable creeping ascent, undeterred by weather or human hands, chilled Green Water's blood in her veins. She raised the knife.

"Stop!" she howled. "Stop, or I'll kill the child!"

Her threat hung in the air between them; Green Water Woman stood poised, her hair streaming in the wind like a black flag. And Spirits paused.

From her vantage point above, Green Water watched her slowly lift her head. The hood fell back, exposing her sister's pale face, revealing eyes filled with endless, greedy darkness.

Then, appallingly, Spirits smiled. "So it was you all along," she called back. "Give me my son, sister, for I bring your doom, and the end of all things."

"Never! I will kill him first. And then you!"

Spirits stared up at her. "No. You will not."

Then her right foot moved, lifted, and she climbed another step.

XIII

And though Spirits kept on climbing, she no longer knew she was doing so. The stairs had vanished beneath her feet. She saw faces floating in darkness: Green Water, Shining Star, and now Smoking Mirror, with a dark, sinuous shape looming behind him.

Vaguely she knew he had summoned his Lord, and the Jaguar had come to defend him. But she felt no fear. If there was any place in all the Worlds for Gods on this day, it was at the peak of Sun Mountain. Jaguar was only the first; He would not be the last.

For now, with a strange, sliding lurch, she felt the boundaries of the Worlds dissolve, the walls which kept them separate vanishing as if they had never been.

The air vibrated; the dead of the Underwater World floated about her in mournful song. And those yet living now rose up to join them, as if anticipating their fate. Finally, she saw the gates of heaven open and spill forth bright spirits. In the heart of the light glowed the bowl, the spike, the empty thrones.

All mixed, jumbled together, in one mad cacophony of doom and destiny. She kept on moving; it was all she could do, and the Gods, demons, spirits, and the dead gave way before her, for she brought the end of the age, and her burden would not be halted in heaven, on earth, or in the underworld.

Finally she reached the platform and stood before them. She opened her hands and showed them what she'd brought.

"Now," she whispered. "Give me my son, and I will give you the gift you have sought unknowing. For I bear it in my hands, and I bring it to you . . . now!"

XIV

Fueled by terror and the raging of his heart, the fumes of the divine pipe seized Smoking Mirror so quickly he barely had time to prepare. He had just begun the inner chant when Jaguar took him, settling into his flesh and bones with the ease of long familiarity.

"I am here," Jaguar hissed. "I am with you." Jaguar shook Smoking Mirror's muscles and tossed him like a doll into the holy somersault. When the High Priest landed catlike on his feet, the ground was enveloped in a cloud. Another filled the wide space at the top of the mountain.

Jaguar peered around, and coughed. His yellow eyes settled on the small woman before Him. He showed His fangs as the sharp white hunger took Him.

XV

Green Water was aware that something had changed. She saw Smoking Mirror flip into a somersault and land, but now she could barely see him. Some dark cloud shrouded him, darker even than the storm above. Cold terror turned her limbs to sludge. She looked over at Spirits, who stood before the Shadow, her hands outstretched as if displaying something Green Water could not see.

"I bring it to You, as well," Spirits told the Shadow, smiling as it loomed over her.

Green Water could stand it no longer. She raised

the knife that still dripped with the blood of the sacrifice, and leaped toward her sister, a shriek of rage tearing at her throat.

XVI

In the end, Spirits found her humanity again. In the same manner as before, she felt herself split apart, and stood as a human woman, watching something that was of her, but not her, as it faced a knife, and a God.

Her life flashed before her like a dream; looking at the faded mind pictures now, she felt unbearably sad. Her fate had been made from the very beginning, and everything she'd done had been twisted to form this moment.

Poor Blue Parrot . . . and poor everybody else, too, even Green Water Woman. Her sister was as much a tool as she was herself.

She watched the knife flash toward the other Spirits and felt a thrill of fear. But before the knife could reach its goal, the platform shook from the weight of the Dark God moving forward. The blade arced up and fell back, but the Jaguar did not. Spirits knew He was a far greater threat than a sharpened stone in human hands.

Then, without any warning, her curious separation ended, and it was she, herself, who stared up into the impenetrable, hungry darkness as the He Who Devours finally showed His teeth.

She could smell His hot breath. His hunting cough rattled in His throat. Slowly, His endless jaws began to close . . .

XVII

As Green Water stumbled toward Spirits with the sacrificial knife upraised, a blast of lightning blinded her, and a gust of rain slickened the wood under her feet. She slipped and fell. Her hand smashed into the wooden railing and the knife dropped clattering into the void.

She was stunned for a moment; she rose slowly, shaking her head. It took her a second to realize the child was gone. When she looked over, she saw the babe in Spirits's arms.

Another fusillade of bolts shook their aerie. Down below the priests and courtiers descended as fast as they could, screaming in terror. She turned to Smoking Mirror.

"Lord . . . !" she cried out in her agony. And the High Priest did turn to her for an instant. She saw him clearly, for the dark clouds which had obscured him had vanished, and he stood as a man.

Then out of the sky reached one long, sizzling bolt. The tip of it touched him. She felt her hair stand on end. His eyes lost their filmy vagueness and glittered bright with terror, for his fate was on him.

The caress of the lightning was hideously slow. The Feathered Serpent ate him in pieces. First his skin glowed, then began to char and bubble. His face burst into flame. At the last his hair began to burn and he toppled, a human torch laid to rest at last. She turned to Spirits, knowing doom was on her, but no longer caring.

"With my bare hands, then . . ." she snarled.

She flung herself forward. But even in her death strength, she couldn't leap the chasm that opened before her. She fell into it, and slid down with the flanks of Sun Mountain, collapsing into the end of time, and was swallowed up. Her scream echoed once, and was gone.

When it was over, Spirits stood on the tiny scrap of platform that yet remained, clinging precariously to the peak. Overhead, the storm began to clear. The earth still grumbled, but even it, finally, subsided. She had one last vision; on the thrones at the heart of the world sat the Two. But They did not see her, for her doom was done, and she was free at last.

It had grown dark. The evening star blazed in the west.

With dawn would come a new age. Before her now stretched the night of all beginnings, and it was cold. Spirits sighed, clasped Shining Star tighter, and began to make her weary way down the ruined mountain. But she moved lightly, for her burden was gone.

She had given it away.

Tomorrow would be a new day.

CHAPTER TWENTY-THREE

I

The day dawned as any other day. In the sky a few clouds drifted, before the growing heat of the sun burned them away. Spirits, holding her child, moved through the desolation slowly.

The air stank of the great burning. On the whole island, not one stick still leaned against another. The temples had been thrown down. Where the royal pavilions had once stood was only charred rubble. The Jaguar Temple was a jagged, ruined shape beyond the muck of the Grand Concourse.

During the worst part of the earthquake and the storm, large parts of the island had turned to sucking jelly. Here and there she saw things of horror: a single arm protruding from the earth, or half a body, now twisting in the death rictus.

Moving like ghosts through the morning mist, a few figures wandered aimlessly. These gradually coalesced about her as she walked. Most were silent. A few wept, or implored her to help them. But she could not. There was nothing here left for her to do.

The mighty monuments of the city, the huge stone

heads, the great altars and thrones, were all cast down and tumbled about. Some had sunk partly into the earth; all were cracked, scarred, chipped.

The desolation was complete. Nothing remained of the city that had wished to rule the Middle World. What was left was only a charnel pit, a graveyard that stank of the blood of its final sacrifice.

She felt them gather around her like ghosts, wailing for what had once been, but was no longer. Shining Star moved at her breast, hungry. She looked down at him, then at the handful of those who'd survived the night, and the end of the age.

She raised her head and spoke. Her voice carried clearly, and struck them like a whip.

"This place is cursed and dead. No Gods come here, nor will for another age yet. Wild beasts will wander here, and wail in pity and terror at what was, but now is gone."

They rustled like dry weeds, rubbing against each other, pressing toward her with febrile eagerness. She raised one hand to halt them.

"We must go. We must leave this place."

They stared at her, blinking. Finally, one said, "Lady? Will you lead us?"

She looked at him, then down at the child suckling at her teat. "I will not," she said at last. "But he will."

By the time the pitiful remnant had crossed beyond the swollen river, the sun was hard up in the sky. It illuminated pillars of white smoke that rose from the wreckage of the doomed city. She turned and looked, knowing it was the last time she would ever see the place.

As she watched, a rainbow slowly took form, arching high over the island. It gleamed with the vanished glory of all that had been, and as she watched it, she knew that as long as men could speak, the story of Great Head City would never end. Finally she turned away. Her feet found the path that led north, toward the mountains and the high plateaus.

In the east, by some miracle, the morning star glowed, undimmed even by the full blaze of the sun. It caught her eye, a steadily burning emerald torch, and she remembered the rest of His promise.

In the morning of the new age, you will come to Me.

She stared at it for a long time, before she raised her hand to lead them on. Her lips moved, but nobody heard.

"Yes, my Lord, my only love. Save a place for me. For when it is time, I will be with you again, in the House of the Dawn."

Then Spirits Walking Woman led them into the bright morning, and was gone.

INTERLUDE

So ends the long tale of the passing of the Age of the Feathered Serpent, and the mortal woman who loved Him. What comes after is known to us, and I will tell that story as well. But now, at the end of the day, as I gaze out from the ramparts of the Pyramid of the Moon, I will lay to rest her memory, for I have written it as well as I can. And in the gauzy veils of dusk I see that nothing changes, though all does change. For They are still with us, the Four, shifting in the endless dance of fire and rain, blood and birth, life and death. I see Their temples and monuments glowing in the gloom, rich with white and gold.

Her name is lost to us, (though I gave her one of my own devise) but I think on her often, that woman who loved a God. In her was both end and beginning, and we are born of her womb.

But there are no temples here for her. She was a mortal woman, and we build only for Gods. This, then, in my words, is the only temple she will have. I pray that it is enough.

Set down by my hand in the Year One Reed:

—White Feather Writer
Chief Scribe of
the Temple of the Moon

ONYX

ROMANCE FROM THE
PAST AND PRESENT

☐ **DEVOTED by Alice Borchardt.** Elin, a daughter of the Forest People, was mistress of the forbidden powers granted by the old gods. Owen, the warrior-bishop, was his people's last hope against the invading Viking horde, and against the powerful ruler who would betray them. They came together in a love that burned through all barriers in a struggle to save France. "Love and treachery . . . a marvelous, irresistible novel."—Anne Rice

(403967—$6.99)

☐ **LILY *A Love Story* by Cindy Bonner.** Lily Delony has no reason to doubt the rules of virtue and righteousness she has been brought up with until she meets the man who turns her world—and her small town—upside down. The odds are against her forsaking her family for an unknown future with an outlaw who shoots first and thinks later.   (404394—$4.99)

☐ **DUCHESS OF MILAN by Michael Ennis.** Once upon a time, in fifteenth-century Italy, two women faced each other with a ruthlessness and brilliance no man has ever matched. Enter their world of passion and evil in Italy's most dazzling and dangerous age! "Two young women who had the power to change history . . . Be prepared . . . you won't want to put this one down."—Jean M. Auel   (404289—$5.99)

*Prices slightly higher in Canada

Buy them at your local bookstore or use this convenient coupon for ordering.

PENGUIN USA
P.O. Box 999 — Dept. #17109
Bergenfield, New Jersey 07621

Please send me the books I have checked above.
I am enclosing $_____ (please add $2.00 to cover postage and handling). Send check or money order (no cash or C.O.D.'s) or charge by Mastercard or VISA (with a $15.00 minimum). Prices and numbers are subject to change without notice.

Card #_____ Exp. Date _____
Signature_____
Name_____
Address_____
City _____ State _____ Zip Code _____

For faster service when ordering by credit card call **1-800-253-6476**

Allow a minimum of 4-6 weeks for delivery. This offer is subject to change without notice.